I0646719

JOEL AUSTIN

PERPETUA

VINCI
BOOKS

By Joel Austin

Frank Sherman Thrillers

For my daughter. May you find joy and adventure wherever you roam.

Vinci Books

vinci-books.com

Published by Vinci Books Ltd in 2025

1

Copyright © Joel Austin 2021

The author has asserted their moral right to be identified as the author of
this work in accordance with the Copyright, Designs and Patents Act 1988.
This work is a work of fiction. Names, characters, places and incidents are
the product of the author's imagination or are used fictitiously. Any
resemblance to actual persons, living or dead, places and incidents is
entirely coincidental.
All rights reserved. No part of this publication may be copied, reproduced,
distributed, stored in any retrieval system, or transmitted in any form or by
any means, including photocopying, recording, or other electronic or
mechanical methods, nor used as a source for any form of machine
learning including AI datasets, without the prior written permission of the
publisher.
The publisher and the author have made every effort to obtain permissions
for any third party material used in this book and to comply with copyright
law. Any queries in this respect should be brought to the attention of the
publisher and any omissions will be corrected in future editions.
A CIP catalogue record for this book is available from the British Library.
Paperback ISBN: 9781036705343

Chapter One

No one drove by the house for hours. The only thing visible through the dirt-stained windshield was a blank canvas of asphalt and concrete. Nothing entered. Nothing left. Horace Filby knew because he kept diligent tallies in a small spiral-bound notebook. It stayed in his front pocket with a mechanical pencil. He never wrote with ink, always graphite. Such a habit meant he always wore shirts with pockets. A modest collection of the collared variety—mostly beige or grey—inhabited his closet. He was particular in such matters. That singular attentiveness carried over to his meticulous notes on the comings and goings in the neighborhood. Make, model, and color. Descriptions of the drivers and passengers. All the details went down in a neat, slanted script… except, that day's entry was blank.

The house in question lay at the end of a compact, tree-rimmed cul-de-sac. Wide without being grand. A post-war addition when such excess came without question. The street was one of a handful that existed on the far edge of town, which was predominantly working class with a smattering of small businesses and a seasonal tourism industry. Most people called it quaint, but that was just a polite way of saying average.

Horace thought the home's location was a poor choice for someone on the run. It offered only one paved exit and the back of the property edged onto farm fields. The homes were small and lumped together as if personal space was unnecessary. It went against the whole notion of the suburbs. Neighborhoods like that bred either friendship or nosiness. Neither trait was ideal for those laying low. In his experience, such people favored rural communities at the edge of population densities. Places where locals don't ask questions or invite those sharing a property line over to a barbeque. Then again, the woman he sought fell far from average.

His employers gave few details when Horace took the job, but that was typical. Although his service suite was broad, finding people was his specialty. The harder to find, the bigger the fee. His current client was paying five times the going rate. It was enough to take the rest of the year off if Horace had been the type to take vacations. Instead, he favored work over play. It suited his reclusive personality, and he was content to spend most days alone in a cheap car watching for his target.

Over time, his file on the woman had grown in height. The cheap manilla folder bulged open at a forty-five-degree angle. Unable to close it, he used a pistol as a paperweight. It was a Glock 22 with no extra frills or additions. Horace craved the conformity of the weapon. Over sixty percent of police officers carried one. It helped convey authenticity when the occasion called for wearing a uniform.

Leafing through the stack of pages, Horace pulled out a well-worn photo. The woman looking back was in her early thirties, slim with a fair number of curves. Horace took her to be attractive by societal norms. Her smiling face was topped with an unruly crop of chestnut brown hair that Horace ignored. He focused on the eyes and the mouth. The geometry of the face was more important to him than hair or eye color. Those things could change easier than a favorite brand of toilet paper. The face, however, took a lot of money to alter—he was one to know, having gone under the surgeon's knife.

It happened after a haphazard job in which the police came close to catching him. He shed the old name easily enough, but getting over an unfamiliar face took time. The woman had no such operation, at least to the best of his knowledge. Bank and credit card statements for her alias did not show the monetary resources. Besides, it didn't fit her pattern.

The file traced her from Chicago to Texas and then to California. Each stop after the Windy City was substantial. She settled down and created a life in small towns. Usually, the woman found work at a local bar. She had a body type that most of the local clientele enjoyed seeing on the serving side of their beer. Her last move from California coincided with a violent episode. Horace understood why she ran from that unwanted spotlight. He also understood the appeal of Stalworth. The town carried a certain level of anonymity or blandness that made hiding easier. That part of the country also carried a rugged individualist streak that favored reinvention, be it personal or professional. It still didn't explain the cul-de-sac choice, but he chalked that up to a constricted rental market.

On or about hour six of his surveillance, Horace felt almost certain she had pulled up stakes and left. Prior to his arrival on the quiet and sterile street, he visited the local watering holes. Only five called the town home, and it didn't take long to find out where she worked. The owner of one bar prattled on about the woman, smitten with parts of her. The man admitted to Horace that he had not seen or heard from her in several days and that, given her recent disappearance, he might have to let her go. Horace smiled politely, paid the bill for his tonic water, and drove directly over to the neighborhood.

The barkeep had divulged other facts that supported Horace's hypothesis. The late nineties Jeep she drove to work was not in the driveway. She had looked edgy in the preceding week and requested her paycheck in cash. Credit card receipts from his contact at Equifax showed she made a large fuel purchase one hundred miles north only one day prior. Horace might have bypassed the house altogether and tried to cut her off towards the Canadian border, but he was too meticulous to leave such a 'T' uncrossed.

After seven hours parked down the street in an old silver Lincoln bought with cash to avoid a rental car record, he walked up the driveway. It was concrete and short. A few faded oil stains marred the otherwise clean gray surface. Grass crept up to the edge, but it was more brown than green. The woman did not have a sense for landscaping or did not care enough to put in the effort.

The house was a solid but lackluster structure. Architectural features were all but ignored. Storm shutters were the only consolation, but those were purely decorative. Cheap plastic curtains in the front window clung tightly together, and the interior was devoid of artificial light. Even in the summer sun, the place felt cold and lonely—abandoned.

Horace circled around the grayish-blue siding towards the back door. He wore an ocean-blue polo shirt emblazoned with the local power company's logo. It concealed the

Glock tucked into his belt. A clipboard and hat rounded out his disguise. Long years had taught him most people ignored a man in uniform meandering through a neighbor's yard.

The back door was metal, originally painted white, now scuffed by time. As useful as a fire break but having no ascetic purpose. People could enter and leave, but it had no character. He tried the doorknob but it was locked. Using a small crowbar that he carried for such situations, Horace pried it open. The old wood frame, more rotten than solid, gave way with a concerted push. A damp crunch met his ears as the lumber disintegrated. Horace glanced inside before slipping on a pair of black latex gloves. He left nothing to chance when committing a crime—a lesson learned the hard way.

Inside, there was scarcely a noise. No hum of an air conditioner despite the summer heat. No music or television noises. Only the faint clanking of an ancient beige refrigerator was audible. He opened the latter and was unsurprised to find it bare except for a box of baking soda and a few condiments. The air was stale but not musty... the woman was not long gone. A few days, but not more than a week. Odors turn after a week. The pantry and cupboards were devoid of contents too. Only one plate and an old plastic cup remained on the shelves. Cheap remnants of an outdoor picnic—a second-hand store purchase.

Beyond the kitchen lay the living room, all bare and lifeless and un-vacuumed. The lack of furniture shrank the space. It appeared small and gloomy. A cable cord protruded limply from the wall like a long rope of black licorice. Two slight indents on the carpet indicated the TV used to sit on the floor.

The bedrooms were upstairs and Horace slowly

ascended the steps, listening for anything out of the ordinary. The house was a simple two-bedroom with a common layout. One room to the right, one to the left, with a bathroom in between. He poked his head in and opened the medicine cabinet mounted over the sink. A lone toothbrush and a sample-sized tube of Crest remained. The sight of such personal items caused his eyebrows to rise, but those things could be bought anywhere. No actual loss in leaving them behind. The shower curtain still hung from plastic rings over the tub and Horace ran his hand across the interior surface. It was drier than Palm Springs. He moved towards the larger of the two bedrooms.

It looked no different from any other rental. Cheap off-white paint, crappy brown carpet, and blinds that were impossible to clean and always got tangled. Horace walked around the room once, then twice. Looking at the floor, he found it peculiar that there were no marks. No furniture had been removed as if none had existed. The woman usually settled in for years, so the lack of fixtures after nine months felt odd. He opened the closet, which held nothing but a hanger. No scuff marks adorned the walls. None of the inevitable wear and tear that rental homes endure.

He moved onto the second bedroom, facing the back of the house. It too had the same cheap paint, carpet, and blinds, but seemed more worn. The coarse brown fabric revealed slight indentations. Nothing substantial, but something akin to furniture. With a delicate touch, he parted the blinds and looked over the vast emptiness behind the house. Something grew out there in the fields but he cared little about the details. Perhaps wheat or barley. Then he remembered he was in Idaho and assumed it must be potatoes. Either way, the intricacies of farming did not pique his interest. He was a city man whose proclivities could only be satiated in large urban areas.

Lost in that mundane thought, Horace took out his phone and dialed a number given to him at the start of the job. He had called it twice before. Three rings rolled by before someone answered.

———————

Two thousand miles away in a curving steel-clad building overlooking the Potomac River, James Abney drummed his fingers against his rosewood desk. Slim and modern, it sat on stainless-steel legs that formed two squares underneath the large rectangular top. It reminded him of the provost's desk at Harvard, only more expensive. The cost of a mid-range car in his case. Not that he sweated the money. Quite the opposite.

A shrill ringtone emanated from inside. He opened a drawer and removed a cheap flip phone. It came from a rundown bodega a few miles from the capitol. A place that had no cameras and only accepted cash. No record of the sale existed, which suited Abney fine.

"What news do you have?"

"She's not here. I'm moving north," replied Horace.

Abney's eyes narrowed. Years had gone into the search, not to mention the hundreds of thousands of dollars. Finding the woman meant a lot to him, but even more to his client. Not just any client. His benefactor. The reason for his success. A man Abney might call his father if he had allowed such a thing.

"Keep at it and remember I'm paying good money for this," Abney growled.

"Of course," Horace replied with an audible sneer.

Abney closed the burner phone and slid it back into the desk drawer, which closed with a soft click. He continued drumming his fingers against the smooth copper-colored top as the quiet action helped him think.

Filby came highly recommended by friends whose problems resembled his own. Despite his reputation, the man was not generating much success. The latest lead carried promise. He'd seen the image—it was her. Older and thinner, but still the same woman. Days had passed with nothing. Then the call came, and still nothing. A seed of doubt grew in his mind, calling into question Filby's abilities. He considered telling his client, but no news equaled failure and Abney did not fail. He built a business on success, results, and getting things done that others could not or would not do. No, the call could wait a little longer.

———

Horace placed the phone back in his pocket and took a deep breath. Clients were clients and money was money, but something about his current meal ticket chafed against his better judgement. He did not like the man or his attitude. He pictured the guy in an over-priced suit, the tailored kind, sitting in some leather armchair in a wood-paneled room. Smoke would waft by from the cigars and hollow laughter would fill the space. An asshole, if he cared to be so succinct.

Horace shook back his disgust and sniffed. Lingering on the stale air was the faint trace of perfume. He sniffed again, this time more thoughtfully. It was a woman's scent. He wondered how long essential oils hung in the air, but the question drifted to the back of his mind. The rear bedroom must have been hers. It made sense. The woman was no slouch. She had disappeared three times. Repetition bred experience, but it also created complacency. Too much success led to sloppiness and slip-ups. The local newspaper took her photo, which ended up online. The algorithms did the rest. His arrival was inevitable.

He turned to open the tiny built-in closet with scuffed wood doors. It was too late. They were already open. Standing in the small, shadowy interior was the woman from the photo. Her eyes were wide but focused and almost shiny in the gloom. Horace went for the Glock concealed beneath his shirt. It didn't matter. The scratched-up revolver in the woman's hands fired first. Knocked over by the force of the heavy grain bullet, Horace gazed at the white popcorn ceiling as it slowly faded to black.

The woman stood over the body for a moment, willing her hands to stop shaking. There was no doubt in her mind the man on the ground was dead. She hit center mass and the wound was fatal. A professional would have fired once more, just to be sure, but the woman was not a professional, not at that.

She reached down, grabbed the Glock, an extra magazine, and the phone before stuffing them into a plain green backpack. She searched for a wallet but found nothing. On the way out the back door, she stopped long enough to send a quick text from her own phone. Then she disappeared into the barley field.

Chapter Two

A six-door cooler of excessive choice towered over Captain Frank Sherman. He had picked the dilapidated liquor store for the opposite reason, looking to limit the possibilities. An old Schlitz sign still glowed neon red in the window and the place had a dingy vibe, yet there he was gazing at so many options as if the number of breweries had multiplied during his last deployment. Row upon row of colorful cans and names greeted his gaze. Each passing second only deepened his confusion. All he saw were IPAs—West Coast, East Coast, hazy, imperial, session, and sour. He rubbed his eyes, sighed, and grabbed something local. The thought of resinous hops in the summer heat didn't spark his taste buds, but it was still an indulgence. Only twelve hours prior, he had boarded a Lockheed C-5 Galaxy out of Iraq. The simplicity of the war was gone, replaced by excessive choice.

The blast of cold air washed over his face like a rogue wave. Everything in his life felt hot—the desert, the war, the flight home, and the liquor store in northern Texas. An old rattling air conditioner on the wall spit out a tepid breeze.

On the other side of the advertisement-covered doors, it was past triple digits. The heat was multiplying.

Sherman took his six-pack up to the counter, looking both sheepish and overwhelmed. The old man behind it had a complexion like one hundred grit sandpaper. He was too grumpy to be an hourly employee, so Sherman assumed he owned the place.

"My boy is in charge of the beer orders," said the man as if that explained everything.

"What do I owe you?"

"Ten bucks even."

A ten-dollar six-pack. Sherman shook his head in disbelief and pro shrugged. He had already offered his excuse. Taking out a bill from his wallet, Sherman went to offer it across the scratched counter when the front door chimed. One of those impossibly loud artificial dings. Sherman turned his head out of habit and watched the distinctive silhouette of a Colt M1911 pistol enter. A hooded figure with some dollar store ski mask followed the gun inside.

"Hands in the fucking air!" shouted the robber. "Cash out, slow like, or I put one through your face."

Sherman raised his hands. A twenty-dollar bill dangled between his fingers.

"I'll take that," growled the masked man. He had bloodshot eyes and yellowed skin.

"Fine by me," replied Sherman, looking the robber in the face.

"What ya looking at, old man?"

A crinkly smile crossed Sherman's mouth. He was not old, but he wasn't young anymore either. Three months humping around the valleys of Iraq had left him lean and tan, but also haggard and scraggly. Twelve hours on a hard metal jump seat had left him in no mood for half-measures.

A single glance at the barrel of the gun told him the whole affair was a sham. The pistol was a knock-off. A .22 caliber replica. His smile widened.

The robber took offense and swung the firearm towards Sherman's head. Over fifteen years of conflict, many guns faced his direction and the army shelled out a lot of money to make sure he survived those encounters.

Before the hammer struck brass, he had taken the pistol from the robber's hand. It clattered on to the peeling linoleum floor with a dense thump. Sherman latched onto the man's wrist and rotated his shoulder forward, straining the joint. Then, with all the considerable force he could muster, he slammed the guy's head into the countertop. No half-measures. A sickly crack sounded as the skull connected with wood. A concussion for sure—maybe worse. The robber crumpled like a fifty-pound sack of rice and fell to the floor unconscious.

Sherman took a pen from a small mason jar on the counter and gently picked up the pistol from the floor, careful not to leave any fingerprints. After placing it near the register, he held out the twenty-dollar bill.

The owner shook his head, shocked not by the robbery attempt but by the casual violence exacted. He mumbled, "It's on the house."

"Suit yourself," replied Sherman.

He stepped over the inert body on his way out. Blood was pooling in the eye sockets. Whatever gash hid under the mask would need stitches… assuming his brain didn't swell too much, then he would need more than stitches.

Sherman opened a can as he stepped into the blinding fever that Texas called July. It wasn't much different from Basra. Cooler, but with more humidity, so it felt about the same. He took a swig and smiled. He had left all his fatigues on base, including his boots. Only the sound of his cheap flip-flops echoed off the buildings as he walked towards nowhere in particular. One can was nearly empty when his phone buzzed. A single one-off vibration. The kind his brain was trained to recognize as important. A communication from the outside world.

He read the text: *Frank help 83219 Ruby.*

Sherman gulped down the last of the can and called the number. It went straight to voicemail—a computerized voice reading off digits. He had not seen or heard from Ruby in over a year. Not since Tillerman died. Not since California.

He opened another can and handed the rest of the six-pack to a homeless guy on the corner, then he started looking for a cab. Something ubiquitous ten years prior was now a rare commodity. Most people would have opened an app on their phone, but Sherman had a thing about being tracked. He valued anonymity at home and abroad. Some habits don't go away.

Six blocks further on, he finally flagged one down as he finished the beer. A faded yellow Crown Victoria with enough miles to drive to the moon and halfway back. The cabbie was in his sixties with a crumpled shirt and oily hair. He nodded in the mirror as Sherman got in the sedan.

"Where to?"

"The airport," answered Sherman. There was no point wasting time in Texas and no point going back for his meager belongings stashed at the base.

The cabbie raised an eyebrow at the bearded man sitting in the backseat with no luggage.

"I don't want any trouble," he said suspiciously.

"Neither do I," replied Sherman. He'd already had enough for one day and things were not looking up.

"Forty bucks then."

Sherman handed over two twenty-dollar bills in advance as a show of goodwill. The cabbie nodded again, and they lurched towards the regional airport, not the army one he flew in to. He pulled out his phone again. Nothing. Next, he searched the number from the text. Unsurprisingly, it came back as a zip code. What shocked him was the location.

"Idaho?" he mumbled.

The cabbie glanced back but said nothing.

Chapter Three

Wheels screeching against rough tarmac woke Sherman up from a deep sleep. The United Express flight was the second of two legs it took to get from northern Texas to western Idaho. One leg went to Salt Lake City and the second got to Boise. A calendar day had passed in between. He'd fallen asleep on both planes before the landing gear retracted. Getting sleep whenever he could was a habit formed over many deployments where it was a luxury easily missed. The guy in the adjacent seat nodded as Sherman unbuckled and rubbed the nap away from his eyes.

"I wish I could do that," said the man, who looked like a faded memory of Sherman's own grandfather.

Sherman raised an eyebrow in confusion.

"Sleep like that," the stranger clarified. "These things get me so riled up."

"Not a fan of flying?"

"That's putting it mildly, but the drugs help."

Sherman smiled as they waited for the passengers in

front to filter out of the plane. Small talk was not his favorite activity.

"What brings you to Boise?" asked the man.

"Just passing through," answered Sherman.

"Ah," he said as if that explained everything he needed to know. "You look like the river type."

What a river type looked like eluded Sherman, but he assumed his tan and ragged appearance gave him some credibility in that department. The hair on his head and face was well beyond army regulations, but his unit ignored that rule and the brass was amenable to looking the other way.

He nodded as if accepting the comment as fact, then followed the old man out of the cabin and into the terminal. They parted ways as his seatmate stopped to wait for some luggage and Sherman moved past the TSA point of no return. He stepped out to the curb with only the clothes on his back.

Morning had just arrived and the airport was empty. A newish-looking Prius sat at the head of a taxi line only two deep. Leaning against the car with his head buried in his phone was the driver. Sherman would not have put money on it, but he bet the guy was from East Africa. Ethiopia or Somalia came to mind... maybe Eritrea.

The cabbie raised his head up from his phone long enough for Sherman to make eye contact. They shared an unspoken understanding and Sherman got in the back seat.

"How goes it?" asked the cabbie. His English was clean but tinted with a colonial accent.

"Looking for an outdoor store."

The cab driver blinked hard like he was staring at some lost breed of human unfamiliar with Google.

"Downtown. Somewhere near the bus station," Sherman clarified.

The younger man scratched his head for a second and nodded thoughtfully. "I know a place," he replied, pleased with himself for remembering the location.

"Drive on," instructed Sherman.

The hybrid moved silently into traffic before the small engine kicked on when the driver floored it. He pressed the accelerator down far enough to negate all the benefits of the car. Sherman watched the colorful display of gas efficiency plummet as they weaved through a smattering of other vehicles. A few minutes later, they pulled up in front of a brick building painted white in some effort to appear newer than the walls underneath. A wooden sign stuck out across the sidewalk.

Gear Exchange, it read.

Sherman handed over some cash, thanked the driver, and walked into the store. Traipsing through rural Idaho in flip-flops and a t-shirt would not work. He needed some extra clothes and something to carry them in. If Ruby's message was real, things would take a grim turn and running around was a foregone conclusion. The question of how bad it would get was still up in the air, lingering in the background like a burnt bag of popcorn.

The store was open, but only barely. Two young guys stood behind the counter drinking mugs of coffee. They looked tired but cheerful. Sherman stepped inside and gave a polite wave or his best approximation of the gesture. The merchandise was mostly upcycled gear and overpriced clothing that did nothing to make the wearer better prepared for the outdoors.

An employee came over and asked if he needed anything. Sherman respectfully refused and wandered around the clothing section until he found a few items worth taking. A backpack, two pairs of pants, a few shirts, new underwear, socks, and some decent boots. The clerk looked at the selection of modestly priced choices favoring function over style and nodded in agreement.

The total came to two hundred and fifty dollars. It was more than Sherman had ever spent on clothing. In fact, he could not even remember the last time he bought clothes. Consumerism held as much mystery as the Loch Ness Monster. Uncle Sam provided all the basics and more.

The purchase went on a debit card linked to an account registered in the Bahamas. There was no name on the account, and only two other people were aware of its existence. A team account of last resort when they wanted to stay well off the radar.

Sherman used a small stall to change and the remaining clothes went into the backpack, along with the flip-flops and shorts. He walked out looking like half of the people on the street. An ATM was his next stop. He found one a few blocks south in the back of a 7-11 sandwiched between the Slurpee machine and a cooler filled with bags of ice. Sherman withdrew the maximum daily allowance from the same account. It was enough to keep him fed for a few days with some extra for other expenses.

From the convenience store, he wandered around the low-slung downtown area. Brick buildings from the McKinley administration mingled with sharp-angled glass towers. It was simultaneously quaint and conceited—new and old. Clean but not spotless, with a thin layer of grit. Overall, Sherman liked it, even though he was on the older end of the demographics.

After a dozen minutes of rambling, he spotted the bus station and grabbed a cheap paper map from one of the plastic holders on the wall. There was not much to show. It had one route east and two routes west. The east bound went through the state and then took a sudden turn south towards Denver like a finger curling down at the last knuckle. He bought a ticket all the way there. It cost three times as much, but Sherman didn't want a record of him stepping off the bus in Stalworth, Idaho.

Even the name struck a chord. The town was an Old English reincarnation of the Western ideal. Loyal, reliable, and hardworking. He imagined Ruby behind some cheesy Western-themed bar slinging whiskey and sarsaparilla. Then he looked around and took in the breweries, upscale restaurants, and copious amounts of hipsters. Maybe he had the state all wrong. Maybe she was living the river life-style—whatever that meant.

The bus didn't leave for another hour and Sherman kept on walking, more to break in the boots than to pass the time. About five blocks off the beaten path, he came across a gun store constructed of two green shipping containers welded together. The place billed itself as a tactical combat emporium. The gaudy hand-painted sign suggested hyperbole, but Sherman had seen stranger names. He stepped closer. The fine print on the steel cladding said China, but he kept that irony to himself.

Pausing for a few beats, Sherman considered the possibilities lying at the end of the bus ride east. Ruby was self-reliant, almost beyond the point of asking for help. She was stubborn and independent and lived on her own. That she had verbally asked for help made Sherman uneasy. Only something serious would have brought her out from behind a year's worth of isolation. Back in California, when the world teetered above the longest of nights, he knew she was running from something or someone. The fake accent, the act—it smelt of desperation. Cumbre County was as good a spot as any to hide. Remote places breed myopic gazes. That invisibility held true until he showed up and added to the cemetery's acreage. Running from the carnage was the smart choice. He didn't hold a grudge.

Gun laws in Idaho were relaxed compared to most states, but they would still record a name. All he had was a military ID and no urge to tie that to a firearm purchase. Beyond the paper trail, he still hoped that he was just chasing ghosts or over-inflated dangers. It was a small kernel of hope, and it faded with each passing hour. He tried the number again with the same result. With nowhere else to go and time running out, he headed back to the bus stop.

The depot was not much more than a bland concrete parking garage with a waiting room tucked underneath. An afterthought of design. Two dozen people were milling about in similar states of travel—not yet departed, and not arrived. Most kept to themselves, as was the nature of bus travel in America. A smooth wooden bench that could have been a church pew called his name, and Sherman leaned back to wait out the clock.

Chapter Four

Miles passed along the interstate as the bus traveled south, then east across the thickest width of the state. Sherman enjoyed the view of green grass, trees, and fields of crops. For months, he had seen nothing but shades of beige, not since his team left West Africa. The thin ribbon of water twisting across the valley brought back conflicting memories. It reminded him of childhood days spent splashing on the banks of the Feather River. It also conjured scenes of corpses floating down the Euphrates during the bloodiest days of the Iraq War when terror gripped the country.

Viewed through a moving window, the war seemed so distant. It surfaced as infrequent notes drifting into the nightly news. People went about their lives, hung flags on their front porches, but rarely talked about the Middle East. They lived insulated lives like most of America. Thousands of miles from the fighting. Some people who recognized a soldier gave him a 'Thanks for your service' remark, and some of them even meant it. The recognition was a friendly gesture, but Sherman didn't crave the attention or the gratitude. He didn't stay for some hope of ticker tape parades or a grateful nation. That was never his motivation, but then again, his once solid moral footing had turned to mud over the years.

"Stalworth, next stop," announced the driver over the distorted intercom.

The bus brakes squeaked as it edged off the highway and bounced into town. Plain bungalows sat behind tree-covered streets. Most of the homes looked like they were built seventy years earlier—the result of a post-war population boom.

The driver turned north on Central Avenue and they passed through a modest brick-clad business district. Most buildings were occupied, which was a luxury for small towns. The place looked solidly middle America. It reminded Sherman of a half-dozen towns they had already stopped in on their way east. The general quietness appealed to him. It was a place where someone could go about their life—someone running from their past.

Sherman grabbed his bag and moved up towards the front of the bus as they pulled into a parking lot. A dingy temporary building sat in the corner. A solitary couple were waiting on a nearby bench.

"Hey, you can't leave here," said the driver as Sherman made his way down the bus stairs with his backpack.

Sherman turned, surprised by the comment. "Why not?"

"You paid for all the way. They'll expect so many to get off in Denver."

The asinine policy reminded Sherman of army red tape. "You gonna stop me?"

The driver was a sizable man, but not a young one. He

eyed Sherman's muscular frame and cool gaze with eyes that looked more predator than human.

"Suit yourself," he barked and shut the door abruptly after the couple boarded.

They left Sherman standing in a noxious cloud of exhaust. The next bus didn't depart until the following day. He was stuck for at least twenty-four hours. Shouldering his backpack, he started walking down Main Street. He needed a meal and a place to start searching for Ruby. The bus depot was as centrally located as it could get. Left or right became the question.

His father always said, "When in doubt, turn right."

With a shrug, Sherman turned left and started looking for a bar. Thinking of Ruby and California and all that happened a year ago, the location made sense. It was familiar territory. The well-worn rut of habit and comfort. The locals out on the sidewalk eyed him wearily like he carried some disease. Stranger danger was something he understood, but their response felt overactive.

Two blocks further, he found a candidate. He stopped in front of a two-story brick building that could have come straight out of a Western movie save for the plastic sign sticking out above the solid wooden door.

Bedlam Bar and Grille.

Knowing Ruby's penchant for bad boys and worse boyfriends, it seemed like a suitable place to start. Sherman opened the door and walked inside the dimly lit space.

The place was empty but for a few locals with elbows glued to the bar, looking solemnly at the TV. From a distance, it looked like they were watching a rodeo. Everyone turned in unison as he walked inside. Each customer held him in a harsh gaze for a few seconds before, one by one, they turned back to the flat screen on the wall. Sherman had passed a test, although he did not understand what.

A wiry man in his mid-fifties with streaks of gray moved behind the bar as Sherman grabbed a stool. He looked uneasily at the appearance of a careworn stranger in his establishment. It took a few moments for him to ask for an order.

"Beer and burger," responded Sherman, looking at the special written on a chalkboard.

"ID," demanded the bartender.

Sherman shrugged. There was no way he looked under twenty-one and guessed the guy wanted to put a name to the face. He obliged and slid over his Military ID. The bartender softened his stance upon seeing an active-duty soldier. From his response, Sherman could see it was a God and Country type of town.

"Thanks," said the man.

Sherman nodded as if to say think nothing of it.

The bartender slid over a Miller longneck and Sherman took a swig. The other patrons left him alone, and he busied himself looking at the pictures on the wall behind the bar. There were hundreds, each attached with a pushpin. Most of the faces looked familiar in the same way high school yearbooks tended to all run together. There were a lot of cowboy hats and tractor supply store shirts. A few people appeared in many photos—the regulars.

His gaze stopped on a Polaroid near the top right corner. It was half hidden behind another picture. It showed a woman standing behind the bar. She was leaner with a different hairstyle and some stress behind the eyes, but it was Ruby. There was no doubt in Sherman's mind. At least his gut had been right, although it was a shallow consolation. It meant that her text was real and so was the trouble.

The bartender slid over his burger and fries. It was hot and greasy. Sherman chewed happily, enjoying his first proper meal in twelve hours. He slid the empty basket back after a few minutes.

Coming over to collect the empty container, the bartender asked, "What brings you to town?"

"I planned to meet a friend. She works here, or so she said," answered Sherman, observing the reaction.

The guy paused as his eyes narrowed and he turned towards the other patrons as if they had said something when they had not. He handed over a beer or two that had gone unordered, then reached for the phone. The way he looked over his shoulder told Sherman he would find trouble sooner rather than later. After hanging up, he grabbed another beer and dropped it off in front of Sherman.

"Sorry about that. You're the second fellow to ask about Audrey in as many days."

The mention of another person searching for Ruby, or whatever she was calling herself, caused Sherman's brow to furrow. He wondered who else was looking for her and why, but he already knew the answers would lead nowhere good.

"And this other guy?" asked Sherman.

"Ask him," said the owner, who was pointing towards the front door.

Everyone at the bar turned their heads. The Chief of Police was leaning against the doorframe, waiting for an invitation inside. Sherman frowned. His track record with small-town law enforcement was poor. One more corrupt cop might cause him to lose his patience.

"Good afternoon, Harold," said the chief.

"Chief," replied the bartender.

"What do we have here?"

The hammer was dropping, and Sherman was sitting right under it. There was no point in running and no point in fighting. He finished his beer and picked up his bag from the floor. The chief stepped forward with an aura of authority granted by badge and experience. He looked a shade under fifty with a few strands of gray streaking through glossy brown hair that parted neatly back. A finger under six feet tall, he was lean like someone who did more than sit behind a desk or driver's wheel.

"This man has been asking about Audrey. Says he's a friend," relayed the bartender.

The chief looked down at Sherman with a hard-practiced gaze and asked, "Well, is that true?"

All the patrons turned to gawk at the encounter. Sherman could feel their stares, waiting for his reaction. There was no doubt they would pounce on him if things turned south.

"The truth is more turbid than that," answered Sherman.

The chief smiled wide and thin. "I think you and I better have this conversation down at the station."

"I figured as much."

With another thin smile, the chief swept his hand toward the door. "After you."

Sherman didn't enjoy walking in front of the only gun in sight, but causing a scene had outcomes he could not predict. With a trace of reluctance, he agreed and sauntered out into the late afternoon light. The chief maintained a safe distance but was not unnerved by Sherman's appearance. Outside, Sherman looked around for a police cruiser, but there was nothing in sight. Maybe it was a stereotype, but he didn't know of any cops that walked as a primary mode of transportation.

When he was young, the neighborhood kids had TP'ed an entire block near the army base. Once the sun rose, the local sheriff drove around the area and pulled down the toilet paper without ever getting out of his truck. It was one of the laziest displays Sherman ever witnessed.

"Station is at the end of the block," said the chief as he pointed down a street Sherman had not explored.

He glanced over, looking for a name tag, but found none. He assumed everyone in town already knew the man, and it was superfluous to announce his name. It felt like that kind of place where everyone knows your name and people eye up strangers wandering the streets.

The two men walked the last block in silence. Neither cared to divulge what they knew in public as if their secrets were a burden no one else should carry. The chief held the front door open when they arrived at a large column-covered building. Dark stone walls contrasted against the white limestone columns. It was both imposing and homely. A beacon for the rule of law that tamed the frontier in the name of progress.

Past the industrial glass doors was a small hallway with the original wood floor. On the right were some city offices. Whatever the place needed to keep things running. According to a small sign, the mayor's office was upstairs. They turned left through another set of frosted glass doors that emblazoned the word POLICE across them, but they split it, so the left door had POL and the right ICE.

The decor of an aging municipality filled the interior space. Thin carpet with well-worn patches covered the ground. The rolling chairs were twenty years old, and the desks were from the 1960s. Sherman counted five of them in use, which put the department size at six, including the chief.

Two cops raised their heads as they walked back into the station. They were on the younger side of thirty and fit. A familiarity surfaced in Sherman's mind like he was looking at a family photo. The chief motioned towards a corner office and Sherman headed in that direction. It was modern compared to the rest of the interior. Calming blue tones adorned the walls and recycled wood shelves held several pieces of art. Even the desk was contemporary, with a metal top and pale wooden legs. A small nameplate etched in glass sat on top.

It read, Chief Talbot.

At least Sherman knew his name.

"I'll cut to the point, Captain Sherman," said Talbot once they had sat down. It appeared the bartender also passed on his name and rank. "Why are you here?"

The chief draped himself across the chair, at ease with his surroundings. He wasn't trying to pressure him with some tactic, which told Sherman a good deal. Either the cop was not worried about a stranger, or he was trying to gain his trust by playing nice. Unless the game was exceptionally long, Talbot did not see Sherman as a threat.

"Meeting a friend. She said I should visit when I had some time."

"And you show up now?"

"I don't get to pick my days off. Uncle Sam does that."

Talbot nodded thoughtfully. He did not strike Sherman as someone who served. He was too young for Vietnam or the first Gulf War. Maybe after 9/11, but there was no edge about him—that scorched aura surrounding those who saw the worst of the War on Terror.

"Well, the other guy asking about her ended up dead two days ago."

"Unnatural causes?" Sherman asked, although he already knew the answer.

"Would you be sitting there if it was another?" countered Talbot.

Sherman nodded with understanding. "How?"

The chief tilted his head to one side, seeing someone across his desk that was accustomed to violence. His town was small and rough around the edges, but few people were of that disposition.

"Someone shot him," answered Talbot after a moment, deciding on his willingness to share.

"Where?" asked Sherman, leaving the question vague.

"The chest."

"You have a suspect?"

"We found him in Audrey's house. You can imagine we would like to have a conversation with her. Perhaps you can tell me where I can find her."

The situation cleared as Talbot spoke. Sherman could see the motivations behind inviting him down to the station. A stranger was one thing, but a friend of a murder suspect was another. The chief yearned for a lead that he did not have.

"I thought she would be working. Haven't heard from her in a few days, not since I told her I was coming."

Talbot was an excellent judge of character. A lie detector of sorts. It was one of the job requirements. He was not sure what Sherman knew, not yet, but it was more than he was saying.

"Stay out of trouble," he instructed.

"Don't worry," replied Sherman. "I never go looking for it."

Talbot snorted in disbelief. "Somehow, I think it finds you just the same."

Sherman raised his hands in mock innocence.

"Where are you staying?" asked Talbot.

"Don't have a place anymore," Sherman answered.

"There is a motel out by the freeway. I can give you a lift."

Sherman had no intention of leaving town. He reasoned Ruby lived nearby and he needed more information. A motel by the freeway was nothing but a waste of travel time and an effort to isolate him away from town.

"I'm more of a B&B kinda guy," Sherman said.

Talbot laughed at the idea, although he knew nothing about Sherman. The idea of the captain sitting down for coffee with some retirees was unbelievable.

"Three blocks south. Betsy is her name. Nice old Victorian house. Get the hash browns," suggested the chief.

Chapter Five

Bacon sizzling in the pan woke Sherman up in the morning. It wasn't so much the smell as the distant memory it dug up. Something warm and happy from his childhood. Waking up at his grandmother's house to a hearty breakfast. The family gathered around the table, congenial and chatty. There weren't many of those... not like that.

Sherman slid out of bed and into the shower. He stood under the cascading hot water for a few minutes, processing what he knew and what he didn't. Some guy was dead, shot in Ruby's house. The location of the wound told him it was Ruby. A professional would have aimed for the head. Given her past life as a doctor, it also meant she wanted him dead. She was fearing for her life and fighting back. He needed to find her, and fast.

After throwing on some clean clothes, Sherman followed the smell of breakfast. He descended a wooden staircase colored like burned sugar and it creaked ever so slightly under his weight. The banisters were smooth and well-oiled from decades of use. Dozens of daguerreotype photos hung on the walls. A visual story of the past. Old faces and old names. English, German, Spanish, and what looked like Basque. Hardy folk filled with hopes of a better life. It was the story of the West.

"I collect 'em," said a honeyed voice from the bottom of the stairs.

Betsy was standing on the landing with a gingham apron wrapped around her slight frame. She was in her late sixties with neatly cropped white hair and eyes that burned with life. Sherman caught another flashback to his own grandmother.

"Do you know their stories?" he asked.

"Oh, here and there. But they're really not all that different."

Sherman understood but knew there was a lot more buried in that history.

"Come on down," cooed Betsy. "Breakfast is ready."

Having eaten only a burger and some bland pre-wrapped sandwich at the airport since leaving Iraq, Sherman felt ravenous. They sat down in a small, sun-filled eating area next to the kitchen. Like most of America, the formal dining room sat regally unused.

The spread did not disappoint. She piled plates up with fluffy scrambled eggs, strips of thick-cut bacon, and golden hash browns. In the center was a sizable carafe of coffee. Sherman beamed. He couldn't remember the last time he had a breakfast of that magnitude.

"Have a seat," said Betsy.

Sherman sat down and served himself a giant helping of everything. Betsy smiled and sipped on a cup of tea but did not eat.

"Not joining in?" asked Sherman between bites of hash browns.

"Oh, don't mind me. I had something earlier."

Given her thin silhouette, Sherman guessed she ate lightly.

"These hash browns are amazing. What's your secret?"

"I cook 'em in bacon fat," she said with a wink.

Sherman laughed and added another helping onto his plate.

"My late husband used to devour them," she added wistfully.

Betsy had an undertone of someone who had loved and lost and kept on living. It didn't surprise Sherman to hear talk of a late husband.

"How long ago?" he asked.

"Oh, Bill died three summers back." She sighed, then looked over at the hash browns and winked again, "Heart attack."

The tacit admission made Sherman smile. He appreciated the company and the meal.

"So, what brings you to town?" asked Betsy with a glint of curiosity in her eyes.

"Visiting a friend," Sherman replied before clarifying. "Or that was the plan."

"Who's your friend?"

Sherman almost said Ruby but corrected himself, "Audrey."

Betsy shook her head softly. "Poor girl. What a mess she's in. Talk of the town these last few days."

"What happened?"

A look crossed Betsy's face. Sherman guessed the meaning—the chief had called before he arrived at her doorstep, and she knew more about him than he did her. How much was still in question.

"Oh, the details are too gory to share in polite company," answered Betsy.

Sherman set his fork down and looked her in the eyes. "Believe me, I can handle the unsavory bits."

She hesitated a moment and then began. "Well, Dolly down at the beauty parlor told me they found a body in her house. An out-of-towner that no one knew. And get this... someone shot him."

Sherman nodded. It was nothing new but he could tell Betsy was a regular gossip mill. She was exactly the source he needed.

"And Harold, he owns the *Bedlam Bar and Grille* where Audrey works... well, he told my neighbor, Suzy, that very same man had come asking around about Audrey earlier in the day."

"And no one has seen her since?"

"Nope. Gone like a frog in the wind."

"Well," said Sherman. "That would explain why she's not answering my calls."

Betsy frowned with sympathy, "I'm sorry. I didn't even ask how you're doing in all this."

"I'm worried," said Sherman. There was no lie in that. "I want to make sure she's all right. This whole mess doesn't seem like her at all." That part held the lie. Ruby was in trouble—or at least running from it.

"She's such a nice young woman," added Betsy in agreement. "Helped me clean on weekends for a little extra money. Never complained. Always polite and such a hard worker."

The sudden change of Ruby's fortune troubled Sherman. No one had come looking for her in California, at least none that he knew. After so many years living on the edge, it attuned his mind to slight changes. An overturned garbage can or misplaced rock. Minute details were the difference between life and death. The difference between going back to base or being peeled off the ground piece by piece.

"Did she seem worried prior to the... uh... incident?" asked Sherman.

"Oh, well, I guess so. I saw her a few days ago and she looked tired, like she hadn't been getting much sleep. I thought it was from working too much at that bar. Told her to take care of herself."

Ruby had been bartending for years. Getting burned out so easily didn't seem like the answer. Sherman kept on probing for more information.

"Was she liked in town?"

"Oh, heavens yes. The boys... well, boys will be boys, and they liked her feminine figure, but everyone agreed she was a pleasant person. Why just the other week she won some drink-making competition, oh, what do you call them?"

"Cocktails," offered Sherman.

"Yeah, that's it. Got her photo in the local paper. Even got reprinted in the *Idaho Statesman*. Can you imagine that? Our little town in the state news."

The comment rolled over Sherman in a wave of concern. For someone on the run, having a picture printed in the local paper was a slip-up. Having that picture reprinted in a state newspaper was a borderline catastrophe. The software existed to find people from images. All it took was money. Lay low—that was the rule. Ruby broke it.

35

"She only told me to meet her at the bar," said Sherman. "Do you know where she lives?"

Betsy demurred for a moment as she decided how much truth Sherman had shared. "Sure. She's over off Vassar Street. Steel blue house at the end of the cul-de-sac."

"Thanks, I know strangers aren't exactly welcome right now."

"Oh, we're a mostly receptive bunch, but small towns close ranks when something bad happens."

"Understood. I appreciate the help."

"Well, I get the feeling you're on her side. Something about you reminds me of my Bill. He was a veteran too, you know."

Sherman smiled. "Is it obvious?"

Betsy chuckled, "You're too collected to be a river rat. Besides, Chief Talbot told me."

It was Sherman's turn to laugh. "I appreciate the honesty and the breakfast. Talbot was right about the hash browns." He turned to take his dishes to the sink.

"Oh, stop that. I'll clean up. Go and find your friend."

"Thanks, Betsy, I'll be back in a few hours."

She waved back to him while teetering to the kitchen with a mass of dishes.

Stepping out onto the covered front porch, Sherman looked down the tidy street loaded with mature leafy trees. Betsy lived in the oldest part of town, and there was a small clump of old Victorian homes standing like sentinels amongst the bungalows. About a half-block away, Sherman spotted a red sedan with too many antennas on the roof to be anything but a cop car. A faint silhouette was visible in the front seat. It appeared that Chief Talbot did not trust him in the least. He'd caught a shadow.

While walking over to the B&B during the previous

evening, Sherman had created a mental map of the area. Whether in Basra or Boise, his brain automatically charted all the streets, angles, and points of interest, besides the best ways in and out. He knew there was an alley behind Betsy's house that would take him around the uninvited guest.

Sherman stepped back through the front door and down a few steps that led to the backyard. It reminded him of a small oasis, rimmed with weeping willows leaning over a small pond brimming with lily pads. He slid through a gate in the wooden fence and took off at a jog down the alley.

Heading south, he passed two blocks in no time. The chance the cop would see him cross the street in his rearview mirror from that far away was close to none. He stopped running and casually walked the last quarter-mile right up to the cul-de-sac entrance. The sight of another cop car, this one plain as day, caught his attention. They parked the Crown Vic in front of a steel blue house, just as Betsy had described.

The choice of the cul-de-sac had confused him. It was a poor choice for someone hiding in plain sight. One entrance meant one exit, which was fine if they were planning for a fight, but not so great if they wanted to run. Then he saw fields of crops behind the house. He couldn't tell what from the satellite images, but the shadows almost looked long enough to conceal a person. The location suddenly made sense.

The cop was too busy with his phone to notice Sherman, so he doubled back and caught a small trail that led to the fields. Golden rows of barley stretched out across the valley and towards the river to the north. The stalks were about three feet tall. It wouldn't offer much concealment, but he didn't need it. An undulating wall of privacy fences stretched from the trail right up to Ruby's house. He hugged the barrier and in a matter of minutes stood on the other side of a gate built into the fence. There was a small latch operable from either side. Small-town security meant anyone could come or go.

Sherman placed his eye against a knot in the fence that had fallen out from years of exposure to the vagaries of Idaho weather. Most of the house was visible through the small hole. Unlike much of the town, the building was two stories tall and looked built within the last twenty years. A result of the neo-suburban boom that invaded many parts of the country.

Slipping through the gate, Sherman dashed up to the house. Police tape covered the back door in a zig-zag pattern. It made for an imposing visual barrier, but not an exceptionally good physical one. Crowbar marks were visible on the doorframe. Someone had broken in. Judging by the damage or lack thereof, Sherman guessed it was a professional. Using a shirt sleeve instead of gloves, he pushed open the back door and squeezed between the lines of yellow tape.

A stale stench of dried blood wafted up to his nostrils—familiar and metallic. His brain could pick it out easier than a normal person could tell the difference between pizza and coffee. The interior was still dark in the morning light, and Sherman took a minute while his eyes adjusted. He was standing in a dining area next to the kitchen. There was no table or chairs, and from what he could see of the living room, it was equally empty. He skipped the fridge and started checking the kitchen. Somehow, people always had a junk drawer, and they always took it with them when they moved like some unknown fear of scarcity drove them to carry it forward from one place to the next. He went through them all and found it at the bottom. It was still full of miscellaneous items—batteries, rubber bands, candles, and matches. Ruby had cleared out in a hurry.

Passing through the living room, Sherman stopped to peek out the closed curtains. The cop remained parked in front of the house with his head still buried in a smartphone. Probably games, news, or porn. The sight did not surprise him. A murder was more excitement than any of those guys had seen in years, but as it faded, only the banalities of procedure endured. Making sure no kids poked around the crime scene was one such chore. Sherman shook his head and walked up the carpeted stairs.

The top floor was simple enough. He glanced towards the street-facing bedroom but ignored it. There was too much exposure and he doubted Ruby would choose it. He didn't need to look into the other room to know it was the crime scene. His nose perceived the truth.

Standing over the crusty crimson stain—doubly dark against the cheap brown carpet—he visualized the events. Sherman glanced down at the floor, then up at the closet. He took a few steps and stood inside the compact space. It all lined up in his mind. Ruby had hidden in the closet, then shot the guy. Chief Talbot said the gunshot wound was in the chest, not the back, so she had waited until he turned around. She confirmed his identity before pulling the trigger. A holdover of her oath to do no harm. Sherman would have shot him in the back. No point in giving the guy a chance.

Parting the cheap blinds, he looked over the farm fields stretching out into the distance. The images on his phone showed a dirt road three hundred yards away by a small clump of trees. Sherman saw them in the distance. Behind the green leafy cluster, there was enough space to conceal a car. It was perfect for parking a getaway vehicle. The place he would park if sneaking into the house.

His mind played through the scenario. Ruby drove into the field and concealed the car. Sherman imagined an old SUV of some sort. It fit with the Wagoneer she owned in California. Then she must have headed inside. The risk was high—she knew someone was or would look for her. The gun proved that. Whatever she had come back for was worth the danger.

The mystery deepened but it convinced Sherman she walked out of the house alive and in one piece. Tangles of the web tugged at the edge of his mind. Evidence of the break-in suggested a professional. A man comfortable operating in the shadows of American life. Chief Talbot didn't mention a gun, but Sherman knew the guy carried a weapon. People like that didn't come cheap. Money exchanged hands, a good sum. Which meant someone out there was looking for her... someone with enough money to buy software that scrubbed through photos. Someone who could afford to hire a professional.

Sirens brought Sherman out of his internal detective monologue. For a moment, he considered his options. An image of the entire Stalworth police department parked out front flashed through his mind. Six officers lining the leafy streets with rifles pointed towards the house. Maybe only four, with two in the back.

There were only two ways out of the bedroom—down the stairs and out the back door or out the window. He ran to the other bedroom and peeked out the blinds. The cop car was speeding away down the cul-de-sac and onto the street. Something more interesting had occurred. Disappointed with his own sloppiness at almost getting trapped, Sherman shook his head and walked out the back door and towards the gate. He slipped through the small opening and stood on the other side of the fence, taking in the undulating fields. It reminded him of a painting. Something quintessentially American, although he could not remember the name or where he had seen it.

The echo of a car door closing caught his attention. Perhaps it was a neighbor or the cop returning from his joyride. Hidden behind the fence, he looked through the missing knot once more. The angle was too oblique to see the nearby homes, but he had a decent view of Ruby's house. Two more doors slammed in quick succession. Not the cop.

A warming sun enveloped the field and earthy smells wafted across on a slow breeze. It was pleasant and comforting. A little bell in the back of his mind said hold, so Sherman waited. Not more than a minute later, three figures made their way around to the back door. Two men and one woman. One man wore a suit, tailored and expensive. The other two wore boots and cargo pants, not so different from what Sherman had on. Hats covered their faces and they moved with a calm confidence. The suit was different. He was all polish and no spit. Ego and arrogance dripped off his thousand-dollar jacket and gold Rolex. They made for an odd trio.

The suit nodded towards the door and the woman slid between the tape. She reappeared a moment later and said something that Sherman couldn't quite hear. It must have been 'all clear' for the other one stepped inside, but the suit stopped him. Tilting his head to one side ponderously, the man gazed out towards the fence and the fields beyond, then he motioned towards the gate. The other man shrugged and started walking in that direction. By the time he opened the wooden gate, Sherman was long gone.

Inside the rental, James Abney gazed around the kitchen with an eye made for detail. An ever so small piece of floor near the wall showed slightly less dust. A small table fit there, made for two at most. A clean fridge and unsoiled stove told him the woman ate at work more than at home. Several stains in one cabinet came in unique shapes. Some circles, some rectangles, some squares. *Booze bottles,* he thought.

Upstairs, he stared at the crusted crimson stain. Filby found her. At least he was good for something. He turned to the woman, looking for answers.

She stepped forward. "The coroner confirmed his identity this morning. Horace Filby. Will he tie back to you?"

Abney scowled at the idea. Four layers of shell companies lay between him and Filby. No forensic accountant on the government payroll could make that connection.

"No."

"Where to now?" asked the man. "The border?"

With a practiced flick of his hand, Abney smoothed out his hair. Cutting it cost more than a steak at Peter Luger, but appearances mattered in his business. They printed 'Lobbyist' on his business card, but the title undersold his abilities. Fixer came closer to the truth but still fell short.

"No," replied Abney.

The other two looked at each other for a moment. Experience told them otherwise, but they hesitated to contradict.

"Where then?" asked the woman.

"I have two spots in mind. One today. One tomorrow."

"Why not the border?" she asked.

"She doesn't have a passport."

"How do you know?" asked the man.

"Because I asked around."

The woman narrowed her eyes. She did not relish her current situation, but some debts required more than just money for repayment.

"Let's go," said Abney, motioning towards the door.

Chapter Six

Ice cubes clinked in the glass of water as Sherman absentmindedly swirled it about. Two hours had passed since he left Ruby's house, but it felt like an entire day. His mind was whirring with activity—the break-in, the shooting, the random team snooping around Ruby's house. He leaned back in a lounge chair, warmed by the morning sun, nestled in Betsy's backyard.

"You find anything?" came a sugary voice.

Sherman turned to see Betsy standing in the doorway with a pitcher of iced tea.

"Depends on your definition."

"Oh?" asked Betsy as she took a seat.

"How much did Talbot tell you?"

Betsy laughed a little at the directness of the question. "A little here and there. He mentioned you served."

Sherman nodded along with the fact. "Can I ask you another question?"

"Of course."

"How much are you going to tell him?"

The question had been on his mind since he walked through her front door. The motel was an obvious choice for Talbot. It kept him secluded, away from the action. Offering the B&B was not a coincidence.

"Oh," replied Betsy with a sly grin. "Aaron is a dutiful man, but he can be overprotective. This town... well, it's home. His daddy was the chief and his daddy before that. His family was here when the first stone was laid."

"So, he's a local boy doing good?"

"Well, there ain't much doing around here."

"Sounds agreeable to me," replied Sherman.

"Oh, sometimes a little fun can be good for the soul. Besides, Audrey is a decent woman. I don't think she'd do something like that."

"I hate to be the bearer of bad news, Betsy, but Audrey pulled the trigger," replied Sherman. He didn't see the point in dancing around the issue.

If there was surprise in her eyes, Sherman did not see it, like she almost expected the fact.

"Some things aren't always what they seem," replied Betsy as she held her glass up in a mock toast.

There was a coyness to her look that made Sherman wonder what other things she had seen and what other stories lingered in her past. He sipped on the iced tea and watched her eyes dance around. There was a kindred spirit lurking behind them.

"What else do you know?" he asked.

"Oh, Frank. Where should I start?"

"What do you know about Audrey?"

Betsy refilled her glass slowly and took a moment. "Like I said, she is a decent woman. Came to town about, oh, nine months ago. Mostly kept to herself."

"Did she say anything about her past?"

"She had a story, that's for sure."

"Sob story?" asked Sherman, although he did not know why. Nothing about Ruby said she was one to cry on cue.

"No, no. Nothing like that. She was moving out of the city, looking for something quiet. You know how expensive those places are these days."

"Not really, but go on," replied Sherman. He had lived nowhere outside of an army base or a friend's couch for fifteen years.

"Well, we've had an influx of Boise folk looking to downsize. Small-town charm and the river are big draws."

Sherman hadn't considered the river and had even forgotten about the comment from his seatmate on the plane. "Yeah, a guy on my flight told me I looked like the river type."

Betsy eyed him sideways and nodded a little. "You have, oh, how do I say this, a grunge to you... like a mangy lion."

The comparison was not so far off from what Sherman saw in the mirror earlier that morning, and he laughed with Betsy. Lurking around the Syrian border had somehow given him the same look as rafting the Snake River.

"So, that was it? Said she was coming to live a quiet life."

"Pretty much."

"And did you buy it?"

"Oh, not really. She was no rich city folk with kids. I believed she was looking for a quiet life, but who was I to pry?"

"Fair enough. What about friends or hobbies? What did she do in her spare time?"

"Mostly worked from what I could tell. I think she mentioned getting on the river when she could."

Ruby had not struck Sherman as an outdoorsy type, but

he did not know her well. In fact, there were few things he knew with certainty. He didn't even know if Ruby was her actual name, although he suspected it was not. She was a doctor in a former life—before all the running began. A faded scar on his bicep was proof of her skills. She drifted towards trouble, but that was where his knowledge ended.

"Any love interests?" asked Sherman.

"There were boys lining up for that honor, but I don't think she was looking for a relationship."

One more tidbit of truth came to his mind regarding Ruby. She did not like commitment.

"Where do you think she is?"

"Honestly, I don't have the faintest idea. Before you showed up, I hoped she was long gone. Now… well, I hope you can help her out."

"Me too," added Sherman after he finished the glass of iced tea. "Thanks for that."

"You off?"

"The amber waves of grain are calling my name."

"Do you like fried chicken?" asked Betsy.

"That's the best question I've heard in months."

She smiled. "Early dinner then?"

"I don't remember an included dinner on your brochure," he joked.

"You're paying for the presidential suite, right?"

"I guess so."

"Well, then. Be back by five."

"See you then," said Sherman, standing up to leave. He headed out the back gate as Betsy watched with a sly grin.

There was no point in going out the front, even if the cop was no longer parked on the street. Talbot was suspicious, too much so to let Sherman wander around town unencumbered. So, he walked down the alley and back towards the small trail leading out into the field. When he came to the opening, nestled between two drooping spruce trees, Sherman headed right and away from the fence.

The hip-high barley swayed in the late morning breeze. A wide summer sun hung in the cloudless sky. Sherman inhaled the aromas of mature grain and thought of how far back the scene stretched into human history. All those farmers that settled down millennia ago. Those ancient Mesopotamian towns that crisscrossed the Fertile Crescent. He had spent half of his adult life fighting in that same land. The irony stuck with him, so did the memories of lost friends and limbs scattered about the packed dirt in the aftermath of an IED.

By the time Sherman reached the small grove of trees, his mood had soured with thoughts of the past. He stopped to lean against the trunk of a wide ash tree. For a moment longer, he dwelled in those curdled memories, then he stooped down to look at the tracks in the dirt.

There were at least a dozen tire tracks crossing the road and running behind the trees. Farm trucks seemed the most prevalent, but the large tread of tractors was also visible. Sherman glanced in either direction down the slender length of barren dirt. Somewhere in the distance, it connected to another dirt road and then another until one ran into pavement and a major artery of transportation. Ruby could have gone either way. They both led out of town.

Sherman was no expert tracker. He had many skills, but trying to read the tire marks on the ground was as confusing as a Tarot deck. Spotting the difference between truck treads was pure conjecture. Too many vehicles had used the road. Hitting a wall, he turned to look between the trees. The ground was dry from the summer sun and he did not see any identifiable footprints. Some scuff marks existed, but nothing that showed a definitive size. He scoured the ground, flicking about leaves and grass.

Stuck under a tarnished penny and next to an empty Chapstick tube was a small receipt folded in half. The Chapstick smelled sweet and sickly like a chemist's version of passionfruit. Sherman smoothed out the paper. It was an ATM withdrawal slip from Yarrow Hill Casino. The name meant nothing to him. Just another place to waste money. But the Chapstick smelled feminine. Maybe it belonged to a farmer, or maybe to Ruby. The scenario was not too far-fetched. The stuff could have fallen out when she took out her keys, but the paper looked positioned under the coin.

As his commanding officer, Major Sanders, once said, "There are no coincidences in our world."

He put the items in his pocket and headed back to Betsy's house. The cop car remained down the street, so he followed the alley and went in the back entrance. It was a familiar pattern and he knew it needed to change. Eventually, the police would catch on to his movements. Complacency in Afghanistan or Iraq had worse consequences, but he wanted no more trouble from the locals.

The back door was unlocked but Betsy was not home. A note on the dining room table read:

Frank,
Gone out for groceries. Make yourself at home.
-Betsy
P.S. There is beer in the fridge

Sherman obliged and grabbed a bottle of something cold. He took a seat outside on the chaise lounge, grabbed his phone, and searched for Yarrow Hill Casino. The map showed it about ninety minutes north of Stalworth and the edge of some state park. His image of casinos formed during the drunken crucible of a few Las Vegas vacations. The quaintness of the pictures posted online surprised him. The building was a stocky two stories tall and had more in common with a Motel 6 than Caesar's Palace. It reminded Sherman of one of those roadside motels with an attached diner he'd seen off Route 66. Except the restaurant was a casino and the hotel looked like it charged by the hour.

"Nice place," he joked to himself.

There was no public transport in that direction, at least none that Google could find. Sherman wandered inside the house searching for something most Americans forgot existed. He found it in a small desk drawer under the landline Betsy kept for guests. The phonebook was slimmer than he remembered them being, and the paper felt even cheaper. A result of razor-thin profit margins in the age of the internet. He flipped it open to Transportation and dialed the only number he found for a taxi service.

A sour old voice answered on the fourth ring. "Stalworth Taxi, this is Bob."

"Hi, Bob, quick question for you," said Sherman. "How much to get up to Yarrow Hill Casino?"

There was a moment of silence as the person on the other end calculated how much money he could extract from the caller. "A hundred bucks each way," was Bob's answer.

"Great. Are you available now?"

Bob tried to sound busy. "Uh, I can shuffle some things around, sure. Where should I pick you up?"

"I'm at the B&B on Cherry Street."

"Oh, it's you. Sorry, friend, I've been told to steer clear."

Sherman chuckled. He should have seen it coming. "Did Chief Talbot tell you that?"

Bob sighed loudly at losing two hundred dollars. "Yeah, sorry."

Sherman hung up without saying another word. *Strike one*, he thought. A ride-sharing app crossed his mind, but they left too much of a digital trail. A credit card tied to GPS data. Leaving no trace of his stay in Stalworth was priority number one. He had been clumsy back in California. The blowback came too close to home. Plenty of sins littered his past, but prison was not the punishment he deserved or wanted. There was a bullet waiting for him out there, somewhere.

Doing nothing took effort. Sherman was a man in perpetual motion. Sometimes he could quiet his natural urge to act, but it usually took a beach and the calming crash of waves against the sand. Idaho had no such amenities, and Ruby's text dispelled any chance of relaxation.

He finished his beer and stood up. The sun tilted past noon. Sherman had a few ideas for getting to the casino— one of which was legal. For half of his life, niceties such as American law never applied. There was the law of war and the rules established by the Geneva Convention, but those were more like guidelines. He wasn't in a conflict zone, nor was he on Uncle Sam's dime, so he suppressed his natural urge to act beyond the confines of domestic law. That meant waiting for Betsy.

Chapter Seven

His patience lasted until the bottom of a second bottle. Then he walked right out the front door and turned towards the small downtown area. The sound of an engine starting rumbled over his shoulder as the cop turned on the unmarked Crown Vic. Sherman didn't mind. He was not trying to hide. Staying inside too long would only create cause for suspicion. His primary goal was withdrawing some more cash. He would need it soon enough, but he wanted to put on a show for Talbot. He strolled down the main street in shorts and flip-flops.

A few other people were wandering around—not too many, even for a weekday. He headed north towards the river. It was hard to miss. The wide ribbon of water wrapped around the town like a horseshoe. Near the river's edge, there were a few small wooden buildings advertising rafting trips and boat rentals. Most were dilapidated, with sagging roofs and fewer amenities than a storage shed.

One, however, welcomed guests with a covered deck and bar. Bluegrass drifted out and friendly chatter filled the air.

There were about twenty people milling about with beers in hand. An old van sat silently in the gravel driveway. Boats piled up on the trailer it towed still glistened from droplets of water, and dozens of lifejackets were drying on a nearby clothesline. The day's rafting group was back from their adventure.

Sherman wandered inside. Betsy had mentioned that Ruby liked the water, and he had time to kill. No one took much notice as he stepped onto the deck. Most were too busy watching replays of their escapades on the TVs to care. Snippets of video showed rafts pitching and rolling in massive rapids as looks of fear and joy contorted people's faces. The adrenaline pumping through their systems was a familiar sight for Sherman. He recognized that momentary sensation of panic and euphoria when life hung in the balance and nothing else existed but the next rapid.

"What can I get you?" asked a voice from behind the bar.

Turning away from the video, he smiled at a tan, no-nonsense woman. Dirty blonde hair tumbled out from under her green trucker hat. She tilted her head, waiting for his response.

"A few minutes of your time," he replied.

The bartender looked around at the crowd, enthralled with their conquest over nature. Everyone had a beverage in hand and no one seemed ready to order another.

"Alright, what do you need?"

"Do you know Audrey? Bartends over at *Bedlam*."

"You a friend?" she replied suspiciously.

"Yeah," said Sherman softly. "I heard she got into a spate of trouble."

"Sounds that way."

"Did she ever get on the river?"

The woman gazed at him for a few moments. "Yeah, she did a couple of trips with us and filled in behind the bar occasionally. We let her store her kayak."

"Kayak?" asked Sherman.

"Yeah, a sit-on-top one. She liked the flat water after the canyon."

"Where did she keep the kayak?"

The bartender pointed towards a small shed near the river. Sherman nodded as one rafter sidled up to the bar for another beer. The shed was four walls and a roof, nothing more. A few kayaks were sitting on metal pegs but they were all small whitewater varieties. Although Sherman knew little about water sports, he could see that Ruby's kayak was missing. He wandered back. The bartender raised an eyebrow as he approached.

"Can I ask you another question?"

The woman leaned in closer. "You wanna know where she's at?"

Sherman nodded, knowing he had not been discreet.

"Let me ask you one first."

He nodded again.

"Where d'you serve?"

Sherman smiled at the no-nonsense observation. He'd seen a shade of the desert in her gaze. "Four tours in Iraq, three in Afghanistan, and a bunch of others I can't tell you about."

The woman listened intently, bobbing her head along with the obvious. "Special forces," she concluded.

Sherman shrugged at the truth.

"So, what brings you here, Lieutenant?" she began before pausing. "No, wait... Captain. What brings you here, Captain?"

"Thanks, Sergeant," answered Sherman, taking a guess at the woman's former rank.

"Staff sergeant. How d'you know?"

"NCOs always know rank, so you can see what kind of trouble is coming down the hallway."

"I'm Maya," said the bartender, extending her hand.

"Frank Sherman."

"How can I help you, Captain Frank Sherman?"

"Audrey's boat is missing. Is there anywhere she liked to go?"

Maya paused a beat. "Lake Ohapite has some nice water. It's two hours north of here."

"Past Yarrow Hill Casino?" asked Sherman.

Maya nodded at the location and the capabilities she saw in the captain across the counter. "The one and only."

"Thanks," said Sherman as he stood up to leave.

"I'm glad you're on her side," added Maya.

Sherman waved as he left. He heard the growl of a modern V-8 as he stepped back on to the main street. The cop had not come into the bar, at least he had seen no one else enter, so he must have been waiting for Sherman to exit. Not that it mattered. He was heading back to Betsy's after a quick stop at the bank ATM. It was dinnertime.

An amazing aroma drifted down the block and Sherman felt the pangs of hunger before he even walked through the front door. Betsy was standing in the kitchen managing three massive cast iron skillets at the same time. She smiled as Sherman slipped inside and took a seat at the table, already piled high with mashed potatoes and salad greens.

"I hope you're hungry," she said with a wink.

"I am now," he answered.

She finished frying up the last few pieces of chicken and

brought over a heaping tray. They both dug in, and for many minutes, he disappeared into the meal. Away drifted the past and the present. The war receded in the warmth of a clean, well-lit home. Betsy said nothing for those precious moments. She was happy to have someone to cook for, and that was enough. After Sherman polished off his third piece of chicken, he came out of his daze.

"Thanks for all of this. It's amazing."

"Oh, it's nothing," said Betsy with a smile. "Glad to share it with you."

"This is not nothing."

Betsy shooed the comment away with her fork, waving it in the air. "Tell me, how did your amber waves of grain fair? Did you find anything?"

Sherman wiped his hands on a napkin before rubbing them together. "A receipt for a casino and some Chapstick."

He held up the empty tube.

Betsy eyed the plastic cylinder. "Passionfruit?"

"Yeah," answered Sherman, suddenly realizing the flavor somehow fit with Betsy. "That came from you?"

She laughed with a hint of embarrassment. "I may have gone overboard at Target. I don't get up there that often."

"No judgement here."

"So, she was at Yarrow Hill?"

"It seems that way. Are there any other casinos around?"

Betsy gave the question a moment of thought. "Not really. There is one in a truck stop on the way east, but it ain't much more than a few slots next to the Subway counter."

"What are your thoughts on me borrowing or renting your car for the day?" asked Sherman with as much sincerity as he could muster.

"Did Bob turn you down?"

Stalworth was certainly a small town, and it kept reminding Sherman of that fact.

"Yeah, Talbot is keen to keep me close."

"I'm afraid the answer is no. A meal is one thing, but the car is too much."

He didn't begrudge her choice. She didn't know him.

"Where are you going?"

"Yarrow Hill Casino."

Betsy smiled wide and thin. "I'll drive," she said to his surprise. "I love playing the slots."

"I don't want to drag you into this."

"Where's your spirit of adventure, Frank?"

"I'm more of an abundance of caution type of guy," he replied.

"How's that working out for you?"

He shrugged, "I'm alive."

Betsy's eyes narrowed. She could see something of her former husband in the younger man. A ferociousness simmered behind his eyes, giving them a feral glow.

"Does eight sound good?" she asked.

"It does. I appreciate your help and thanks for the dinner."

"Oh, we're not known for our dining around here. Fine or otherwise. The only decent place is the Mather Hotel."

Fine dining. The phrase reminded Sherman of his remaining task for the evening—the man in the expensive suit. He had not mentioned the trio snooping around Ruby's for a reason. The scrap of paper was innocuous and held no tangible value other than as a thin string worth tugging on until it unraveled. The three strangers were a threat—a genuine danger. One that Betsy needed to be insulated from, lest it spill over into her world.

"Sounds fancy," he said.

"Very."

He smiled and they continued to talk about the town and its peculiar past, illustrated in such stark detail by the photos on the wall.

"How long has your family been here?"

Betsy looked up for a moment as she added up the generations. "Oh, since the railroad."

"Forgive my lack of history knowledge, but that was quite some time ago. Right?"

"It was," she admitted.

"And they never left?"

"Some of us have come and gone, but we never leave."

"There is something comforting in that."

Betsy smiled. "Do you know the Idaho state motto?"

"No."

"Esto Perpetua."

Sherman thought for a moment. "Let it be perpetual."

"Not so bad with languages, are you?"

"I speak a few."

Betsy said nothing but curiosity dotted her cheeks.

At the end of the meal, Sherman once again tried to clean up, but Betsy refused. Doting on someone was making her happy. Excusing himself for a walk, Sherman headed towards the Mather Hotel.

The evening was still young and he was happy that Betsy ate at such an early hour. It gave him time to look for the competition. Caught up in the casino and the lake, he had not stopped to consider where the trio was staying until Betsy brought up the hotel. A man with a taste for fancy suits wouldn't be staying at some motel by the freeway and eating at Denny's. That just didn't compute. Someone with a gold Rolex would demand better.

Walking gave him time to think. If the dead guy was an employee of sorts, it stood to reason he was their only link to Ruby. Why else come looking? And if they were looking, it also made sense he did not pass on any recent information. Stalworth was the last point of contact between the dead guy, the trio, and Ruby.

The hotel sat back against the river on the west side of town with a circular driveway flanked by tall pines. Old gas-lamp-style streetlights lined the drive, and Sherman couldn't tell if they were authentic or not. The age of the place said they were, but appearances were often deceiving. Having got a better look at the building itself, it had a frontier chic that reminded Sherman of some National Park hotel. Rock and wood were the materials of choice, and the whole facade blended with the surrounding trees. The grounded qualities struck a chord and he immediately took a liking to the place.

An enormous oak door with cast iron handles opened into a cavernous space. Sherman stepped inside and was greeted by a middle-aged woman with black hair that fell over the sides of her glasses. She stood behind a concierge desk for hotel guests.

"Can I help you, sir?" she asked, a bit surprised to see someone so casually dressed.

A grand-looking staircase behind the desk went upstairs and Sherman could see a bar straight ahead. A small sign pointed to the restaurant, which appeared to connect to the bar.

"Just here for a drink," he said with a smile.

The woman motioned with her hand. "The bar is straight ahead."

"Thanks."

He passed through a pair of heavily polished French

doors and back in time about one hundred years. The bartender was wearing a vest and bowtie with a white apron tied around his waist. The wooden bar top wrapped around a central stone wall in a lowercase 'r' shape, so that end looked beyond the wall and into the restaurant itself. Sherman took a high-back chair with good sightlines across the sea of white linen-covered tables and waited.

The bartender, whose name tag read Stan, sauntered over. He was younger than Sherman by a few years and didn't eye him with the same suspicion as the woman at the front desk.

"What can I get you?" he asked.

"Bourbon," replied Sherman after looking up at the shelves of golden liquors glowing softly like a warm fire.

Stan looked at him for a moment as if considering what the man would appreciate before returning with a half-filled lowball glass. Sherman sniffed at the amber liquid and pretended to know more than he did. The small dining room buzzed with activity, and he wondered why all those people were in an insignificant town like Stalworth. The bar was almost empty and Stan was only intermittently busy making drinks for the dinner crowd.

During a lull, Sherman asked, "Busy night?"

"Most are locals," answered Stan. "They come from around the county."

"Do you get many guests in the hotel?"

"Not so many at this time of year." Stan nodded towards the table Sherman was discreetly looking at. "I think they're the only ones staying right now."

Three people sat around a thick square table—two men and one woman. Servers in white tuxedos were shuffling dishes about and refiling glasses of wine. All three were at some stage of devouring a porterhouse steak. Sherman recognized them immediately. The suit was sitting like a king ruling over his empire. While they had changed out of the athletic wear, the younger two still looked out of place. They ate quietly, deferring towards the older man who gestured when he talked. The guy looked to be in his late forties with a few silver streaks in his hair that Sherman had not noticed that morning. He had an aura of confidence brought on by years of ordering people about. A man of clout.

The longer Sherman watched, the more he saw the man check his phone, which sat facing up next to his steak. His constant looks down, between sweeping gestures and small talk, gave Sherman the impression the suit was not the top rung of the ladder. He was still on someone's leash.

"City folk?" asked Sherman.

Stan shrugged. "The boss has a real thick southern accent. We don't get many like that up here."

"Really!" said Sherman in mock interest. Shared disdain created conversation. "He got some good ol' boy kinda name?"

The bartender snorted with laughter. "Yeah, kind of. Abney is the last name."

"Sounds entitled."

"Got the looks to match," joked Stan.

Sherman agreed. He watched the group eat for a few more minutes. Long enough to form an opinion. It started with the younger two. The man had jet-black hair that got buzzed short. The woman had hers in a ponytail that kept the dirty blonde strands out of her face. They sat upright with straight backs and eyes that darted around the room, looking for the unknown. Sherman recognized something in the hollowness of their gaze. An emptiness of spirit or compassion. Maybe not killers, but close enough that they would act without question.

Mr. Abney was not altogether different but he looked more a fixer than a doer. With piercing gray eyes, he stopped staff in their tracks and demanded complete acquiescence from those around him. He had taste and the money to buy it, which meant he worked for someone with deep pockets. Deep enough to send a loyal lieutenant and some wannabe hitmen out to rural Idaho.

"Another?" asked Stan.

"I'm good," replied Sherman as he slid across a twenty-dollar bill.

"Change?"

"No, thanks. Have a good night."

The bartender nodded as Sherman slipped back out through the posh interior and into the cooling night air. A faint gurgle sputtered to life as he walked down the street towards the B&B. Dim shadows danced on the sidewalk, lit by the faint running lights somewhere down the block. Talbot was not giving up his surveillance.

Chapter Eight

A few faint stars clung to the fading night when Sherman awoke. The alarm on his phone was still twenty minutes away. He had taken a quick shower the night before, so he slipped into his remaining clean clothes. By the time he stepped on the top landing of the stairs, the smell of freshly brewed coffee was enveloping the house. In the kitchen, Betsy stood dressed and ready to go.

"I thought you might be an early riser," she said before holding out a mug.

"I would have waited."

"Why waste the time? I'm guessing there is more to the story than you told me."

"Some things are best left unsaid."

Betsy looked at him long and hard like she was drilling through a shell of self-righteous gibberish. "I'll let you have your secrets, but if you need help, you must turn on the lights."

A small smile cracked across Sherman's face. There was

little that escaped her attention like a diminutive eagle. "Alright, I'll tell you on the drive up."

"Oh, good. I packed some leftovers for lunch and made some breakfast burritos for us."

"Of course, you did," replied Sherman with admiration.

Gathering up the coolers, Betsy led the way into the garage. A small blue RAV-4 sat parked in the tidy space. Everything about the woman was orderly and precise. Energy radiated out from her and Sherman felt like he was just along for the ride.

"You better hop in the backseat. We don't want Carl out there to see you."

"You know about that?"

"It's a small town. I know his mama. We play canasta together. Besides, all this hullabaloo is the most excitement those boys ever had."

Sherman suddenly got the impression that it was Betsy who was not telling him the complete story.

"Alright, lean down," instructed Betsy.

She pulled out of the garage, drove down the alley, and swung around on the street in front of her house. The car slowed and then came to a stop. Sherman slid down to the floor below the back seat. Betsy rolled down the window.

"Good morning, Carl, I brought you a breakfast burrito." She handed a small bag out of the window.

"Thanks, Betsy!" called a voice as they drove away.

For a few more minutes, Sherman stayed on the floor, laughing softly to himself. Finally, Betsy flashed him a thumbs-up, and he climbed over the armrest and into the front seat. They were on the far side of the river and headed north on a two-lane state road. Farms bracketed the surrounding area like a jigsaw puzzle of squares and circles.

"You're devious," joked Sherman between sips of

coffee. An unwrapped burrito sat on its foil in his lap. The aroma of bacon and green chili wafted up.

"Oh, I have my moments," replied Betsy with a flick of her wrist.

Thin stripes of brown grass hemmed in the black asphalt, making it look like a strange sandwich. Beyond the dead grass lay fields of green alfalfa. The mountains faded on the horizon when the valley sunk downward as if pulled by some hidden weight. Betsy kept the speedometer close to the legal limit and an impish smile stretched across her face. Miles passed with no discernible change. Every time Sherman glanced out of the window, they appeared to be in the same spot as before. It reminded him of driving through Kansas as a kid. Miles of nowhere.

"So," Betsy began as she threw a sideways glance. "Are you going to tell me what happened?"

"My very unprofessional opinion?"

"Self-depreciation aside, I think you're probably very good at your job, Frank."

"I am," replied Sherman in a modest tone.

"Good, now tell me what I am driving into."

"Audrey," said Sherman, almost mincing the names, "shot that guy in her house. I think he was searching for her."

"She was on the run?" asked Betsy, but her question carried minor surprise. It was more of a confirmation of something she already knew.

"Yeah. From what, I don't know. But I am not alone in looking for her."

"Oh," said Betsy.

"Three people showed up at her house just after I left."

"Looking for her?"

"I think they all share the same employer and are here to finish what the dead guy started."

"And what's that?" Concern etched into Betsy's face.

"I don't know," answered Sherman.

"What's your unprofessional guess?"

"A bullet," said Sherman without hesitation. He would not sugarcoat it. Betsy deserved the truth.

"Oh, I see," she replied after a few moments of silence.

"We can turn around," offered Sherman.

"No," she said definitively. "Tell me, Frank, what do you do in the army?"

Sherman glanced over at her expression and the way her eyes narrowed with a not-so-distant memory. "Something tells me you already know."

"My husband, Bill. He came back from Vietnam with a look like yours." She swirled a thin finger in his direction. "There was a gleam in his eyes like he was measuring everyone up, waiting to pounce."

"So, I look like a cat?"

"Goodness, no," answered Betsy with a laugh. Then she looked at him again and took a more serious tone, "You're something much more primeval."

Sherman took her description as a compliment, but he wondered how his eyes compared to the two henchmen in the hotel. Had all his compassion drained away? Was he no different? Just another trained killer living for the next job.

More miles of identical fields passed, one after another, until it all became a smudge of green. As more time elapsed, the internal map in Sherman's head had them closing in on the casino. The ground began to rise and mountains poked over the distant horizon.

"Almost there," said Betsy.

Sherman nodded politely at what he already knew. As

they crested over a slight rise, there was a garish sign announcing their upcoming destination. Red block letters, set against a cheesy Western landscape, advertised the casino. *BEST THING IN A HUNDRED MILES* read the sign. The specific absurdity of it made Sherman laugh out loud. The notion grew stranger as the building itself came into view. It looked even shabbier in person than the pictures online. A squat length of faded paint with doors facing an enormous sea of parking. Spliced onto the far right side was a windowless structure. Neon letters above the roof announced it was the casino. Betsy pulled into a spot on the edge of the parking lot that he pointed out.

"We should go in separately," suggested Sherman. "I don't want anyone making the connection."

A sparkle of understanding crossed Betsy's expression. "Suit yourself, James Bond."

"Go ahead, I'll follow in five minutes."

"That's not much time for the slots."

"Five minutes of pennies?"

"I play two at a time," she added with a mischievous grin.

"Okay, ten minutes. I'm gonna head over and check out the ATM. I'll let you know when it's time to leave."

Betsy was already halfway out the door before he finished his instructions. "Toodles."

Given the hour and the location, the parking lot was crowded. People were coming and going in varying states of depression and euphoria. A sliding scale of gambling success. Few looked like they could afford the losses. They drove off in battered pickups and shoddy minivans. Sherman watched the throng of people come and go for ten minutes, then he followed them inside.

Past the windowless double doors, he spotted Betsy a

few rows in, sitting between two slot machines. A giant plastic cup full of pennies was in her lap. She dropped in the coins and pulled the handles for both machines simultaneously. A wide smile spread across her face and she winked at him as he walked by.

The ATMs lived in the back of the casino next to a few tellers for cashing out winnings. Set against the corner was a small video camera. It overlooked the machines. Sherman kept his head low. It was easier for someone to get the security footage from the casino than from the ATM. He inserted the card tied to the account with no name and withdrew the maximum daily allowance. It was an agreeable place to get money out. No one thought twice about withdrawals in a casino.

Not wanting to draw more attention to himself, Sherman wandered down the aisles of slot machines. He stopped to play a few nickel slots, using some change clinking about in his pockets. It only took a minute or two to lose it all, but he got a solid view of the place. It was not huge, considering the size of the parking lot. The main doors led to five rows of slots on either side of the entryway. The tellers and ATMs were on the far wall. To the right was a restaurant hidden from view. It advertised all-day breakfast and an all-you-can-eat snow crab buffet. The latter gave him pause in such a remote, landlocked county.

Sherman followed the signs and entered a carpeted dining room with rows of booths lining wooden slat walls. He guessed it was supposed to be Western-themed, but it looked more like a prison than a restaurant. A waitress smiled at him as he entered and stopped to ask if she could help.

"Cup of coffee to go," he answered.

She nodded towards a self-serve station tucked in a corner as if the process for caffeination was self-evident.

"Thanks."

He filled up a paper to-go cup with some stale brew, poured in one of those small disposable half-and-half containers, and wandered towards the entrance, which was also the exit. One way in, one way out. Sherman meandered long enough to catch Betsy's eye. The cup of pennies in her lap was half-empty, and she nodded as he exited.

A steady stream of patrons was still wandering through the parking lot. Sherman slid back into the Toyota and scanned the asphalt field. He guessed Betsy had another ten or fifteen minutes of pennies left, give or take the slight chance of a jackpot.

Thinking of his own transaction, Sherman's mind slipped into Ruby's trip inside. She had not struck him as the gambling type, at least not in a legalized casino manner. She took risks, but not monetary ones. The only reason for coming was to get cash out, and the only place to spend that cash outside of the casino was the lake. Spotty service meant his phone took a while, but he finally found an outdated website advertising cabins for rent. A loophole in the state park system allowed someone to rent a few of them out during the summer. *Cash Only* splashed across the homepage.

In the middle of connecting all the dots in a neat little line, from Maya's comment about the lake all the way through the casino and to the cabins, Sherman spotted Betsy exiting the building. She walked with a gleeful prance through a group of people entering under the neon sign.

Three figures stood out. He sat up straighter in his seat. Even from across the parking lot, he recognized the fancy suit and swagger of Mr. Abney. The henchmen were following dutifully behind, dressed in off-the-rack versions of the same attire. They reminded him of the feds he'd seen at Quantico years ago.

"Damn," he muttered as they walked through the front door like they owned the place.

Betsy slid into the front seat with a satisfied smile. "Up two hundred bucks!" she announced as she started the engine.

"Good luck or do you have a secret?" asked Sherman, not taking his eyes off the front door.

"Oh, I know things," she began before noticing his gaze. "Trouble?"

"Remember the trio I told you about?"

"Sure."

"They just walked inside."

"Oh."

"How do you feel about another drive?"

"Where to?"

"Lake Ohapite."

"Frank! Are you holding out on me?" she asked.

"I wasn't sure before now, but it's an excellent place to hide. I think she got out cash here and then rented a cabin at the lake."

"I see... well, no time like the present," replied Betsy.

She pulled the SUV back onto the state highway and headed north once more through groves of pine trees.

Chapter Nine

Lake Ohapite spread out before them like an emerald ink blot, reflecting the wall of pine trees enclosing its edges. It was long and narrow, with small channels spreading out into the nooks of the old valley. They had passed the dam on the way up—a thick wedge of rock and earth blocking the river's natural flow. The cool mountain air and shimmering water brought some solace to Sherman's nervous system, raw as it was from years of life lived on the edge.

"I haven't been up here for years, not since Bill passed," said Betsy as they drove towards a small outpost of buildings.

"What's it like?"

"Peaceful," she replied with a smile. "We'd come up and get a cabin for a week. They have paddle boat rentals and a burger shack if you don't feel like cooking."

"Nice and quiet?"

"Oh, it gets busy during the summer. Lots of kids run around being loud and messy, but it's mostly families. Ten o'clock is quiet time at night."

Busy was good for hiding. No one would question a person getting supplies or ordering a burger. Lots of faces also meant it was harder for an employee to remember a single woman. The commotion was good, except for the cabin itself. Sherman guessed Ruby would pick the most isolated option. Neighbors could be nosy when there was nothing else to do. Simplicity breeds curiosity.

The website contained a rudimentary map. Basic shapes cobbled together in some word processor. It showed a main strip of cabins surrounding the store, restaurant, and playground. On the far edge was a lone building. It was the furthest cabin from the central gathering areas. *The ideal spot*, reasoned Sherman. He tried to pull up the satellite image on his phone but there was no service. He went back to the already-loaded website.

"Keep going past the store," he instructed.

"Shouldn't we ask?"

"No, I don't want to bring unwarranted attention. Besides, I know where she'll be."

Betsy glanced over with the question on her lips. "How?"

"It's where I would be."

Her eyes narrowed. "How well do you know her?"

"It's complicated."

Betsy laughed. "That well."

Sherman shrugged. Truthfully, he didn't know Ruby all that well. A one-night stand followed by some harrowing days that culminated in her running from Cumbre County. She stitched up his arm and saved another man's life. That was about it. But she was friends with Tillerman, and that counted for everything in his book.

"That's it up there," said Sherman, pointing towards a brown smudge between the pine trees.

Gravel crunched under the tires of the Toyota as Betsy pulled into the driveway. She turned off the engine and they both stood outside the SUV for a minute. Sherman wanted to give Ruby time to see who it was. She was armed and probably scared. Catching a friendly bullet was not how he wanted to go out.

Betsy strained to see any movement inside. "Is she here?"

Sherman nodded towards the mid-nineties Jeep parked around the side. "Is that her vehicle?" he asked.

"Yeah."

He snuck around the side of the house. The car indicated her presence, but she would have come outside— assuming she was still alive. Past the back porch, the rays of light filtered through the trees from the lake beyond. A lone figure was visible near the shore. A woman, sitting alone on a rock.

Sherman stood there for a few moments to be sure. Her hair was different and she was thinner, but it was Ruby.

"Hey there," he said somewhere between a shout and his normal voice.

Her head snapped in his direction with a look of fear and surprise. Those sharp edges melted as she recognized his face.

"What took you so long?"

"You could have given me directions."

"No service up here," added Ruby a bit sheepishly.

She had not done more for fear of being tracked. Also, she secretly didn't think Sherman would show up. Sending more information could have led to greater disappointment.

Betsy stepped out onto the beach, and Ruby lowered her head and nodded.

"Hi, Audrey," said the older woman.

"It's Ruby."

Betsy smiled one of those maternal know-it-all smiles. "I figured it was something different," she said and pointed to Sherman. "This one always paused before saying your name like he was making sure he got the right one."

"Are you going to tell Aaron?" asked Ruby.

"No," replied Betsy with a decisive shake of her head.

Ruby understood whatever that meant. Although the details of why she would not tell Talbot were lost on Sherman.

"Thanks, Betsy."

"Of course, honey. Now, I think I'll head back to the slots. Call if you need me. I'll keep the room open, Frank."

"Can you leave my bag on the porch?" asked Sherman, not wanting to leave what few possessions he had.

"Sure thing," she said with a wave over her shoulder.

As the older woman disappeared between the trees and the shadows beyond, Sherman turned to Ruby. "So, why am I here? Other than the dead guy in your house."

Ruby nodded towards the front porch. "It's not a short tale."

Once they settled down on two Adirondack chairs, she took a deep breath and started.

"I grew up in the Northeast. Connecticut, but not the fancy part. Blue-collar parents. House, yard, white picket fence. Nothing special other than my dad was a drunk, abusive asshole. I was smart enough to apply for some colleges. Got through on federal aid and did good enough to get into medical school."

"Why medicine?" asked Sherman out of curiosity.

"I used to stitch up my mom so she didn't have to go to the doctor. It saved her the embarrassment and my dad a ten-by-ten cell."

"Kind of you."

"Kindness had nothing to do with it," she said with a chuckle. "I got the hell out of there as soon as I could. Never looked back. I was almost more upset with my mom for not leaving, but I wasn't gonna stay one extra minute with that father of mine."

"Understood."

Sherman had father issues of his own, but the man was not abusive. Exacting and demanding, but not physical.

"I ended up taking a job down south in Alabama."

"Can't get much further."

"Nope. My dad... he hated the south. Too much warmth and humidity. It fit me fine. I'm sure he still brags about his doctor daughter as if he paid my way through school. That bastard never gave me a cent."

Sherman waited for the turn like a gambler at the poker table. All stories like hers had one. It was inevitable.

"One day, I met someone. Mason Knight was his name. He was fancy, cute, and attentive. Told me he came from old money. A local boy. All good-mannered and well-groomed. We started dating. Things were good, even better than good. We moved in together and he finally popped the question. I said yes, of course. I don't remember when things changed, but they did. He got possessive like I was property. He kept mentioning that his family had money and that I shouldn't be working. It was his job to take care of me."

"You don't seem like the type to buy into that bullshit."

"I'm not. The signs were there, Frank, I just ignored them. I justified away his behavior like it was some southern phenomenon." Ruby sighed and rubbed her face. "Things just got worse from there. One night, I was going out to meet some colleagues... you know, grab a few drinks, blow off some steam. As I was walking out the door, he grabbed me by the wrist and started yelling at me. Shit like, 'Where are you going?' and 'No wife of mine is going out dressed like a slut.' I lost it. All that old shit with my parents came rushing back and I pushed him. There was this look in his eyes, I can't even describe it. Almost like it gave him permission. Next thing I know, he punches me hard in the stomach. I puked everywhere."

Sherman nodded but didn't interrupt.

"That was just the beginning. He kept hitting me and I kept making excuses for him until I realized I was no different from my mom and he was worse than my father. One day, I snapped. I was barely working by then. Too ashamed to face all those people. I told him I would resign and stay at home full-time. I went into the hospital and stole a bottle of liquid fentanyl from the pharmacy. I got home before he did. Got dressed up nice and fixed him an Old Fashioned. It was his favorite. Laid it out for him all nice and then I put enough opiates in there to kill an elephant."

Ruby looked up from her story to check Sherman's reaction to the news that she committed the premeditated murder of her husband. His bearded face didn't budge.

"He dropped dead on the spot. I put a few fentanyl patches on his arm to throw off the cops and emptied the safe. He had some cash, some valuables, and a USB drive. I left for Chicago that night."

She shook her head, long and low. "I thought I could start over there. A delusion. I can see that now. I used my middle name, Ruby, and switched back to my maiden name."

"The past never forgets."

"So it seems. My sins followed, but not in the way I imagined. I pictured the cops knocking on my door, but it wasn't the cops who showed up. They were men sent by Mason's father. My roommate opened the door. They shot him in the face. Door opened, life over. I ran out the back and over to my office. Took whatever valuables I had and got the first bus out of town. That was the day I ran. The day it all ended."

Sherman, who had said little, finally spoke. "You let him off easy. I would have put a steak knife through his kidneys."

A smile broke across Ruby's face. "Jesus. Frank, it is so good to see you. I'm sorry for dragging you into this. Shit, I'm sorry for leaving back in California."

"That's just smoke on the wind. Besides, I was in a frying pan called Texas before you reached out."

"That's where my bus ended up," added Ruby. The look in her eyes was somewhere deep in the past. "Are we calling this an improvement?"

The lake glinted like a field of broken bottles, and the citrusy smell of pines drifted on the breeze. Sherman soaked in the stillness.

"Yeah, I'll take this any day."

Ruby was still hugging her knees like a small child waiting for terrible news. "I'm scared, Frank. If one found me, more are coming."

He nodded and slid his chair closer to hers. "You're right. I saw at least three in town."

Ruby bit her lip and looked absently across the water.

"Does the name Abney mean anything to you?" asked Sherman.

The sound of the surname snapped her head to attention. "Yeah, he was Mason's best friend. They grew up together. Thick as thieves, literally."

"Well, criminal or not, he is staying at the Mather Hotel with two government-looking sidekicks for muscle."

"We need to leave," said Ruby as she stood up. "I should have never dragged you into this. We could be in Canada by nightfall. Maybe take that west back to Oregon."

Her eyes darted about as she tried to map out a route that ended with herself still breathing. Sherman looked at his watch. Two hours had passed since Betsy left. Gone was the morning light. A harsher glare had taken its place.

"If we're going, it should be now."

"What?" she asked, suddenly aware of her surroundings again.

"I'm guessing you paid for this in cash."

"Yeah."

"I'm also guessing you got the cash out at the casino."

"Yeah. Where are you going with this?" she asked, looking even more worried.

"If I watched the security footage, would I see you gamble?"

"No."

Sherman nodded at the accuracy of his own assumptions. "Who drives to a casino, takes out a bunch of cash, but doesn't gamble?"

Ruby shook her head in disgust. "Someone renting a cabin at the only other place within fifty miles. Shit, I thought I was being careful."

"It gets worse."

She sighed. "They were at the casino."

"Showed up as we were leaving."

"I'll grab my things," she said.

Sherman stood up and walked inside to help.

"It will only take me a few minutes," came Ruby's voice from the bedroom.

Sitting on the dining room table was the matte-black polymer frame of a Glock 22. Next to it was an extra magazine.

"Souvenirs?" asked Sherman.

Ruby poked her head out of the doorway and looked in his direction. Her face darkened when she saw what he was talking about. "Oh. Uh, yeah. I kept it in case you showed up."

"Had your doubts, did you?"

"Frank, I haven't been sure of anything for seven goddamn years."

Sherman grabbed the gun and pulled back the slide long enough to see brass. Then he ejected the magazine. Still full. The extra one, too. It made sense. He didn't see any extra holes in Ruby's bedroom walls.

"What did you use?" he asked.

"Snub nose Smith and Wesson."

"Thirty-Eight or Three-Fifty-Seven Magnum?" Sherman asked. He had a good guess but was curious.

"Magnum. It was dirt cheap."

"Solid choice up close," he replied while imagining the damage it had inflicted.

Ruby came back with a small duffel bag stuffed to the gills with clothes. But that was it. Seeing Sherman's questioning glance, she added, "I sold the rest of my shit after they posted that picture online."

"You knew they were coming?"

"My gut said yes."

"Gotta listen to it," he added.

Instinct or gut or whatever they called it had saved Sherman more times than he cared to count. His DNA carried it like eye color or height. His old man had it and his father before that. Family lore said it went back to the Revolutionary War, although Sherman didn't believe the story. Those men died, so not that great, but so does everyone eventually. Someday, it would fail him too.

Sherman motioned towards the door. "Let's get you out of here."

A thin smile crossed Ruby's lips. She was grateful for his sudden appearance. They did a quick sweep of the cabin. Nothing remained inside except for a lone bottle of beer in the fridge. Ruby had emptied the trash earlier that morning, not wanting to leave any evidence of her stay. They were halfway to the front door when the muted sound of tires crunching on gravel ended their departure.

Chapter Ten

Through a narrow part in the curtains, Sherman could see a big black SUV parked near the top of the driveway. It blocked Ruby's Jeep and their easiest exit. Common folk would have pulled further in and left space for someone to leave. Decency demanded it, but the SUV was neither decent nor common. It was a Suburban or Tahoe. As the years passed, Sherman could no longer tell them apart. They were both big and getting bigger.

The two clean-cut sidekicks from earlier were out of the vehicle and surveying the area with a keen interest for what was inside. Black sunglasses and black suits were the attire of the day. As they advanced towards the house, Sherman could see they carried the big stick of entitled authority. Everything about them smelled of government money.

If Mr. Abney was in the car, he was keeping a low profile. Tinted windows blocked Sherman's gaze, but he guessed the man was in the back seat, watching it all unfold. This only increased his level of suspicion, which was flooding faster than a slot canyon during a rainstorm.

Sherman cracked the bottle of beer and poured half down the drain. It was a prop that portrayed a lazy afternoon on the lake. Nothing more, nothing less. Then he tucked the Glock into his pants at the small of his back and stepped outside. They met his appearance with narrowed eyes that would have turned the stomach of the average citizen.

"Can I help you?" he shouted.

The bottle bobbed about in his left hand like it was number four or five of the day with more to come.

"Good afternoon, sir," answered the woman. "We're with the FBI."

They held up their badges, which looked real from twenty yards. With so much disinformation flying about, Sherman gave them as much authenticity as a Facebook post. He took a few steps closer to the front steps to get a better look, but they had put them away.

"We'd like to ask you a few questions," the woman continued.

"FBI? Seriously?"

"Yes, sir," replied the woman. The talking had fallen to her, and for excellent reasons. She had charm. Men found mild voices less threatening.

"This is Idaho," replied Sherman. "We like our government to stay in Washington and don't take kindly to people poking their noses where they don't belong. Besides, I heard rumors of some fake feds trying to scam old folks around here."

The agents exchanged a quick glance and reluctantly pulled out their badges again. Holding them high enough for the gold to glint in the sun, they waited for the all-capital blue letters 'FBI' to sink in. Sherman squinted and leaned forward a bit. He had excellent eyesight, but the writing was small. The pair had not announced themselves, which told him they didn't want their names revealed. The little stunt was Sherman's best effort to gain an advantage.

As the woman was closer, Sherman could read the last name well enough. Harris. Her partner was further back and to the side. Tactically, it was the right move, allowing him to draw his weapon without worry of hitting the woman in the crossfire. The extra distance made it hard for Sherman to see his name. Tarney or Tomwell was his best guess. He still couldn't see past the tinted windows of the SUV.

"Okay, sorry about that," Sherman said. "What can I help the Federal Bureau of Investigation with?" He waved the beer bottle about and pretended to take a swig.

"We're looking for a woman by the name of Audrey Latimer. Do you know her?"

He didn't, at least by that name, and answered truthfully, "Afraid not. What does she look like?"

The woman's eyes narrowed at the switch in power dynamics. "Brown hair. Green eyes. Five foot six. One hundred and twenty pounds."

It fit Ruby's current appearance but he feigned surprise. "Sounds like my girlfriend, but her name is Sarah."

Inside the cabin, hidden against the wall, Ruby cringed at the name. Sarah was her college roommate and they hated each other, but at least it was common. An average name. She tried to think of what name she'd given the creepy guy at the rental desk. Nothing jumped up from her memory, but it wasn't Sarah.

"Is your girlfriend inside?" asked Agent Harris.

"She took our boat out on the lake like, oh, thirty minutes ago. We got into a tiff. Said I was drinking too much. I said she didn't buy enough beer."

"And her name is Sarah, correct?"

The agent was trying to catch Sherman with facts he did not possess. That much was obvious to him, but he nodded anyway.

"This cabin is rented to Karen Jones."

There was no point in changing his story. That would only draw more suspicion, so Sherman just shrugged like the question annoyed him.

"I don't know any Karen either, but we paid fair and square for this place. Ain't no one gonna try to take our money away," he replied and took a blatant step forward.

"Sir, please stay where you are," instructed Harris.

Tarney or Tomwell cleared his coat away from the holster underneath. Sitting inside it was a Glock—the same model as the one tucked away under Sherman's shirt. Given the evidence, it convinced him they really were feds. They walked and talked like them.

Then his glance landed again on their vehicle. The make said FBI. The license plate said Idaho. The car itself screamed rental. Bonafide agents would drive something with government plates. Even if those badges were genuine, they were not on Uncle Sam's time. *Moonlighting*, thought Sherman, if that was a thing. The gig economy of corruption. Special Agents for hire.

"Sorry," he replied with hands raised. "I'm just a little overwhelmed right now."

"It's okay, sir," answered Harris. Her face registered some relief at the de-escalation, although her partner didn't appear to agree. "Must have been a clerical error at the rental office."

Harris nodded towards Agent Tarney or Tomwell, who moved his coat back over the holster and edged back towards the SUV.

"You didn't say why you want to talk to this Karen woman," added Sherman.

"Person of interest in a murder investigation," said Harris as she got back in the car.

Sherman let out a long, controlled exhale and did his best impression of someone lost in the circumstances. Inside, Ruby was sitting on the ground. The revolver hung limply from her hands with the barrel facing down into the pine floorboards. Her lips were quivering as Sherman stepped back inside and closed the door.

Behind the tinted windows, settled in the back seat of the Suburban, Abney watched the events unfold. He had an eye for detail. It was a source of pride. Nothing went unnoticed. The man who came out of the cabin appeared intoxicated, leaning to the side and gesticulating with the bottle, but his feet said otherwise… like they were ready to pounce at any second. Tan and ungroomed counted for little in Idaho, near the river, but there was a hardened physique under the shirt. Abney knew the type. He worked with men who had that same look.

The agents slid back onto the leather seats and dutifully buckled their seatbelts. Neither looked backward. They watched the man in front of the cabin who was watching them right back.

"Why didn't you search the place?" he asked.

"We didn't have a reason," replied Harris.

"You have a badge—you don't need one."

"And if he complains to the locals and they ask questions?"

"A technicality," replied Abney. "He doesn't strike me as the type to report such an infringement."

"What type is he then?"

Abney sniffed at the retort. "The kind that would trounce you two in a fight."

Tarney turned his head, not so far as to look back over his shoulder, but far enough to catch Abney with one eye. "I doubt that," he growled.

"Either way, I have a plan."

"Care to share?" asked Harris.

"That's in my purview, but we'll need some locals."

Harris bit her lip but nodded anyway. Debts and repayment and all that. She pulled the shifter down and reversed back up the drive and onto the narrow road circling the lake.

Ruby had not moved from her hiding spot. "What the hell was that?" she asked as Sherman stepped back inside the cabin and closed the door with mock anger.

"Deep pockets."

"But they're not really FBI, right?"

"Real enough, but not right now."

"What does that even mean?"

"They're not here on official business," Sherman clarified.

"That's even worse. You're telling me the old man has two federal officers on the payroll."

"At least two," he informed her. Then Sherman caught her gaze and held it there. The time for half-truths had come and gone. "Tell me more about your ex-father-in-law."

"Terrance Knight," she sputtered.

A sharp crack of recognition echoed in Sherman's mind. He knew the name, even if most Americans didn't.

"You mean the Vice Chairman of the U.S. Senate Select Committee on Intelligence—Senator Terrance Knight of Alabama?"

"Yeah, him," Ruby mumbled.

The gravity of the situation pressed down on her chest, and she struggled to take a full breath. Her mind recognized the signs of a panic attack but could not shake the tendrils of fear overtaking her nervous system. It took all her energy not to hyperventilate.

Sherman rubbed his overgrown beard. "Well, that explains a lot."

And it did. A ranking member of the most important committee in the U.S. government had considerable clout. Terrance Knight had that and then some. From what Sherman recalled, the man was a shadow player. Someone who stayed behind the scenes, pulling the strings, having the laughs and raking in his winnings.

"You should go, now," groaned Ruby after a minute of calm breathing.

"Not a chance," Sherman retorted.

"Why not? It ain't your fight."

"Neither is any of it, I didn't start this damn war, but that doesn't stop me. You're as good a reason for killing as the President of Afghanistan or some warlord in Somalia."

"Your principles will be the death of you, Frank."

"Good. Better than a battle without merit. And I've seen my share of those."

Ruby slid back up, using the wall as a runway. She turned and kissed him hard on the lips. The previous year dropped away, and for a moment, they relieved the passion of that night in California.

With her hands still clasped around his neck, she asked, "Now what?"

Sherman started with the obvious. "We can't stay here."

"Canada?"

"Do you have a passport?"

"No," was her mournful reply.

"I know a place, but we need to wait until dark. I doubt those agents have gone far."

"Frank, I can see your devious wheels turning."

"Betsy has a room at her place."

"You can't be serious," exclaimed Ruby. "She is Chief Talbot's aunt."

The revelation caught Sherman by surprise, but the logic behind it made sense. Unable to sequester him at the freeway motel, Talbot suggested someone he could trust. Someone in the family. It was comically simple and he kicked himself for not making the connection earlier.

"Well, if Talbot doesn't show up, sirens blaring, before we leave, I'd say Betsy is on your side," he offered.

"Not telling is just an omission. Sheltering a murderer is an accessory."

"No jury would convict. It was self-defense," said Sherman.

"The second one, maybe, but not the first."

"They both were," Sherman tried to reassure her, but his own moral compass had wobbled over the years.

He stood and leaned against the kitchen sink and gazed absently out over the trees, standing like bony brown fingers around the lake. Events tumbled through his mind as if driven by a mechanical agitator. Some were small and innocuous. They fell through the tiny holes. What remained clattered about, making an awful racket. Multiple murders, a powerful man, and corrupt FBI agents. Under all of it was Ruby, looking flattened by the weight.

Most would have fled such a situation, driven away by fear. Sherman didn't work that way. Fear was not a problem, and problems were not to be feared. A solution always existed. Options emerged even in the bleakest of situations. His entire existence rested on a keen ability to assess a problem and quickly come to a solution. Ambush, IED, or dirty feds—when you broke them all down, the answer was practical. The legality of that answer mattered not. Surviving to the next problem... that mattered.

Hours passed as they kept out of sight.

They sat on the smooth pine floor with the curtains drawn, waiting for darkness and watching for movement. Ruby offered a bottle of bourbon, but Sherman waved it away and she slid it back into the duffel bag. He wanted a clear head. She wanted to survive the night. Having such myopic hopes and dreams only fanned the fires of depression and hopelessness. At least she wouldn't die alone. Not yet. The thought brought her some comfort.

"Are you happy?" asked Ruby, finally bridging an hour of silence.

"I'm not chasing happiness," answered Sherman.

"What are you chasing?"

He shrugged and took in a deep breath. "I'm not sure anymore."

"Me either," she replied.

"Looking for meaning in this mess?" he asked.

Ruby's chest deflated inward with the thought. She had sought little other than the bottle and trouble since that night in Chicago. Solace, it seemed, was not on the menu.

The guilt of all those skeletons in the closet dissolved any hope of happiness and dreams for a future.

"I can't imagine much past the end of my nose. It feels like I'm one step away from the edge. Except, I can't see my feet, and blind hope is the only thing that moves my legs forward."

"Like running at night," Sherman admitted. "You don't know what's below your boots, but it's solid until it's not."

Ruby turned and glimpsed a sympathetic smile. She had not expected him to understand, but it felt like he did. "Yeah, just like that."

Chapter Eleven

Two hours past sunset, they finally stood up from the worn wooden floor and stretched away the waiting. Nothing of note appeared in the distance. No SUV waited in the shadows. No FBI agents lurked in the gloom. The corrupt feds remained a threat, but a hidden one.

Sherman swept the perimeter one last time. Habits and all, they don't go away, some of them for excellent reasons. Then he motioned for Ruby to get in the Jeep. She snuck out the back door and crouched low in the darkness. Once inside amongst the faded leather interior, Ruby laid down on the floor behind the front seats. A lost world of randomness greeted her eyes. Wrappers, bottle caps, and coins clung to the frayed carpet. She tried to remember the last time she cleaned the thing but failed.

"You ready?" asked Sherman after slipping inside. He slid the seat back a few inches but didn't turn around.

"As ever."

"Stay down until we make the highway," he instructed.

"I might never get back up."

"Not your style," said Sherman.

"Whatever I'm doing isn't sustainable, might as well try something new."

"I can pull over now if you want to give up." Sherman was in no mood to fight for a cast-aside cause. Lost causes and long shots were one thing. Hopelessness was something else entirely.

"Oh, fuck off. I may lapse into a pool of wallowing occasionally."

"Only if it's shallow."

"It is for now. I suppose that could change depending on how the next few days go."

"Ain't that the truth," muttered Sherman.

"Frank, have you ever been on the run?" asked Ruby quietly.

"Have I ever been in this position? No. But I've faced some poor outcomes."

"How did you keep your head above water?"

The question bounced off his memory like a tennis ball tossed lazily against the side of a house. A hollow thumping sound like mortars popping out of their tubes. A few months before, Sherman and his team ran operations near the Syrian border. Summer waited in the wings and the fighting season raged on.

A nasty guy surfaced, who went by the *nom de guerre* of *Hisada*, which, translated from Arabic meant reaper—as in the grim reaper. Egotistical, but maybe the guy watched too many movies. It didn't matter. His name made it on a piece of paper. That paper ended up in front of Sherman. What happened next was not a surprise.

A small cell of *Hisada* loyalists roamed tracts of the southern border between Iraq and Syria. Loosely affiliated with the Islamic State, they played their own game. Most of their attacks were small-scale. Personal grievances or crimes of opportunity. Nothing to stand out in a pile of other crazies. That was until *Hisada* dreamed big. He exploded a truck inside the police station. The blast killed scores of cops and civilians. It put *Hisada's* name on two lists. One that circulated in cagey chat rooms devoted to the struggle against America and one housed on a Department of Defense server.

Hisada lived outside of Baghdad when taking a break from jihad. A nice little apartment. Wife. Two kids. He even drove a minivan. A regular suburban soccer dad, minus the sadistic streak that involved flaying his victims before cutting their throats. In his younger years, Sherman used to wonder what drove men like *Hisada* to such depravity. Over time, his curiosity faded as the reasons never changed. A war without end birthed craziness. It was inevitable.

At some point, the man slipped up and called home for a kid's birthday. Intelligence got up on his burner phone. A real coup, given that he switched weekly and moved constantly. The window was tight, and Sherman's team mobilized without the due diligence of a well-planned operation.

Dawn broke as they entered a town picked at some intelligence briefing. The rising sun washed away those shielding curtains of night. Their helicopter hit a mechanical snag and ended up two hours late. Sherman knew things were heading south, but orders overruled better judgement.

The dogs barked as they came down a quiet little street not wider than a seventies sedan. The dogs always barked. They smelled the blood drifting in on the wind. Most people ignore the howls—some at their own peril—but that morning, the owner heeded the warning. He stepped out to see why sleep had gone the way of the winter birds.

For a guy in his late fifties, the owner ran fast. It took half a block for Sherman to catch up and tackle the man to the ground. Before the chokehold took effect, the owner managed a chilling scream that made the dogs bay in some morbid call and response.

The mission ended with that scream. Compromised was the word used by commanders in some far-removed office. It had too many syllables for Sherman. Anything over four letters was a luxury.

Bullets started snapping overhead. Just a few guns at first, then more joined the racket. Soon, the air hissed and sizzled with a tangle of metal. Retreat was the only option.

Sherman pulled his men back but they got stuck in a warren of tiny one-room homes. Each seemed to grow out of the next in an endless cluster. With no way out, they went through. His men knocked down one wall after another until they came out on the other side of town.

Two trucks sat out front of the last structure. The militia inside them were smoking cigarettes and waiting for the fight to arrive. It came fast and without formal announcement. Sherman saw them first. Five men of various ages. Some old. Some young. All of them died on the spot. They spared no one. Not the old. Not the young. No one.

Sergeant Gournsey dragged out a corpse from behind the front seat and took the wheel of the first truck. Sherman helmed the second and off they sped. Half the town followed. A dueling convoy of vehicles bent on burying the other.

Shell casing bounced off the steel bed of the trucks and onto the ground below as they sped across miles of feature-less desert. Bullets pinged off metal or crunched through glass. There was nothing else to hit besides sand. Sherman kept the truck in fourth gear and wailing like a banshee in protest. The villagers gained a little ground, then someone took a round through the chest and they backed off for a few minutes before trying again to close the gap.

The back and forth lasted twenty minutes or fifteen miles. That brief block of time stretched into a week in Sherman's mind. All his concentration ebbed into that truck. Nothing else existed or ever would exist. That cab contained the entire world.

He kept driving until the Apaches got on their frequency. A friendlier voice he never heard. They started the attack from over two miles away. No one chasing the Americans saw anything until the first dozen men disappeared into a cloud of fire and smoke. They tried to turn around—to go back home to warm beds and families who loved them—but that chance fell away miles earlier.

After the missiles came the cannons. Twenty-millimeter rounds poured down from the horizon like an afternoon storm. Hundreds of high explosive bullets strafed up and down the convoy until no one remained to tell the story. And through it all, Sherman never stopped staring at the road in front.

Ruby reached up and poked him in the shoulder. "Well?" she asked, still wondering how he managed terrible situations.

He shook away the drab memory of smoldering wreckage. "I just keep on driving."

"You were thinking too long for that. Where were you?"

"The edge of sanity," answered Sherman as they pulled onto the main road south. Then he added, "You can move up front."

Ruby slid her slender frame over the front console,

brushing against Sherman. They both smiled unencumbered grins. Neither cared much for modesty and both felt comfortable in their skin. Time and circumstance had erased that peculiar human embarrassment.

A pair of headlights split the night as they settled in for the drive. Intermittent traffic had crossed their path. People coming and going from the casino. A smattering of locals. Nothing much else out there was worth the gas. Sherman wasn't the best driver. His mind watched for ambush points and IEDs, not arbitrary yellow stripes on the ground. Despite that fact, he knew no one had been behind them on the last straightaway. Such an incongruous fact nagged at his mind like a foxtail stuck in his sock.

The lights intensified as the vehicle closed the gap. A minute before they existed as dim pinpricks in the distance. That changed to a respectful quarter-mile. Sherman's eyes stayed glued to the mirror as all the separation fell away. High beams were practically in the Jeep and they could hear the loud throaty growl of a big domestic engine.

Ruby turned around. Her face strained under the sudden fear. "Frank," she said nervously.

"Hold tight," was all he could think to say.

The words scarcely tumbled from his mouth before the vehicle crashed into the back of the Jeep. The impact jolted them forwards into suddenly taut seatbelts.

Sherman couldn't see much other than the lights, but he guessed it was a truck. One with a heavy-duty grille. A collision like that would have deployed the airbags. In his mind, that proved the make of the vehicle. Such a conclusion also meant it was not the FBI agents from earlier.

The truck backed off for a moment. Sherman knew they were building up some speed for another hit. He floored the accelerator, but the old Jeep had more torque than top end.

Another thumping collision rocked them about. Metal crunched and screeched in protest, and Sherman struggled to maintain control. Once was a scare tactic, twice was a threat. He wasn't in the mood for a third time.

As the truck backed off for another ramming attempt, Sherman slammed on the brakes. Out of instinct, so did the other driver. The sound of screeching rubber filled the air as eight thousand pounds of metal and plastic shuddered to a halt.

Sherman was out of the Jeep even before it fully stopped. Ruby had to lean over and pull the emergency brake to keep them from rolling off the road. Only then did she notice the Glock, which had been wedged between seat and console, was missing.

Outside, the sweetness of cooling air mingled with an acridness of burned rubber and overworked brakes. The truck was thirty feet behind the Jeep, engine idling, brakes still depressed. The red glow of taillights faded like embers into the surrounding fields. Years of hostility taught Sherman to act first and deal with the results afterward. Caution advised to wait for the next move, but actions beget reactions. In his world, threats were met with violence. He started shooting.

Staccato flashes danced in the darkness like tiny fireworks. Ruby watched, almost transfixed, as Sherman pulled the trigger. Five rounds went through the driver-side windshield in what felt like a long blink, although her eyes remained locked open. Another five bullets crashed through the passenger's side. The ten sharp cracks rolled together into one long wall of sound. With the casualness of a drunk popping off another bottle cap, Sherman exchanged one magazine for the other in case someone else showed up.

Sliding right in a wide arc, he approached the truck from the driver's side. The engine still idled, and he could see no movement inside. Not wanting to give away easy shots, Sherman moved towards the door from a blind spot in the mirrors. From his angle, in the middle of some state highway in Idaho, the shattered windshield twinkled with a crimson hue.

With a quick jerk, he opened the door and peeked inside. The driver was a bloody mess. Five out of five bullets found center mass. His head lolled to the left and only the seatbelt held him in place, but somehow, his foot remained on the brake. The guy was youngish, late twenties, with an extra layer of pudge from too much partying and not enough work. Sherman didn't recognize the face at all. It was not the feds or Abney or any other local he remembered.

Across the cab was a passenger. He had fared better, but only slightly. Ragged breaths still rose from his chest but no fight remained. Sherman could hear a collapsed lung. A slow and painful death. Again, the face brought no memory to life. He looked like the driver. A mid-twenty-year-old white kid with jeans and cowboy boots. Nothing unusual from what Sherman had seen in town.

The kid, for their ten-year age gap was an eternity of experience, looked at Sherman. No spark of recognition passed across his eyes. They were just two strangers gazing at the abyss. The Glock hung at Sherman's side, feeling almost weightless in that moment. He raised the pistol and fired once more, finishing what he tried to do a minute earlier. Murder—plain and simple.

Others preceded those two and more would follow. The

difference between there and here, war and home, once had mattered. Time took a toll on such intricately carved differences until everything looked like a used cutting board. Those defining marks, those lines one dared not cross, became indistinguishable from any other and blood ran between them all. In Sherman's world, there was no room for gray. Nuances did not matter. You played to survive. No rules. No excuses. The two amateurs understood that at the end... or not.

More nicks of light glittered across the lonely valley as if from holes in a sheet of black plastic. Sherman moved quickly to gather up the phones and wallets. He found a shiny Colt 9mm pistol in the glove box. It was unloaded. The magazine lay nearby. He tucked them into his pants. Neither man appeared ready for a gunfight. One gun with no bullets. It made little sense. A question of innocence tottered through his mind. Was it just some twisted youthful joke? Drunk kids being their dumbass selves. Or was it something else?

Such questions did not find simple answers. Not on the side of a state highway with two bodies still warm in the cab of a truck riddled with bullets from the gun he still carried. Not with more cars coming down the road. The twin lights of consequences would shine brightly if he did not get moving.

Reaching inside, Sherman twisted off the lights and kicked the driver's foot from atop the brake. The truck lurched forward, and he turned the wheel hard right towards a hay field. By the time he got back into the Jeep, the front end of the pickup was gliding across green grass.

"What the hell!" yelled Ruby.

Sherman shrugged and sped south. His evasiveness did nothing to calm her nerves.

"Frank," she growled. "This isn't Kabul. You can't go around shooting people."

The irony of her words fell hard, and a lump of hypocrisy clogged her throat.

"Sorry," she added after a few minutes. "I don't know if I'm the glass house or the stones. Either way, I should keep my mouth shut."

Sherman laughed at the comment. Even if the world were made of glass, he would still be throwing stones. Nature or nurture, it did not matter.

"Don't be too harsh on yourself," he concluded. "My world is a grim place."

"Us or them?"

"Always us. That's the rule."

"No matter the price?"

He nodded.

"Even here?" she asked, knowing the question selfishly covered her own actions.

"Here and there are only concepts. They teach us to turn it off, but..." his words trailed away.

"Not so easy to unlearn what keeps you alive."

Sorrow and understanding crept into her facial expression. Sherman watched it unfold across her defined cheeks and over her brow.

"Not when it means death," he replied.

"At any cost," she repeated.

"Or until you tire of paying. It comes at a hefty price."

"Like my principles?" asked Ruby.

"Or your soul," added Sherman.

"I don't see the afterlife going all that well for me."

"Catholic?"

"Lapsed."

"Well then, it never would end well."

Ruby laughed, but it felt hollow, and she cut it off. She considered turning herself in and facing whatever music deemed worthy of playing. Running was a youthful pursuit. It took and took but rarely gave back. All she could say about the last few years was simple—she was still alive. Nothing more. Not much less.

"Still going to Betsy's?"

"Nothing changes," answered Sherman.

"Why not?"

"Because nothing has. They are still after you. The private investigator, the feds, those two yokels, all of them came from the same spool of thread."

"Dear old daddy?" she wondered.

"Him and Abney. Grief and revenge go well together."

"Even after all these years?"

"Did time heal your wounds?"

Ruby still bore the scars inside and out. "No, not really," she replied softly.

"There you go. Senator Knight is not the forgetting and forgiving type. You don't get that far in politics without a long memory and a short fuse."

"Do you have a plan? I assume you do."

"Get to Betsy's house," answered Sherman.

Ruby narrowed her eyes. "Then what?"

"Keep you safe."

The asinine answer made her simmer with anger. "Until what?"

"The next door opens."

"Frank, your plan sucks."

"It's short term."

"Parking meters are short term. This is something else."

"Suspend your disbelief for a moment and trust me. I've gotten this far."

Point taken, thought Ruby. Sherman came across the country from a single text and found her without help. Short-term or not, his plan was keeping her breathing.

"Okay, Betsy it is."

Sherman nodded, not with the pleasure of being right, but with the acknowledgement of their partnership. They were reading from the same page and that mattered.

"Here," he said, tossing over the wallets and phones. "Take a look."

Ruby opened the glove box for light and started investigating the wallets. Both phones were locked with pictures of smiling women, likely girlfriends or lovers. She threw them out the window. Without a passcode or biometric, they were nothing but paperweights. The wallets contained more secrets. Each had ten crisp, mint condition hundred-dollar bills. Straight from the bank. That kind of new. A thousand bucks a piece to run them off the road. She held up Franklin's many faces for Sherman to see.

"Blood money," he replied.

Most of the contents were trivial. More credit cards than means allowed. Memberships to an assortment of grocery and big-box stores. A few BOGO coupons for a local Dairy Queen. Proof of health insurance, the minimalist plan with an obscenely high deductible. Good for youthful people who don't get sick or don't survive to bear the debt. Ruby tossed a few random receipts next to the cash and shuffled through a stack of business cards.

"Was he sitting on this thing?" she asked with an element of disbelief.

"Yeah, probably had a wad of napkins in the other pocket to even it out."

She couldn't tell if he was joking or not. Both men carried awfully large wallets and almost nothing of value.

Ruby had always assumed men only kept the basics in their back pocket. It became apparent they carried clutter too, no different from her own purse.

"Do you have this much crap in your wallet?"

"I don't have a wallet," replied Sherman.

The answer was so direct and simple, it almost took her by surprise, but then she thought about the man sitting next to her and it all made sense.

Chapter Twelve

Steam still poured from the bathroom when Abney answered the flip phone waiting on the nightstand. Water dripped from the showerhead—one of those fancy types that sits directly overhead imitating the rain.

"Any news?" he asked.

A wet bathrobe sprawled across the carpet next to the inert body of a youngish woman. Her unconscious but still breathing form lay crumpled at the foot of the bed.

"We found the truck," replied Agent Harris. "Both of the locals were shot dead."

"I was right," Abney added, feeling pleased with himself.

"It appears so," replied Harris.

"Where are we with an ID?"

"Not far, but the guy is or was military. The grouping he fired was exceptional. My gut says special forces."

Abney turned over the news in his mind. All the details fit together nicely with the man at the lake.

Harris continued, "Local LEOs will find the truck soon enough. We could wait for the roadblock."

"No need. They won't catch him. Keep digging and report back to me at breakfast."

"Are you sure she's with him?"

"I think the shooting proves that."

Harris hesitated. "Many people carry in this part of the country."

"But they don't shoot up their neighbors."

"They might if those neighbors were trying to run them off the road."

"Did it appear to be road rage?"

Harris bit her lip and acknowledged, "No, it didn't. An execution more like it."

"See you in the morning. Eight, sharp."

Abney hung up the phone without waiting for a response and placed it neatly on the nightstand. Then he dragged the woman back to the bed.

———

With miles to nowhere and two bodies in the rearview, stopping created risk. Staying on the highway, the major north-south road, had similar issues. If the cops found the truck, which would surely happen, setting up a roadblock was one radio call away. Sherman was no cop, but he knew how to hunt. Not animals, he never developed that taste, but people. Those on lists compiled by intelligence officers and handed down to field commanders. A few innocent—or falsely accused—individuals got killed, but such statistics happened in war. A tiny blip, an anomaly in the data. Nothing more.

The first time was different. Scalding with rage and

indignation, Sherman pinned one such officer against the wall and demanded an explanation for why his team shot an unarmed farmer. How did he get on the list? The guy did not blink or offer some banal comment about collateral damage. He took the time to walk Sherman through the process. All the steps, the signoffs and the quality checks. Every detail. Only then did Sherman apologize. The officer was not to blame for a broken system. It all stunk. Starting with the war itself.

Knowing the obvious reaction to finding two dead guys on a straight shot highway was a roadblock, Sherman turned at the next marked road. A small white signpost with black lettering announced some country byway. The lack of a 'No Outlet' sign reassured him it went somewhere, which, at that moment, was west. Down the dirt track they went and kept going until the traffic on the highway looked like the dim lights of an airplane passing overhead. Then he turned left at the next sign heading south. Sherman repeated this west to south process until they reached the interstate, which ran north of the river with few turns.

"How did you know those roads connected?" asked Ruby.

"I looked at a map."

She frowned. He had done nothing but stare out the windshield since the shooting stopped. "When?"

Sherman shrugged. He did not remember looking but could recall all the details. "Maybe two days ago."

Ruby inhaled as if to ask a question, but the breath lingered instead. She barely knew Sherman but remembered enough from California to know he possessed unusual skills. Memorizing an entire county map came as no surprise. Neither did the shooting. She'd seen that before firsthand. The former doctor squirmed at the sight of such wanton carnage, but Sherman's presence lifted her spirits. A strange sensation for someone used to relying on her wits alone to survive.

"Are we going to Betsy's house?" she asked.

"Not yet. I'm guessing the cops will recognize your Jeep."

"Then where?"

He pointed up ahead to a large, well-lit sign standing tall on the side of the interstate. It advertised one of those 24-hour truck stops. The complete package. Fuel. Restaurant. Showers. Everything someone crossing the country in the small compartment at the back of a semi-truck might need.

Ruby looked down at the fuel gauge. Half remained. "Gas?"

"I was thinking about dinner. When was the last time you ate?"

It took her a minute to recall. Breakfast was a granola bar. She tried to remember lunch. Did she have it? A gnawing sense of scarcity tightened in her stomach like a knot. Then she remembered the two guys in the truck and the blood splattered against the window. Her stomach twisted in the other direction in some strange duel between morals and reality. Hunger won out.

"Breakfast, I guess."

"Good, I'll buy."

"Let me," she replied, holding up the money from a dead guy's wallet.

Sherman smiled and exited past the sign.

They parked in the asphalt lot out back, hidden between inconsistent splotches of illumination. It was an enormous space, full of other vehicles and semis. Truckers from all over stopped there. Sherman pointed the rear of the Jeep towards an empty field, hiding the damage from searching eyes. Ruby went to get out, but he held out his hand for a second. She stopped and looked around the area and then back to his face. Sherman's eyes didn't dart around so much as inhale the surroundings.

"How far out does the city limit go?" he asked.

"Are you asking if we're in it?"

"Yeah."

Ruby glanced over at the exit number. "I don't think so. This is more a State Police kind of spot."

Sherman stared for a few more seconds and then put down his hand and opened the door. They followed a long shadow until it fizzled out in the neon lake ringing the truck stop.

The restaurant had its own entrance inside of the larger building, opposite the convenience store and down the hall from the showers and coin-operated laundry. Save for a motel, the place covered all the necessities. A wiry woman in her late forties with speckled blonde hair smiled when they entered. Sherman asked for a booth in the back facing the door and the windows. The waitress didn't bat an eye, like it was a common request. Cops, most likely, or veterans. Some habits don't stop with a change in country codes.

They slid into the booth with Sherman watching the entrance and Ruby doing her best not to face any of the other patrons. A glossy menu lay on the table. Nothing unusual about the fare. Meat and potatoes with a few salads containing the same ingredients. The options suited Sherman fine. He ordered some fried chicken with mashed potatoes and coffee. Ruby picked a patty melt with fries. Did she order the same thing a year ago in California? Or did he? Sherman couldn't remember.

The coffee came. Stale, black, and strong. He splashed

some cream on top and sipped slowly, watching for any lingering eyes.

"Should we call Betsy?" asked Ruby, taking her cell out.

"There's a payphone down the hall."

"Really?"

"Unless they kept the sign up for show."

"Have you seen one recently?"

"A payphone?"

"Yeah."

Sherman laughed. "No, I suppose not, but if any place would have one, it would be here. They have an arcade, which suddenly seems outdated."

"With everyone on their phones."

"Yeah, remember when that was a thing?"

"I used to go with friends to check out the boys," answered Ruby with a hint of embarrassment in her voice.

Sherman gave an empathetic nod to a changing world. He'd done something similar whenever his location allowed. Growing up in the army meant moving around a fair bit. Not as much as some, but more than the average American.

"Should we call Betsy and ask for help?" she asked.

"We need a place to lie low."

"Why not run?"

"Too much risk. They can tie your Jeep to at least one murder, two more if anyone saw us. Plus, we have the feds to consider. They have access to better toys. Databases. Cameras. Wiretaps. And they're onto us."

"The truck?"

"What else."

"How did they know?"

"I don't think they did. It felt like a probing mission."

"Probing?"

"Defenses. Probing defenses. A smell test to see if we are

for real. Look for an old nineties Jeep and try to run it off the road. If they killed some innocent folks, no big deal. If they killed us, all the better."

"And?"

"Well, they know a few things. We are traveling together. We are armed, and one of us can shoot. Hopefully, they will assume we are heading for the border and try to stop us. That puts the pressure on a search outside of town."

"And we'll be in town?"

"Maybe."

"And if Chief Talbot shows up at the Bed and Breakfast?"

"I was already staying there. He recommended the place to me."

"I already failed with my attempt to hide here twice. Let's see how we fare with your plan."

They finished eating and Ruby left an eighty-dollar tip. *Blood money,* she thought. *No point in saving it.* Past the restaurant entrance, they made a right and walked down the hall, past showers and a small dingy arcade with a few scattered machines blinking brightly. Towards the end of the corridor, below a square blue sign, existed a lone payphone. An entire bank of the heavy-duty devices once inhabited the space, but only the one remained. Small metal panels covered the empty spots.

Sherman reached into his pocket and pulled out a few quarters he kept for the situation. Normally, he didn't keep change or money for the matter. Such things hadn't mattered for years. The larger bases in Iraq and Afghanistan served decent food, but no one paid for it, at least not directly. Loose change on some firebase in the wilds of the war had less value than a chocolate teapot.

The quarters clinked as he inserted them into the

machine and dialed the number. Despite the nighttime hour, Betsy answered on the second ring as if she had been expecting the call.

"Hello."

"Betsy, it's Frank."

"I thought it might be you."

"We could use some help."

"Oh, what do you need?"

"A place to stay. Someone came looking for us."

"The unsavory type?"

"Afraid so," answered Sherman.

"Oh, I have plenty of room here, but there might be a better choice."

"I'm all ears."

"Bill kept a hunting cabin to the south in the mountains. I haven't been there for a year, but it was still stocked last time I visited."

"Are you sure? This might land you in some hot water."

"Oh, life is nothing without a little adventure."

"Thanks, Betsy. How do we find it?"

"I'll meet you. There is a gate at the base of the road. It's got one of those community locks on it."

"What time?" asked Sherman, thinking they could lie low through the night if needed.

"Forty-five minutes."

Sherman glanced down at his watch. It was on the cheap side of sturdy with the time, date, and one of those rings used to tell directions. It read a little after eleven at night. A midnight arrival seemed reasonable.

"Are you sure? It's getting late."

"Will your unsavory pursuers stop because of the hour?" asked Betsy.

"No."

"Well then, I'll give you the directions. Do you have something to write with?"

"I don't need one."

Betsy laughed and gave him a turn-by-turn route to the gate. He stayed still and absorbed the information. It superimposed onto his existing mental map of the area like adding color to an old painting.

Once she had stopped, he said, "Thanks. See you there." Then he hung up.

Ruby stood close enough to hear most of the conversation. She shrugged when Sherman glanced over. It sounded like a plan. As good as any of the ones floating around her head. Much better than the sinking sense of despair she had felt in the days before.

Chief Talbot awoke to the shrill beeping of his work phone. He grabbed it with a sense of urgency, not wanting to wake up his wife and knowing something was wrong. Calls at midnight rarely happened in Stalworth. His mind went over the possibilities—drunken brawl, drunk driving accident, drunk and disorderly conduct, drunk kids breaking and entering. The theme was common and consistent. He answered with a quiet hello and recognized Officer Torres' voice.

"Chief. There's been an incident."

"Who drank too much?" he growled.

"Uh, no, nothing like that. A shooting. On the road to the casino. Just inside the extended city limit."

"Jesus. Did anyone get hurt?" asked Talbot, still groggy.

"Yeah. They're dead."

All those tired brain functions snapped back into action and Talbot said, "Tell me everything."

"I'm standing right next to it. A passerby called it in. They spotted a truck off to the side of the road. They got out to help. Engine was still running. Two guys inside are shot to hell. Blood is everywhere. It's a damn mess."

Talbot was already pulling on his pants and buttoning up his uniform. "I'll be there soon."

Three dead in three days. That put the murder rate at 30 per 100,000 people. Ten times higher than New York City, but not as bad as Baltimore. *A slight consolation*, thought Talbot.

He laced up his boots, smiled at his wife who somehow remained asleep, and headed off into the sour night.

Chapter Thirteen

Flashing lights blanketed the horizon. Talbot squinted into the reds and blues. The entire department was there. One car blocked the road to the north and one to the south. A prudent choice. That left three officers to secure the crime scene and look for clues. Talbot supervised. At least traffic was sparse. Word would leak out, but slowly. The morning would be hell. The mayor would descend the stairs with that pompous step of his and demand answers when Talbot had none.

"Chief," yelled Officer Raquel Torres.

Talbot walked over to where the woman was standing. One of the few officers in his department with a future in law enforcement. Most had family ties to him or the mayor. Small-town problems. He didn't blame them. His father was chief, and his father before that. It remained an insular department.

"Shell casings. A lot of them," said Torres, shining her light on the pavement.

Talbot took a picture with his phone and then stooped

down to pick one up with a pen from his shirt pocket. On the bottom of the brass was a headstamp around the rim reading *R-P 40 S&W*. He withdrew a magazine from his gun belt and removed a single round. Stamped on the bottom was *R-P 40 S&W*.

"Same ammo," he said aloud.

Torres nodded. "Should I call the gun store and get their sales records?"

A good question. A competent question. The others might have skipped right over it, but Talbot already knew the answer.

"No, we order it from a store in Boise. They don't sell it here."

"Too late for a roadblock?"

"Too late," agreed Talbot.

"Where does that leave us?"

Talbot wandered off into the field. He stepped over the broken barbed wire fence. A tangle of metal and wood strung between the still-standing posts. The officer on scene had turned off the engine—fire risk.

He looked inside at the gas gauge—near empty. A needle width above the bottom line. No one would drive that stretch without at least a quarter tank. The nearest gas station was thirty miles in either direction. A twenty-five-gallon tank at fifteen miles per gallon. Ninety miles of range at the start. Now almost empty. It idled for a while. An hour, maybe more.

The front grille of the truck looked bent around the edges like a cheap spoon. Except it was one of those after-market pieces. A heavy-duty chunk of steel. Only a decent collision would bend it. Another car. Not something new or plastic. Something old and heavy.

He flicked on the flashlight from his belt. Not the big old

heavy Mag-Lites that cops used to carry. It was small and easy to use. He had a collapsible baton for situations that called for blunt force. The front grille glinted in the white LED. Talbot leaned closer and ran his finger across the metal, scrutinizing them in the light.

Something old and heavy and beige, he thought.

Torres edged closed.

"They hit another vehicle," announced Talbot.

"Trying to get away?" she asked.

Talbot leaned in again and then stood up. "I don't think these guys are the type to run. I'm guessing they were the aggressors."

"I guess they hit the wrong guy," replied Torres.

"Yeah," added Talbot. An image of the army captain flashed through his head. Those eyes of his like something out of a National Geographic issue devoted to predators. "The wrong guy indeed."

It took a few extra turns to align with Betsy's directions, but Sherman found the route. They came from one black stripe across a field and connected to another. County roads. No names, just numbers. Ruby drove. Sherman navigated. The better choice, he reasoned… easier to shoot that way. The two locals might have lived if he had fired a few warning shots.

"Take the next right," Sherman instructed.

Ruby peered ahead into the fading gloom at the edge of the headlights. She slowed down a touch.

"Where?" she asked, forgetting that Sherman had never been there.

"Less than a quarter-mile."

Betsy said about two miles from the last turn. His mind said they'd done about eighty percent of that total. Ruby slowed down further. They were doing twenty-five miles per hour on a narrow road bent on avoiding the mountains altogether. It snaked around them and between them, but not up them. The path of least resistance.

A red glint caught Sherman's eye. Taillights reflected off to the right. "Stop by the tree," he instructed.

Ruby rolled to a stop beyond a thick pine. A small dirt track no wider than a truck appeared. She eased the damaged Jeep into the narrow entrance. A Toyota Rav-4 waited twenty feet further down. Sherman recognized the license plate. Still, he waited. No need to rush out. Good habits and all.

Betsy got out first. Ruby killed the engine and followed suit. The two women met in the emptiness and exchanged brief pleasantries. Sherman checked the road behind them. A few minutes after midnight and not a soul in sight. No lights. No sounds, except for cooling engines and insects and hushed tones filled with worry.

"Did you find it okay? Most people miss a turn or two," Betsy asked as Sherman returned from the road.

"Yeah," replied Ruby. "No problems. Frank here is a walking atlas."

"You gave excellent directions," he replied.

The older woman laughed softly at some inside joke no one else knew. "Glad to hear it. Audrey… sorry, I mean Ruby, was telling me about some trouble on the drive here."

"The less you know, the better."

"Oh, that kind of trouble."

"Afraid so," replied Sherman.

Betsy nodded thoughtfully and slowly. Her movement barely visible in the faint glow coming from the dome lights inside the cars. "I'll open up the gate. The cabin is four miles in on the left. Can't miss it."

"Thanks," said Ruby. "You've gone above and beyond."

"Friendship is important these days. Too many people forget that."

Sherman agreed but said nothing. Betsy opened the gate, and they followed her through, up the dusty track. A dozen feet later, she pulled onto a thin grassy gap in the trees and they passed with a wave. Ruby kept driving.

The density of pine trees grew with the altitude gain. More feet, more trees. The low beams cut a narrow arc of light into the forest. Straight and tall, the shadows slid as they crawled over the rutted road.

"You think she'll tell Talbot?" wondered Ruby.

"She should. I suppose we'll find out in the morning."

"And if he shows up?"

She hesitated.

"I won't shoot him if that's what you're worried about."

"Not to complain, but you were quick on the trigger back there."

Sherman thought he had shown restraint. Two times that truck rammed the Jeep. Two was a lot. Zero was ideal. In Iraq, the truck would not have made it within a hundred feet. Any further and it would be scrap metal for the locals to pick apart in the morning—assuming they could pull the bodies out. Sometimes it all melted together in a horrible slag of metal and men.

"An abundance of caution," he said.

"Still, they were just kids."

He glanced at her but said nothing.

"Us or them, right?"

Sherman nodded. Survival. Nothing more. Nothing less. It seemed odd to him that such an idea resonated so poorly.

Given her history of running, she must have taken it to heart. She shot a guy in her house. That took a basic calculation. Weighing his life against hers.

The thought triggered some gap in his memory. A board without a nail. A fact to tie down.

"I forgot to ask… why did you go back to your house?"

"Stupidity. I forgot some paperwork in the junk drawer. Have you ever had that moment when you just don't know what to do with the mail, so you stuff it in whatever space is convenient?"

"I don't have a home, let alone a junk drawer, but I get your point."

"Oh. Well, it related to my Jeep. Insurance or registration or some such paperwork. Leaving it felt risky. So did going back, but I did it anyway."

"And the guy. Did you know him?"

"Never saw him before."

"He was asking around town. That picture of you winning the cocktail competition. It went online."

"I know. Another stupid mistake."

"No judgement here."

"But you are here," said Ruby. "That's my fault."

Stars twinkled gaily overhead, and Sherman looked up through the windshield at their endlessness. "This beats Texas."

"Gum stuck on the pavement beats Texas," she mumbled.

"Up ahead," said Sherman.

A small driveway emerged to their left. Narrow and rutted. Nailed to an old pine tree was a sign. It read *Talbot*.

"She's a devious one," he muttered.

"We're hiding here. In the Chief of Police's cabin?"

"Technically, it was his uncle's cabin."

"I better stay dressed. You have a habit of being harassed by the cops early in the morning."

"I never go looking for the trouble," he protested.

"Doesn't matter. You and me are alike. It always finds us in the end."

Sherman took the Glock and slid out into the night. "Be right back."

Ruby watched him disappear into the gloom like a rock sinking into the ocean. A minute passed. Then two. She could feel her anxiety building. Stacking like Lego blocks of fear. But before they went any higher, Sherman reappeared. Striding back into view in the same spot. She rolled down the window.

"All clear. There is room to park around on the right side. It should keep it out of view."

She followed his instructions and parked the Jeep just beyond the cabin. He was already inside when she reached the front door.

Not much had changed since Bill Talbot bought the place thirty years before. It still had four walls, a roof, a chimney, and an outhouse. He added a small camping stove, some secondhand chairs, and a decent bed, but the place kept its rustic vibe. To Betsy's credit, the pantry still contained canned food and water. She wasn't wrong. Sherman found two old rectangular sleeping bags in a closet and unrolled them on the bed.

"Presumptuous," joked Ruby.

"Don't know what you're talking about. I'm self-contained."

He locked the door, stuck the pistol between the bedframe and the mattress, and lay down. Their neatly zippered separation lasted three minutes and not a second more.

Chief Talbot's watch read two in the morning. The coroner had come and gone. Only the tow truck remained. Most wrecks could wait a day. The bloodied remains of the pickup could not.

Another officer sauntered over. Everyone called him Carl, even though his birth name was Eugene. A mix-up from childhood. Talbot knew the story but stopped listening years before. It wasn't worth the energy.

"Late night," said Talbot.

"Yeah, seems the entire town is up."

Talbot frowned at the lack of detail.

"Saw Aunt Betsy driving off just before I got the call."

The frown furrowed deeper.

"She headed south out of town."

"Did you see Mr. Sherman today?" asked Talbot.

"No one left the house, except for Betsy. Offered me a breakfast burrito this morning on her way out."

"Which way did she go?"

"North, I think."

Talbot took in a deep breath and tried to suppress the joy he felt when he considered firing Carl.

"Go home, Carl. Get some sleep and then see if Mr. Sherman is there in the morning. Knock if you have to."

Chapter Fourteen

A synthetic ding woke James Abney from a dreamless sleep. His eyes popped open as his brain searched for the source of the sound. Another ding, the reminder bell confirmed it. He rolled out of bed and looked at the stark white screen. It displayed a single line of text. A question.

Status?

Seven characters long. Not much of a message, but the weight behind pulled on his nervous system like an undertow. It came from his benefactor. The man behind his success—Terrance Knight.

Five thirty in the morning East Coast time. About average for a wake-up call from the Alabama senator. Early to rise. Late to bed. It maximized his time. Abney knew that but hoped for a few more days. His first plan succeeded. The two dead locals proved she was not working alone. Identifying the mystery man would take time, but Abney's working opinion was straightforward. A man from her past, a military man, was helping her. The details remained unwritten, but those facts created a rough sketch of his options. His gut said they ran, but not far. Men like that were practical. Running brought risks. Minimizing risk was important. Staying close accomplished that.

Abney typed out his response.

Target is close. Forty-eight hours. No more.

He avoided deadlines when possible, but the senator backed him into a corner. He felt confident. Things change. They always do. In D.C., two days could overtake an eternity. Two days bought him time. With that thought in mind, he slid back into bed, flushed with plans.

Shadows danced across the cabin walls—thin and long. Pine needles fluttered about their narrow width. Sherman noticed them first, then the birds announcing morning. A dream lingered like the coals of a nearly extinguished fire. The texture faded within the first few blinks, but it involved his sixth-grade teacher and a volcano made of mud. The more he reached for the memory, the more it crumbled. An incoherent echo of the night.

He stopped and listened to the breeze blowing and animals chirping. Normal and reassuring sounds. Everyday noises with no hint of menace. Ruby stirred, those initial moments straddling the world between sleep and consciousness. Then, without warning, she sat straight up like a catapult unleashed. In her uncontrollable haste, she almost punched Sherman in the face. He rotated his nose out of the way at the last second and her elbow slid under his cheekbone.

Ruby sat there naked and breathing hard in the unheated morning air. Fears came and went like the tide.

Finally, her gaze settled on Sherman's bearded face. Tan and ragged and smiling.

"You look like the Unabomber," she said with a sigh.

"Good morning to you, too."

Slipping out of bed, she took the sleeping bag with her, more as a guard against the chilly mountain air than any leftover modesty. Sherman watched her search for clothes with discernible appreciation. He did the same and found most of his under a rustic chair made from bicep-thick pine logs.

"Your scar collection has grown," noted Ruby as she slid into her underwear.

The latest stuck out, fresh and pink. A three-inch slice mixed with burns just below his ribs—gifts from a Russian-made cluster bomb. Syrian teenagers had grabbed it out from the wreckage of a car as Sherman's team passed by. A stroke of luck, dumb or otherwise. The kids ended up more bits than solid, like an onion in a food processor. Sherman's vest took most of the damage, but a chunk of metal cut through. Superheated by the blast, it lodged just under the Kevlar and burned away. Gournsey yanked it out with his bare hands... yet another act for which Sherman owed the sergeant.

"I like to have something to show for my work."

"You have a twisted sense of humor."

"I know."

Ruby pointed towards the chair. "Can you hand me that bra?"

Sherman tossed it over.

"Did this place come with a coffeemaker?"

A few wide cedar planks made up the pantry. The organization made no sense. Then Sherman realized it was alphabetical. Soup sat next to canned salmon. Tuna next to turmeric. The coffee sat at the top. Right before creamed corn. A dusty can of the instant variety. Sherman scooped a few spoons worth in two cups and fiddled with the camp stove. It took a minute to find a propane tank and matches, but he got everything working. They sat there in silence, waiting for the water to boil. Only after her first sip did Ruby let go of the fear.

"Looks like we have enough for a few days," she began.

"Easily."

"Do we just wait?"

"It's not so bad up here," he gestured at the view from one window.

Ruby glanced at the contorted pile of sleeping bags and smiled. "Not too bad," she agreed, but a memory from California surfaced along with a question. "How long do you have here?"

Sherman had no definitive answer. It was the hard truth of his profession. Most soldiers had predictable patterns of time at home. He did not. "Honestly, I don't know. A week at least."

Ruby's chest tightened at the thought of losing her lone support. Starting over stood like a long shadow, blanketing her future. Everything felt like free fall. Her life was a wreck. More of the same made her want to add bourbon to her coffee. Anything to dull the creeping sense of despair.

"I'll stay as long as I can," added Sherman, sensing the fear pooling in her eyes.

"Thanks, but it's not your fight."

"I think we're beyond that now."

She took another sip and nodded. "I suppose that bridge is burned and gone."

Sherman agreed but didn't get the words out. A faint buzzing caught his attention. Not louder than crickets on the wind, but his ears sensed trouble. A base conclusion hidden from all the logic and justifications of higher brain function. His eyes darted about in a disorderly search for the unknown.

"What is it?" asked Ruby. Her fears fed off his expression.

"A car. Someone is coming."

She strained to hear anything but the breeze. It took a moment but she finally heard it. The hum of low gears in the distance.

"What should we do?"

"Get your shoes."

The sneakers were next to an old wooden crate, but it took Ruby a few seconds of frantic searching to remember. She got them tied with haphazard loops as the sound grew louder. It had a gurgly quality associated with engines and vehicles. Sherman slid the Glock into his waistband.

"Stay out back. You'll know when to run."

Ruby numbly bobbed her head in recognition and hid in some trees behind the cabin. She couldn't see the front anymore, but the sounds grew unabated.

Sherman did not need to see anything before dismissing it as the Suburban and the FBI. No trained agents came in like that. Not without back-up and first surrounding the area. Moonlighting required a level of cunning. Driving right up made little sense.

Two Ford Explorer SUVs roared into view through a sliver between the pines. Police models. Recent productions. A year old. Sherman stepped out from behind a tree and stood off to the side of the driveway. The vehicles pulled in and blocked the gravel entrance.

Chief Talbot slid out of the first SUV, followed by a man from the second. The guy reminded Sherman of the blob that followed him around town. Not once did he get a good look, but somehow, the proportions felt right. A second later, Betsy's Toyota slid around the corner and stopped behind the cops. Talbot didn't turn, which meant he already knew.

"Mr. Sherman," yelled the chief from a respectable distance, still standing behind the ballistic door panel.

"Chief Talbot, to what do I owe this visit?"

"I'm afraid it's a professional matter. Can we have a word?"

"I'll allow it."

"Do you mind stepping closer to us? I don't want to yell."

It was a good tactical question and Sherman understood it at once. Talbot wanted him out in the open. Easier to win a firefight if the other guy had nowhere to hide.

"I'm fine here."

Talbot's square jawline hardened a little further. He wanted a peaceable outcome but knew enough about Sherman from his handiwork to understand he was dangerous. Decision time arrived. With a glance backward at Betsy, he closed the door and walked away from the hardened cover. Her trust in the captain moved Talbot's legs forward.

The chief came within fifteen feet before stopping. He glanced back at Carl, who looked unnerved in the changing circumstances. Sherman watched him eye up the angles and take two causal steps to the left. Enough room to allow the other officer to shoot without worry of friendly fire. He appreciated the risk and the gesture of good faith. Would he do the same in Syria or Afghanistan? Likely not.

Behind the two cops, Betsy stood fuming with hands on her hips. A storm raged in her eyes with enough fury that

Talbot could feel her gaze on his back. She looked at Sherman and shook her head with an apology.

"I'm sorry, Frank," she yelled. "Aaron's not as dumb as his daddy."

Sherman smiled at another effort worth appreciating. He understood the events without knowing them.

"I'm guessing your man saw her leave last night."

Talbot nodded. "He went to check on you this morning. The rest was easy enough to pin down."

Behind the chief, Carl hid in the door's crook and leveled his service pistol straight at Sherman's chest. Never had he drawn his pistol outside of target practice, but Sherman could see a certain comfortableness in the man's expression.

"I have a few questions for you and Audrey," Talbot continued.

The battered Jeep remained hidden around the corner, so either Betsy told him or he was fishing. The older woman's comment rang in Sherman's ear.

Not as dumb as his daddy.

He considered the angles and reckoned putting a bullet through Carl was reasonable. The kid looked shaky enough and stood at a range where it mattered. That left the chief. How often do small-town police draw their weapons? A few times a year, he reasoned. Small-time stuff. A domestic dispute that escalated or a break-in. Speed became the issue. Sherman was quick, even with the awkward positioning behind his back. Repetition creates proficiency. It was not the first time, nor the last. Doable from a technical perspective. Morally, it crossed a line and few of those remained in his world. Too few. No, he wouldn't take a giant leap over the edge of his principles.

"I assumed so," replied Sherman.

"Do you mind asking Audrey to come out?"

"Let's hear your questions first."

"Captain, I'd like to keep this low-key, but people died. It's my duty to investigate and enforce the law."

"No need for rank here. I'm just a concerned citizen willing to cooperate within reason."

"Within reason?" asked Talbot. The qualifier hung like a distant storm rolling across the valley.

"There are safety concerns."

"For whom?"

"Audrey."

"Okay."

"I want to set some ground rules," added Sherman.

"This isn't a playground, Mr. Sherman, you don't get to dictate terms. I'm trying to be civil. My aunt says you're a decent man."

"Did she explain the situation?"

"No. Said it best came from your lips."

Betsy nodded decisively in the background.

"Kind of her."

"She's a forceful woman," added Talbot delicately. "I'm happy to discuss your concerns on the drive back to the station."

"That is not wise."

Talbot swallowed down his rising anger. He considered himself a calm person. Not one to react out of hand. But he hated incomplete stories and pictures without details.

"I can't help with what I don't know," he replied.

Sherman saw the frustration flare. The chief was out on a limb, standing in the open, and trying to help. He looked at Betsy for confirmation. She nodded.

"We'll come into the station, but you need to keep this

off the record for now. If our names get entered into that database of yours, well, my opinion will change."

Stark words, but truthful. It wasn't just his career on the line, but their safety. Within a few keystrokes, the FBI would know of their whereabouts.

"Agreed. Off the record."

"You okay with that?" shouted Sherman over his shoulder.

Ruby leaned around the corner, having heard everything. "Do I have a choice?"

"You always have a choice," Sherman answered.

"Off the record?" she asked Talbot.

Talbot nodded. "Just questions."

"Okay, but we ride together."

"Fine by me," agreed Talbot.

They all nodded with some unspoken pact.

Sherman raised his hands above shoulder height and looked at the other officer, who never lowered his weapon during the entire conversation. "Carl," he began, taking a guess it was the same cop who had followed him around town. "I'm going to turn around and slowly drop something. It's a pistol. A Glock 22, just like the one you're holding. I'd appreciate it if you could refrain from shooting me in the back."

"Stand down, Carl," ordered Talbot.

The officer lowered his gun but kept his eye on Sherman as he followed his own description. The pistol clattered onto the gravel below and Sherman turned back to face the trio.

"I'm gonna need to handcuff you both," added Talbot. "It is standard procedure, and I can't risk the safety of my officers."

Sherman turned around and nodded towards Ruby,

hoping she wouldn't run. Things might turn sour if that happened. "Chief, I'm placing a lot of trust in you right now. Don't let me down."

"The feeling is mutual, Mr. Sherman."

Cold metal encircled Sherman's wrists. Such unpleasantness had occurred once before during a training exercise run by the CIA, on the 'Farm' outside of Langley. Enhanced interrogation techniques were the topic that day. At least waterboarding was not in the police manual for Stalworth, Idaho.

Ruby followed suit and Talbot led them both over to his SUV while Carl retrieved the gun from the driveway.

Betsy came over to the vehicle and apologized, "I'm sorry, Frank. I didn't mean for this to happen. Aaron's an honorable man, he'll keep his word."

"Thanks, and this was not your fault. Things just happen."

She smiled as Talbot shooed her back to the Toyota.

The Ford came without traditional back seats. A single sheet of molded plastic took their place. It was easy to clean —just spray it down with a favored disinfectant and move on. Even the seatbelts were custom. They closed the opposite direction. It allowed the officer to secure a subject without leaning over them. Sherman's six-foot frame barely fit inside, and his knees hit the hard-plastic barrier. Ruby sat glumly next to him. Her shoulders slumped forward, dejected, depressed, and bewildered.

Talbot started up the twin-turbocharged V6 and backed out of the driveway. Carl followed with Betsy somewhere behind them both. The odd convoy descended the mountain and back towards Stalworth.

Chapter Fifteen

James Abney lay on an overstuffed chaise lounge, basking in the morning sun. The Snake River was visible just above his outstretched feet as the cool water sparkled and danced with a mild wind. Harris and Tarney had brought him up to speed over a breakfast of two eggs, extra runny, with a double order of sausage. He skipped the included bowl of fruit and toast.

The agents' retelling of the night was dry and colorless. A common state school vernacular. No panache. They spoke in the stodgy and clipped speech so common in government bureaucracies. By the second egg, he knew nothing of interest had changed. The shooter remained at large, and the police had no leads.

He had set his eye on a lithe Hispanic woman who worked as a housekeeper when the phone rang.

"News?" he asked.

Harris swallowed another chunk of her pride and replied, "Our source in the department called. They detained two persons of interest. One male, one female."

A mile-wide smile revealed Abney's white teeth. "Excellent news. Intercept them before they get into the station."

"Under what pretext?"

Abney shook his head at the agent's lack of imagination. "Use your badge. Issues of national security. You don't need a warrant for that."

"And then what?"

"I will not spell this out for you, Harris. Pay your debt off and get back to your boring studio apartment and that tabby cat of yours."

Harris hung up without a word, and Abney went back to leering at the woman in her black-and-white maid's uniform. The day was looking up. His forty-eight-hour deadline would last only until lunch. Time remained for some extracurricular activity.

The handcuffs dug into his wrists and Sherman slouched a little to relieve the pressure. Ruby teetered on the edge of a breakdown. She leaned her head against the window and gazed at the valley below. The vibrations made her face itch, but she ignored the sensation because scratching her face was impossible.

"How did you know Carl's name?" asked Talbot. The minor question sat like a pebble in his shoe—inconvenient and irritating.

"Are we starting this now?" asked Sherman.

"I suppose we are?"

"Betsy gave him a breakfast burrito."

Mental puzzle pieces snapped together for Talbot. "You were in the car when she headed north."

"I was."

"Why?"

Sherman looked over at Ruby. She shook her head with sharp movements.

"Audrey here ran into trouble a few years back," he began. "The guy you found in her house was looking for her."

"That true?" asked Talbot, looking at Ruby in the mirror.

"It is," she answered weakly.

"Why?"

Sherman answered, "A domestic abuse situation that escalated."

The chief eyed them carefully, trying to discern the length of yarn being spun around him. "Okay, sounds like you ran from an untenable situation. That happens all the time. Did you shoot the guy?"

Ruby glanced at Sherman, who nodded reassuringly. He had no plan of letting Talbot press charges. The army taught him to survive. If it came to it, he would check all the boxes in the manual.

"He had a gun," explained Ruby.

"We didn't find one," Talbot countered.

"You have it now. Carl picked it up from the ground."

"You're saying the guy from your house was armed, even though he was an Idaho Power employee."

The change in narrative caught Sherman flat-footed, but the reasons unfolded over the next few seconds. Scraping the web for images took time, money, and skill. The same skills needed to hack into a company database.

"You confirmed that?" he asked.

"A recent employee. The woman from H.R. couldn't tell me where he worked, only that he just started."

"And his address?"

"Boise."

"Did you check it out?" wondered Sherman.

"We requested that Boise P.D. look into it."

"Did you hear back?"

"Not yet," admitted Talbot.

"Then you have no confirmation of his story."

"Nor do I have reason to doubt it."

A valid point, thought Sherman. He liked Talbot and hoped the situation would not force him to hurt the guy, but the outlook kept growing worse.

"And the gun, the one that Carl picked up and purportedly belonged to the deceased. Did that get used last night?" Talbot asked.

Trying to deny it made no sense. Ballistics would tie it together, even if the science proved circumspect. Any competent prosecutor could present that to a jury.

"It did."

"Care to explain how two men died?"

"Multiple GSWs to the thorax and abdomen," explained Ruby with a monotone voice that reminded Sherman of the doctor lurking in her past.

Talbot glanced back with a touch of surprise at the unexpected answer. "I saw it. Something I'd like to unsee. But why are they dead?"

"They tried to run us off the road. Rammed the Jeep twice. I nearly lost control. When they started in for a third try, I hit the brakes and got out."

"And started shooting?"

"Yes."

"Audrey. Care to give any color?"

"My name is Ruby, not Audrey."

Talbot didn't pause a beat. The switch felt logical.

Something he expected. "Okay, Ruby. Is Mr. Sherman's retelling accurate?"

"Yes."

"Did you recognize the men in the truck?"

"I kept my head down, so I didn't see much."

"Mr. Sherman, did you recognize them?"

"No, and I don't think they knew me," answered Sherman.

"Did you exchange words?"

"Not so much."

"Then how do you know?"

The hypothetical case against him unfolded in Sherman's imagination. Chief Talbot already had the pieces. Neat crimes with excuses he could not prove. Agreeing to get in the car felt like a mistake. Both cops were wearing vests. He should have shot them center mass and escaped during the confusion. A search party takes time to deploy. Escape and evade. Easy for him, but maybe not so much for Ruby.

He dodged the question. "They didn't shoot first."

"I'd like to believe you, Mr. Sherman. But even with Ruby as a witness, I don't see your self-defense argument playing well with a jury."

"You assured me we were just talking," retorted Sherman.

"And we are," replied Talbot. "I'm stating the facts as I see them. What you've given me is not enough. There is more to this story, I know that, but all I see right now are three murders. Manslaughter, if you plead the charges down."

Only one card remained. The FBI agents. Sherman toyed with the idea of telling the chief but didn't. It came down to proof. There were no witnesses. Betsy never saw them at the casino. He alone saw them at the house. And Ruby was the only witness for their interrogation at the cabin.

Ruby shook her head, low and slow. "I'm sorry, Frank, I should have never got you involved."

"Don't apologize," replied Sherman. "I came here with my own two feet."

Past the alfalfa fields and across the valley, the town appeared as neat black lines of asphalt set against the serpentine river. Sherman liked the view, so serene against the ebb of recent events. Seeing it through the plexiglass barrier of a police cruiser lessened his enjoyment. Getting out percolated up as the top priority.

Talbot eased to a halt at the first four-way stop on the edge of Stalworth. Carl and Betsy turned left. They went straight. Sherman watched the woman drive away. At least she wouldn't be there to see if the situation turned upside down. He hoped it wouldn't get too messy. A few broken bones were fine. Dead cops? Not so much.

All the scenarios unfolded before Sherman. He picked through them one by one. Discarding the drastic endings. Lost in that thought, he almost missed the large black SUV parked next to the stop sign before the police station.

"Frank," said Ruby with alarm.

Talbot stopped as two people in black suits got out of the vehicle and approached the police cruiser. They were holding up badges with thick blue letters. FBI.

"Hold on," said Talbot as he got out of the car.

"Chief, wait," yelled Sherman, but Talbot slammed the door before the words could reach his ears.

All the color faded from Ruby's face and her breaths came quick and ragged. The fears of arrest and prosecution paled compared to the fate standing before them. She glanced at Sherman. His eyes narrowed to a flinty stare. Not fear or acceptance, she thought, but something else. A prehistoric glance of opportunity, like some caveman sizing up his next meal.

"We should have told him," said Ruby.

"They got here too quickly… like they already knew."

"How? He said off the record."

"I don't think he called it in. Maybe it was Carl or someone else in the department."

"They can't just take us, right?" asked Ruby.

The thought of leaving the police cruiser, which only minutes before felt like a prison, was frightening. The heavy plastic barrier and bullet-resistant siding shielded them from outside forces.

Agent Harris gestured towards the car as the three law enforcement professionals were deep in conversation. They watched Talbot shake his head sharply several times in defiance. Then Harris pulled a sheet of paper from her suit pocket and handed it over. Talbot took time to read everything before handing it back. When he looked over his shoulder at the SUV, Sherman knew they were in trouble. A defeated crease turned down from the corners of his mouth. It was the FBI. The feds. A cop from some Podunk town in rural Idaho didn't stand a chance against them. He came over and opened the back door.

"Chief, don't do this," pleaded Ruby. Her voice cracked and tears burned behind her eyes.

"I'm sorry. My hands are tied. They called it a matter of national security. Even had a letter classifying you as a person of interest in the death of a foreign agent."

"The power company guy? You believe that?" asked Sherman. Throwing the dead guy under the bus was a smart move by Harris and he knew it.

"What I believe stopped being important the moment they pulled out their badges."

"Did you tell them my name?" demanded Sherman.

Talbot shook his head. "You're not listed on the document, but they claimed you as an accomplice."

Agent Tarney approached the vehicle and yanked Sherman out from the back seat. The guy was powerful. His suit hid the gym-built muscles underneath, and he twisted forcefully on Sherman's bicep. A test, or show of power, from one professional to another, ramming home the helplessness of the situation.

"I want my handcuffs back," said Talbot as the agent maneuvered Sherman towards the Suburban.

"We'll send you some fresh ones," barked Tarney with a dismissive glance.

"I really must insist," Talbot growled.

Harris walked over with industrial-strength zip ties. Two thick white plastic loops. A cheap, effective replacement for steel. Tarney slid them over Sherman's wrists and yanked hard. They bit into his skin like a dull knife.

Standing to the side, Talbot watched dejectedly. By keeping his job, he had broken his word. The self-inflicted betrayal sat like a stone in his stomach.

"Talbot," yelled Sherman while struggling against Tarney, who was pushing him inside the SUV. "Check the license plate."

Tarney slammed the door. Sherman's voice faded, muffled by the dampening material inside. Talbot stood there grasping for meaning in the comment. It landed as a non sequitur.

The Suburban burbled to life and Talbot took a step back towards the police cruiser. Agent Harris gave a brief wave. A courteous, professional gesture like a holdover from some previous generation. The chief almost waved back in an automatic, congenial, small-town response. But he didn't. He shook his head, huffed an obscenity, and tried to think of the future. At least the body count would not go any higher.

When he got back to the police station, Officer Torres was waiting. A manilla folder lay in her outstretched arms like some school kid who took home too many books from the library.

"Chief," she shouted as he walked up.

"I hope this is something good," he said glumly.

"Don't know if I'd call it good, but I found Horace Filby's car parked down the street in Mr. Berryworth's driveway. He always seems to have some fresh junker, so we didn't notice until they came back from vacation."

"Which was today?"

"He called an hour ago. I found this under the front seat. Check out the first page."

She held out the folder. The top stuck out at a forty-five-degree angle. Chief Talbot flipped it up to reveal the picture of Ruby. An extensive background investigation lay underneath. All the details of a life lived on the run. The realization hit him harder than a surprise jab to the gut. Horace Filby was not working with Ruby. He was stalking her. Looking for the opportunity to strike.

"Their damn plate isn't federal," mumbled Talbot as he threw the folder back at Torres and jumped back into the police cruiser.

Chapter Sixteen

Dull vibrations on the table caught James Abney's attention, which was otherwise preoccupied with the naked housekeeper unconscious on his bed. She took some coaxing, but it had been worth the effort and now the phone call dampened his gathering excitement.

"What!" he barked into the phone.

"Your package is in tow," said Harris, gulping down her disgust.

"Splendid. Disposal is part of the job. Call me when it's done and bring me her belongings."

Abney ended the call. The morning continued to brighten. His long-suffering trouble was nearly over. Five years of waiting and searching. Five years of suspense and fear and guilt. The unknown hanging over his head. All of it was almost over.

Agent Harris tossed her cell phone onto the dashboard. It skittered across the faux leather surface. Every conversation with the man unsettled her further. She looked in the rearview mirror at the two faces glaring back. At least there was an end in sight. A tiny ray of light in her otherwise murky life. Only four months earlier, her existence fit together better than a well-paired pinot noir. The sleek studio apartment with exposed brick and stainless-steel accents. Her sporty German car. The fat tabby cat named Stellan. A lovely life. Perfect, except for a languishing career. Then, James Abney showed up. A dapper wrecking ball.

She called it entrapment, but the blame for the entire dogged affair lay on her shoulders. Greed or entitlement pushed her towards the agreement. A few phone calls later, and she received a transfer to Major Crimes. Then she got a promotion. Serious cases. Recognition from the higher-ups. All that for a single favor hidden somewhere over the horizon. An issue for future Harris. Until it wasn't. Until Abney called in his marker and she took a week of precious leave and flew to rural Idaho.

That was table scraps compared to the choice of sitting in the back seat. Two people for two careers. Tarney was in the same boiling water. His story was so similar, all you had to do was exchange the last names to discover identical mistakes. An eye for an eye times four. The instructions from Abney were clear. Killing the woman would negate her debt. Scout's honor, he had said. Although, she doubted the man had ever been a Boy Scout. The strange man was a bonus. Not for them, but for Abney. The cherry on top of the icing that covered the cake. Oh, how she hated her own stupidity. Harris tried to focus on that lone ray of light. It was almost over.

Sherman eyed the woman thoughtfully. She looked younger up close. Late twenties. Still glowing from college and career advancement. An up-and-comer. Dyed hair. Nicer watch than she wore earlier at Ruby's house. Even her suit appeared pricier from a few feet away.

She kept glancing back in the mirror, weighing her options like a customer at some fancy butcher shop. Was it worth the expense? How would her friends view the choice? The stare felt shallow, and then he knew why. It was the look of someone who had already decided but felt the need to justify it to themselves… as if accepting the price tag for her next meal.

The guy in the passenger seat was no different. He had the same blank stare. The same curdled smile. He was older, but only by a year or two. While the woman expressed a dejected acceptance of her role, Tarney's face hinted at a smile. Maybe not pleasure, but something close.

"Why are you doing this?" cried Ruby. She sobbed and shook against the tightness of the seat belt and zip ties. The agents triggered the auto-lock mechanism when strapping them in and everything they did only further restricted their motion.

Neither Harris nor Tarney said a word. They sat stony-faced with lips pursed tightly together. Sherman wondered if they taught the look at Quantico. All the agents he knew carried the same expression as a broom to sweep away unwanted questions.

"Are you gonna just sit there?" Ruby demanded. "What about our rights?"

"Ma'am," replied Harris in her sternest tone. "It's for

the best if you remain quiet. My partner would prefer to duct-tape your mouth shut."

"You're not even going to pretend to be real cops."

More indifferent glances, but no words. Ruby looked at Sherman for help but she could already see his thoughts racing.

The change of circumstances switched his mind into complete survival mode. All other considerations disappeared. Anyone standing in his way was an obstacle. A problem that needed a solution. Everything was permissible in that pursuit. No one got a pass, even if their paychecks came from the same government.

"How much did Abney buy you for?" he asked. Psychological warfare was a critical piece of any decent battle plan. It felt right to start by spreading some dissent and disinformation.

Harris glanced at the mirror. The name got her attention, even if she tried to suppress the impulse to react.

"I'll assume it wasn't just money. You two don't look so easily bought," added Sherman with a sneer. "If not money, then power. Did he pull some strings? Maybe you got that promotion or corner office. Hell, maybe you did it for a closer parking spot!"

Tarney took the bait and whirled around to face Sherman. "You need to shut your goddamn mouth, or I will break it and tape the pieces closed."

Sherman took a mental note of who cracked first. The man had thinner skin than Harris. Reaction was a weakness to be weaponized under certain circumstances. He thought about antagonizing the man further but knowing was enough.

"And the man Abney works for. You must know whose dirty work you're doing, right?"

At the invocation of a third party, Agent Harris raised an eyebrow in curiosity.

"Oh, I see... you don't know," continued Sherman. "Does the name Terrance Knight mean anything to you?"

Both agents recoiled ever so slightly at the name. The senator had many detractors on both sides of the aisle, but his name rang loudly within the law enforcement community. Harris took it worse than Tarney, at least from Sherman's point of view. She at least choked down some semblance of disgust on hearing the name. Agent Tarney gave an eye roll at the acceptance of fact with no regret over the bargain he'd struck or the price or the man who owned his debt.

Politics aside, Sherman didn't care much either way. Left or right, the wars never stopped. Promises made and then broken. Truth of it was the whole notion of democracy rested on the sword. All the way back to the rocky hills of Greece. Governments came and went. Some carried bigger sticks than others, but it all boiled down to force. Swords and spears. Bullets and bombs.

Senator Terrance Knight waved a righteous stick clothed in piety and American exceptionalism. Lots of speeches. Words that gave credence to certain views and claimed mantles of righteousness. His views were not new. Both aisles straddled those lines in their storied pasts. Still, Sherman considered him a pompous prick.

"Words are cheap," spat Tarney.

"Really?" asked Sherman incredulously. "You're not just the slightest bit curious why they sent you out here?"

Neither agent responded.

"I'm just spitballing here," Sherman continued. "But the lovely woman sitting next to me has something of value to Mr. Knight. Doesn't your inner detective chafe at that incongruence?"

Still nothing but silence.

"Come on. You're smart people, notwithstanding your moronic choices leading up to this debacle. But overall, you two seem competent. Think about it. What is he hiding?"

Ruby sighed. Reason was getting them nowhere.

"I killed his son," she admitted.

The two agents tilted their heads at the admission. A minor display of curiosity. They couldn't help but be interested despite the situation.

"Sounds like revenge," replied Tarney. "Justifiable."

"Her or him?" asked Sherman rhetorically.

"Doesn't matter to me either way," replied the agent.

The conversation stalled. Sherman could see appealing to instinct was futile. He pushed against the seat belt to see how much wiggle room existed. Not much was the answer. Agent Tarney put the effort in to pull it all the way out, so it locked down tight. A smart move given the constraints of a rental car. Shifting a bit left, he got a thumb on the seat belt release button. *Step one*, he thought.

Step two involved timing. Ruby shot a glance at his effort. Genuine terror filled her eyes, pushed out by the tears. His plan involved waiting for a turn, but the road was straight. Sherman was about to wing it when a siren pierced the quiet luxuriousness of the SUV cabin. He turned enough to see red and blue lights strobing in the distance.

Agent Harris glanced at the rearview mirror and then over at Tarney. His expression hardened and motioned towards the shoulder of the road. She eased the SUV over and stopped. Tarney hopped out and gave a friendly wave.

Chief Talbot stepped out and approached the SUV and the FBI agent walking in his direction. Between the file and the rental car, his alarm bells were ringing loudly. Despite those reservations, somewhere in the back of his mind, he trusted the fellow cop. Maybe there was some simple explanation. A lack of vehicles or extraneous circumstances. Or something else.

"Chief, what can I do for you?" asked Tarney as he pulled up short about ten feet away.

"Probably nothing," replied Talbot with a friendly smile. "But I'd like to see that document again."

Tarney nodded slightly. "I could have emailed it to you."

"I'm old-fashioned."

"Did you have concerns?"

"It's a small town. I even check my punctuation."

"And the lights?"

"Oh, I don't get to turn them on that often," replied Talbot with a sheepish grin. "Do you have the paperwork?"

Tarney made a show of checking his pockets but came up empty.

"My partner must have it."

Talbot shrugged.

Agent Tarney turned back towards the SUV and took a step before whipping back around with practiced ease. He fired a single shot from his service pistol and hit the Chief of Police just above the left eyebrow. Talbot crumpled to the ground like a house of cards collapsing under its own weight. The agent watched him fall and then grabbed the spent cartridge from the pavement.

Inside the Suburban, Ruby let out a muffled scream that slipped out of her throat but died in the ensuing silence. Harris watched the incident unfold in the rearview mirror and, upon seeing the body hit asphalt, let out a deeply prolonged sigh. She could not think of any lines left to cross. Strangely, it made the dirty work of disposing of her two passengers feel less foul.

Watching another human life disappear did not give Sherman pause, but a little door closed in his mind. Any thought of leniency for the agents vanished behind it. He twisted right again and gently released his seatbelt but held it in place with his hands.

Step two, complete.

Agent Tarney slid back inside the Suburban, and Harris glared in his direction.

"He knew," replied Tarney.

"It didn't look like he knew," she retorted.

"He knew."

"It could come back on us," she replied.

"It won't."

Harris shook her head but knew what he meant. They could pin it on their guests in the backseat. It might take some doing, but they had gold badges and IDs with big block letters that said FBI. That was enough in rural Idaho.

She pulled back onto the thin state road. The place they had picked out earlier that morning was only three miles away. Harris committed the details to memory after breakfast. Leaving nothing to chance was her new motto. Their phones were back at the motel and they disabled the GPS on the Suburban when they rented it. She wanted to force Tarney to do the shooting. It felt like penance for the cop, but she knew such hopes were futile. Her debt would still stand, Abney would make sure of it.

Sherman watched the thoughts wash across her face. He harbored no illusions of what it meant when they got in the Suburban but held out hope for Harris. She looked like someone out of their depth but still capable of swimming back. That was gone.

Step three, he thought.

As soon as Harris brought the SUV up to speed, Sherman released the seat belt and shifted his weight onto his right foot. Step four involved timing, aim, and luck.

"You're a shitty shot," he growled in Tarney's direction.

As expected, the agent turned his head to the left, not all the way, but sufficient to get one eye on the voice behind him. It was enough. Sherman leaned back to give himself some extra room and swung his left foot as hard as he could towards Tarney's face. He was aiming for the nose but hit the man's lower lip, hard with the steel toe of his boot. The sound of teeth cracking from their bone foundations filled the air, and a thin spray of blood splattered across the soft cloth-covered ceiling. His head snapped back from the sheer force and slammed into the window. The back of Tarney's skull left a small crater of shattered safety glass.

The sudden savagery caused Harris to swerve a little as she reached for her gun. She cleared leather but her right hand couldn't quite rotate far enough to point back. Her elbow hung in the open between the seats. Sherman kicked straight at and through it. The joint snapped and bent back at an unnatural angle like a crudely drawn 'V'. Waves of pain overwhelmed the agent's brain.

Convulsed with shock, Harris yanked the wheel hard and sent the massive vehicle hurtling into a copse of trees on the side of the road. The sound of crunching metal and plastic filled Sherman's ears right before he flew forward. Newton's Third Law of Motion in action. Unfortunate but necessary was the last thought he had before bouncing off and between the two seats and into the console. When his eyes finally opened, Sherman was looking up through the broken front windshield with his head on the dashboard. A slimy trickle of blood slid down between his eyes. Something hurt above his forehead, sharp and aching. Painful, but not fatal. He moved his toes and fingers. No tingling, which he considered a decent sign. Although, a center console airbag would have been nice.

The SUV was ringing with warning bells and hissing from the damaged motor, but he heard the driver's side door open. Harris fell out onto the dirt below and screamed with pain. Sherman could see her good arm reach inside and search for the gun, which had fallen on the floor. He slid to his right and landed the heel of his boot on her knuckles. The woman screamed again and fell backwards away from the vehicle.

His arms remained tied behind his back and blood covered part of his right eye. Harris was shaking out her left hand, which looked bruised but functional, while her right arm hung limply at her side like an uncooked hotdog. Sherman considered it a fair fight. Then Harris opened a shiny pocketknife, and the odds went in her favor, but only just.

Chapter Seventeen

The road stayed empty. No one drove by the wrecked Suburban or the Chief of Police lying dead across double yellow lines. There was no one to witness the odd duel between two handicapped strangers. No one except for Ruby and, to a lesser extent, Tarney.

Harris took a step towards Sherman with the knife clenched tightly in her left fist. She held it low and awkwardly to the side. Not her dominant hand. The off hand. The one used for flashlights and badges, not for knives. Not when her right arm hung there, useless and screaming in pain. She could shoot with her left. Quantico taught that much, but nothing could have prepared her for that kind of fight.

From her first step, Sherman could see Agent Harris lacked practice. But a knife was a knife, and if she got lucky, he'd bleed out in the dirt. The entire premise of the encounter became avoiding the sharp bits. He started by circling to his left, which made it harder for her to take a solid swipe. Swinging across the body takes more time.

There is the wind-up and then the slash. An expert can do it in a blink of an eye, but not Harris. Not with her broken arm and the waves of pain rocketing through her system.

She stepped in again and slashed towards Sherman, who stepped back and left. It went on like that for a few more times. Long enough for Sherman to get a feel for the woman's speed and timing.

Slash—miss. Slash—miss. Slash—*ouch*.

Sherman felt the familiar pain of flesh sliced open by steel. It burned and ached but did not feel deep. Bandage? Yes. Stitches? Maybe. She was quicker than he thought.

After some adjustments, he stepped straight back onto his left foot and quickly unloaded with his right. The kick was quick and didn't have much follow-through. Missing big had its own risks, but it was enough. His steel-toe caught her wrist and sent the knife tumbling into a pale-yellow clump of dead grass.

"Listen, this wasn't my idea," pleaded Harris upon seeing her advantage sail away.

Sherman glanced quickly back towards Tarney, who had not moved. He never mixed fighting and talking. It distracted from the important part—winning.

He kept circling and said nothing.

"Really," continued Harris. "I'm sorry. I can help. Let me help. I know things about Abney. Details you need to hear."

Sherman stutter-stepped to the right and caught Harris mid-plea. She didn't have time to react to his sweeping kick that hit just above her ankle. The force toppled the agent sideways onto her good arm. It was enough to break her fall, but having landed on top of it, it left her defenseless. Sherman slid over and landed one hard kick across her temple. He could see the lights go out as Harris sprawled across the powdery dirt.

It took some searching, but he found her knife stuck blade-first in the grass. Cutting through the thick plastic cuffs took longer, but he got free. Sherman glanced at his reflection in the passenger window and took stock of the situation. He was bleeding from a contusion on his forehead. A deep cut. Stitches for sure, but not a skull fracture. The laceration on his arm was already clotting. Harris barely caught flesh, but it made a fine addition to his ghastly appearance. Blood-soaked hair and clothing with crimson splatters on his boots and pants.

He reached inside the open driver's side door and found the Glock under the gas pedal. It was clean, new, and loaded. Sherman looked across at Tarney's half-open eyes, leveled the pistol at them, and fired. The window behind the agent's head shattered completely. What remained of his head hung awkward and limp in the suddenly open space.

Then he remembered Ruby. Prior to that moment, his existence extended no further than the agent's knife. Those slashes and his next move encompassed everything. No future. No past. Only the present. When it ended, he found her sitting bathed in disgust and relief.

Unable to move, Ruby had watched the preceding minutes with rapt attention. Her world also shrank to a few square feet with any hope of a future hanging in the balance. She had a plan if Sherman lost, but it got no further than head-butting Harris and running for the road. Maybe a car would pass by and someone would come to her aid. More likely, she would catch a bullet in the back and that would be the end of her sad story, or so she thought.

Sherman opened the back door and freed Ruby from her constraints. She looked at him and then at Tarney and Harris. All Ruby could do was shake her head and feel her still-breathing body, the warm morning air and the silky dirt under her feet. The smell of dry summer grass and the pine trees brought home the aliveness of the moment. The triumph and euphoria. And the cost, so plain and clear.

Tarney was dead. She knew that before Sherman pulled the trigger. Brain damage from the kick, the window, and the crash had already put him on the organ donor list and not as a recipient. The bullet sealed his fate and ruined any chance of harvesting what remained, but she would not lose sleep over it. Harris was another story. She was still breathing shallow and labored, but alive.

"Frank. We need to go," she said, almost surprising herself.

"I know. Go and get Talbot's Explorer. I imagine the keys are still inside."

She looked back across and down the road. The Ford sat idling about two hundred yards away.

"Are you sure?"

"Yeah. And grab any keys or ammo he has on him."

Ruby wanted to ask if he was serious but already knew the answer, so she said the only thing that came to mind. "You need stitches."

"Later. We need to leave before anyone shows up."

Sherman turned to Agent Harris and her unconscious form lying on the ground. From inside her suit pocket, he grabbed a business card and wrote a single phrase. *Go home.*

He wasn't sure if he meant it for her or Abney, but the message was the same—stay and die or leave and live. A basic message. He tucked the card in her pocket and walked back to Ruby, who was waiting in the driver's seat.

"Is she still alive?"

Sherman squinted towards the Suburban. "For now."

"Where do we go now?" asked Ruby. An overpowering sense of claustrophobia had descended upon her.

"Back to the cabin."

"Seriously?"

"I'm guessing you have something they want."

"They want my life and revenge for what I did to Mason. What more do I have?"

"Whatever you took that night."

"The money is long gone, and I pawned the jewelry last year. Whatever I took from that safe, I've spent or sold. I've got nothing left."

"Back at the lake, when describing that night, you mentioned a USB drive."

Ruby looked into the distance. "You're right, I did."

"Where is it?"

"With some of my stuff in the Jeep, but there is nothing on it. Just a bunch of gibberish."

"You looked?"

"Years ago. I'm no computer whiz, but the file looked corrupted or something. I opened it up in Notepad and it had nothing but random letters and characters."

The oddity of keeping something useless in a safe struck Sherman as unusual. "Drive on," he instructed.

———

Twenty minutes later, Officer Eugene 'Carl' Ortman received a phone call from a primary school friend. The man lived on the fringes of town and the law, but friendships counted for something in Carl's world. He had stayed in touch over the years and even helped the guy out of a bind over some stolen electronics.

Carl tapped the flashing green button. "Shaun... what's up, buddy?"

"Well, I was just driving into town on Shaver Road, you know the one, and I passed something you might want to see."

"What is it?"

Shaun hesitated. "It's best I don't say. Just come out here. I'm about three miles from the old quarry. And hurry."

Carl ended the call, confused and frustrated. If his friend was in another jam, he wanted to know before showing up on the scene.

It didn't take him long to cover the distance in his Police Interceptor. He used the flashers. He always used them. The red and blue lights reinforced his sense of power and importance. A visual business card that also went over well with the ladies. There were several from his local bar that liked a bit of excitement and danger. In a town with little crime and less nightlife, a ride in a police car felt like the wild side.

Even at sixty miles per hour, Carl could see something strange unfolding before his eyes. Shaun's truck sat off to the side of the road, nearly covered by the pine trees. Further on was another car. Something big and black. It too was off in the trees. But most peculiar was the shape in the road. It started off as just a dark brown speck shimmering with the heat. Then it grew in definition. By the time Carl stopped, he knew it was a body.

Shaun stood to the side with his arms crossed and a nervous squint in his eyes. He kept looking at the horizon like a kid waiting for an angry parent to arrive home.

"Remember," he shouted towards Carl. "I called you."

Carl glanced at his friend and then at the body on the pavement. They wore some sort of uniform, and he almost mistook them for a FedEx driver at first. Then the details coalesced and Carl knew exactly what he was looking at—a dead cop.

His first instinct was to grab the radio attached at his shoulder, but something stopped him. He suddenly recognized the form splayed out across the double-yellow lines as Chief Talbot.

He could also make out the model of the car in the trees. A Suburban. Carl made the connection and loosened his grip on the radio. He walked over to Talbot's body. A single gunshot wound to the head. Close. Professional. The wheels in his mind raced. Powered by some expectant energy, he ran down to the black SUV.

Two bodies were visible. One man and one woman. Neither were the two he expected. He peered in the open door of the vehicle. The male agent was dead. A medical degree was not needed to make that leap. He turned towards the woman. The one he had talked with a few days before. She lay on the ground taking short but stable breaths. Her arm was bent back at a gruesome angle and there was a large contusion on her forehead. Carl pulled in a deep breath and scratched his chin. The wheels spun faster. He grabbed a business card from his wallet, turned it over, and dialed the number.

James Abney sipped from a top-shelf margarita while glancing at his phone. He did not recognize the caller, but the area code was local. Few people had his number. It existed outside of the average. So, when people called, he answered.

"Who is this?" he demanded.

"Uh, Officer Eugene Ortman, but people call me Carl."

Abney paused for a moment. Harris told him about recruiting a local police officer. An asset. "Of course, Carl. What can I do for you?"

"Well, I found something that might interest you."

Abney took an even longer pause. He looked at his watch and unease surged through his system. Harris and Tarney should have called. But they had not. And now he was talking to some provincial cop who believed he had something of concern.

"Don't be shy, Carl. Spit it out."

"I know I wasn't supposed to call this number, except for emergencies, but I thought you'd want to know there's been an incident over on Shaver Road. You probably don't know where that is, but it leads out of town. At any rate, I'm standing here next to one of your FBI agents. A Mr. Tarney, I believe."

Abney tapped his fingers on the bar with growing frustration but held his tongue. "Would you be so kind as to put him on the phone?"

"Oh, he's dead."

"What?"

"Yeah, shot through the head. Along with Chief Talbot."

Abney paused a beat to take in the news. "And Harris?"

"She's breathing, but only just. Got her ass kicked by the looks of it."

"Can she talk?"

"No, she ain't conscious."

"Do you have any good news, Carl?"

"I believe so."

Abney could feel the lawmen angling for something. Money or a promotion. Maybe the whole shebang. Maybe he wanted to be chief. *Someone like him*, thought Abney, *couldn't dream any bigger.*

"Care to elaborate."

"Well, I reckon you have a bit of a problem right now. Those two lovebirds are on the run and your dogs are dead. Judging by the brass in his pocket, I'd say it was Mr. Tarney who killed Chief Talbot. But we must wait for ballistics to confirm."

A great sigh welled up in Abney's chest and he tried his best not to lose his temper. He was a practical man and could see that Carl represented a necessary evil. Another step on the ladder or wheel that needed greasing.

"We are at a crossroads, Mr. Ortman. I am without associates, and you seem like a capable man. Perhaps we can work together for the foreseeable future."

"I'm glad to hear you say that," replied Carl. "An idea just popped into my mind."

"Pray tell."

"Well, I can make the bodies disappear. Ain't no problem there. But there is still the issue of those two outsiders and my, uh, compensation."

Angling indeed, thought Abney. "What did you have in mind?"

"Old Talbot's job. I figure you could help persuade the mayor. He responds well to large campaign donations."

Abney almost laughed out loud. Hicks never dreamed on a grand scale. They were too content with their mean-ingless lives in obscure towns.

"I might consider such an offer if the two lovebirds disappeared from the area."

"Permanently?" asked Carl.

"Is there another way?"

"I suppose we have a deal then."

"Not quite. First, I require an act of good faith."

It was suddenly Carl who paused. "That seems fair. What is it?"

"Agent Harris. I'm afraid she won't survive her injuries."

The officer glanced over at the unconscious agent. "I see."

"Good. Call me on this number when the rest is done."

Abney put down the phone and took another sip of his over-priced cocktail. His watch showed ten minutes past noon. Forty-one hours remained on his promise. The morning's conquest faded, and a pall spread over his face.

Chapter Eighteen

The light filtering between the pine trees appeared flat and lifeless in the summer afternoon. Stubby shadows leaned away from the trunks like an afterthought of physics. Sherman peered deep into the forest. His eyes devoured the details. Tiny shifts in the wind. A fluttering butterfly or bird fleeing up from the ground. A dry crack in the under-growth. It was a puzzle unfolding, and his mind turned over each piece with great care.

"Everything okay?" asked Ruby. She had come out to the front porch of the cabin, having taken a break from rummaging through her stuff.

"So far," he replied without taking his eyes off their surroundings. "Did you find the USB?"

"Not yet."

"Keep digging."

Ruby turned and walked back to the Jeep. The remnants of her life lay strewn about on the deep brown dirt. Deteriorating cardboard boxes rested on piles of pine needles and most of her clothes moldered in black plastic garbage bags. Somewhere in the mess was a dark blue case. The kind a cheap optician used when selling eyeglasses. She knew it existed within the pile. Finding said item was proving difficult.

Near the bottom of the back seat, next to a roll of duct tape, it finally surfaced. Black stains had dulled the original blue, and most people would have thrown it away without a second thought. Ruby carefully opened the lid and peered inside. A brief rush of anticipation raised her heart rate. She felt it pounding in her ears. The small rectangular stick remained inside, right where she left it all those years before. Ruby let out a sigh of relief and pocketed the piece of plastic. Only then did she hear Sherman's low whistle.

A famous country music song twanged loudly in Carl's pocket. He answered the phone with a hurried expectation.

On the other end, his friend, Shaun, spoke in hushed tones. "We're here. I see the chief's car."

"Good. Be careful. I mean, double-wrapped careful. This guy is no slouch. Dude looked like he could have shot us both without a second thought."

Shaun understood the aftermath. He witnessed it on the road out of town. But seeing the sum does not unveil the equation that created it.

"Just keep your promise."

"Don't worry," replied Carl. "You won't have anything to worry about. You have my word. A perpetual get-out-of-jail card."

"I'll call shortly."

Carl put the phone back in his pocket and smiled a small, conceited smile. In the distance, he watched as the black Suburban burned, engulfed in flames. Bright orange and red. They leaped up twice the height of the vehicle and sparks shot up like a Roman Candle.

Cleaning up the mess took a few calls. Close-knit communities have inherent bonds. Every generation knew a complete spectrum of people, from cops and crooks to farmers and lawyers. They grew up together and it was not a stretch for Carl to find the friends needed for such an operation. It cost him. But not money. Favors. A problem for future Carl.

His first call went to an old buddy who owned a rusty tow truck. Steven, or Steve-O as they called him, did some honest day's work towing cars for AAA. At night, he stole cars from neighboring towns, but Carl never said a word. It wasn't his town, and friendships mattered.

It took some negotiating, a few carrots and the big stick that Carl's badge represented, but eventually, Steve-O agreed to help. Part of the agreement included extra help in the form of Steven's younger brother, Ralph. The guy was a bowling ball in more than just a shape. Nicknames such as 'Rowdy' and 'Wreck-It' followed in his wake and not without justification. The boy liked to party hard and did not much give a damn who he knocked over or out.

Steven and Ralph showed up fifteen minutes after Carl set up some flares on the road to make sure no one got too close a look at the crime scene. Shaun helped him move Talbot's body into the Suburban behind Tarney's.

Despite appearances and a checkered history of stupidity, Carl was astute and ambitious. He recognized several facts early on and they guided his actions. Foremost was that Sherman, or whatever Talbot called him, did not kill the Chief of Police. That much was obvious. The shell casing in Tarney's pocket and the one round missing from his Glock proved it. From the carnage in the SUV, he knew the man was more than just dangerous. He was brutal. Shaun gave a low whistle when they first looked inside, which summed up Carl's impression too. Even the most out-of-hand bar fight never ended that badly.

The battered but still breathing Agent Harris served as proof of his theory. Her wounds were vicious in a no-holds-barred sort of way. As Carl looked at her, a single word kept popping into his mind—survival. It explained the brutality. The unmitigated violence of the situation. Like a cornered bear.

It also meant he had leverage over Mr. Abney. The man wanted Audrey and Sherman dead. Carl felt working with him warranted the risk, like an educated guess at the poker table. He saw the cards on the table and bet big.

The problem with going all in was simple. He needed to dirty his hands. Carl didn't relish the task. No hidden sadistic streak ran through his heart. But he was a realist. All his chips lay on the table. There was no turning back.

Carl took Agent Tarney's service pistol from the holster and walked over to Harris. An argument for staging a suicide passed through his mind, but he quickly dropped the idea. No one would find the bodies. Not where he planned on disposing of them.

With nothing left to say or do, he mindlessly walked over and pulled the trigger. A single mechanical action. They tossed Harris in the back with Talbot. Then Steve-O and Ralph towed the Suburban three miles down the road to the same spot the FBI agents had unknowingly picked out earlier that morning.

Their instincts were right. The old quartzite mine was the ideal spot. Closed for years, the mine was a deep gash in the mountainside. The rock went down more than across, so the open pit was deeper than normal. After a few years, the company went bust and moved on to cheaper stone. The pit slowly filled with a sickly green water and the locals stayed away for fear of contamination. There were plenty of nooks and crannies to hide a body or three.

Carl had dreamed of something a little bigger. They lined the bodies up under a large slab of quartz that had been cut from the mountain but never sliced up into smaller pieces. It reminded him of Stonehenge, or at least pictures of the place he'd seen on some documentary while drinking away the night. Shaun only saw a big rock, but his imagination took a beating from his father when he was young. With the help of the tow truck, the men toppled the plinth on top of the two dead agents like an oversized mallet. He moved Talbot and the gun that killed him to a chest freezer at Shaun's house. A contingency of sorts.

As the plan unfolded so neatly, Carl decided it was time to move onto the next stage, which was the removal of Audrey and Sherman. With the boys already pumped up from the disposal activities, they didn't take much convincing to drive up the mountain towards the cabin.

Earlier that morning, while Carl retrieved the gun Sherman had dropped, he glimpsed the Jeep hiding. It meant nothing to him but going back felt like the move to make. It didn't take much to confirm his suspicion. With Talbot's vehicle missing, Carl checked the GPS program the department used. The little red dot blinked vibrantly. Almost the same spot from that morning.

Carl felt elated as he slid back into his police cruiser and drove to the station. He even stepped into Talbot's office and tried his chair on for size. The plan was airtight.

Chapter Nineteen

The three men reminded Ruby of those green plastic toy soldiers. The kind kids used to play with when they played with physical toys. She knew them by name. Regulars at the bar. Shaun, Steve-O, and Ralph. They walked in that order down the dirt drive towards the front door like a trio of dogs running after a cornered raccoon.

Each man carried a weapon. Practical guns—shotgun, hunting rifle, and a self-protection revolver, the kind hunters used when they faced boars or other wild animals. Ruby knew the types. She saw them all over town. Stacked neatly in the back windows of trucks. Lined up like sticks on the walls of homes. Hidden behind thick steel doors in safes. Having one was just a fact of life. No different from a flag on the porch or a microwave in the kitchen.

None of them noticed Sherman hiding in the shadows to their left. Having seen Talbot murdered hours before, he was in no mood for a conversation. The guns spelled out their intent and no words would change that.

From the trio's perspective, Sherman appeared from

nowhere. A phantom of the afternoon light. When the shooting started, it arrived without warning.

At the head of the line, Shaun carried a long hunk of steel and wood called a Remington 870. A classic shotgun. Reliable and a boon for hunters. Not so great for extended firefights as it only held five shells. Given its size, it also failed at swiveling quickly in reaction to a threat. But Sherman felt it was the most dangerous weapon of the lot, and its owner appeared to be the most capable shot.

The group of wavering pines concealing Sherman stood about thirty feet from the driveway with a scrubby line of bushes between them. The first three bullets hit roughly where Sherman aimed, which was center mass. Shaun staggered a step to the right and then collapsed in a heap on top of the shotgun.

The brothers stumbled over themselves, trying to get away from the sudden onset of violence. They knew of it but didn't understand it. Killing a deer or duck required a smidge of savagery. So did beating up a rival or some poor sap at the bar. Violence hid amongst all those actions, but they diluted it. They only stuck a toe in those cold, cruel waters. Sherman, however, was trying to keep his head above the rising tide.

Tripping over his panicked feet, Steve-O fell backwards and fired an unaimed shot up into the swaying pine needles overhead. The oversized revolver bounced harmlessly away and into a thick clump of sagebrush. The greyish-green foliage all but gobbled up the weapon. Sherman held his fire and snapped towards the final human shape.

What he saw looked almost spherical. Not perfectly round, for Ralph was more height than width, but close to it. The younger brother stuttered a step to the side in confusion from the quickly changing circumstances. The barrel of the hunting rifle in his hands swirled about like a child's doodle.

Inexperience aside, the kid was not cut out for such a life. Sherman knew that immediately. A look of confused terror said he wanted nothing more than to be sitting at home enjoying his mother's pork chops. The look was nothing new. Sherman had seen it dozens of times before in unprepared adolescent men sent off to die in distant lands. They all had some version of that expression. While geography may have varied the cuisine, the look remained the same.

In a moment of compassion, Sherman shot Ralph in his shoulder or the area of the sphere that looked most like a shoulder. The force spun Ralph around and he dropped the rifle in between guttural screams.

In reaction to seeing his brother shot, Steve-O glanced at Sherman and rolled onto his stomach to look for his missing revolver.

"You can try," said Sherman.

Hands went up towards the sky in reply.

"Frank?"

Ruby's voice was fraught with fear and tangled in her throat.

"All clear," answered Sherman out of sheer habit.

She poked her head out the door and looked stunned. Not at the carnage, but the participants. She stalked outside like a mother hen and shouted at the brothers.

"God dammit, boys," she raged. "What the hell are you doing here?"

Sherman glanced in her direction but kept the Glock pointed at the spherical kid. "You know them?"

"Yeah. They're regulars at *Bedlam*. These two idiots are brothers," she replied while pointing an accusatory finger.

"And him?"

Ruby glanced down with clinical detachment at the slumped figure with blood seeping into the dirt. She nodded in recognition.

"Yeah, him too."

Sherman turned his gaze on the brothers. "Anybody else out there?"

Steve-O shook his head slowly as if to emphasize the answer.

"If that's a lie, you die first. Understood?"

The nodding continued.

Ralph was rolling around on the ground, moaning between heavy breaths. Sherman grabbed the rifle from the ground and the revolver from the bush and placed them on the porch. He didn't bother with the shotgun or the body on top of it. Shaun was not getting back up. Not then. Never.

"Care to tell me why you're here?" he asked.

Ralph was leaning so far back on his one good short pudgy arm it looked like he might topple over at any moment. Despite all the name calling, he desperately wished to be a bowling ball rolling away from the surrounding mess. Sherman started the follow-up threat but didn't need to finish.

Shaun's phone started ringing. It wasn't a standard noise, but a god-awful Nickelback song popular when he was in high school. Sherman glanced down at the name on the screen. A bold white font read: CARL. It even had a picture of the officer lying prostrate on a couch with a rather cartoonish penis drawn on his forehead in Sharpie. It was an old photo from one of those disposable cameras. The sort of people gave away at birthday parties or school outings.

"Carl," he said aloud.

"The cop?" asked Ruby.

Steve-O nodded so meekly he might have been mistaken for a Russian serf from the nineteenth century. Everyone watched the call go to voicemail.

Sherman looked towards Ruby with a question dancing in his eyes. "What do you know about Carl?"

"He is no Einstein, but the guy looked a few moves further out than most. He keeps it hidden though, like being bright is a crime or maybe just uncool. You can see it shimmer in his eyes when one of those two say something dumb."

"An up-and-comer?"

"There is some ambition in there too."

"So is Carl making a play for Talbot's throne?" The question floated towards the brothers.

Ralph nodded his cantaloupe-shaped head while Steve-O shrugged. They wore a certain acceptance on their faces, like a seal caught in the jaws of an orca. As if their situation was inevitable and all those rotten turns in life stretched it until it broke. The tan stranger with the beard was an inevitability.

"And this Mr. Abney, is he the king maker?"

This time neither brother gave any reaction because they knew little. Planners they were not.

"These two aren't executive material," answered Ruby, taking their silence and history as evidence.

Sherman waited for the rest of the story because there was always more with such an intro.

"The clumsy one is Steve-O."

A youthful flashback filtered through Sherman's mind. "Like Jackass?"

"I guess," shrugged Ruby. "The obese GSW is Wreck-It."

The name held no more meaning for Sherman than an ancient Norwegian fable.

"Wreck-It Ralph," she continued.

Still nothing.

"He's a cartoon character," she began, but stopped. Explaining a Disney character to a man like Sherman was a waste of breath. "Never mind that. His name is Ralph, and the corpse is Shaun. And they all drink at the bar."

Ruby's voice climbed higher with the last sentence. The thought of regulars trying to kill her brought her anger to a squealing boil.

Sherman turned towards the brothers and gestured with the pistol in ominous circles. "That doesn't sound very civil. Murdering your bartender is poor form. Carl must have really sweetened the deal. What did he offer?"

The brothers looked at each other. They exchanged some information in that briefest of glances because Steve-O began talking in a soft but gravelly voice.

"Carl told us he'd run that two-bit hack, Jeffrey Sills, out of town."

None of it made sense to Sherman, so he turned to Ruby for translation.

"He's the local drug dealer."

"Carl said we could take over."

"Pills, weed, opium, what?" asked Sherman. The last narcotic brought out a particular ire as the War on Terror only increased opium production in Afghanistan. He saw it unfold as farmers converted to the cash crop.

"A bit of everything," squeaked Ralph. He was holding his shoulder like it might fall off.

"Is that fatal?" Sherman asked Ruby. He had a good guess but saw men die from less.

Ruby leaned over and looked at the wound. With so

much mass to pass through, the bullet never left. No clean through-and-through. The copper jacketed round was still in there somewhere.

"He might die from sepsis in a few days if not treated."

Sherman leaned over the wounded man. The pistol dangled in front of Ralph's eyes.

"Okay. Here is the deal, boys. The time has come to leave the nest. Head south over the mountain. Maybe find a fresh place to live in Wyoming. Or maybe just keep heading south until you feel safe. I don't give a damn either way. But if I see you again, anywhere or at any time, I'll come for you. Not right away, but soon thereafter. When you're asleep in your bed, all cozy and warm. Or maybe you'll be stuffing your face with some juicy burger, fries, and a shake. Life will be grand. And then it won't. Either way, I will make sure you know it was me who pulled the trigger."

The brothers exchanged another one of those looks that only siblings can understand. They nodded in unison.

"Good," replied Sherman. "Leave now and you might make it to the other side before dark."

Hesitantly, the men rose to their feet and started walking uphill. They glanced backwards with anxious expressions, like they expected a bullet at any second.

"One more thing," shouted Sherman, and the brothers froze as if waiting for the bullet. "What happened to that mess on the road out of town?"

"We buried the feds," Steve-O answered.

"And Talbot?"

"On ice at Shaun's place."

Sherman waved them on like brushing off dirt from his shirt. The contingency plan did not surprise him. A sound idea. Carl was no slouch. If something happened, the officer could always stage Talbot's death and blame it on Sherman.

Once they were out of earshot, Ruby said, "Frank, was that kindness?"

"I'm getting soft in my old age."

"I can't imagine what that looks like."

"Do you think they're dumb enough to come back?"

"Yeah."

"Shame."

Ruby shrugged her shoulders with indifference.

"Or not," quipped Sherman as he picked up Shaun's phone.

He held the dead man's thumb over the small button at the bottom of the device. It unlocked and went to a photo of a naked woman with little square icons covering portions of her body. The phone record was sparse, but the last incoming and outgoing calls were to Carl. He deemed the rest as unimportant. The texts held nothing of interest, although a prosecutor might have built a case or two.

"Anything?" asked Ruby.

"Just the calls from Carl."

"Nothing from Abney?" she asked.

"Too low on the totem pole, I suppose."

Something occurred to Ruby. A question so simple she'd forgotten to ask it earlier. "How did they find us?"

Sherman nodded towards Talbot's Ford SUV parked near the cabin.

"You knew they'd come?"

"Just sussing out the enemy."

Ruby flailed her arms about. "And you just forgot to mention that?"

"I didn't know who would show up."

"Frank!"

"Look. Someone gave us up. Now we know who. We also know he's not a complete idiot. Maybe not too bright for sending those three up here, but you're right, he's sharper than the average pencil. He checked the GPS."

"The GPS?"

Sherman motioned towards the police cruiser.

"Seriously?"

He nodded.

"Are the cops going to come next?"

"Depends on Carl. It seems to me there are two ways. One above board and one below. He'll either throw us to the wolves and blame us for Talbot's death or call Abney and bring in reinforcements."

"Reinforcements?"

"If they had FBI agents on the payroll..." Sherman didn't need to finish the sentence. Ruby could fill in the blanks with an alphabet soup of agencies.

"What does your gut say?"

"That I need to make a call."

It left Ruby staring at his back as Sherman stepped around the cabin and dialed a number seared into his memory. The man on the other end answered with a single word.

"Where?"

"Stalworth, Idaho."

"I'll be there in the morning."

"Keep it off the grid," reminded Sherman, even though his friend needed no such reminder.

"Ain't no other way."

Sherman slid the phone back into his pocket and returned to Ruby and her worried look. He glanced at his watch. The simple waterproof Casio model showed the time and little more. Twenty-past-one in the afternoon. Still lunchtime.

"We need to keep out of sight until tomorrow morning."

"What happens in the morning?"

"Help."

A sinking sensation pulled sharply at Ruby's stomach. Sherman had never asked for help. Not once in California. At least not before she ran.

"Do we need help?" she asked.

"I don't think Carl is playing above board."

Chapter Twenty

The phone in front of Carl remained silent. He kept glancing at the black rectangle, willing it to ring. Anything. A beep or ding or ring or song.

The call would never come. His friends were dead. If not outright, then dying on the mountainside. He could excuse one missed call, but not ten. After that, it went straight to voicemail. No ringtone. No computerized voice reciting Shaun's number. Nothing but silence. It taunted Carl with a blank screen and forced him to choose.

Calling Abney was admitting failure. Having stepped out and placed his neck under the butcher's cleaver, Carl could not back down. It went against his principles. Even the thought felt like shaving with forty-grit sandpaper.

The opposite call would also invite unwelcome scrutiny. Carl figured he could stage Talbot's death. Pull the chief out of the freezer and make it look like Ruby and the stranger did the killing. But if he started that rock rolling, there was no telling how many cows it would knock over. Invariably, questions would arise. Discrepancies he could not account for. Torres would figure out something was amiss. Her detective skills eclipsed his own —a fact that Carl begrudgingly admitted, but only to himself.

That left him with one option. Family. He picked up the phone, opened his contacts, and scrolled down to a name— Floyd Dooley. He did not relish the conversation for one simple reason. The Dooleys hated the Ortmans. A schism from three generations back.

The enmity traced back sixty-odd years before Carl was even born. Details were murky, but from what he gathered, the two families shared mutual kin. A great-grandfather in the dusty past. What could have been a great extended family turned to bloodletting. According to his father, the culprit was land. Somehow, the Ortmans gained possession of more than their fair share, and the Dooleys cried foul. When matters could not be settled in a civilized matter, the two did not take it to court. They loaded rifles and went to war.

Once the bleeding stopped, the Dooleys left town and moved over the county line. Their tentacles reached right down into the underbelly of the area. All sorts of shady dealings.

Things had thawed over the years and the cousins met on friendly terms, but the relationship hung by a frayed scrap of thread. Calling the family patriarch further raised Carl's blood pressure.

"Who is this?" demanded a rancid voice.

"Mr. Dooley, sir, this is Carl Ortman. Do you have a minute to talk?"

"If it ain't the great lawman himself. Did one of my boys get pulled over or something?"

"No, sir. Nothing like that."

"Then what in bleeding Christ's name are you calling me for?"

"Well, sir, I have a proposition for you."

"A proposition, eh? Did you go queer, boy?" Floyd sneered. "What could I possibly need from you?"

Carl had little to offer, so he gave old-man Dooley the same offer Steve-O and Ralph received.

"The pill business in Stalworth."

There was a pause as Floyd considered the offer.

"You ain't got the juice for such a promise. Talbot tolerates that scumbag Jeffrey Sills because he ain't got ambition. No way you gonna change his mind."

"What if Talbot was no longer Chief of Police?"

Another long pause followed.

"I'm listening," Floyd hissed.

"Sills will disappear. The oxy trade is all yours, provided you help me get rid of a problem. Well, two problems to be exact."

Faint traces of laughter came through the phone, and it made Carl's skin twitch.

"Alright, Officer. If what you say is true, which I ain't believing just yet, me and the boys could help you out of this situation."

"I have proof. Meet me in an hour at the old appliance repair shop on the east side of town. You know it?"

Floyd made a wet sucking sound through his front teeth. "I know it. You better be good for this."

"I am," replied Carl, then ended the call. He looked at the blank screen for another second before clearing his lungs of any residual air—as if exhaling would expel the conversation.

He slipped back into his police cruiser and headed towards Shaun's house.

James Abney's plate had more blood on it than a boxing ring. Lunch consisted of sirloin steak. It was almost raw, and blood clung to the flesh like condensation on a can of beer in summer. A side of potatoes swam in the red juices. He was in the middle of slicing off another chunk when his phone vibrated softly against the white linen tablecloth.

The sole character of text was a question mark sent by Terrance Knight. Abney stopped cutting and placed the knife down on his plate. He gingerly dabbed the corners of his mouth with the napkin and set that down too. Only then did he pick up the phone to respond. Thirty-six hours remained.

"The plan is unfolding," he typed back.

He waited for a reply. Some cross remark or vulgarity. Nothing arrived. The uncertainty made his lip curl into a sneer. He hated not knowing.

Abney scrolled for a second and called Carl Ortman.

"Mr. Abney," answered the officer.

"Do you have any updates on our mutual concerns?"

There passed the briefest of pauses before Carl answered, but Abney took a mental note.

"They found the car up in the mountains. I'm calling in some, uh… reinforcements to help."

"Is that necessary?"

"I don't want any mistakes."

The last word rose an octave higher, and Abney sensed a lie. His entire reputation rested on his abilities of perception. Seeing the weak point in people and then twisting it until they broke. Abney felt something shift in Carl's voice, but he said nothing.

"I'll call back tonight for the good news."

Carl swallowed. An audible gulp. "Of course."

Abney ended the call and picked up his knife. He sliced off another chunk of steak and slowly chewed the rare meat. An image of the man from the lake drifted through his mind. The way he carried himself was instantly recognizable. Abney knew the type. He warned the FBI agents, but they failed to accept the obvious fact. The man was a weapon.

People who said they didn't want to make mistakes were just trying to cover up one they already made. Abney guessed whoever the officer sent up the mountain was dead. Getting reinforcements was the first sensible thing to come out of Carl's mouth. He picked up the phone once more and dialed a number from memory.

"Sir," answered a familiar voice.

"Who do we have near Idaho?"

A few keys clicked in the background. "Bayless landed in Seattle this morning."

Abney knew the moniker, even if it was fake. Their paths had crossed twice before. The woman was a professional. Not like those FBI nitwits or the locals.

"Redirect her to me."

"Understood," said the voice before the call ended.

Reinforcements, thought Abney. *The first decent idea to come out of the damn mess.*

At half-past two in the afternoon, Carl Ortman stood in a narrow parking lot covered with dirt and weeds. The sky was a pale smokey blue. Behind him was a defunct appliance repair store that belonged to Shaun. Plywood covered the windows, but the attached house still stood. Years before the business boomed, back when Shaun's father was alive. Any mechanical knowledge or engineering ability died with him and so did the business. Some abilities skip a generation.

A metallic howling sound announced the Dooley clan's arrival. Carl heard it coming long before any vehicle arrived. He knew the car. A 2006 Monte Carlo SS. The old man loved it like a first-born son. Carl thought it a joke, but he sure as hell would not voice such a thought. Not then. Not when he needed their help.

The big red Chevy roared into the dirt parking lot and sat there growling. Carl stood still and waited for Floyd Dooley to make the first move. The engine revved as both men held their ground in some invisible pissing contest.

Carl broke first and walked towards the coupe. The driver's side window slid down a few inches and he peered inside at the patriarch behind the wheel. Floyd smiled back with yellowish teeth. His corrugated brow arched with the effort.

"Mr. Dooley," said Carl.

"Eugene."

Carl frowned at his birth name. Only family used it, and despite their shared DNA, he did not see the Dooleys in a familial light.

"What you're here for is inside."

Floyd looked at the old storefront and then glanced around the car at his two sons. The older one took up the entire front seat. Lee Dooley looked just like his old man, only bigger. As if genetics had added twenty-five percent to everything. His brother, Glenn, was the opposite. Thinner in all facets except that thin toothy grin, which they all flashed. Both were close to Carl's age.

The two brothers nodded. Floyd turned off the ignition

and thrust open the door. Carl jumped back to avoid being knocked to the ground. He gritted his teeth at the second insult.

All three Dooleys exited the vehicle, and their collective gaze made Carl look away uneasily. He felt like a prize pig at the state fair, waiting to be turned into sausages.

"We ain't got all day, boy!" demanded Floyd. "You invited us."

Carl took a breath and motioned towards the store. He was second-guessing the invitation. Dealing with Officer Torres started looking like the better option. He didn't think the Dooleys would turn him in, but after the last few days, he knew stranger things could happen.

They walked around the boarded-up shop and entered through the back door. The chest freezer was in an office. The Dooleys got a bit agitated standing in the dimly lit space. Both brothers paced about while Floyd looked hard at Carl like he had tricked them.

"Enough suspense. I ain't agreeing to nothing until I see what cards you're playing with."

Carl nodded towards the freezer.

Floyd scoffed while the brothers stepped back towards the door. "I ain't a fool. You can open it your damn self."

The old man had a point, Carl conceded. He stepped forward and swung open the thick plastic top. Floyd stuck his head over and peered down at the contents.

"God damn, boy. I didn't think you had it in you."

Carl shook his head. A tinge of remorse surged through his chest. "I didn't pull the trigger."

"It don't matter to me if you did," replied Floyd with a rumbling laugh. "We ain't going to say anything."

The three Dooleys formed a semi-circle around Carl,

backing him towards the wall. Instinct pushed him to reach for the holstered gun, but fear stayed his hand.

"Tell me about your problem," Floyd continued.

"Problems—plural."

Floyd flashed a smile full of stained teeth. "Go on."

"Audrey, the bartender at *Bedlam*, you know her?"

The old man glanced at the youngest brother, who nodded his narrow skull.

Carl continued, "She's causing some trouble and needs to leave town. Permanently."

Glenn whispered something to his father, but it looked like Floyd already understood the situation.

"Don't half-ass your story, Eugene. You don't stuff the Chief of Police in a freezer over some big-titted bitch."

Carl sniffed the stale air. "She has an accomplice."

"Who?"

"Talbot called him Mr. Sherman, but I think he was a captain in the navy or something."

"Why do you say that?"

"I heard him use the rank," answered Carl. He considered telling Floyd the guy could probably shoot the wings off a fly but kept that bit of information for later.

"And they need to leave town?"

"Permanently," Carl reiterated.

Floyd showed that thin smile again. He knew the drill. A deep hole somewhere far from town. The kind where no one looks at the bottom. He used a few over the years. It became family lore and the reason Carl called him.

"Fine, but we need to discuss remuneration. Your offer, it feels a few ounces under a pound."

Carl may have been a cop, but he was not in the business of equality. The demand rang out as a threat and nothing more. "My offer stands as is," he retorted as the two brothers slid a foot forward.

The patriarch raised an eye in surprise and the deep ruts on his forehead tilted to one side. He made another wet sucking sound through his teeth that sounded like runoff in a sewer. Then he chuckled. "Come on, boys, we're leaving."

The resonant stubbornness left Carl with no choice. He did not want to give an inch for fear of the mile to come, but didn't see another option.

"Wait. You can have the bitch."

The three men turned as shades of disgust flashed across their faces. Floyd spoke for the group.

"I don't need a stubborn mule."

"She's worth something," Carl suggested.

"Killing is one thing when it needs doing, but you got the rest all twisted up in that dirty Ortman head of yours. That ain't our price."

"What is your price?"

The brown teeth flashed again.

"Lee here needs a job."

Carl eyed his cousin, many times removed. "And?"

"A slice of whatever seizure racket you have going on."

Civil forfeiture was standard practice in many small towns. It helped cover budget shortfalls. The local cops would pull over some suspicious-looking individual and take their cash or car until the owner could prove its legal provenance.

"Talbot stopped that years ago," replied Carl.

"And you will restart the practice. With Lee in charge."

The knot of tension in Carl's stomach twisted tighter. He had little choice but to nod in agreement. "If I'm chief, I'll bring Glenn on board."

"And?"

184

"And restart the civil forfeiture program," he added with reluctance.

Floyd extended a hand etched with grease and dirt. A hand hardened by years of toil. Carl took it and winced as they shook over the premeditated murder of two people.

"Where do we find these problems?" asked Lee.

"They were up at the Talbot's hunting cabin."

Lee glanced over at his father, who looked lost in some memory of the past. It took him a second to place the location, but the corners of his eyes deepened with recognition. The son understood the look.

"See you soon," sneered Lee.

As the Dooleys walked away, Carl had some consolation. He knew at least one of them would not live to tell the story. He saw the stranger and his handiwork up close. No way would the Dooleys come out unscathed. Maybe Lee would catch a bullet and that part of the deal would die too.

Chapter Twenty-One

Gas slowly pooled under the Ford SUV as Sherman stood watching. It trickled from the puncture in the fuel line. Not wanting to burn the entire forest down, he had parked it in the middle of the dirt road. Shaun's body sat lifeless in the driver's seat. A message of sorts. If someone cared to look hard enough at the DNA.

The flare hissed in his hand for a moment and the trees glowed red despite the sun overhead. Ruby came out of the cabin as he tossed it under the SUV. Her face scrunched in at the center as fire enveloped the vehicle. Sherman stepped back, but the scene did not ruffle his morality. All of it was immoral, including the entire concept of war, but if he thought too long about that, he would not survive. It became just another passing thought like a reflection caught in the corner of your eye.

"Are you sure this is a good idea?" Ruby stood next to him, hands on her hips.

"No."

"Thanks for that convincing."

"It's an unconventional choice," he added.

"And that's good?"

"Until it isn't."

"Do you think she'll see it that way?"

"I'm guessing the murder of her nephew will do the talking."

It was an hour's drive from the Talbot cabin to Betsy's house. A circuitous route that went east and south before turning back west. The direct approach, from A to B, shaded under twenty miles. Sherman could do it in four hours but reckoned it would take them all night. Hiking downhill in the dark with minimal moonlight was not Ruby's strong suit. What came as second nature to Sherman was a novel experience for her.

"We should go."

Ruby watched the sun's long shadow disappear into the gray dusk. "Lead on."

Sherman smiled, nodded down the hill, and started at a gentle pace. In the distance, his ears picked up the faint hum of an engine. Maybe a neighbor. Maybe reinforcements. He did not plan on finding out.

Miles slowly disappeared behind them as they swerved between the pines, dancing in the silvery light. Ruby was quiet, lost in her own regrets and fears. Images of the Horace Filby haunted her consciousness. The look on his face when she pulled the trigger. The immense volume of the gunshot and how quiet it sounded when he fell on the carpet. Guilt gnawed at her moral certainty like an earwig on a lettuce leaf.

"Let me know if this is too personal, but I have a morbid question."

Sherman looked over with a smirk she could not see in the dark. "Okay."

She tried to get the question out. "When did you first...?"

"When did I first kill somebody?"

"It sounds terrible when you say it like that."

"It's a long story."

"Life is a long story," she countered.

"We hope."

Ruby took a deep breath and Sherman continued.

"I was on leave in Jerusalem. Iraq part two was about to kick off and command had seen fit to give us a break from crawling through caves chasing the Taliban in Afghanistan. I was still green. Spring leaf, recent growth, green. My team had partied hard in the Old City. To this day, I'm not sure where. During the debauchery, I took a drunken walk. Not just merrily pissing on some church drunk. No, I was walking with one hand on the ground, seeing everything sideways drunk. All the cars I passed were stretch limo versions of themselves. Camry limo. Accord limo. Each car was a blurry streak two or three times the actual length. With stupid drunk mode in full swing, I went down some random darkened alley. These three guys jumped out from the shadows or wherever they were hiding. Shit, they could have been just standing there, I was too blitzed to notice. One guy comes over towards me and I just start puking... throwing up everywhere. Well, the guys think this is hilarious and are laughing at some poor American sod who can't hold his liquor."

Ruby laughed at the thought of Sherman too drunk to walk, but motioned for him to continue.

"The guy keeps walking up to me, laughing the entire time, and just kicks me over. Shoe right to the chest. So, I'm on my back, still retching up all the beer I've had, my cheek rubbing up against some cold cobblestone. His buddies didn't feel like missing out, so they walked over, but, jerks that they were, practiced some knife play on me. I was freaking out."

"I bet," she said.

"When they first jumped out, I was like fuck it. Too drunk to know I was in deep shit. Then I was ten pints lighter, and the adrenaline was in full force. It was fight, flight, or fuck, and the latter two were pretty much impossible with my level of inebriation."

"Were you armed?"

"Yeah, I had my service pistol. A Beretta tucked into my waistband like some wannabe gangster. I reached around my back, still lying on the street covered in vomit, and grabbed the handle. Have you ever used one?"

"A Beretta? No."

"Well, the safety is this little lever on the right thumb side of the gun. It was loaded, full magazine plus one in the chamber. I could feel the metal click. Even now, I remember that sound—the feel of the switch moving into place."

"And?"

Sherman looked back at her silhouette.

"I killed three men that night. Put two rounds center mass on each of them. Then I got up and left another round in their cerebellum to be sure. It felt mechanical... like I had done it a thousand times. Afterwards, I puked some more and more and more. The dry heaves lasted until morning."

Ruby stood still in the pale glow and cooling night air. The story stabbed deep, but she didn't know how it made her feel. In some sense, they were both justified. Fighting for their lives. But she also saw the other side of the coin, where they were to blame.

"There is no wrong way to feel about what you did," added Sherman.

Ruby wanted to believe him and find comfort in the knowledge but could not find the words to agree.

Only the soft glow of embers remained when the Dooleys found the SUV. They had seen evidence of the fire a mile east. Thick black smoke, acrid with chemicals, stole upward into the fading light. An omen of malcontent. They took their time arriving at the cabin.

"Is that what I think it is?" asked Glenn, peering into the twisted and charred remains of automotive engineering.

"It ain't much," replied Lee.

"I think I see teeth," Glenn added.

Floyd poked about with the barrel of his rifle. A lone tooth fell through what remained of the floor and onto the blackened earth below. "Boys, we have a conundrum here. If Talbot is on ice, who the hell is this?"

"Mr. Sherman?" Lee wondered out loud. He may have been the older of the brothers, but it did not make him the wisest.

"You think we were Carl's first call?" asked Glenn. "Someone else tried first and failed."

"Your brother is right. We ain't the first to try our hand."

"Shaun?" asked Lee. "I didn't see him at the house."

"Stands to reason," replied his father with a sigh.

"They must have run," Glenn conjectured.

"It would be the smart move," agreed Lee.

Floyd kept looking at the wreck as if his eyes would

eventually find meaning. "It don't matter if they ran or not. We agreed to remove them from town."

"Permanently," added Lee.

"Don't you see, boy. If they skipped town, we won. If they show up, we'll bury them. Waiting for them to show up is all we have to do."

Glenn understood the basics of the idea but not the details. "Where?"

"Where you always go. The damn bars. You can start at *Bedlam*. Lee will go to that place by the river."

"And you?"

"I'll try that uppity hotel in town. A bourbon will do me good."

Betsy heard a knock on the door. Soft and faint in the fading hours of the night. The old alarm clock on her nightstand read 3:45 AM. There were no guests. All the keys hung on the wall by the front desk. She slid on a robe and padded down the stairs toward the front door. No one was there.

Another knock came, slightly louder than the first. Betsy turned towards the noise. It came from the back door. Her eyes narrowed with suspicion. No one used the back door. All guests came and went through the front. Friends came in that way too. Then she remembered the last person to be outside, and she raced to open the door.

"Frank," she squealed. "What are you doing here?"

Sherman and Ruby stood off to the side, hiding from the interior light. Betsy could see the exhaustion etched on their faces.

"We could use a room," Sherman replied.

"Of course. Come on in."

Despite their rather open relationship, Sherman hesitated to enter. He was carrying two rifles. One AR-15 from Talbot's SUV and the hunting rifle Ralph left behind. He took the precaution of wrapping them up in his jacket, but even that bit of camouflage did little to conceal the weapons.

"Betsy, I'm afraid this is not a social call."

The woman glanced down at the rifle stocks protruding from the dark green jacket and understood something terrible had occurred.

"We have some awful news," added Ruby.

Betsy shut the door and the three of them stood motionless in the kitchen for several seconds. No one wanted to speak first, but Ruby finally summoned the courage.

"Your nephew is dead."

Chapter Twenty-Two

The red-eye flight from Kentucky to Idaho Falls landed thirty minutes late for reasons unknown. It departed on time. It landed behind schedule. No explanation was offered or requested. Sergeant Raylan Gournsey made it off the plane by 7:00 AM. The emergency exit row cost him a few minutes, but he needed it. His massive six-foot-five frame required extra room, but the price for a few inches more legroom was a step too far. Sleep still tugged at the corner of his mind. He grabbed the nearest cup of coffee in sight from a brightly colored kiosk between his gate and the exit. It cost twice as much as any other place of similar quality and tasted burned, but he did not care. He promised to be there in the morning and nothing would change that.

With coffee in hand, he sauntered down to the lone baggage claim carousel. The kind that looped through the building. One half exposed to the outside air and within a stone's throw of the plane. The other end snaking comfortably inside. His bag was already circling. An old army green canvas duffel. Not shiny. No wheels. *Efficient ground crew,* he thought.

From the terminal, he looked for long-term parking. Fewer people came and went from those types of lots. Often, they were far away and out of view. A sign showed the path and Gournsey walked the two hundred yards. The regional airport was too small for a shuttle bus. Maybe a golf cart, but nothing bigger. Fifty vehicles sat waiting for their owners to return. Hulks of metal sparkling in the summer sun.

Gournsey walked down the rows and checked them carefully with the eye of a butcher at the county fair. He wanted a truck because it was Idaho and most people in Idaho drove trucks, or so it seemed to him. He wanted an older model for security reasons. Manufacture dates further in the past contained less electronic parts and less chance of fancy alarms that needed time to bypass. Early 2000s was ideal. Earlier still was better if it ran well. Nothing fancy or shiny. Statistically, white, black, and silver dominated the color palette in terms of sales. Far better than red or blue, which tend to remain in the memory. Memories that populate police reports and eyewitness accounts.

A grayish Ford F-150 caught his gaze. The paint carried deep scratches, and it had a well-worn appearance that veered towards ragged. A few seconds was all it took to get the door open and start hot-wiring the ignition. The truck ran well enough and Gournsey pulled out two tools from his checked bag and got to work. Within minutes, he unscrewed the license plates from the truck and swapped them out with plates from a newer model nearby. The entire affair took under four minutes. The ticket stub was on the dashboard and he paid thirty dollars to get out, but it was cheaper than a rental. And no one was the wiser.

After a brief stop at some fast-food joint for a breakfast sandwich and more coffee, he merged onto the interstate heading southwest. His phone was off with the battery removed and he smiled at the open road. The way people used to travel. Free of distractions and navigation and the constant harangue of the outside world. It took an hour to see his destination listed on a mileage sign. Fifty-seven miles to Stalworth, Idaho. He'd be there by 9:30 AM.

Not bad for two hours' notice and a last-second flight that was thirty minutes late, he thought.

The smell of dark roasted coffee wafted throughout the room as Sherman sipped the scalding brew. Ruby sat like a wet leaf on a kitchen chair with a mug in hand. The few hours of sleep had done little to replenish her energy levels. Caffeine was the only option.

They heard the creak of stairs, and then Betsy entered. She looked exhausted and haunted. Hours earlier, she learned of her nephew's death. No tears flowed but Sherman could see a part of the woman's soul broke. She sat down at the table and gave a weak smile.

"Sorry for not having breakfast ready," Betsy apologized. She couldn't drop the pretense of hospitality and sit with her grief. The wound was too raw.

Ruby shot her a look that vibrated with both understanding and anger.

Betsy shrugged off the glance and offered, "There are some scones in the fridge."

Sherman stood and fetched the plate, placing it gingerly in the center of the table next to the coffeepot.

"I want to call his wife," Betsy pleaded.

"I know," replied Sherman with a bite of scone in his mouth.

"When can I?"

"I can't say. Either they figure it out and you can call, or they don't and you have to wait a few days."

"Figure what out?"

"That he's dead," answered Sherman. He had filled in only the thinnest of details. The hour was too late or too early for anything more.

Betsy rubbed the back of her neck and looked blankly at the tablecloth. She wanted to do or say something. Anything to fight back against the pain. She loved Aaron like a son. The one she never had. As a child, he used to stop by in the summer in the afternoon heat, when he was supposed to be doing chores, and eat vanilla ice cream. Betsy never told Bill or his brother—Aaron's father. It was their little secret.

"Can't we tell Carl what is going on?" she asked. "Maybe he will understand."

Not even Sherman's poker face could hide his animosity. It slid out from narrowed eyes and furrowed deeply into his brow.

"What now?" asked Betsy.

"Carl is neck-deep in this mess."

Betsy's jaw hardened. "What, pray tell, does that mean?"

"He's working with the fancy suit. Making a play for power."

"I brought him a goddamn burrito," she hissed at her own misplaced hospitality.

"I want to be clear, Betsy. You are taking an enormous risk in having us here."

"He's serious," agreed Ruby.

A thin, mischievous smile crept across Betsy's face. One

that Sherman recognized from their adventure to the casino. "Oh, sometimes you need to live a little. Besides, I want to give that little twit, Carl, a piece of my mind."

Neither of them challenged her resolve.

A sudden knock at the door made Ruby jump a few inches off her chair. She was not expecting a visitor. Sherman glanced up, took a breath, and moved out of sight. He wasn't worried. Trouble rarely knocked. It appeared through a cloud of splinters as the door burst open. Besides, Gournsey agreed to a morning arrival.

Betsy steadied herself and answered the door with a sweet smile. "Hello there," she said, and then paused for a beat longer than normal. "What can I do for you, Carl?" The last word caught in her throat.

Ruby froze. Her eyes wider than silver dollars. Sherman slid out the Glock from under his shirt. It was not the voice he expected to hear. He would happily shoot the officer on the spot and sort the rest out later.

"Hey there, Betsy," replied Carl. "This is a bit of an odd question, but have you seen Chief Talbot since yesterday morning?"

Unadulterated rage simmered in Betsy's eye sockets, but she focused on keeping her facial muscles calm. "Oh, can't say that I have. Why do you ask?"

"Well, I'm sure there is nothing to worry about, but we haven't heard from him in twenty-four hours. Not since he took off with that Mr. Sherman. The one who was staying here."

"The one you were tailing?" she retorted.

Carl nodded sheepishly, "Yeah, that one. The depart-ment is concerned something is, uh… amiss."

Betsy held her tongue for a second, considering her desire to let the man have it. Instead, she replied, "I'll let you know if I hear from either of them."

"Thanks, Betsy. That would be a grand help."

They smiled politely and Betsy closed the door. She took a deep breath and let out an exhale capable of blowing out a hundred birthday candles.

On the other side, Carl lingered for a moment. People assumed his dull looks equated to limited intelligence. A familiar assumption—one that he played upon for his own benefit. Standing out in a crowd came with risks, just like driving a shiny red car. He preferred flying under the radar in something benign and unthreatening.

In that briefest of exchanges, something inside piqued his interest. The Bed and Breakfast had three rooms. He knew that much for certain, yet there were only two keys on the wall. He turned and looked at the quiet, leafy street. No out-of-state license plates caught his eye. Nothing that might be a rental car. He did not see much of anything. The stan-dard assortment of local vehicles. A few sedans and a few trucks. Nothing more.

Having spent most of the night on the mountain, exhaustion crept into his thoughts, along with a strong desire for a cup of coffee. After the Dooleys left the Talbot cabin, he arrived. Spotting the SUV took no time. A solitary column of smoke rising in the woods gave the game away. Figuring out who was sitting in the driver's seat didn't take much deduction either. Shaun had not answered his phone for hours. Murder was a forgone conclusion, given every-thing he knew about the strange Mr. Sherman. While that list was short, it gave him pause. The two dead guys on the road north to the casino rushed into his memory like a flash flood. Their lifeless bodies angled and contorted. And the blood splattered everywhere. Enough to fill a gallon pail or paint a wall. Those images were bad enough, but what really made him sweat under his polyester uniform was the grouping. The shots themselves. They struck the windshield, one on top of the other. Orderly and precise. Not the work of an amateur. A professional. Someone who had done such things before. Someone capable of doing such things again.

He wondered what to do next. A simple question that was the only question. Coming to an answer was not easy. Carl pondered on the problem for hours as the stars wandered across the night sky. A beautifully empty black void dotted with faintly shimmering light. He gamed out all the possibilities. The pitfalls and potential ways of getting caught. Dozens of scenarios. He honed them down. Whit-tling away until there was only one.

Showing up on Betsy's doorstep was the first act of a slow play. He needed to express and document concern. Only raising the alarm if needed. Otherwise, no one would believe him when he pointed a finger at someone and hung the blame for Talbot's murder around their neck.

Chapter Twenty-Three

Raylan Gournsey sat slumped in the front seat. An impressive feat for someone of his size. He watched the local cop come and go from the Bed and Breakfast. He waited some more in an abundance of caution. Then he got out and knocked on the door. Sherman hadn't given him anything but a city, yet it only took one look at a map to guess the place. The motels were too far out and the hotel too fancy.

A second visitor within twenty minutes startled Betsy. It took all her concentration to smile when she answered the door. Her mouth dropped open when she saw the man standing on the other side. A six-foot-five mountain with hands big enough to pulp a cantaloupe. Not to be caught flat-footed again, Sherman pointed the Glock at the door frame.

"Can I help you?" Betsy squeaked.

"Howdy, ma'am, I'm hoping you have a vacancy."

The voice was wonderfully polite. It caught Betsy by surprise. "Oh, well, we don't have room," she began.

"It's okay, Betsy, he's with me," said Sherman.

The diminutive woman gestured, and Gournsey stepped inside. The two men smiled and hugged it out to the women's surprise. They shared a deep, unspoken bond that glowed with strength.

"Thanks for coming," Sherman said.

"Had your doubts?"

"Not for a second."

"Are you going to introduce me to these two lovely ladies?"

Sherman turned and saw both women gazing at the stranger in their midst.

"Ruby and Betsy, I'd like to introduce you to Sergeant Raylan Gournsey. The finest thing born in Kentucky since bourbon."

Gournsey eyed up Ruby carefully. A few stories passed Sherman's lips since California and her name drifted by after a few beers. Nothing more than a passing description and few wistful words, but he suddenly knew the why of it all. The captain had a soft spot for doing the right thing, and God help anyone standing in the way.

"It's a pleasure to make your acquaintance."

Betsy, having suddenly remembered her occupation, retrieved one of the two keys hanging on the wall and handed it over. "Please, let me know if you need anything. I'm sure you two have some catching up to do."

"You are sweeter than a honeybee," Gournsey cooed. The woman reminded him of his own grandmother.

Betsy blushed a little. "Thanks."

Sherman motioned up the stairs. Ruby followed, and the three of them settled into Sherman's room. The two men sat close and faced each other, while Ruby hung on the outskirts, unsure of the stranger or what he represented.

One thing she knew—the men were closer than brothers and capable of unspeakable violence.

"Alright, Cap. Care to fill me in?"

Sherman nodded towards Ruby. "She is in trouble with some nasty folks. I need your help to sort it out."

A wide smile crossed Gournsey's face, knowing he called it correctly. "Start from the beginning."

A terse recitation followed, containing everything Sherman knew, while Ruby interjected with her own colorful personal history. It began with Mason Knight and the running with a detour to their interaction in California. Sherman held nothing back. All the details lay on the table. The whole sordid affair. The body count from Horace Filby to Shaun and everyone in between.

"Damn, woman. You've had the house dropped on you."

Ruby looked at the ground and nodded. She didn't need the sympathy, but it felt good for a passing moment.

"What now?" he asked.

"Would you chase a woman across the whole wide land for scum like Mason Knight?"

"Kin is kin. We've killed for less. But it strikes me as odd."

"What part?"

Gournsey took a breath and began, "Terrance Knight never cared a minute for anyone but himself. I met the man once at some parade event. All pomp and circumstance. Narcissus had less self-conceit. I just don't see him caring that much, even about his own blood."

"You're speaking my truth, which brings me to what Ruby took from the safe of the duly departed, Mason Knight."

Gournsey grinned. "I'm all ears."

Ruby produced the USB drive and placed it on the small table.

"Have you looked at it?"

"Gibberish," replied Ruby.

Gournsey glanced at Sherman. "Encrypted?"

"That's my guess."

"Area 51? Who killed Jimmy Hoffa?"

"I'd settle for leverage," Sherman answered.

"Let's see what's on that spoonful of silicone."

"We need a clean laptop. I don't want to involve Betsy, and she bought her desktop when the first Bush was president."

"What are you two going to do while I'm out shopping?"

"Sharpen the knives," said Sherman with a smile.

The town of Stalworth had one big box store. A Walmart on the outskirts of town, one exit east on the freeway. It sat next to all the other chains one would expect to see in rural parts of the country. Gournsey found it without trouble. He could have sniffed it out *sans* the internet. Places like that had an order about them. Big things went on the edge of town, next to the major arteries crisscrossing the country. There might have been a store in town, but the blandness and ubiquity of Walmart ensured anonymity. Everyone and no one went there.

He parked the truck between two similar vehicles midway down the massive asphalt field. The late morning sun shimmered across a cloudless sky. Shopping carts piled high with essentials traversed across the blacktop. Gournsey smiled at the normality of life and entered through the extra-wide front doors.

The bowels of the store lay in the electronics section. Past the food and clothing and 'As Seen on TV' section of crap. Past eight-foot-tall walls of cereal and canned goods of all sorts. The sheer number of things always amazed Gournsey. He grew up poor. Multi-generational poverty, stretching back to the Civil War. That much of anything besides coal made him uneasy.

An employee named Sam sidled up as he was looking over the laptop selection. The name tag had a thick, all-caps font. Big block letters seared like a brand into the thin metal rectangle.

"Can I help you, mister?"

Gournsey eyed up a thin, pimply face. "No."

"Are you just looking? Or are you serious?" replied Sam. He looked up at the massive frame and had no doubts that the man could rip the metal cord attached to the demo computer right out of the wall.

"Serious enough."

"Consider this Dell. It has a 2.4 GHz Quad Core processor and..."

Gournsey cut him off with a glance. "I'll take the cheap one."

"Of course. Anything else? A mouse and keyboard? Would you be interested in the, uh... warranty?"

"Does it prevent me from coming in here again?"

"Not exactly."

"Then no," growled the sergeant.

After Sam scanned the item, Gournsey handed over the debit card linked to an account with no name.

"This isn't valid unless you sign the back," Sam squeaked.

Gournsey gave the kid a look that tore through his soul like a hungry Pitbull with a porterhouse.

"I guess we can make an exception."

"Oh, we will," replied Gournsey and ripped the bag out of the cashier's hands.

Having failed to recover from the night before, Betsy moved from coffee to coffee with whiskey. Just a splash of a mid-shelf variety. The kind people buy only when it's on sale. Sherman caught up with her in the kitchen. A weak smile whisked up from what remained of her energy.

"You look like a brewing question."

"I have one. I'm afraid it's personal."

"Oh, are we at that stage?"

"I'm afraid so."

"Go ahead," she replied after taking another sip for some courage.

"Do you own a gun?"

"This is Idaho," she replied as if that explained everything. A self-evident answer.

"I meant something a little more tactical. Something your husband might have used."

"What are you implying?" Her voice rose with the question in what almost sounded like remorse.

"Call it a hunch, but I think Bill had an affinity."

Betsy said nothing but her brow slanted down in the middle.

"You said he came back looking like me," Sherman continued. "I'd wager Bill and I were more similar than either of us would like to admit."

The creases on her forehead deepened. They were thick

with indecision. When her face slackened, she spoke as if the choice to share was natural.

"When Bill came back from the war, from Vietnam, things were different. I guess I knew he'd change some, but not like that. Part of him stayed back there in those rice paddies and elephant grass, but something else came home too. A thirst for the darker waters of his soul. Uncle Sam saw it too. How could they not? They appealed to his pride and asked him to help now and again. Use that skill set paid with blood. We lied, of course, and told everyone he sold insurance. A traveling salesman. Can you imagine that? Nonsense, but perhaps better than the truth."

"Which was?" asked Sherman. Although, he already guessed at her answer.

"Sometimes he trained men like you. The chosen few. Gnarled and hardened, inside and out. Other times, he pulled the trigger himself. Some skills don't dull with time. The details were not mine to know, but a wife sees past the spoken word and into the shadows in between."

Sherman listened and nodded with understanding. He knew of such consultants. Ex-soldiers continuing their career path beyond retirement or their expiration date.

"I'm not here to judge," he added.

"Oh, I know. As you get older, things have a way of catching up with you. Those you could justify in the good times creep back into your consciousness like a slow stream of ants. It starts with a few and then, suddenly, the whole damn kitchen is filled with them."

The sensation was familiar to Sherman. He'd felt it a few years back. A few years beyond when most soldiers leave the service. A few years past his prime.

"You're not alone in that either," he replied.

"Certainly not," added Ruby. Her own actions hung like

a stifling blanket over her face. She had lived with regret for years. It burrowed into her soul and stayed.

Betsy sniffed her coffee. "There is a gun safe in the attic. It's under an old painter's tarp. The code is my birthday. Four. Twelve. Fifty-Six. All of Bill's old stuff is up there. I don't pretend to know what it's for, I haven't touched it since he passed. Didn't know what people might think if they saw it."

Sherman stood to leave but put a hand on her shoulder. "It doesn't make him any worse than the rest of us."

She bobbed her head around. Not up and down, nor side to side. "It reminds me of an old D. H. Lawrence quote. You know him?"

"I know of him, but don't ask me to name any books."

"I taught English literature in another life. You're no different from any high school student.

Sherman smiled, unsure if he'd been insulted or accurately described.

"Anyway," Betsy continued. "He once wrote: 'The essential American soul is hard, isolate, stoic, and a killer. It has never yet melted.' I used to think he didn't understand us. Maybe I'm wrong."

The assessment felt as accurate as any, Sherman thought. His father was a killer. All his friends were killers. And most certain of all, he was a killer. Cloaking it in uniform didn't change the facts.

"I can't say he is wrong," replied Sherman. "I've known nothing less. But, I've also seen some kindness in my years. Maybe, not to split hairs, we are somewhere in between. Some ice, some melt. A river slowly thawing in the spring sun."

Betsy wanted to give some reply, but the door opened and Gournsey bounded in from his shopping trip. Whatever poetic reply she harbored remained where it began.

"Did you find something?" asked Sherman.

"Send me to the markets of Marrakech before marching me into Walmart."

"That bad?"

"We have too many choices."

"Did you make one?"

"After some deliberation, yes, I found a laptop."

"You could have used my computer," Betsy interjected.

"It's better this way," Sherman replied.

"Why?" she wondered. "Are you hacking into the Pentagon?"

The two men exchanged a glance that held nothing back and confirmed her worst suspicions.

"Oh, perhaps it *is* for the best."

Sherman remained silent.

"I'll leave you to it. Do I need to write the code?"

"No, thanks. I remember it."

Betsy nodded and took one more look at the trio. Then she took her coffee and the bottle of whiskey into the backyard.

"Code?" asked Gournsey, a little perplexed.

"For the gun safe," answered Sherman. "Turns out her husband ran in similar circles."

"Small world."

"Too small."

"What's first?" asked Gournsey.

"Let's get this ball rolling. I imagine the Senator did not skimp on his encryption."

Chapter Twenty-Four

Senator Terrance Knight adjusted his suit jacket with a casual flick of the wrist and glanced at the watch underneath. The Rolex glowed like pirate's gold in the soft indoor light. A colleague gesticulated wildly behind the podium on the Senate floor, but Terrance's thoughts flowed elsewhere. Nineteen hours remained in Abney's promise. Out of a generous forty-eight-hour total. The senator leaned back in his chair and ran through his usual decision-making process. Honed over the years, it was foolproof and entirely one-sided.

He started with the risk, which was catastrophic in scope. Next came the solution. Nothing had changed in that department. The girl needed to disappear, along with the USB drive. Only the means remained. Up to that point, Terrance's trust lay in Abney. A boyhood friend of his son and one of the most capable fixers near the capitol. Under less forgiving circumstances, he would have allowed the full time to elapse. If the risk was lower. If his entire career and legacy were not at stake.

One iron in the fire wouldn't do. Even with the two FBI agents, Abney had failed. Maybe that was his mistake. One woman, one bullet. It seemed easy enough. The lack of results said otherwise. The trust he once placed in Abney eroded over twenty-nine hours without results. It left Terrance with one choice. He quietly left the Senate chamber and hastened back to his office. A prepaid phone sat in his desk drawer. He inserted a fresh SIM card, dialed a number from memory, and waited for the familiar voice to answer.

"How may I direct your call?"

"It's me."

"Sir, good morning. What can I do for you?"

"Who do we have near Idaho?"

The voice paused for a moment and the faint clacking of keys sounded in the background. "Bayless is arriving shortly."

An operator of her caliber in play sent a chill down the senator's neck. "Who requested her?"

"Abney."

Things were worse than appeared. He should have called earlier.

"I need someone else. Someone I can trust. And I need them now."

"Cummings is in California. Straeger is in Montana. And Granger is still in Florida."

Terrance sorted through the list, turning over each name in his mind like a playing card. Granger and Cummings were his top choices. Not necessarily because of skills, but he trusted them. They were company men. They toed the line and did the deeds. Colonel Straeger was the better hunter. He'd done a few jobs after retirement, all successful, and they had crossed paths in uniform over the years. Terrance remembered Straeger standing ramrod straight like his spine grew from steel. The epitome of a jarhead. Square jaw, hard hands, and harder eyes. A soldier's soldier.

"Straeger is closest. Make the arrangements."

"Yes, sir."

"Tell him this comes from the top."

"Yes, sir."

After the call ended, Terrance removed the SIM card and broke it in half. He poured himself a finger of scotch and sat down in an overstuffed leather chair to consider the unfolding events. Given this risk and Abney's recent incompetence, he felt justified in adding a player to the field. Overreacting came naturally.

The interstate did not spear dead straight across the valley. It meandered next to the river like a fly above a plate of meat. Karen Bayless did not appreciate the deviation. She considered it a waste of time and material. Point to point should involve the shortest line. Cut out the fat, the sightseeing, the points-of-interest and all those damn brown historical markers. She wanted none of it. A-to-B. That was it. Anything else was frivolous.

Her spartan mentality continued with her choice of rental car. Economy—always economy. Never Full-Size or even Intermediate. A Ford Fiesta or similar, which was the model she drove into Stalworth. Silver with Washington State plates. An obvious tourist. The moniker was not an impediment. She was not trying to blend into the local population. Not that she ever had a problem blending.

At five-feet and four-inches tall, Bayless was exactly

average. Sixty years ago, her one-hundred and thirty pounds would also have been average, but things had changed in the American diet. Either way, she looked unremarkable. Short brown hair framed a face that was neither attractive nor unattractive. Her dark green eyes did not sparkle with energy. They were not liquid or deep or particularly memorable. People often overlooked her in crowds or mistook her for a waitress at restaurants. She became part of the backdrop to any moment, cloaked in her own dullness. A mid-thirties extra on the set of a family sitcom.

None of that bothered Bayless in the least. Banality was her greatest asset. She dressed conservatively and wore no makeup or jewelry. No cleavage or tight dresses, no tattoos or piercings. Nothing but short brown hair and insipid green eyes. Run-of-the-mill, save for her occupation. At that, she was a rare commodity. A self-trained killer for hire on the payroll of the biggest organizations.

Daughter to an Italian loan shark from Miami, she grew up shaking down two-bit crooks and retirees in floral shirts who made a poor bet or two. Business was good and it stayed in the family. Even the hardened criminals could see her viciousness had no end. During high school, she graduated to witness intimidation and theft. The latter started petty but blossomed into larceny and grand theft auto. Nothing for show or bling. It was always a family matter.

Bayless turned pro at nineteen—an awfully young age for someone not born in Mexico or El Salvador. It began with two Cuban brothers muscling in on her father's slice of the pie. They were hungry and ambitious young men who wanted more of the American dream, or whatever they saw in Scarface. Not long from the island itself, the brothers were cruel and inventive. They introduced methods of torture hitherto unseen except for the dungeons of Havana.

Despite their paranoia, the brothers loved Mafia movies. Scorsese was their favorite director, so anything that he directed, they watched. Bayless bought a ticket to a Goodfellas re-release. She sat down right behind the two men. Both turned to look at her, but their gaze lasted less than a blink and registered nothing of alarm. When the first gunfight erupted on screen, she fired a .22-long pistol point-blank into the back of their heads. It took a second for the crowd to understand what happened, and by then, Bayless was long gone. In the aftermath, even the person sitting next to her could describe nothing but a young white woman with brown hair and a gun.

The government took notice several years later, but not in the usual fashion. Bodies kept piling up, but they were all criminals. The work was clean and the collateral damage remained small. Then came something of an international incident. The loan shark father found himself in business with some Iranians moving opium to fund Hezbollah and other proxy groups. In the post-9/11 world, the US Government only cared about drugs where there was terrorism. It was a small slice of a large Venn diagram. The Iranians fit nicely in the middle.

After a few months, an old adage held true. There was no honor among thieves. The Iranians shorted the old man. Sanctions were biting the economy, and Tehran shifted its focus elsewhere. Bayless decided that one slight was one too many. She pushed a stroller packed with explosives next to their car and walked away. The explosion made the nightly news. Iran blamed the Israelis, who blamed the CIA. Insults flew and a few rockets hit Tel Aviv. Things quieted down over time, as things always seem to do, but the agency did not forget. It took them time, but they tracked Bayless down. When they caught up with her, the agents came, not with handcuffs, but a job offer.

Bayless did not consider the preceding nine years as she pulled into Mather Hotel. The job and her life had intertwined so completely that one did not exist without the other. Past recollections of another way, a different path, were nothing but vague echoes of memory. Frayed thoughts of the past that skittered like mice in the dark.

She parked the Ford in the lot's corner next to a group of tattered cars she assumed to be employees. Maybe the manager got a close parking spot, but the maids would have to walk the furthest. The woman at the front desk glanced up and almost scolded Bayless for being late before seeing the rolling suitcase trailing behind. She forced a smile.

"How can I help, ma'am?"

Bayless smiled at the noun. Many people used it in her presence as if it was her default word. "I have a reservation. Karen Bayless."

The clerk typed in a few keystrokes and looked up again. "Welcome to Mather Hotel. We have you in room 220." She handed over a key and a small packet of local tourist information. "If there is anything you need, please let us know."

The normal expression Bayless wore in such situations was cheerful and humble. Like being at the fancy hotel was a treat, and she was so glad for having the opportunity. Most took pity on the person wearing such a bewildered look. Often, they would give information beyond the acceptable norm. Maybe on another guest or some happening at their establishment that no one else knew. Social engineering at work.

From his stool at the bar, Abney watched Karen Bayless wander over to the elevator and head up to her room. A pleasant guilelessness exuded from her stride. *If only people knew,* he thought. The woman had murdered more people than Charles Manson. For that gruesome fact, he admired Bayless. Otherwise, he found her physical plainness repulsive like boiled chicken or canned green beans.

The *maître d'* appeared at his elbow and motioned towards a table tucked away in the corner.

"Your table is ready, sir."

"Thank you, Charles."

"I have a guest joining me for lunch. A rather prim woman with brown hair."

"Of course, sir. I'll send her over."

"Much obliged."

"Can I get you a drink?"

"Yes, Charles. An Old Fashioned."

"Right away, sir."

Abney sat back in his chair, smug and self-satisfied. He knew Charles thought him a conceited asshole, which made their exchanges even more gratifying. Hustle and decorum brought him joy as if acknowledging the natural order of things. The *maître d'* worked for him, and he wanted to be sure the man knew it.

The drink arrived promptly, and for the next few minutes, Abney sat sipping in silence, waiting for Bayless to arrive. There was no doubt in his mind that she would. The note he left in the middle of her bed spoke to his expectations, including lunch and dinner. There was a certain deliciousness in such a flagrant violation of her privacy. It was the only pleasure he would find with the woman.

It took Bayless five minutes from check-in to arrive back

downstairs. She glanced through the thick oak doors at the bar and walked up to the entrance, wide-eyed and smiling. Charles took one look at her and swept his arm towards the corner table and Abney's sly grin. He looked like a shark waiting for an unsuspecting fish to swim by. Her eyes narrowed almost imperceptibly at the edges, but she maintained the silly guileless expression. Charles pulled out her chair and they exchanged brief pleasantries before he handed over a menu.

"Something to drink?"

"Oh, water is fine. Thank you."

"Still or sparkling."

Bayless gave a patented look of surprise and amusement. "Why, sparkling sounds lovely."

"Of course, ma'am."

The *maître d'* turned and left, but there it was again. That word—ma'am.

"Welcome to Idaho," cackled Abney and raised his glass.

The smile vanished from her face like a wispy cloud against an advancing storm.

"Get to the point, Mr. Abney. Why am I here?"

"What? No banter or small talk?"

"If I wanted banter, I'd cut off your balls and listen to you squeal."

Abney's smile widened with a tinge of stunted lust. *If only she had as much physical spunk*, he wistfully thought.

"Two targets. Primary is female. Early thirties. Long brown hair. Buxomly. Secondary is male. No description, but dangerous."

"Tertiary?"

"A USB drive in her possession."

Bayless took no notes. She did not have to. Her memory captured more detail than the IRS during a tax audit.

"Payment?"

Abney smiled. It always came down to money. "One million per target."

"Including tertiary?"

"Including the USB."

While Bayless never moved her mouth, Abney could see her eyes smiling at all those zeroes.

"How do you know the secondary is dangerous?"

"They both are."

Bayless tilted her head ever so slightly to one side and narrowed her sterile green eyes.

"She killed our private investigator. He did the two FBI agents that followed and two local hacks, but idiocy played a large part in their untimely deaths. However, the shooting was superb from what I hear."

"How superb?"

"You must talk to the local law enforcement for that information. I've set up a meeting after lunch between you and Officer Carl Ortman. He's interjected himself into the proceedings."

"Rules of engagement?"

"Burn the town down for all I care," answered Abney glibly. Only after the words came out did he consider Bayless might go through with the act.

"Does that pay extra?"

"No."

"Then I'm all clear."

Charles strode over and set down a bottle of sparkling water. "Are you two ready to order?"

Abney looked down at his watch. Seventeen hours

remained on his promise to Terrance Knight. *No time to waste*, he thought.

"I believe we are," he answered without glancing up at his table mate.

Chapter Twenty-Five

A grease-stained paper bag sat between Carl's legs. Strewn on top were the remnants of a double cheeseburger and a few stray fries. His usual lunch order. Only, he ate uneasily and not with his typical gusto. There was too much on his mind. It wandered over and across all the worst-case scenarios his imagination could conjure. The truly terrible stuff. He'd seen the endings foretold. The two guys in the truck. The FBI agents. Shaun. It all ended with him in a box. Either a cheap pine under six feet of soil or a ten-by-ten concrete cell in prison. The latter he considered a stroke of good fortune.

Lost in that thought, he did not see Abney approach his police cruiser. The knock on the window made him jump and his greasy lunch ended up all over his pants.

"Damnation," he muttered to himself while rolling down the driver's side window.

"Officer Ortman."

Carl wiped off a ketchup stain and looked up. "Mr. Abney. How can I help you?"

"An update for starters."

Carl looked at the woman standing behind and slightly askew. He asked, "Who is that?"

"My associate."

"Associate?"

"Think of her as the closer."

Bayless gave a demur smile.

"We don't have much baseball here," replied Carl.

"Fine. Think of her as the inevitable conclusion to your incompetence."

"I liked the baseball reference," he mumbled.

"Karen, this is Carl. Carl, this is Karen. Please fill her in on all the details. You'll extend her any help she might require. Is that understood?"

Carl nodded. "I understand."

"Good. I'll let you two get acquainted."

As Abney walked away, Carl glanced over at Bayless, who fixed him with a glance that could melt ice. It was not her cluelessly joyous expression. No point in putting on a show when talking shop. She didn't like local help, be it Italy, Iraq, or Idaho. Locals were a liability. They talked. They were overconfident and lazy and easily swayed by the prevailing winds.

"Where should I start?" he asked.

"The beginning will do."

"Of what?"

"Of why I am sitting in this goddamn car," she growled.

Carl hesitated for a moment but didn't see another way to get her out of his cruiser. "I suppose it started with Horace Filby."

Bayless didn't blink.

"The woman in question killed Horace in her house. Well, so we think."

Bayless still didn't blink. Her eyes just bored right into Carl's head like the light at a dentist's office.

"Then this Mr. Sherman shows up in town and things get worse. Two guys from the next county over ended up shot to pieces on Casino Road."

"Tell me about that."

"A damn bloody mess. Looked like they tried to run a car off the road. Ran into a bunch of bullets instead."

"I was told the shooter was good. How so?"

"Five rounds each. Center mass."

The rote statistic did not impress Bayless. Any decent shooter could do that. Even a terrible one could manage if they stood a few feet away.

"Through the windshield, no less," added Carl.

"And the other two?"

"The FBI?"

"Was there someone else?"

Carl paused for a second, "Yeah, a friend of mine."

"Never make friends in this business."

"Is that advice?" asked Carl. He fancied asking what her business was but thought better of it. She didn't seem like the sharing type.

"More of a fact."

"Is that so?"

Bayless ignored the question. "Tell me about the feds."

"Your friend, Abney, brought them to town. I assume he had his reasons."

"It's not their arrival I care about."

"Their departure. Got it. I guess that began when Chief Talbot and I picked up Mr. Sherman and Ruby on the mountain. They came quietly enough. I think the feds scooped them after that. I showed up for the aftermath."

"What aftermath?"

"Talbot died on the road. GSW. The agents met a different fate."

"Christ. Do I strike you as the squeamish type? Details and right quick."

"Someone beat them to death."

"Someone?"

"This Sherman guy, I assume. I don't think Ruby can do that level of damage."

"Was he handcuffed?"

Carl nodded. "Last time I saw him."

Not easily impressed, Bayless had to acknowledge certain facts. A certain skill set. "Anything else about this mystery man?"

"Talbot called him 'Captain' like he was in the navy or some shit."

"How old did he look?"

"Mid-thirties."

"You're an idiot," replied Bayless. "A Navy captain is career-track, just below a rear admiral. This guy is in the Army or Marine Corps."

"Does that make a difference?"

"No," she answered with a nostalgic glint in her otherwise matte eyes. "They both bleed just the same."

An urge to run swelled in Carl's stomach like the morning after a bender.

"How did you know where to find them? You and Talbot."

"Talbot knew. It was his uncle's cabin."

"Where do I find his uncle?"

"Stalworth cemetery."

Bayless exhaled with gale force. "An aunt then?"

"Betsy. She runs the B&B on Cherry Street. You can't miss it. The big old Victorian house."

"Thanks, Officer. We'll talk later."

The sentence sizzled as it came out of her mouth, all heated and full of intensity. Carl swallowed hard but stuck with his choice. The alternatives, all those terrible outcomes, scared him more than a diminutive woman named Karen.

For the next dozen minutes, Carl did nothing but stare ahead and drum his fingers on the steering wheel. Change was coming. If there had ever been a chance to stop it, that chance was long gone. Only one option remained—survive the ending, whatever that took.

Back at the police station, the atmosphere was morbid. Over twenty-four hours had elapsed since Talbot disappeared. It did not take much acting for Carl to match the mood. Everyone feared the worst. He knew the worst. Crumpled and bloody, lying dead in the middle of the road. All those unfulfilled dreams. The wife and child left aching for knowledge or closure. He knew all about it because he stuffed Talbot's still warm body in the freezer. Because he killed an unconscious woman. Because he squished her corpse under four tons of granite. Because he would do it again if needed.

"Where have you been?"

Carl looked up to see Officer Torres standing over his desk.

"Patrol."

"It wasn't on the board." She pointed to the whiteboard Talbot installed to coordinate shifts and patrols.

"I needed to do something," he answered. Lying was easier when sprinkled with truth.

Torres looked at him for a moment. Her soft brown eyes

narrowed and tilted towards the side. It was her detective look. Carl knew it well. Her investigative prowess intimidated him on an average day. Seeing it directed across the desk made his stomach jump like a dolphin.

"Tell me again what happened up there?"

"At the cabin? We've been over it twice."

"Once more won't hurt anyone."

"Once more is a waste of time. Time we don't have. We should be out looking for him."

"Where else are we supposed to look? Without more info, he could be anywhere. They burn his cruiser to the frame. And the last person you saw him with is in the wind."

Carl raised up his hands. "What more can I add?"

"I don't know," she sighed. "I think there is something else going on here."

"What?" he asked, leaning in.

"He said something about a license plate and then just took off."

"What license plate?"

"I don't know. He didn't say. He just got in his SUV and burned rubber."

"With Mr. Sherman and Ruby?"

"That's the thing. I don't know if they were in the vehicle or not."

"They were in the vehicle. Where else would they be?" Carl asked. Torres was veering off track and needed direction back towards safer ground.

"Like I said," she sighed. "Something ain't right."

Chapter Twenty-Six

The coffee shop was trim but not overly fancy, and no stainless steel or unvarnished woods adorned the walls. Exposed brick gave the place a warm glow, but it was built from the stuff, so Raylan Gournsey didn't hold it against them. The inside smelled of espresso and baked fruit. Homey and inviting. A clean, well-lit place. He liked it. Plus, it had Wi-Fi, which had proven harder to find than he initially thought. Betsy's internet was out of the question. Too easy to track and far too slow. She was of a generation used to certain speeds and had never cared to upgrade past DSL.

Gournsey ordered an Americano. It came piping hot. He let it cool while powering up the laptop. Someone wrote the password in clean script on a piece of paper that resembled something from a fortune cookie. Nothing fancy. Not etched into small chunks of wood with a laser. There was no QR code to use on his phone. Just paper and pen. He appreciated the simplicity, if not the speed.

As plans went, it was relatively simple. They had a USB.

It contained encrypted files. Therefore, they needed to decrypt the files. The simplicity ended there. The concept of codes traced back to the first written words. As soon as humans learned to read and write, someone wanted to obscure what they were saying from others. The technology had changed over the millennia, but the sentiment remained.

It took Gournsey over an hour to get everything ready. The Tor browser, Bitcoin wallet, and dark web address. Buying a program was a waste of time. The laptop didn't have enough processing power to run half of them, and it would take months to crack even a simple encryption. He needed a specialist. Which was where he started his search.

Spend enough time on the dark web and you meet people. Nothing concrete. No first names or places of birth, although buying such info was easy enough. But, with enough interactions, people got a sense for each other. Gournsey had spent his fair share of time in the strange underbelly of the World Wide Web. Most of it was gun-related. He collected weapons that could not be bought through legal channels and relied on the discretion and anonymity of illegal ones.

He started with a known entity. A friend in the online sense, who directed him to another user and another. This daisy chain of trust continued until someone with the right skill set started chatting back. From there, it was just a matter of negotiation. The price was set and they placed Bitcoins in an escrow account run by a mutual acquaintance. Trust only went so far in a faceless world. The timeline was not so easy. The estimate ranged from twenty-four to two-hundred and forty hours. A day or ten, depending on the encryption. Gournsey uploaded the file to an FTP site and sent the link.

Then he closed the laptop and ordered another Americano to go. A clock on the wall that could have come from his elementary school read two in the afternoon.

Outside, late summer warmth languished along the main street with a certain urgency. The last gasps of heat before autumn winds pulled down the leaves and ushered in winter. Gournsey crossed the street and headed away from the Bed and Breakfast. Something prevented him from retracing his steps. An abhorrence of patterns scorched into his mind by years of foot patrols. All those claustrophobic alleys and hard-packed walking paths left him wary of return trips. Too many friends perished in those thick, ear-splitting blasts.

Gournsey meandered. He sauntered. He looked in windows and poked his head in bars. Most of all, he watched his back. Specifically, the red Monte Carlo that appeared and reappeared in his wake.

Behind the wheel, Floyd Dooley tapped his long dirty fingers against the console. The hotel bar had not suited his disposition and only some middle-aged hairdresser checked in. He'd moved on to the Talbot widow's B&B. From down the street, he saw everyone coming and going, including Carl and the guy who showed up after. A big bearded man who looked every bit the type of soldier to burn an SUV to the frame with someone inside.

Lee and Glenn were sleeping off their all-night stakeout in the back seat, which meant they were hungover and useless. He watched the guy head out in a truck and return with a box. Not big, but not small. Glenn looked up and informed his tech-ignorant father the package in question was a laptop.

Hours passed. They waited in silence. Booze evaporated from the brothers' pores like mist above a rancid swamp. When the man emerged, they watched him walk down the street and into a coffee shop with a small silver rectangle sandwiched under his arm.

"That him?" asked Lee.

"Fits the bill," suggested Glenn.

"He walks like a snake-eyed gorilla," Floyd confirmed. "Like he owns the damn street."

"What now?" asked the brothers.

"Why do you suppose he is going to the coffee shop? I'm sure the old Talbot hag has a coffee pot always warming in the kitchen."

Glenn answered, "The laptop. I bet the B&B has terrible internet."

"Risky, isn't it? Coming out like that?"

"Maybe he doesn't want to be tracked. That is a new computer under his arm."

More time passed, but not much more. They stayed within sight after the coffee shop. Floyd moved the car up a few blocks, then a few blocks further.

"What is he doing?" asked Lee.

"Looking for us," replied Floyd.

"Did he see us?"

"Maybe. Maybe not. But it's an old trick," explained Floyd. "Walk around aimlessly and anyone following you will pop out like a stripper's titties."

"Is he looking for us?"

"He's just looking," Floyd assured. "Which means we got the right man."

Circling around Main Street, Gournsey veered north towards the river. The vivid red Monte Carlo remained visible down the block. Twice was a coincidence, but the vehicle had crossed his path four times since arriving. Soon, the happenstance would turn into a problem and he enjoyed solving problems.

The warm winds cooled within a block and the smells of water reached his nostrils. Gournsey stood watching the lazily moving stretch of river for several minutes. The unhurriedness reminded him of childhood and summers spent on down by the creek with nothing to play with but his imagination and nature. It spoke to an innate desire to be outside under the sun and the clouds. For he was, at his core, a country boy.

From the northern tip of town, he turned and headed back south-west. Ghosts of industry cropped up along the river. Old hulking chunks of iron and steel leered back from a once useful past. Long forgotten machines rusted behind fences. Proud brick buildings still stood undisturbed one hundred years after construction. History stalked the streets and narrow alleyways, but with a particularly western youth. Not like the haunted hollers of Kentucky, but Gournsey enjoyed it.

As the commercial outcropping gave way to residential homes, Gournsey turned and walked back towards Cherry Street. In the compactness of the Stalworth, it did not take him long to reach Betsy's front porch.

On the inside of the closed door, Gournsey peeked through the front window. Deep down the street sat a small smudge of red. Back where they started.

"Problem?" asked Sherman.

"I caught a tail."

"Who?"

"Locals, I think."

"Cops?"

"No. They look like hayseed highwaymen. Driving a red Monte Carlo."

Sherman's eyes rolled without moving. The verbal confusion he once felt faded over the years. Only the humor remained. "Concerned citizens, perhaps. Maybe they don't like your type in town."

"You're onto something there."

"They don't know what I look like," replied Sherman, suddenly realizing what he had missed.

"How descriptive do you think they got?" asked Gournsey. "Big military guy?"

"Something more colloquial, but racing in the same lane."

"From a distance, without context, we look similar enough. I'm much better looking, but they couldn't see that far."

Sherman laughed. "I'm offended that they think you are me."

Gournsey feigned a wounded look. "You should be so lucky."

The two friends were still laughing when Ruby walked up. She gave them a questioning glance but decided it was an inside joke. There was no point in trying to determine the punchline.

"Any luck with the file?" she asked.

"I got in touch with an acquaintance of a friend of a friend. He or she is looking into it."

"That sounds nebulous," Ruby replied.

"The dark web usually is."

"Dark web?" she gasped. "Isn't that full of crazies?"

Gournsey frowned. "The internet is full of crazies. Reddit and 4Chan are full of crazies. The dark web isn't any worse. It is the place where all the normal internet psychos go to buy their drugs and guns."

"Can you trust this person?"

"No," answered Gournsey in a flat tone.

Ruby turned to Sherman with a look of concern mixed with confusion. "I thought we were decrypting the file."

"We're trying," he reassured. "But the senator has access to high-end software. It's not something that our Walmart laptop can do. Passing it off was the only option."

"How long will that take?"

Gournsey shrugged. "A few days at best. A lifetime at worst."

With a clouded future the only thing in sight, Ruby sat down. She took a deep breath. Her natural inclination was flight. Running was the first and often final answer. She usually stayed until the first breeze of discontent. Then she packed up and left town. By her own calendar, she was four days overdue.

Ruby bit her lip and a brief flash of anger lashed out towards the two men for keeping her tethered, then she chuckled to herself about gift horses because Sherman was the only thing keeping her alive.

"Are we waiting here?" she asked.

"For the time being," Sherman replied. "The sergeant spotted some overly interested locals in town. Do you know anyone who drives a red Monte Carlo?"

"New or old?"

"Newer," answered Gournsey.

Ruby had an expert eye for cars and faces. A byproduct of bartending and several poor choices in boyfriends. She searched through her memory. Only a vague image came back.

"Nothing concrete," she replied. "Someone from the next county over, but I couldn't say who."

"Not local?"

"That depends on your definition. You say local, but Betsy might consider the man a foreigner."

Sherman turned towards the back door and the other two followed. They found Betsy sitting in silence under the shade of a willow tree. The bottle of whiskey was a few fingers thinner, but she had not abandoned her wits. She looked up as they approached.

"Oh my, don't you make quite the trio."

"Do you know anyone who drives a newish red Monte Carlo?"

"Does it have two stupid stripes down the middle? Like that makes it any faster."

"In fact, it does," answered Gournsey.

Betsy gave a mournful little sigh. "I believe that car belongs to Floyd Dooley."

"Can you tell us more about Mr. Dooley?"

She pursed her lips and took a deep breath, readying herself for a long story. Sherman smiled. Small-town gossip was a wonderful resource.

"Floyd is what you'd call a nuisance in these parts. In a big city, he'd be known as a drug dealer, but small-town words for small-town problems. He and his boys live over in Copperton. Been there for years... since some schism between the families."

"Which families?" asked Sherman.

Betsy chuckled at the answer. "Between the Dooleys and the Ortmans."

"Carl!" gasped Ruby.

"None other."

The officer's name did not surprise Sherman. Logically, it made complete sense. Where else could he turn for help but family?

"How much of a nuisance?" asked Gournsey.

"Oh, there have been rumors over the years. Bodies and ghosts and all that. They're nasty people. Not to be trusted."

"I don't plan on doing much talking," Gournsey replied.

"In that case, you should surely check the attic. Bill wasn't much for talking either."

"Thanks, Betsy," said Sherman before leaving the woman to her thoughts and her bottle.

Chapter Twenty-Seven

Given the afternoon hour, Abney would have usually taken his drink at the pool overlooking the river. The transition to warm air, cool water, and evocative views had not happened. He was still in the hotel lounge, sipping on a highball glass filled with whiskey and bitters. Fourteen hours remained on his promise to Terrance Knight. The stupidity of his proclamation weighed heavily like shoes in a swimming pool. Booze eased the edges of his panic, but only just. He needed action.

The lounge had an unobstructed view of the front door, which was the reason for Abney's indoor seating arrangement. Within two drinks, Karen Bayless returned from her conversation with Officer Ortman. The woman headed towards the elevator but Abney caught her attention and forced her towards his couch. She gave a smile that was pure conceit, and Abney patted the expensive leather seat next to him. Reluctantly, she sat down.

"What did you learn?" he asked.

"Plenty."

"Details, please, Ms. Bayless."

Her eyes flashed a rare twinkle of energy. "We need to discuss our terms."

A sharp smile crossed Abney's face. "I set the terms."

"There is always room for negotiation."

He finished the drink and whirled a finger in a tight circle high in the air until the bartender nodded. "Three million is plenty."

"Three for the bodies, one for the drive."

"Greed doesn't suit your complexion," Abney hissed. "It brings out the splotches."

Bayless didn't blink.

"Fine," he conceded. "One extra, provided you have some information."

"I know where they are."

Abney sat up straighter at the news. "Where?"

"In town."

He laughed at the obvious simplicity.

"I'll confirm tonight," she added.

"No. Confirm now."

"Now is not good."

"If you want the extra million, you'll confirm now and have this business settled by morning."

"Two days is better," Bayless insisted, knowing such an operation took time to plan.

"You have twelve hours."

"No one said this was time-sensitive."

"Now you know."

She stood up to leave.

"Do it tonight," Abney insisted.

If she was angry, it didn't register on her face. Bayless merely turned and headed towards her room. A few minutes later, she returned with her rolling suitcase trailing behind. Abney said nothing as she left through the front door. He barely glanced at her exit or the man holding open the door.

Colonel Charles Straeger, retired, glanced down at the woman exiting from the hotel. She looked familiar in an average way. But there was something about her eyes that stuck out. A matte expressionless devoid of delight like the gloss of life had been rubbed away. Determined and capable and dangerous, but mute.

Walking up to the front desk, he slouched a little at the shoulders. People noticed posture, so did software. Altering it, even just a little, gave his interactions a common quality. He spent forty years in the army walking ramrod straight, head held high. Every bit the alpha male. That worked when the uniform mattered. Civilian jobs had come with a few new lessons in camouflage. Even his hair changed. The buzz cut gave way to inches of gray. Still neat and straight, but not short. The beard was a recent addition. Gone was the constant shaving, replaced by the occasional trimmer. Those he met appeared at ease. They treated him like a well-off grandpa who stayed in shape.

"Welcome to Mather Hotel. How can I help you, sir?" asked a smiling middle-aged woman.

Straeger beamed and gave a fake name and matching credit card.

"I have you for two nights."

"Yes, ma'am."

"Great. Room 209 is all ready for you. The elevator is in the corner. The lounge is open to all guests and we have an excellent trout special tonight in our dining area."

"Sounds wonderful," replied Straeger, a wide and easy grin looping across his face. He picked up his bag and glanced towards the bar and lounge. A sideways glance, just long enough to see someone he knew from a photograph. An image sent and deleted once he memorized the face.

The colonel forewent the elevator and took the grand staircase up to the second floor. Even in the throes of retirement, he found luxury to be a strange condition. The room was exquisite with muted tones and heavy wooden accents. Comfortable but not baroque or kitschy. Still, it had more than he needed or wanted.

He placed his suitcase on the king-size bed and methodically unpacked the contents. Underneath the clothes and sundries lay another compartment, hidden from prying eyes. A specialty space built for a specific rifle. He owned other cases for other weapons, but this one held a Blaser R93 rifle.

The Tactical 2 variant had a unique feature that made it suited for such jobs. Unlike most rifles, the user could remove the barrel from the gun with only two screws and reassemble the whole thing in thirty seconds. It was not the movie world, where an assassin assembled their sniper rifle from ten different parts. Guns like that do not maintain accuracy. The Blaser did.

Satisfied everything was in order, Straeger locked the case and crumpled up a small receipt from his pocket. On his way out of the room, he placed it carefully behind the door. An old trick he learned in Beirut back in the nineties. Nobody searching a room bothered to rearrange trash on the floor.

The bar had emptied after the lunch rush, and when Straeger arrived, there were only three other customers. A retired couple from Minnesota on their way to visit a daughter in Oregon and a well-to-do local who enjoyed bourbon. Abney had not moved from his chair in the lounge. Only the drink in his hand was new.

Straeger sat at a polite distance from the couple and the regular. He didn't want a direct line of sight into the lounge as it was too obvious. The stool at the end caught a reflection through the glass. It worked well enough to see a smug, intoxicated face. He ordered a vodka with lots of ice. The best drink for sitting long stints at a bar. No one could tell when the drink ended and the ice took over.

"Sir," said a voice from behind. It was the short-haired woman from the front desk. "We have a package for you." She handed over a box marked next-day air.

Inside was a phone. A simple model like some knockoff Blackberry. Straeger powered it up and waited. A few minutes later, it vibrated softly against the thickly lacquered bar.

A single word appeared: *Status?*

Straeger tapped the keys gingerly like a cat inspecting a new toy. *Just arrived. Our friend is here.*

Make sure it's done and dusted by tomorrow morning.

The colonel lingered over the reply for several moments. *Vague and oblique,* he thought. The message politicians favored. Not the Terrance Knight he once knew. The 'get shit done' senator from Louisiana who always sided with the military for more funding. That man was direct and Straeger appreciated directness.

Grimacing, he replied.

Anything else?

Stay put. There are other problems to solve.

A low growl escaped from Straeger's throat—not loud, but enough for the bourbon drinker to hear.

"Trouble with the missus?"

"Isn't there always," he replied with a knowing grin that was not a complete lie.

Mrs. Straeger had left years before. Not long after the birth of their daughter. They rarely spoke directly, and conversations were often mediated through the muffled tones of lawyers.

Uncle Sam had taken all his time before and after retirement. A fact that his ex-wife consistently underlined. Moving to Montana was a chance to get away from that past, but it seemed to carry on like nothing had changed.

"I tell her I'm at the office."

"A safe bet."

"Until she sees the credit card bill…" the local trailed off.

"Try cash," Straeger suggested. "If they still take it around here."

The gentleman laughed and nodded emphatically. "Kids these days. If it ain't on their phones, it doesn't exist."

From Mather Hotel to Cherry Street took Bayless six minutes to traverse. Two walking to the car and four minutes of stop-and-go traffic. Residential streets. Wide enough for parking and lazy walks and block parties. She disliked the delay, or any delay. Wasting time did not suit her nature.

She parked across the street, slow and easy. No circling of the block or any effort at reconnaissance. Such actions draw attention from those hard-wired to look for patterns. Based on what she heard, one target was such an individual. Better to approach from the front with a bag in tow and play the tourist card.

On the way to the front porch, Bayless put on a show in case anyone was watching. She slowed and glanced around with a big smile on her face. A self-satisfied look from one who found the cute, off the beaten path, boutique lodging. Without further hesitation, she walked right up to the door and rang the bell. Then she stepped back so anyone on the inside could see her.

A heavy ding echoed around the inside of the house and, a few seconds longer than it should have taken, the door opened. Bayless smiled. Betsy smiled. They stood there in mock politeness. A duel of propriety.

"Hello there. How can I help you, dear?" asked Betsy.

"Well, hello there to you too. My name is Cynthia, and I was passing through the area for work and thought I could use a night to treat myself. I saw this on Google and thought, heck, Cynthia, you deserve a little break. Your sign in the window says Vacancy, so I'm hoping you have a room available."

Betsy glanced over at the small hand-painted sign still hanging next to the front door and silently cursed her oversight. In the shadows of the parlor, Sherman's chest tightened. The voice was silky smooth as if covered with cream.

"Oh dear," she began. "I'm afraid I just rented it this morning to a delightful couple from, uh… Indiana."

"Drat," replied Bayless. The look of disappointment on her face would have fooled a con artist. "Is there any other place in town?"

"Mather Hotel is lovely this time of year," suggested Betsy.

"You wouldn't have a brochure for them, would you?"

Betsy smiled and lost her composure for a second. "Of course, honey. Step on inside."

Bayless smiled and complied with her own backhanded suggestion. "What a lovely place you have."

Betsy eyed the woman with an inkling of unease but kept on smiling. "Why, thank you. I am terribly sorry about the sign. Sometimes old age gets the better of my mind. Here is a brochure. The directions are straightforward if you need them."

Bayless glanced around the home some more. Charming, cozy, and full of character were the words used in the review she read before driving over. Ostensibly, Cynthia craved that combination and her face eagerly showed it. Beneath that mask, Bayless despised warm and cozy. She liked clean lines, stainless steel, and gray paint.

She took the brochure from Betsy's outstretched arm. "Thanks for the suggestion."

"Of course. Again, I must apologize for my oversight."

"Not at all. I'll still get my treat." And with that, Bayless skipped down the stairs and drove off.

Four minutes after that, she pulled into her old parking spot at Mather Hotel and considered all she had seen. Starting with the innkeeper. Bayless could tell the woman was putting on a show. *It took one to know one,* she reasoned. The smile turned up a bit too high on the edges. The muscles twitched slightly in a sure sign it was forced.

Despite the old woman's protestations to the contrary, there was a vacancy. Three pegs adorned the wall with neat numbers painted in vibrant colors. Two were missing. One was not. Two rooms rented, not three.

Then there were the smells. Two distinct olfactory notes. A faint whiff of perfume. Cheap and lightly applied, but not from the woman. She smelled like the kitchen. The perfume was from someone else. Then there was the sweat.

Musky and coarse. Without a doubt from a man. Not old or young but someone in the prime of life.

Bayless saw enough to form a plan. Simple yet effective. She smiled at the ease of the reconnaissance and entered through the front door, bag still trailing behind her like a loyal dog. Abney spied her entrance and cocked his head to one side, looking for confirmation. She didn't stop but gave him a wink. An almost imperceptible gesture, but it was enough for Abney. He picked up his drink and staggered towards the pool.

Chapter Twenty-Eight

Betsy watched the woman leave through parted blinds. Only once the car turned the corner did she flip the vacancy sign around. Unwelcome guests did not sit well with her. They never had. She feared it with Bill in Vietnam. The looming knock on the door that never came, and she feared it every time he left after that. Maybe the police. Maybe the army. Maybe someone worse.

"Sorry about that," she sighed. "I should have turned over the sign earlier."

Sherman smiled but did not hide the pistol in his hand. Neither did Gournsey when he stepped out of the kitchen with Talbot's AR-15 in the crook of his arm.

"Boys? I don't think those are necessary."

The men exchanged a glance that said differently. Betsy's uneasy smile turned into a deep frown. Thick trenches burrowed into her forehead.

"What does that look mean?"

"Our commander has a saying," Gournsey began. "There are no coincidences."

Betsy looked incredulous. "That lady?"

"You think they all look like Bill?" asked Sherman.

"Low blow, Frank."

"Sorry, Betsy, but soccer mom is a good disguise. No one would second guess that woman being in the room."

"But she seemed so nice."

"It wouldn't be the first time," added Gournsey.

"The Kurdish financier in Erbil," suggested Sherman.

"Or the Russian oil workers in Angola."

"Gruesome. Oh, remember that Iranian scientist in Damascus?"

"Yeah, they found... what? Twenty percent of him?" prodded Sherman.

"At most," replied Gournsey.

"Enough," snapped Betsy. "I get it."

"Get what?" asked Ruby, who had just emerged from her hiding place upstairs. "Who was at the door?"

Betsy looked at the soldiers and then up towards Ruby, who was standing on the stairs. "I'm making some coffee."

"What is going on?" Ruby asked, perplexed by the sudden change in attitudes.

"Trouble," replied Sherman.

"My luck doesn't go any other way," she added dejectedly.

Gournsey smiled and gave her a pat on the back. "Don't worry. His luck is no better."

"Not comforting," Ruby snarled.

The Kentuckian shrugged his mammoth shoulders and nodded towards the attic. There was nothing left to discuss because they did not have any concrete information. No need to let the imagination wander. It did that well enough without external prodding.

The three of them followed the second-floor hall back

until it ended at a tiny off-white door. No standard-size opening, the dimensions were at least a foot shorter than the closet doors on all fronts. The brass knob creaked and jiggled as Sherman twisted it open. Ruby had to duck on the way through, which meant Gournsey had to become a contortionist to reach the ladder leading up to the attic.

Grunting and twisting, he asked, "Was her husband a damn leprechaun?"

"This is no smaller than that tunnel near Kandahar," Sherman replied.

"I got stuck in that tunnel."

"Wasn't that Bagrahn?"

"No," growled Gournsey. "We blew that one up."

"Really?"

"Really."

The memories ran together in Sherman's mind. Fifteen years of the same thing erodes all distinctive edges.

Odors of mothballs, rat poison, and history enveloped them as they stepped into the attic. Dozens of moldering cardboard boxes sat stacked two or three high. The place reeked of the past. A hundred years at least. How Bill got a gun safe into the space was a question Sherman could not answer. It seemed unfathomable, but the thick steel doors still twinkled in the corner. Ruby brushed away the cobwebs lacing off from the corners.

Sherman knelt and gently spun the dial back and forth. It opened without a sound, still oiled from years of tender care.

The sergeant danced around like a child, unable to contain his excitement. Christmas brought less joy than the potential contents of Bill Talbot's safe. Squeezing through the narrow confines of Victorian architecture would surely be worth it.

"What the hell," uttered Gournsey.

Ruby sighed. "Is there another safe?"

Only dust and a small yellowed envelope remained in the safe. Fifty square feet of emptiness as if it could hold all their dismay and anger. Sherman grabbed the envelope and flipped it open. Inside was a note from Bill to Betsy and dozens of hundred-dollar bills. He didn't read the note. He didn't need to. The reason had no bearing on their current predicament.

"What does it say?" asked Ruby.

"It's not for my eyes," he replied, then turned towards the ladder.

They found Betsy putzing around in the kitchen, making coffee and half-heartedly prepping dinner. Sherman handed her the envelope with a ceremonious nod. She flipped it open and gasped, then started reading the note.

For a minute, she said nothing, but her eyes drooped in the corners as some anger inside her melted further.

"It's a Christmas present from Bill," she began. "An apology for all those years of uncertainty. For all the lies I told on his behalf. He sold the guns and told me to buy something nice."

She stopped for a moment and then looked up at Sherman. "Nothing at all in the safe?"

"Dust."

"Oh, Bill. I had no idea. I'm sorry for y'all."

"We'll be fine."

"He always made these treasure hunts for Christmas. Leaving me clues throughout the house. I wish I had known about this one. He died a few days after he wrote this note."

Ruby gave her an empathetic smile. "He really loved you."

"That he did," replied Betsy with a wistful look towards

a picture on the wall. She reached back into the cupboard and brought out the whiskey once more.

All eyes turned to her and the shard of history she was reliving. They lingered on her features, which, at once, seemed both younger and older. Then Sherman nodded towards the parlor. There were things to discuss. Things that could not be ignored.

The ornately carved hands on the cuckoo clock read quarter to four. Sherman hadn't noticed the intimidating ode to German timekeeping. Nor could he remember any annoying song going off, but his mind weeded out the unnecessary sounds. Background music barely registered, while the lone whistle of an incoming mortar roared like a Motörhead concert.

"Who's first?" asked Gournsey. He was leaning against the wall with the rifle in his hand, peeking through the parted curtains. The gun looked like a toy in his giant palms... like one of those cheap knockoffs with an orange tip.

"What do you mean?" asked Ruby.

"The sergeant is suggesting we winnow down the field."

She blinked a few times to straighten out the details in her mind. "The Dooleys?"

"Or the woman."

"What woman?" she asked.

"The one that stopped by asking for a room."

"What does she have to do with anything?"

Sherman looked at Ruby, not with anger or condescension, but with genuine disbelief. After all that she had gone through, there was still a decent bone in her body. One that gave a stranger the benefit of the doubt.

"Gournsey thinks he knows her or of her."

"What do you mean?"

"I briefly met her once," Raylan began. "At least I think it was her. She had blonde hair back then, but the build and age are the same. Same eyes too—mirthless and green."

"I'm sure you've met a lot of women."

The sergeant did not take his eyes off the street. "Not in Iraq. Not like her. Anyway, we met with an NGO group. Aid workers trying to build wells up north. She was with them, I think. Dust storms drove us inside and everyone got to chatting about the war. She seemed superficially nice, but I can tell a faker when I see one and she was trying hard. When the storm stopped, we parted ways. I never saw her again, but a half-dozen Kurds ended up at the bottom of those wells."

"And she's here for us?"

"She's here for the money," answered Sherman. "We're just the means."

"For fuck's sake," she groaned. "I should have burned it all down when I left."

"That's how I end my relationships," Gournsey added, jokingly.

"Can we run now?"

"Not a good idea with those three parked down the street."

Ruby jumped up and glanced under Gournsey's arm. A small smudge of red was visible two blocks away on the opposite side of the street. Through the sun's glare, it looked like a paint stroke on canvas. If she had seen such danger a month ago, her heart would have sunk with despair into her stomach. As it stood, she felt a rising sense of anger. Despite her question about running, she stood taller. *Perhaps,* she thought, *there might be a way out.*

"Who's first, then?" she asked.

Sherman took a breath and nodded with admiration. Ruby was not giving up, and he liked her even more for it.

"The Dooleys."

"You think they'll take the bait?" asked Gournsey.

"If they have us two confused, I think so."

"Are you trying to get them to follow you?" Ruby asked. Both men nodded.

"And if they don't follow you?"

"We'll have a real mess on our hands," answered Gournsey, clearly relishing the outcome.

"And if we sweeten the pot?" she asked.

The two soldiers turned and smiled. Neither questioned her motives nor highlighted the risk. They were in it together.

"Like flies to shit," Gournsey added.

"We'll leave just before dusk. There is a good spot towards the Talbot cabin."

"At the base of the mountain?" Ruby asked, fidgeting a little with the looming adrenaline.

Sherman nodded. "Exactly."

Gournsey asked, "And the cutthroat?"

"I'll deal with her tonight."

"I should do it."

"No, she might recognize you."

The certainty of the conversation confused Ruby. "How do you know where she'll be?"

"The same place as Abney and the FBI agents," Sherman replied.

"Mather Hotel?"

"He kept Harris and Tarney on a short leash. I bet it is the same with this one."

Dozens of logistical questions tumbled into Ruby's stream of thought. How would he know which room? What would he do? How would he stay hidden? All reasonable and pertinent questions, but she asked not one. There was no obvious explanation of how Sherman knew what to do and how to do it. *Experience*, Ruby reasoned. Brains rewire themselves with repetition, creating new neural pathways between often used memories and reflexes. No different from a doctor thinking in clinical terms, Sherman thought tactically like every enemy he ever faced. Then an additional question edged into her mind. A sour thought that gave Ruby a queasy feeling.

"Why not kill Abney too?"

"I plan on it," answered Sherman. A simple statement of fact, like a person announcing they were going to the grocery store. "Just not yet. We need him to get to Terrance Knight."

Ruby sat back down. There was nothing else worth asking about the woman or her deceased husband's best friend—at least nothing that she wanted to know. Only the next few hours mattered. "Now what?"

"Let's see what Betsy cooked for dinner. After that, you and Gournsey are going to walk right out the front door and get in the truck. I'll meet you in the alley at the end of the block. Then we're going for a drive."

"And if they don't follow us?"

"Then the sergeant here gets his wish and Stalworth has a belated fireworks show."

Chapter Twenty-Nine

It took Floyd Dooley all of five seconds to reach for his phone and start mashing buttons. Two figures crossed the empty street under a raspberry-sherbet-colored sky. One was big and bearded. The man from the coffee shop. They hid another under a jacket, but Floyd knew a feminine figure when he saw one. A man and woman, just like Carl's description. The guy looked anxious. He glanced around the street, twisting his neck one way and then another. The woman ran and ducked into the cab of a truck.

Floyd turned the ignition and the Monte Carlo growled to life. He held the phone in the crook of his neck and waited for the call to connect.

"Mr. Dooley," Carl answered. "I was hoping to hear from you. I pray you're calling with good news."

"Two people just left the Bed and Breakfast. A big bastard with a beard and some chickety."

"What did she look like?"

"Can't say. The bitch was hiding under a jacket and running like a fox."

"I trust you know what to do."

"Don't be a smartass, Eugene. Carry your end of the deal and we'll do the same."

"Call me afterwards... like immediately."

Floyd Dooley answered the demand by ending the call. He glanced over his shoulder. "Safeties off, boys."

The truck stole into motion and made a U-turn, then a right. Floyd eased the Monte Carlo onto the quiet section of pavement and followed on a parallel street. Behind a stop sign on Main Street, their paths met, and the Dooleys got a brief view of the truck as it passed. The bearded guy was behind the wheel, looking stern and vigilant. Edging just above the door, they glimpsed an unruly mop of brown curls—long, wavy, and shiny.

"You see that?" asked Glenn.

"Trying to hide like a rat," answered Lee.

Glenn turned to his father, "Pa, what's the play?"

"They're running scared," Floyd explained with amped confidence. The plan tumbled out of his mouth in rapid succession. "We follow them past the edge of town. Force 'em off the road. Expend some brass and leave a nice bonfire for Carl to clean up."

Lee pointed up ahead. "They're turning towards the mountains."

The patriarch bobbed his head with joy. "Perfect. There ain't shit out there but miles of lonely road."

Floyd Dooley was right about the area's seclusion. As the town faded, so too did witnesses. Homes, where they existed, sat back from the road guarded by tall stands of pine trees. If not for the occasional mailbox cemented into the ground and the gravel driveways cleft into the earth, no one else would have known. What began as a straight ribbon of asphalt suddenly climbed and stooped with the changing elevation. A powerful scent of conifers clung to the evening warmth.

Hidden behind the thin steel walls of the pickup bed, Sherman enjoyed the view passing above. White cumulus clouds floated by, bathed in pink and orange. They billowed like sails across a vast expanse of blue. It took him back to the years of his youth. Friendlier days, when life came in lavish sprints of uninterrupted joy. Back before shiny things lost their luster and a tree fort was worth more than gold. A few of those memories remained. Sketches of something lost but never truly forgotten.

The time and place were missing, but he remembered the feel of grass on his back. Green and damp and smelling of rain. Giant white creatures careened overhead towards the sea. He watched them form and twist, willing new shapes into existence as they passed. For years, whenever Sherman saw a cloud, he bemoaned that naïve innocence. Suddenly, he craved the shininess of an afternoon under an open sky and an unburdened imagination.

A sharp swerve of the truck ended his wistful hopes. Gone was the smooth pavement. Washboards rattled the suspension, and Sherman held his head for fear of scrambling those cumulous memories. He knew exactly where they were. Almost to the foot. All he had to do was study the map or satellite image for a few minutes. After that, his mind kept track of the rest. Sherman knew they were approaching the spot long before Gournsey slowed or tapped on the roof of the truck. It was just one of his skills.

Dust plumes merged and wavered in the air as Sherman jumped out of the pickup bed. A faint mist of brown lit by the setting sun. They picked out the exact location. It came at the start of a wide looping right turn that pulled the rutted road through a grove of quaking aspen and into an open field of gray scrub and wavy yellow grasses. From the shadows and into the light. The last mile before any real incline. A point of no return for the Monte Carlo as they could not follow much further.

The aspens were old and thick and closely spaced. A single giant living organism sprawling across the hills. Hundreds, if not thousands, of trees growing together. In the failing light, Sherman disappeared into the shadows. He held the hunting rifle requisitioned from Ralph. The well-worn walnut stock felt smooth and warm and solid. Familiar like an old friend or lover.

Of the three weapons in their possession, the only one confirmed to work was the Glock he took from Agent Harris. Sherman had pulled some extra ammo from Talbot's SUV before burning it, so he had two full magazines and the rifle. It had an 8x scope mounted on the sight rail. Some zoom, but not a lot. Enough, he reasoned. Even though he had no proof it worked, it appeared functional. Trusting another person's weapon was a dangerous game, but they had no other choices. Walking into the sporting goods store was not an option.

Hidden amongst the shadows, Sherman heard the Monte Carlo coming fast. They had missed their chance on the pavement when the coupe had the speed advantage. Floyd Dooley was trying to correct his mistake before the road deteriorated any more.

Gournsey slowed the truck and checked his rearview mirror. A flash of red burst from the shadows and skidded on the dirt. *Predictable,* he thought.

"You remember the plan?" he asked Ruby.

She nodded. "Stay low until the shooting stops."

"And you don't hear my voice when it's over?"

"Keep driving."

"You're a natural."

"I'm good at running."

The joke landed on the sticky side of truth, and Ruby took a breath. Gournsey started swerving the truck back and forth, imitating a panicked driver. The big Ford lurched off the road. Substantial quantities of dust rose all around like ash from an erupting volcano. Gournsey shifted into park and slipped out with the AR-15 before the air cleared.

The breaks gave a little squeak as Floyd brought the Monte Carlo to a sudden stop. Its engine burbled in the relative mountain silence. Only a distant warbler added to the noise of the chase. All three Dooleys paused for the briefest of moments with their eyes glued to the truck and the dust and possibilities unfolding before them.

"Let's finish this dirty business," instructed Floyd.

Anticipation shone from Lee's eyes like a kid on Christmas morning. He enjoyed the chase and the violence that followed. Glenn harbored no such joy. He was cerebral and distant, a planner, not an implementer. Both brothers carried venerated versions of Ruger rifles. Lee carried the larger caliber Mini-30 while Glenn shouldered the Mini-14. Solid choices for hunting deer or varmints or humans.

Unlike his sons, Floyd carried an antique. A revolver passed down for three generations from his grandfather, who carried it across the blackened and pitted fields of France in the Great War. Family legend said it killed three Germans at the Battle of Soissons in 1918. In the decades that followed, a few more bodies fell in front of its sights. There were newer guns and there were better guns, but they didn't have a history. A legacy. One that he planned on passing down to Lee when the time came. The boy was cruel and pigheaded, but Floyd had only himself and genetics to blame for that.

He opened the driver's side door and stepped out. Lee followed suit, but Glenn struggled to squeeze out of the back seat. They built the coupe for speed and fun and late-night racing, not ease of access. He folded down the front passenger seat and tried to get out. The rifle caught on the seat belt. He struggled some more, but it only made things worse.

"Jesus, boy. Hurry the hell up," yelled Floyd.

Another reason that Lee deserved the revolver, he thought.

Across the car, his better son shouldered his rifle and took patient aim at the truck.

One hundred and twenty yards away, Sherman took a breath and exhaled. He aimed for center mass, a foot below the neck and middle of the spine. It was not his gun, and therefore, prudent to maximize his chances of landing a shot. The crosshairs of the scope stood still, and he squeezed the trigger. A thumping crack rolled out over the valley and echoed up the mountains. The round struck high and right, just under Lee's shoulder blade. He lurched forwards and spun to his left, sinking towards the front seat and Glenn, who was still trying to exit the vehicle.

Glenn looked up at his brother's face, contorted with shock and fear and pain. In that second, everything changed like a quick slap to the face. Doubts blossomed into terror and all the air in his lungs leaped out.

Having seen the ballistics, Sherman made a quick adjustment to the small dials on the side and top of the scope. He slid the bolt back and forward to load another round.

Across the coupe, Floyd flinched, froze, and then ducked at the sound of gunfire. The sound was not new. Thousands of times within his lifetime he had heard those distinctive pops. Yet, in that moment, it took on a whole new quality and texture. Fear rippled down his spine. He turned towards Lee and a novel sensation gripped his stomach like a vice.

Smears and globs of blood covered the window like spray paint used too long in one place. It resembled the paint job on the Monte Carlo, but a shade darker and still wet. Lee's face was pale and etched with pain. His eyebrows pulled down and away from the wrinkles across his fore-head. Floyd knew he was not the best father, but the sight of his firstborn at the edge of life felt like hot iron searing his soul.

Lost in that terrible moment, Floyd didn't see Gournsey lean out from behind the truck. He didn't see the AR-15 or the man behind it. He didn't see the muzzle flashes or hear the gunshots. He didn't even feel the impact or the pain.

From Gournsey's barrel to Floyd's skull only took a heartbeat. The sergeant did not miss. Not from thirty yards. Not with a rifle.

Two rounds. Two hits. Nothing left to chance.

Floyd Dooley went down in a messy heap that only the dead can manage. Twisting further out, Gournsey placed the front windshield of the car in the iron sights. There was movement inside and he could clearly see another man leaning against the passenger side door cling to the roof and life. Someone inside the car was yelling out of panic and fear. A familiar tone. One he had heard too many times from friend and foe alike. It started high and warbly then ended low and guttural. Gournsey sighed down to his toes.

Lee lost his grip on the door and sank onto the dirt road. His shirt was slick with blood that looked like motor oil stains in the fading light. Everyone watching knew there wasn't any fight left in the man. His fate was a forgone conclusion, determined seconds ago by ballistics.

The only choice left was Glenn's to make. Fight or flight or surrender. He was lying down in the back seat, clutching the rifle and desperately thinking of a decent outcome. Shooting his way out felt impossible. He was smart enough to know they had driven into an ambush. A result of his father's own hubris and greed. The Monte Carlo was still idling, and running was an option, if fleeting. Assuming he made it into the front street without getting riddled with gunfire, Glenn doubted he'd make it very far. Maybe there was still a chance to parlay. It was a long shot, the Hail Mary of last hopes, but it was all he could see.

He tossed the rifle out of the open door and yelled, "Don't shoot. Please don't shoot."

The act surprised Sherman and Gournsey. Neither could remember the last time the Taliban or ISIS surrendered. Years? Maybe more. Sherman slung the rifle, grabbed the Glock, and jogged towards the car. Gournsey didn't take his sights off the backseat.

"Hands out," shouted Sherman.

Glenn complied and shoved them out into the open like a swimmer desperately coming up for air.

"Slowly, slide out."

Again, Glenn did as instructed and wiggled his way out of the coupe. He instinctively kept his hands in the air and looked over at the commanding voice. A sudden understanding dropped his jaw and curled his lip. Their mistake was profound. There were two men, not one.

"Not who you expected?" asked Sherman, reading the confusion on Glenn's face.

"No... not exactly."

"He's behind you."

Glenn slowly turned his head and saw Gournsey's bearded face squinting back. "This wasn't my idea," he began.

"It never is," replied Sherman.

"I mean, I didn't know, uh... I wouldn't have done anything."

"That gun just for show?" Gournsey asked.

"No, but I would, uh," Glenn continued, searching for a viable excuse or justification for his actions. The only words that felt right were an apology. "I'm sorry."

"Contrition is a good start," added Gournsey.

"What's your name?" Sherman asked.

"Glenn Dooley, sir."

"You a good man, Glenn?"

"No, sir. I reckon I've been less than good."

Gournsey laughed at the honesty. "There ain't one among us, but what does your future hold?"

Glenn swallowed down the bile creeping up his throat. "I suppose that is up to you."

"Where are you from?"

"One county over," answered Glenn, pointing west.

Sherman glanced across the gloom. Thick blotches of pine trees hugged the mountainside and rocks. "How far?"

It took Glenn a minute to work out the distance. No one had ever asked him before. "About thirty miles."

Gournsey and Sherman exchanged a brief look. The

sergeant shrugged in agreement. The kid seemed alright to him.

"Start walking," Sherman instructed.

Glenn pivoted from one man to the other, trying to figure out if they were serious, or if he would catch a bullet in the back. He reasoned there was no other choice. Hesitantly, he took a few steps.

"Wait," yelled Sherman.

Glenn's heart almost stopped, but he forced himself to turn around.

"Who got you into this mess?"

"Carl," he muttered.

"Louder."

"Carl," he shouted.

Sherman nodded at the confirmation.

"Talbot's in the freezer," Glenn blurted out. He wasn't sure why, but it seemed like the right thing to do. A little more good karma couldn't hurt his situation.

"Where?"

"Old appliance repair shop on the road east. It belongs to a friend of Carl's named Shaun."

The dead man, thought Sherman. "Keep walking, kid."

Glenn didn't turn around again that night, but he could see the faint flicker of a fire reflecting off the trees he passed. The Monte Carlo, he assumed. Maybe his brother and father too. Not that it mattered. Dead was dead, Floyd had taught him that much.

Chapter Thirty

The waiting game continued well past sunset and the end of Carl's shift. It spanned dusk and into darkness. No calls came. No news arrived. Nothing but the ever-present chirping of crickets. With only the cooling night air for company, Carl held vigil. Seven o'clock rolled by like a distant freight train. Eight o'clock followed with more urgency as if the engineer was really laying onto the horn.

All those worst-case scenarios danced in the bushes and whispered in the wind. The police cruiser felt suddenly, and incredibly, small. Carl opened the door and stood up to stretch and escape his growing claustrophobia. The wheels of worry were spinning loosely in his imagination.

Fifteen more minutes, he thought, looking at his watch, but no more. Back in high school, if the teacher was that late to class, everyone got a free period. His next step had less joy than smoking cigarettes behind the gym, but Carl needed to do something.

He checked the phone one last time in a vain hope for

some communication from Floyd Dooley. Nothing but the time popped up on the over-lit screen.

"Damn," muttered Carl as he closed the sedan door.

Across the street was the Bed and Breakfast. The gentle width of asphalt suddenly stretched and took on the endlessness of a drive through Kansas. All the consequences of crossing that road tumbled through his mind like coins from a slot machine. Each outcome was shiny and new and almost always fatal.

Night settled down across the valley while Carl reconsidered his choice. It did not take long to reach the same conclusion. Limited choices and all. It was the only play left if he wanted to find Ruby and Mr. Sherman. Shaun died trying and every synapse of reason suggested the Dooleys met the same fate. Betsy was the logical choice. He thought of the scary woman named Karen Bayless. She'd been in town less than an hour before knocking on the front door. He knew the old woman had information. It was the only info, which made it the only choice.

The front light snapped on. A timer, he assumed. Weathered porch steps squeaked under his weight as Carl reached out to push the doorbell button. The sound echoed around the house and footsteps rattled the glass in the front door before it opened.

Betsy looked out at Carl through a narrow opening between door and jamb. "What can I do for you, Carl? It's getting late."

"Later than you know," he answered without considering his words.

Betsy looked back quizzically.

"Never mind," he muttered. "Sorry to bother you again, but we've reason to believe Audrey hurt someone else."

"Oh, no," replied Betsy, mustering oodles of mock surprise. "Who got hurt?"

"Uh, uh," shuttered Carl. He hadn't thought very far into his story. The truth, that her friend had almost surely murdered his kind, was unsayable. "One of the neighboring Sheriff's deputies," he finally lied.

"Dear me. Are they okay?"

The lies came quicker and easier. "Not sure yet, he's in critical condition. They shot him up pretty good."

"They?"

"Audrey and your guest, Mr. Sherman."

Betsy was not in a giving mood. Nor was she completely sober. She swung open the door in a grand gesture. "Former guest," she corrected.

Carl looked at the barren wall with no keys dangling from their hooks and the No Vacancy sign hanging in the window. His eyes narrowed with frustration and anger.

"Where are they?" he demanded.

"Who?"

"Damnit, Betsy, you know who."

"I told you everything I know."

"I don't think you have," replied Carl. His voice was dangerously quiet. A low growl of sorts.

"That makes two."

"What does that mean?"

"Where's Aaron? Where is your boss?"

With the tables suddenly turned, Carl took a step back. It was small, but Betsy noticed. Her words had put him on the back foot.

"Dead," answered Carl, regaining his composure.

Even though Betsy already knew that fact, it still stung to hear it from someone else. There was a particular finality in the way Carl said the word… as if her nephew was just another statistic in a large data set.

"Oh, no. Has anyone told his wife?"

The question hit Carl hard and fast. Only his own consequences had mattered. Never did he consider the aftermath for everyone else. Talbot's death was an opportunity for exploitation, but Carl did not want to hurt his family. They were good people and deserved to know. Unfortunately, the truth was too dangerous. It left him exposed.

"I'm on my way over after this," he lied.

"I should call her now."

"No!" he yelped. He was not ready to reveal the truth. There was planning and staging yet to do.

"Why not?"

"It's my responsibility," he answered solemnly.

"To tell her? Or his death?" Betsy couldn't help herself. The words sort of tumbled out, loosened by whiskey and a growing self-righteous anger.

As far as anyone knew, Talbot left with Ruby and a stranger from out of town. Torres was the last person to see him alive. Any suspicion fell far from Carl's shoulders. He was making sure of that. Keeping up the act. Yet, there was Betsy accusing him of misdeeds.

His voice hardened. "What do you mean by that?"

"I think you know exactly what I mean."

"I'm only gonna ask you one more time. Where are they?"

Betsy stood tall with her back erect and fire in her eyes. "You are a pitiful excuse for a man. You haven't got a shred of loyalty in that yellowbelly of a body. Bill would have whipped your hide for talking like that. Get the hell off my porch!"

Carl leaned in closer. "Bill ain't here. Hell, I don't think anyone else is here."

Grabbing the door with both hands, Betsy heaved it closed but Carl stuck his boot forward. The heavy wooden panel thudded against the reinforced leather toe box. Whatever reservations he carried, moral and practical, melted away in the harsh fluorescent porch light. With a burst of his shoulder, Carl returned the gesture and slammed the door into Betsy. Her lip cracked from the force and she stumbled back into the house, bloody and shaken. Carl stalked forward, closing the door behind him.

"You should have told me. It didn't have to come to this."

Betsy retreated towards the kitchen and the drawer full of knives. Adrenaline coursed through her body, but Carl was bigger and younger. He caught her wrist and twisted hard. There was a dry pop like an acorn smashed on concrete, and pain surged up Betsy's arms. She tried to scream, but all the air had drained from her lungs.

Carl grabbed the diminutive woman around the throat and pinned her against the wall. A numbness blanketed his thoughts, and he applied more pressure on her wrinkly neck.

"Where are they?" he yelled.

Panic welled up in Betsy's eyes as she fought for breath. The end was coming, she could feel it.

"Where?" repeated Carl with spit flying.

Betsy raised her hand and pointed out the window. Carl turned towards her outstretched arm and loosened his grip, only to have his anger flared when he saw what finger she was using. He went to tighten his grip on her soft flesh when Betsy brought her knee up hard and fast. It connected with his crotch and Carl bent forward in retching agony.

The extra foot of space gave Betsy an opening, and she lunged towards the kitchen. She got two steps before Carl regained his balance and clipped her ankle. Falling with two good arms and youth hurts. Hitting the ground with one broken wrist and sixty-plus years of wear and tear constituted something entirely different. Betsy did her best, but her good shoulder took the brunt and sent waves of pain across her chest and back.

Carl stood over her. Little beads of sweat clung to his forehead, and he was breathing hard. "Where are they?"

"I don't know," Betsy gasped. "They left hours ago."

"Are they coming back?"

"No," she whimpered. "They're headed north. You'll never find them."

"I don't believe a God damn word you just said. The keys are still missing Betsy, the fucking keys. They're coming back here. Maybe we'll just stay up and wait for them."

Betsy didn't reply. There was nothing to say or do. She just looked up at the ceiling and drifted off into the memories of her life with Bill. The warmth of his smile and his firm hands holding her own. Then a sudden, sinking irony gripped her, and she wondered how many times her beloved husband had wielded comparable violence. How many people suffered from those hard hands? How many people did he kill? Did they feel the same unbearable fear and desperation? The questions were almost worse than the pain in her shattered wrist.

An intrusive squawk came from the radio still attached to Carl's uniform. "Carl, it's Torres. We have a problem."

He took out his service pistol and pointed it at Betsy, then put a single finger over his lips. Slowly, he reached across and pressed the talk button.

"What is it?"

Betsy held her tongue out of some misguided hope for a better ending.

"There is a car on fire out east on the unpaved county road past the Mitchel place."

"Call the fire department."

"They're already there."

"So, why are you talking to me?"

"It's filled with bodies."

Carl's head dropped and hung there. "What kind of car?"

"They couldn't tell the make or model, but something red. We need your help."

The Dooleys were dead. Torres confirmed it.

"I'm busy."

"We all are," Torres snarled. There was an edge in her voice that made Carl reconsider his response. Her suspicion would only grow if he didn't show up.

"Fine, I'm on my way."

Carl stood looking at Betsy's contorted body on the floor.

"It looks like our conversation has taken its course."

Betsy still said nothing. Words held no weight when the scales of power were so imbalanced. Logic or reason or compliments could not change that. She watched his silhouette take another step forward and raise up the pistol.

Chapter Thirty-One

For Terrance Knight, the hour was late, but the night still reverberated with youthful exuberance. Drinks flowed and smoke billowed out of oak-paneled rooms. Dozens of men mingled and chatted and drank. Almost all were at the top echelons of government or industry. Knight circled like a shark in an ocean full of chum. He bared his whitened teeth with a hollow smile and shook copious amounts of hands.

Only after the olive in his third martini found itself high and dry did the senator step out onto the balcony. Two junior staffers occupied the space, each was desperately trying to impress the other with tales of access and power. Knight glared with polished indifference and the men stumbled inside to resume stroking their egos.

The first call he made was brief. It comprised few words but overflowed with intent. When done, Terrance took a moment to enjoy the well-lit spectacle of the Capitol Building, not so far away. He loved the view, but even more, he loved his proximity to the power that lived inside its walls. Money and power, those twin elixirs, were alluring beyond words. The district never got old, it only got greedier.

The second call reached James Abney mid-sip of an over-priced glass of Bordeaux. An extravagant expense, but he was celebrating the coming conclusion to a god-awful mess.

"Sir," he answered. "Good evening."

"Cut the formalities and tell me a story. By my watch, you only have nine hours left."

Abney glanced at his watch out of habit. He knew exactly how much time was left on the proverbial clock. "Our esteemed colleague has a reservation tonight. Things will be tidy by morning."

"I expect to hear good news over my coffee."

"Without a doubt," replied Abney with the certainty of too many drinks.

———

No one spoke on the drive back to Stalworth. For Sherman and Gournsey, it was not the quiet after the storm. Quite the opposite. Return trips were often fraught with more danger. Any decent climber knows the descent can be more precarious than the ascent. Accidents happen when people let their guard down, assuming the danger has passed. The soldiers said nothing because they had no attention to spare for idle conversation.

Ruby said nothing for other reasons. She could not shake the image of those bodies burning or the violence leading up to the fire. The crackle and hiss of metal and bone turning to ash continuously played in her mind like a morbid white noise machine. After hearing the shots, she glanced in the mirror. There was no helping the father, but she could have saved the son. At least, that was her clinical opinion from the floor of the truck through a mirror. Relapsing back to that state of mind calmed her nerves. Despite all the drama and the stakes involved, being a doctor had caused less stress than her current lifestyle. A life spent running was no life at all. Not only was she causing harm to others, but she was also refusing to help those in need. Two strikes against her Hippocratic oath.

A question kept sticking in her throat until it finally jumped out. "Why did you let him walk away?"

"Should we have burned him too?" asked Gournsey.

"Call it professional curiosity, I suppose."

"The boy didn't need killing."

"I'm against all harm, including any he might cause against us in the future."

"He ain't got no fight left."

Ruby wanted to know why or how the sergeant could claim such knowledge, but she stayed silent. From the look on his face, it was clear that two bodies were more than either man wanted. Despite their propensity for solving problems with violence, neither cared for the aftertaste.

As they neared the Bed and Breakfast, Gournsey slowed to turn into the alley running behind the house. Sherman opened the door for Ruby and they slipped out into the relative darkness. The warmth of day ebbed away, and a cool layer of air clung to the ground like a tick on a dog. They paused in silence for the truck to disappear around the block.

She waited for Sherman to take the first step, but he did not move. A little voice buried under all our evolution was yelling. He never understood what triggered the warning, but he always listened. Call it intuition or gut or whatever, the word mattered not. Only the feeling was important.

"Stay behind me," he instructed.

"Is something wrong?"

"Too early to say no."

"What?" she asked, but Sherman was already creeping into the backyard.

She watched him with a strange sense of admiration and fear like someone watching a leopard stalk through the forest in a nature documentary. It was both thrilling and frightening. Sherman moved with such ease and self-assuredness that Ruby would have testified the man could see in the dark—medical impossibilities aside.

A faint light shone through the back door as Sherman slid inside. It came from a low-wattage ceiling bulb in the kitchen. By the time she got inside, he was kneeling over something while Gournsey looked on from the hallway. It took Ruby's brain less than three seconds to recognize the object on the floor and switch into clinical mode.

She rushed to Betsy's limp form sprawled out on the floor. Her initial glance did not inspire much hope. The old lady was a mess.

To her immense relief, Ruby found a tepid pulse and shallow breathing. Betsy was alive, but that was it. Taking a visual diagnostic, Ruby saw at least three major traumas. All serious. All worse when combined.

A deep laceration above the left temple was still bleeding. Judging by the depth of the cut, and the bruising already forming, Ruby knew that Betsy got slammed. Maybe a thin pipe or the butt of a pistol. It looked bad, much worse than the cracked lip. Blood covered her face like the wide strokes of a paintbrush.

Massive swelling and discoloration around Betsy's wrist pointed to trauma number two. Everything Ruby saw suggested a spiral fracture. The kind you get by twisting the arm hard. Usually associated with those twin evils of domestic and child abuse. Someone had beat her badly. Someone willing to hurt a nice, retired woman for no apparent reason. No money was missing from the register and the fancy TV was still on the wall.

Then there was Betsy's shoulder injury. Ruby knew a dislocation when she saw one. Not a big deal for someone young, but it was a serious issue for the over-sixty crowd.

She looked up at Sherman. His face sagged at corners with sadness and anger, but he kept his emotions tamped down. Years of practice, she reasoned.

"How bad?" he asked.

"She needs to be in a hospital."

"You know that can't happen right now."

Ruby did but seethed against the reminder. "I'll do what I can but she needs help by morning."

Sherman gave a sympathetic nod. "Understood."

"Good. Now find me all the first aid supplies you can."

He didn't budge, and Ruby almost started yelling when Gournsey appeared with two red bags. One large and one small. Only a glance had passed between the two friends. She forgot they saw such carnage all too often.

Using the meager supplies at hand, she stopped the bleeding from the cut on Betsy's head. With enough gauze, she got the wound bandaged and cleaned. Luckily, the woman was still out cold. A concussion or skull fracture was a real risk, maybe even internal bleeding. Ruby ticked off all the potential outcomes. A scar was the best of the bunch. Stroke or death ranked highest on the possibility scale.

She set to work on the arm as Gournsey and Sherman gathered in the front room.

"The door was unlocked," said Gournsey.

"Forced?"

"No."

"Then someone she knew."

"Makes sense."

"Did you see the gash?" asked Sherman.

"I did."

"Look familiar?"

"If by familiar you mean the edge of a pistol magazine, then yes."

"Carl," muttered Sherman a bit dejectedly. "Was he planning on coming back?"

"The door suggests so, unless he didn't think it through."

"It must have gotten heated. That's a lot of injuries stacked on top of each other."

"So, maybe he just forgot on the way out."

"He doesn't strike me as the forgetful type."

Gournsey spitballed some ideas. "Interrupted?"

"Or he didn't have the resolve to pull the trigger."

"Do you want to pay him a visit?"

Sherman looked at Betsy and then back to the front door. "No, I think we have a bigger threat."

"The spook from earlier?"

"I believe so."

"The iron is hot."

"It certainly feels so."

"Tonight?" asked Gournsey.

"When would you show up?"

Gournsey thought about the hypothetical question. The answer was straightforward. Always keep the pressure on your enemy.

"Tonight," he replied.

"Then I have somewhere to be."

The sergeant looked at the door and then at Betsy as if

considering the possibilities for the next few hours. "The second floor is more defensible."

Based on the layout, Sherman agreed with his friend. A single staircase followed by a long hallway was the only way upstairs. Unless they were up against a full-out SWAT incursion, it was the safest spot. Save for a fire, in which case Betsy was in for some more trauma when they tipped her out the window as they never exited through the front door.

"See if you can rig up a stretcher."

Gournsey didn't respond. He just moved off to engineer what they needed.

He returned a few minutes later with a wondrous combination of wooden shovel handles and bed sheets. A simple solution. One as old as conflict. Two pieces of wood and something to hold the body. Most people would have double-checked the construction, but Sherman didn't need to. He trusted Gournsey implicitly and had for years.

Chapter Thirty-Two

A quiet hum filled the lounge as clinking glasses and plates faintly filtered in from the dining area. Karen Bayless sat in one of those oversized leather chairs that seem to swallow the occupant. The lack of utility bothered her more than its relatively uncomfortable nature. Too much space and form for the function. Limited choices forced her hand, and she sat looking awkwardly down at her laptop screen. Efforts to book the first plane out in the morning had failed. She kept searching but a long layover seemed inevitable.

"Fucking Idaho," she mumbled almost inaudibly.

"What was that?" shouted Abney with slurred consonants as he emerged from the bar.

Bayless could smell the liquor sloshing around his guts.

"Nothing," she replied tersely and closed the laptop.

Abney tilted his head and tried to decide if he would sleep with her if he kept drinking. He found the very thought amusing and almost revolting. The kind of decision one regrets only after sunrise reveals the blunder's true scope.

"Shouldn't you be preparing? I just got a call from the top. We must clean this mess up by morning. Spotlessly clean."

Why those in power used such generic, colorless language eluded Bayless. Clinical and precise, that encapsulated her thought process and vocabulary. The people writing checks described nothing of substance. Only euphemisms existed in their world. Clean words for messy actions. She preferred the straight-up, no milk or sugar versions. No 'mess to clean up', only a house to burn and guests to shoot. Every other descriptor was superfluous.

Bayless stood to leave. "I hope our paths don't cross again."

"Oh," mocked Abney. "And what happens if they do?"

"I'll cut your balls off and put them in a blender. Preferably you'll survive long enough to see it."

He smiled wide and thin, and his eyes seemed to sparkle. "That's the first sexy thing you've said."

Disgusted and annoyed, Bayless turned and headed up to her room. Abney may have been a twit, but he was right about one thing. She needed to prep.

Out came a large suitcase, the kind that didn't go through airport security or customs. It arrived in her possession through a series of dead-drops and third parties. Built from a standardized list, and aside from the pistol, someone could purchase most of it without raising local suspicion.

On top were her clothes. Plain items with no designer labels or loud colors. Bayless pulled out a pair of black yoga pants and a dark blue long-sleeve pullover. When paired with black trainers, the ensemble looked like someone out for a nighttime run. She looked like any woman might after going to the gym or some exercise class.

Below the clothing and assorted personal items was

another compartment. She felt around the inside for the small latch that opened it up. With a tiny click, the bottom pulled up and revealed what would surely lead to her incarceration if sent through a TSA screening.

A Sig Sauer P229 pistol chambered for 9mm ammunition and suppressor lay in the center with two extra magazines. Bayless preferred the Germans or Austrians over the Italians or even Americans. In her opinion, they just made better guns. Function over form was what she liked in a weapon.

In the leftmost section was a series of edged instruments ranging from knives to scalpels. Then came a Taser and two pre-filled syringes. One contained a sedative capable of knocking out a three-hundred-pound man. The other had a cocktail of drugs that would stop the heart of an elephant. She'd used both to good effect, although Bayless was not one for poison. Too indirect. Too impersonal. She liked the knives best. They were simple, no-nonsense, and effective, just like her.

Under all the weapons and tools of her cruel trade was a thin coil of gold chain. Bayless picked it up and twisted it around her pointer finger. First one way and then the other. A ritual of sorts. The chain belonged to her mother. It was the only thing she had left. Her only remaining connection with the past.

Bayless never knew her mother, who died from cancer when she was only two years old. Not the kind with a sudden diagnosis and death three months later. No. It was slow and agonizing.

Sometimes she thought about the fear and sadness her mother must have endured during those grueling chemotherapy sessions. Sitting there alone, always alone, knowing she would not see her daughter grow up. Hoping for a wonderful future without her.

Bayless let the thought wash over her once or twice and then retreated behind her wall of silence. She did not dare stay too long, lest she fall into the abyss of genuine emotion.

Growing up, her father never mentioned her mother. Not once did he explain what happened or how she died. No bedtime stories about how they met. Not even a picture on the mantel. Bayless only learned the truth from her grandma when she was ten. By then, it seemed almost impossible she ever had a mother. An entire life erased as if it had never happened.

If she missed out on maternal love, the paternal side provided nothing of substance. An uncaring man, Bayless fought for scraps of recognition from her father. Straight As on a report card barely elicited a raised eyebrow. Gold medals at track competitions went unnoticed. So did high SAT scores and college acceptance letters. Only when she took an interest in the family business did her father finally give her the time of day.

The deeper down she went into the muck of her father's business, the more her value became tied up with violence. The first time Bayless heard the words 'I'm proud of you' come out of her dad's mouth was after she murdered the two Cubans in the movie theater. The words felt like manna from heaven, and she yearned for more. She chased those good feelings down a long dark hole, all the way into a CIA training program.

The gold chain softly clinked as she set it down and took a deep, focusing breath. Her plan was good but walking through it was an important part of the process. It focused her mind to the task at hand.

She started at the beginning, which was Mather Hotel.

Driving over to the Bed and Breakfast made sense over walking. No one walked around at night unless they were stealing something. That and she needed a speedy exit. Bayless placed the car keys on the bed. The first item in a pile of gear she made for each mission.

On her reconnaissance earlier in the day, she noticed a fancy gas stove in Betsy's kitchen. Big and stainless and expensive. A chef's stove. For the plan to work, she needed to cut the gas hose connecting to the appliance. A four-inch matte black knife went next to the keys. The blade could cut through most things from ligaments to hoses of all types.

Some lock-picking tools followed in order to get through the back door. Although Bayless hadn't seen one in person, images from the website provided all the needed info. It was an old door. Not original, but close enough to have an unsophisticated lock. It amazed her what intelligence she could get without ever setting foot in a building. Websites, Google reviews, and real estate photos were a treasure trove of information.

Next came a curious-looking black cube. It was small and only two inches on any side. A dial on top labeled with Cyrillic letters hinted at its Russian origins. Bayless bought them by the crate. Each box contained a timer, lighter fluid, nozzles, and an electric sparker. Operation was a snap. Turn the dial, walk away, and soon enough, three-inch flames would shout out from the sides. Pair that with a propane-filled room and there was no need for fancy plastic explosives. The best part, in her opinion, was the little contraption melted away in the explosion and fire. It left no trace of an ignition source. The FSB, ironically or not, called it a *topka*. Russian for firebox.

Finally, as if a cherry on top of the sundae, out came the Sig Sauer pistol. She checked through all the important parts like a mother checking on her child after a nasty fall. Each piece received loving care and inspection. Bayless loaded in a magazine and pulled back the slide with a satisfying click. She loved that sound. It gave her an empowered, everything will be fine, type of feeling.

The yoga pants hid nothing, so she loaded everything into a slim messenger bag. It was black and looked expensive. She had learned over the years that people ignore oddities if they appear nicer than average. Something to do with envy overriding suspicion.

Bayless went through everything one more time with staccato precision.

Drive to B&B – keys, check.
Enter back door – lock-pick, check.
Cut gas line – knife, check.
Start fire – *Topka*, check.
Shoot everyone that leaves – P229, check.
Drive back – keys, double check.

She zipped the bag closed and swung it over her shoulder. An oversized mirror edged with heavy dark wood caught her reflection. A sudden sense of age leered back at her like a newly discovered freckle. The face staring back looked older than she felt and worn on the edges. The crow's feet around her eyes had grown longer and deeper. Bayless lingered until she grew self-conscious and uncomfortable with her moment of shallow reflection. Looks didn't matter, she reminded herself—only action.

No epiphany barged into her consciousness. Nothing like self-doubt or regret crept into her thoughts. She rounded that corner of no return at nineteen years old and never looked back. Shadows were haunting, so Bayless focused on the future. The next mission. Sometimes the next few minutes.

With a robust shake of her head to tamp down any wriggling emotions, she grabbed the keycard off the ornate oak desk and stepped up to the door. Standing on her toes, Bayless craned her neck one way and then the other, looking through the peephole. She always checked the hall before leaving the room. Paranoia was second nature in her line of work. Seeing nothing but fading red carpet and outdoorsy paintings hanging from the walls, she opened the door. Then her breath caught between her nose and lungs.

A man stood on the other side, staring back at her. He was bearded and lean and hard, with eyes like a cat. Fear danced across her face as panic flooded her brain like a tropical storm.

Chapter Thirty-Three

For twenty minutes, Sherman had slunk through shadows and edged down alleys. An apparition of trash cans and power poles. Getting to Mather Hotel was easy. Arriving unseen was not.

In the recesses of broken shadows near the back entrance, he waited until some staff member came out for a smoke break. It was all but guaranteed to happen. The five-gallon bucket of sand had more butts than his grandmother's ashtray, and she smoked two packs a day during his childhood. Even the bushes reeked of cheap tobacco. Only a matter of time, he reasoned, before someone indulged their addiction.

It took less than five minutes. A testament to the power of cravings. Sherman never understood that vice, but he was no stranger to the human condition. Several psychologists and two ex-girlfriends claimed he was addicted to adrenaline. They were not wrong, but he knew there was more nuance to the problem. Excitement alone was not his vice.

A pale-faced whippet of a man emerged into the soft yellow glow. He took a metal folding chair from inside and propped open the door. A prevention against the self-locking mechanism and his manager's ire for taking too long a break. Sherman watched him from the shadows, inhaling and coughing, then repeating the process.

Lost in thought and the comforting hiss of nicotine, the guy didn't notice Sherman slip out of the darkness and through the open door. He took the first stairwell available and headed up to the second floor. A professional would not stay on the ground floor. Too many ways in and not enough out. Too much risk. Jumping one story was workable if the need arose.

He knew from the bartender that only a handful of guests were staying at the hotel. Gazing down the heavily lacquered hallway, with its maroon carpets and brass fixtures, only two rooms appeared occupied. The hour was late for most people, but still early for what the woman had planned.

Sherman padded softly down the reddish hues towards the first room with light spilling under the door. He came to a stop several feet short and hugged the wall, listening for sounds. A conversation seeped out, all flat and tinny. It went on for several seconds before changing to a man selling Dodge trucks out on Interstate 84. He moved on.

A late-night TV binge didn't resonate with Sherman. It was a distraction, something to drift away from reality. It did not bring focus to the task at hand. The woman was a professional, not some third-rate shooter from Spokane.

The second room was smack in the middle of the hotel, equidistant from each exit. Again, Sherman stood quietly a few feet from the door and listened. At first, he heard nothing. Then came the muffled footsteps of someone crossing the room and maybe the delicate thump of a suitcase landing on the bed. He wasn't sure on the second sound until a zipper confirmed what his mind already knew.

Someone on the other side was packing or unpacking. Not unreasonable if they had an early flight out or a long drive back to Boise. A hole of doubt widened in Sherman's mind. Had he picked the wrong target? Should he be standing at Carl's door instead?

All that uncertainty ceased a moment later with a single solitary sound. Even through the closed door, he recognized it without any doubt. The well-oiled metallic clack of a pistol slide being pulled back and released. Locked and loaded. He had the correct room, after all.

Flattening himself against the wall, Sherman inched forward until he was within reach of the door handle. The door was thick and solid and ornately carved from some species of wood he could only guess. Shadows danced in the narrow space underneath. Someone was moving around the room. Back and forth they went for several minutes as he waited and watched. Finally, the feet came closer and stopped. The peephole darkened for a moment as the occupant checked the hallway. Sherman was decently sure they could not see him but figured he would find out momentarily. When the handle turned, he stepped forward, steading himself to give the door a hefty kick if needed.

When the heavy thing opened, it left him staring at the woman from earlier at the Bed and Breakfast. Cynthia or whatever name she came up with for that briefest of interactions. She wore dark clothes and carried a bag slung across her back. On the way out, no doubt. She caught his eye and panic crept into her bland, expressionless face.

Karen Bayless did what anyone would do when confronted with a stranger unexpectedly on the other side of her door. She tried to close it fast and with as much force as her arm could muster. It was exactly the move Sherman predicted. Flight was human nature at its simplest.

He swung his right foot forward and landed the bottom of his boot a few inches from the door handle. With all 180 pounds of force behind it, the door slammed back into Bayless with a resounding crack. Her right shoulder took the brunt and a merciless snap of agony raced through her arm. Between the pain and the sheer momentum of the door, she staggered back several steps.

Seeing an opportunity, Sherman moved inside and closed the door. No pistol was in sight, and he favored the odds in an up-close and personal fight. Eight inches of height and a good fifty pounds of mass gave him a distinct starting advantage.

It took Bayless a few seconds to recover from the initial shock. Her shoulder ached and throbbed, but she could move it around. Not broken and not great, but she was still in the fight.

They stood there in the golden light cast from a fixture predating the First World War. Neither one of them moved like two predators frozen from a sudden encounter in the jungle, sizing each other up. Sherman was in no hurry to break the deadlock. He knew the door struck hard enough to cause soft-tissue damage. The way she favored her left side meant any strikes from the right would be weak and muted.

Besides the physical advantage, Sherman guessed the gun was in the messenger bag slung across her body. Where else could she hide it? Not in her snugly fitting pants or clingy shirt. The bag contained all her gear. Although he left open the possibility there was a blade up her sleeve. She was a professional.

Bayless had killed bigger men. Mean, brutish men with rippling muscles and oversized egos. Men with an over-inflated sense of their own physical superiority. It came down to speed and precision and knowing where to strike. Years of practice produced the first two, and a CIA training course gave her the rest.

It took but one look for Bayless to know, without a wrinkle of uncertainty, that Sherman was not one of those men. The casualness with which he stood. The calloused hands dangling loosely at his sides. The inquiring eyes that seemed to swallow all the details in the room in a single glance. Taken collec-tively, it pointed towards a different type. A dangerous type.

She had lost fights before. Not many, but enough to see the odds slowly stacking against her. The risks were lower back then. When she lost, it was schoolyard stuff and a few bar brawls at a time when she felt slighted by the opinions of others. Most were men, some were big, others mean, with a few women smattered in the mix. The losses were painful, but not consequential. A broken bone or two, but nothing more. Not all or nothing.

"I scream and they come running," she bluffed.

Sherman's gaze held steady. "There's no one else."

"I always work with backup."

"Did you have a backup in Kurdistan?"

The reference to a former job made her squirm a little like she was two chapters behind in history class. "Always."

"Scream then."

She did nothing.

"I thought so."

Bayless palmed the knife hidden below her sleeve and

stalled for time. Time to think. Time to act. "How did you know about me?"

"It was bold of you to show up at the house like that. Little Cynthia out for a weekend away."

"You'd be surprised how often that act works."

"I don't doubt it. You're good."

A picture formed in her mind like a puzzle comes together from the outside in. "Have we met?"

"No, not personally. But you met my friend, the other man in the house."

"Oh, so you have backup?"

Sherman smiled and shrugged.

"Outside of Kirkuk," Bayless continued, digging into her memory. "A bunch of you boys were pretending to help the locals. Trying to wear some mask of generosity while still carrying your rifles."

"He said something similar about you. An aid worker if I remember correctly."

When Bayless smiled, her eyes narrowed and thin lines formed around her mouth. "No one questions a helping hand."

She stepped right, testing Sherman. He stepped left, mirroring the direction and making sure she couldn't reach the door.

"What now?" she asked.

"I imagine your bag has the answer to that question."

"It's just a job. I think you understand that."

Sherman did. "Have you ever quit mid-contract?"

"No. Have you ever disobeyed a direct order and run mid-fight?"

"We call that a tactical retreat."

"The CIA calls that treason."

"You don't strike me as the patriotic type," added Sherman.

"You don't know shit about me," she snarled back.

"Broken home. Criminal background. Recruited, not enlisted. Am I close?"

Her eyes narrowed, and Sherman could tell he'd hit a well-buried nerve. He kept digging. "You started young. Small-time stuff. Not much to brag about or get in trouble over. Probably didn't get noticed much at all. That changed around, say, eighteen? Got your hands wet and liked it. Must have made a splashy impression to get recruited. Accidentally kill a terrorist or something?"

Goaded into action, Bayless pretended to lose her temper. She started pointing at Sherman with her left hand while opening the knife with her right hand out of view. She spewed some obscenities to muddy the waters.

Sherman didn't move. He waited for what was coming next. The move was inevitable. People abhorred inaction. Stillness never made it into our DNA.

Bayless swung quick and low, aiming for the femoral artery on the inside of Sherman's leg. Men meet confrontation eye-to-eye, not down at their waists. They expect a punch to the nose, not a blade to the thigh.

Not Sherman. He watched the arm whip low and fast towards his legs. She played to her relative strengths. It was a smart move, but to him, it was the obvious one. Twisting his torso towards her hand, he caught her wrist with his right knee.

The force of the impact spasmed her hand open, and the knife thumped onto the carpet. Sherman kicked it under the bed as Bayless stepped back to regroup.

"Tactical retreat?" he repeated.

But Bayless had four million reasons to keep going. She

feigned a punch and sliced her leg towards Sherman's knee, hoping for some ligament damage. He raised his leg in time, and they both winced from the equal and opposite reaction of bone and tissue.

Undaunted, she stepped left and sent two quick kicks towards vital areas. Sherman dodged the first one aimed at his groin. The second came fast on the heels of the first and went straight for his neck. It connected with his shoulder and stung like a four-seam fastball from his high school baseball days.

When she twisted again, Sherman stepped in to close the gap. Her knee landed hard on his side between his pelvis and ribs, but his elbow connected with her left collarbone. A sickening pop rippled out from under her skin and Bayless reeled backward in pain.

Her left arm crackled when she moved, and they both knew he broke it. For a bar fight, that would have been the end. Only the ambulance ride to a hospital remained. But they weren't brawling over spilled beer or wounded pride, or testosterone-filled egos. Their fight would only end when someone stopped breathing.

Bayless pulled on a small piece of black plastic that connected to the front of the messenger bag. Out came a small push dagger. Having grown up in the south, she knew it as a gimlet knife on account of the handle's shape. A two-inch blade of last resort and close encounters.

Grimacing against the pain in her left shoulder and the bruise from the door, she lunged at Sherman in one last attempt to connect steel to flesh. It didn't work. He caught her wrist and twisted hard until the arm bent backward at the elbow. Using his body weight, Sherman pushed until the knife plunged into her stomach.

Falling back onto the bed, Bayless looked down in

shocked horror at the damage. Blood streamed out of the wound, growing worse with each successive heartbeat. It soaked through her shirt and onto the flower-patterned comforter she despised.

Sherman knew it was over for the fight and her life. The blood was bright red and well-oxygenated. He'd severed one of the iliac arteries. A trauma center could have done something, but he made no moves to call 911.

In simple terms, the threat no longer existed. Neutralized, as the government liked to say, painting with a bland brush over terrible events. Sherman stopped for a moment and then walked back out of the room. He padded down the hall and stairs until he passed the metal folding chair and the back exit.

The door opened with a sharp scratching sound like a fork dragging across a steel pot, and Sherman eagerly slipped out into the welcoming darkness.

Somewhere across the wooded grounds, he turned and glanced back towards the hotel. A lone light caught his eye. The damp yellow glow from one of those old-style lampposts he'd seen days earlier. But it wasn't just the illumination that stood out. It was the shape standing underneath waiting to be seen. Even from that distance, he could make out the details.

A man in his late fifties stood ramrod straight, unperturbed by the hour or the darkness. His grey hair was closely cropped but well beyond regulation. Strong cheekbones jutted out and his jaw was sharp enough to cut glass. Sherman knew the face all too well.

Chapter Thirty-Four

Gournsey exhaled slowly and asked, "Are you sure it was him?"

Sherman nodded. His eyes were red and tired and longing for sleep.

Ruby could sense the apprehension in the room, but her questions remained unanswered. "Who?"

"Colonel Straeger," repeated Sherman.

"I heard you the first time," she retorted. "Who is he?"

"Retired, or so I heard," added Gournsey.

"I guess we heard wrong."

"Is this bad?" Ruby asked.

"Yes," answered Sherman before closing his eyes and slipping into the abyss of sleep.

She turned to Gournsey and held up her hands in confusion.

"He's a shooter," explained Gournsey as if the word was all that she needed to know.

"Just what we fucking need." She glanced at Sherman's inert form on the bed. "Is that blood on his shirt?"

Gournsey turned and took a quick look. "Yup."

Ruby stepped forward in alarm.

"Not his," Gournsey added, knowing her next move was to check for wounds.

She sighed and rubbed her temples. "I'm going to check on Betsy."

The alarm dinged relentlessly until Abney fumbled enough to tap the snooze. A bourbon haze blurred his eyesight. Sunrise was still an hour away, but only fifteen minutes remained on his promise to Senator Terrance Knight. It took a moment for Abney to focus and switch over to his encrypted messaging app. It took another moment to realize that it was empty. Nothing from Bayless. Nothing from Carl. Nothing. His stomach knotted and bile leaped up as if trying to escape the night of booze and excess.

"That bitch," he muttered while dialing her number. It rang on and on before going to voicemail.

Abney dialed it repeatedly. His panic rose and the number of minutes ticked down. Finally, he slipped on some pants and padded down the hallway to her room. The door was closed and no light slipped out from underneath.

He tried the door. Locked. Not the deadbolt, but the doorknob itself. Straining to hear, Abney pressed his ear against the wooden surface and concentrated what remained of his senses. Nothing stood out. Panic boiled over and he flung himself against the door like a wounded animal. On the third try, it broke open.

After stumbling inside with his shoulder throbbing from being treated like a battering ram, Abney switched on the light. All his hopes tumbled away in the moment it took between the room filling with a pleasant yellow glow and his brain registering the morbid scene. Dread escalated like a rock rolling downhill.

Bayless lay motionless on the bed with skin whiter than a porcelain sink. Blood covered the blankets and sheets and carpet below. Some appeared dried, some less so. A knife lay haphazardly on the floor like a forgotten toy.

Abney dared not move. He ran his hands roughly through his hair, rocking back and forth as if in a trance. Of all the outcomes he had considered, the one before him was the worst. Failure never crossed his mind. Not with all those resources. The FBI agents failed, but that was a fluke. Two easily bent cops never stood a chance. Bayless was different. She was a professional. An agency-trained killer. Not like some hacks living beyond their means on the fancy side of the Potomac.

A voice sounded down the hall and Abney closed the door seconds before someone knocked.

"Everything alright, sir?"

"Fine," yelled Abney.

"Are you quite sure?"

"Quite."

"I see some damage to the door."

Abney cracked it open, just enough to see the manager on the other side. "Add it to my bill."

The man looked at the broken frame and then back to Abney as if considering what level of damage warranted a call to the police.

"We will," he concluded and walked away.

Abney slumped to the floor behind the closed door. His stomach revolted, churning with the extravagance of the previous night combined with the horror he was looking upon. He called the only person left in the town.

The hour was early, and it took a few rings for Carl to answer. "Mr. Abney. What's the urgency of a pre-sunrise call?"

"We have a problem."

"I know, I know. I was going to call you this morning."

"What? How do you know?" asked Abney in confusion.

"Wait," replied Carl, groggy from a night in the woods. "Start over. Why are you calling?"

"Meet me at the hotel. Room 220. Come now."

"Can it wait?"

"No!" screamed Abney and ended the call.

For the next ten minutes, Abney did his best to clean up the mess. He hated every moment. Pungent aromas harassed his senses. Blood stuck to his shoes, and the carpet squished as he crossed back and forth. Her still damp flesh glared back at him as if begging for some unsaid action.

It took a few hesitant efforts to get the messenger bag off. Each time Abney leaned in, he glimpsed those lifeless eyes and had to back off and take a breath. He was no stranger to violence, but inflicting harm was different when he didn't have to deal with the aftermath. People on the payroll cleaned up the mess, he created it.

A soft knock on the door announced Carl's arrival. The deputy was inspecting the broken frame when Abney opened the door.

"About time, Officer."

Carl leaned his head to the side and gazed past Abney's blood-stained frame.

"What on God's holy earth happened here?"

"I told you, we have a problem."

"With all due respect, Mr. Abney. You have a problem."

"Oh, for fuck's sake. I didn't kill her and that's the problem."

Carl looked at the man with his chiseled jaw and fancy haircut. His once invincible shine of power was tarnished and cracked. Doubts about the horse he'd hitched to crept into Carl's thoughts. "Best to start talking, Mr. Abney."

"She was supposed to deal with them last night. The details were arranged and promises were made."

"But not kept," Carl interjected.

"Yes, what an astute observation, Officer. Our mutual problem, this Mr. Sherman, got to her first."

"Not just her," added Carl.

Abney narrowed his gaze and focused on the officer's eyes. "What do you mean by that?"

"Well, not to heap shit upon your sty, but I got a call last night. A noisy neighbor up in the mountains called in some disturbance up on Sill Creek Road. You know where that is?"

Abney shrugged his shoulders but Carl didn't wait for the answer before plowing onward.

"Anyway, no reason you should. Like I was saying, a neighbor up there called in a fire. Nothing big, but something off the road caught his eye. A car, he said. A red one. Now, by the time we got there, not much remained. Mostly ash and charred metal. But we found enough. It belonged to the boys following Mr. Sherman. They called me this evening, telling me they were on his trail, aiming to end this problem you speak of. All we found were their teeth and a few burnt bones."

"Are you playing me, Mr. Ortman? Do you take me for a fool?"

"No, sir. I am not, nor do not."

"Then you expect me to believe that one man killed your men in the mountains during dinner and then murdered our under-skilled colleague in the middle of the night?"

Carl flashed back to the image of Sherman standing comfortably in front of two armed men. He appeared so calm, like he was talking with a neighbor across the street about an upcoming football game. Even in handcuffs, he didn't seem perturbed. Momentarily inconvenienced, but nothing more.

"I imagine that is exactly what happened."

"And what do you plan on doing?"

The question had already occurred to Carl during the night he spent sleeping in his cruiser parked off some unmarked dirt road. A precaution against the problem plaguing them. He played through all those scenarios once more, but with an updated data set. Three more dead and his cover blown. Betsy had said as much before he smashed her face with the butt of his pistol. Even if she died, Carl saw no realistic path to the chief's chair. He had dreams but was not an unrealistic person. Run when the cattle's fat, his father used to say. Carl took that to mean don't wait until there's only skin and bone left.

"To be completely honest, Mr. Abney, my money is on running. Somewhere far from here."

"Running?" he scoffed. "It's too late for running."

"It's never too late."

"I will not end up like her."

"Like Ruby?" asked Carl.

Abney shook his head at the thought. "She killed my best friend. Did you know that? Spiked her husband's drink with fentanyl."

"And then ran?"

"And then ran like a rat from a sinking ship."

"An alive rat."

Abney curled his thumb over his knuckles and squeezed until they popped like a string of fireworks. The force helped him think. "You're going to kill them."

"Me?"

"Yes, Carl, you."

"I'm leaving town."

"I'll give you the same amount as Bayless."

Carl chuckled. East Coast people and their emphasis on money. "How much?"

"One million," Abney lied, figuring he could pocket the extra three.

"You'd pay that much for two people?"

"My employer is a man of iron will and deep pockets."

Carl rubbed his chin and thought about such an absurd amount of cash. His mistake with Betsy had left him exposed enough to run. Shooting two more people and retiring to a beach in South America was not that far a stretch.

"Fine. One and a quarter."

It was Abney's turn to be amazed at such Western ignorance. Haggling over such a tiddly sum. "Deal. Get it done this morning."

"This morning?"

"Yes, this morning or keep driving out of town."

Carl nodded. "Understood."

"Good. Now, what are you going to do about the body?"

"Nothing. You called the cops, I showed up. Now the department will be gunning for our problem too."

"Sounds risky."

"Any worse than trying to clean this slaughterhouse up?"

"Point taken," replied Abney.

297

"Good, I'll make the call. Did you grab everything of interest?"

"Yes, I'll move it to my room."

Carl took out his phone and dialed Torres. Unlike him, she answered right away despite the hour.

"What is it, Carl?"

"We've got another body."

"Shit. Where?"

"Mather Hotel. Room 220."

"Okay, I'll be there in fifteen."

He hung up and looked at Abney. "You better make yourself scarce or the blame may fall in your direction."

"You better make sure it doesn't."

Back in his room, Abney swirled a glass of twenty-year-old scotch and mulled over his choices. They were grim. His entire reputation rested on getting results. This debacle would not fare well in the Capitol. Questions would arise that he could not answer. Explaining away failure entailed twisting the truth. He was good at spinning words into facts. Turning six or seven bodies—the exact number eluded him —into a success felt beyond his abilities.

He got out a notepad from the desk drawer and started writing ideas. He knew sooner rather than later, his phone would ring. Senator Knight would demand answers and he would only have knotted threads of events in response.

Sirens trilled in the distance. The wail grew louder and shriller in the morning silence, then it stopped. Abney stripped off his blood-stained clothes and placed them in a burn bag. He lit a match, tossed it in, and turned on the shower. The antique brass clock on the wall read two minutes past six in the morning. He was already late.

Chapter Thirty-Five

Long, thin shadows fell across the Potomac River, hinting at autumn. Terrance Knight breathed in the cool air on his morning jog. A habit he'd started as a freshman senator thirty years earlier. Two members of the Capitol Police trailed inconspicuously behind, blending in with the other runners. A perk of being head of the Senate Select Committee on Intelligence.

Knight glimpsed his watch. Time was up on Abney's promise. The boy had never failed to deliver, but firsts were rarely pleasant in politics. Doing nothing would be seen as a weakness by those involved in Knight's side business. The one he paid Abney handsomely to keep out of the public eye. Maybe a demotion was in order or some friendly competition for his pocketbook. Anything to tarnish the stellar reputation Abney maintained.

The cell phone in his windbreaker pocket vibrated. Knight stopped to look at the number and waved the two guards away. He recognized the number and wanted to keep the forthcoming conversation private.

"Yes."

"Good morning, sir," began the familiar voice. "I believe we have an issue of great importance."

"I'm listening."

"A friend across the river reported they discovered a certain file during a routine scan of FTP sites."

Knight's polished poker face cracked at the edges and his upper lip quivered ever so slightly.

"Does anyone else know?"

"Our friend marked it as non-essential and moved on but did his due diligence on the sender and recipient."

"Do we have a location?"

"An IP Address and an email from the original source. The recipient covered their tracks."

"Do you know if they opened it?"

"No."

"Send me the details by messenger."

"Of course, sir."

"Outstanding work. Tell our friend he'll get an extra bonus this time around."

"Understood."

Rage simmered behind Knight's placid exterior, and he could feel his heart pounding in his chest. A nightmare years in the making had materialized, and for the first time, he did not know what to do.

Concerned by the sudden stillness, one cop walked over and spoke up, "Senator?"

The sound of the woman's voice snapped Knight back into the moment. "Sorry," he answered. "Lost in thought."

"Everything okay?"

"It will be. Can you give me another moment of privacy? I need to make a few more calls."

"Sure thing. We'll be ready when you are."

The senator took out a piece of paper no bigger than a fortune cookie and dialed a number written in small, clean script.

A voice, gruff and hard at the edges, answered. "What is it?"

"I'd like to discuss a change," replied Knight.

———

The bottle of scotch sitting on the oak nightstand was two fingers short of empty. James Abney had already drunk a hand worth and showed no signs of slowing. The call was coming. He knew it was only a matter of time, and despite the booze and the brainstorming, no answer emerged. Helplessness tightened its weighty grasp around his chest, driving him to drink larger swigs from the $200 bottle. The notes written on hotel stationary lay crumpled in the wastebasket. The handwriting grew more slanted and hurried with each successive paper.

Failure stung his shallow ego worse than any wasp or bee. It burned straight through everything like the chunk of white phosphorus he dropped in high school chemistry class. Years had passed as he searched for his best friend's killer. Horace Filby came close only to end up in a county morgue. They buried the FBI agents under enough stone to build a moment to their incompetence. Even Bayless, a woman of unique talent, failed and the string of bodies behind her covered a country mile. The only option left was Officer Carl Ortman. Abney took another sip at the thought of such luck.

"One stupid bitch," he muttered to himself.

A delicate knock sounded on the door. He looked through the peephole at high cheekbones and local police uniform. Lust surged through his drunken body, and he opened the door.

"Sorry to bother you, sir, I'm Officer Torres. Do you have a few minutes to chat?"

Abney was naked under his bathrobe and did not hide that fact. He motioned inside, but Torres didn't move.

"I'll be brief," she seethed.

"Fine," Abney replied dejectedly. He didn't have the mental capacity for stronger advances. "What questions?"

"Did you hear anything strange last night or earlier this morning?"

"Nothing comes to mind."

She pointed to the bottle. "Were you drinking all night?"

"No, but perhaps I should have been."

"Why would you say that?"

"You could have joined me."

Torres didn't flinch, but it only increased Abney's libido.

"Sir, did you burn something in here? I smell smoke."

"I sat around a campfire."

Torres eyed him carefully. "The manager said your reservation is for one more night. Is that true?"

"I suppose it is."

"We'll be in touch," Torres replied tersely.

"I hope so," he growled before slamming the door.

Abney grabbed the bottle and sipped lustily on the brown liquid. Another knock reverberated through the door, soft but assertive. He opened it with no pretense of modesty, letting the bathrobe continue to hang open. A drunken, toothy smile creased his face.

The self-satisfaction melted quicker than butter in a hot pan. Those wonderfully well-defined curves were not on the other side of the door. Instead, it was a man's face staring back. A mid-fifties male with short, cropped grey hair and a harshly sharp jawline. A faint whiff of recognition floated through Abney's liquor-addled brain. He knew the face and the eyes burning right through him, no different than he used to do as a kid with ants and a magnifying glass.

"Who the fuck are…" Abney began.

Colonel Straeger's hand struck just below the Adam's apple and sent Abney spinning to the floor in a fit of coughing. Struggling to breathe, he was only vaguely aware of the door being closed.

"Sit down," Straeger instructed.

Abney did as he was told. His mostly naked body felt unpleasantly exposed and vulnerable with the sudden intrusion. He struggled to shift enough fabric from the bathrobe to cover his crotch.

"Who are you?" Abney rasped.

"Rather an existential question coming from the likes of you, Mr. Abney."

"Okay, so you know who I am, that's fine," Abney chattered nervously. He couldn't help himself. Genuine fear made him ramble. "I'm guessing someone sent you here, of course they did, why else would you be here? And it must have been someone from Washington. I can explain why I haven't called yet, I, uh… I had some local issues and…"

Straeger cut him off. "Christ alive, be quiet already."

Abney sat mutely like a kid waiting in the principal's office for his share of the punishment. He hoped it wouldn't be too severe.

"Senator Knight sent me to help you out."

Confusion filled Abney's eyes. "Why did you hit me?"

"You opened the door with your dick dangling about. A quick punch to the throat was the least you deserved."

Shame made his ears turn red. "Sorry about that."

"Give me an update on your situation here,"

commanded Straeger as he wandered around the cluttered room strewn with bottles and dirty clothes.

Having provided no window into the true scope of his failures, Abney felt cornered by the question. "Like I said, there were problems with the locals."

"You're a clever man, Mr. Abney. Clever men contrive better excuses than that."

Abney's gaze followed Straeger around the room as he rifled through items like someone looking for a bottle opener in a stranger's kitchen.

"We've run into some technical issues."

"Technical issues? I love the words you suits use for the baser acts of human existence."

"Okay, okay. There's a player in town. Someone we couldn't have anticipated."

"Always happens with the best laid plans. What do you know about this person?"

"Last name of Sherman. Ex-army or something like that."

Straeger stopped and looked Abney in the eyes. "Something like that."

"Do you know him?"

"How many else?" asked Straeger, waving off the question.

"What do you mean?"

"Who else tried?"

"A few," Abney whispered.

"Ah, more vaguery. I require specifics."

"Three from our payroll," Abney admitted.

"And the others."

Abney squinted. He didn't know the exact number. "A few more."

Straeger began placing a suit on the bed. "Let me

arrange the facts. One person, supposedly this Sherman character, killed three people on the Senator's payroll and a few more locals."

"Yes."

"Finally, some clarity. I was thinking your reputation might be undeserved."

"What's your plan?"

"Mine? To get you dressed. The Senator will be here in a few hours."

Abney could not hide his surprise. "What?"

"I'd wear something smart. You know how old-fashioned the Senator is with appearances."

"Wait, what are you going to do?"

"Solve your problem," answered Straeger.

"How? The woman down the hall was one of the best we could afford. Go look and tell me how that turned out."

"I already did. Messy scene in there, but a clean cut."

"What?"

"Her wound. It was a clean strike to a vital spot. Severed one or two major arteries."

"You sound impressed."

"Death should never be taken so lightly, Mr. Abney. I'm talking about the skill required to do that. That is something I can appreciate."

Abney felt nauseous and confused.

"You know what doesn't take skill?" continued Straeger. "Drugging a woman with flunitrazepam or, as your prescription states, Rohypnol." He held up a small orange bottle that rattled with a few pills.

"Wh-what?"

"You see, Mr. Abney, I've been here for a few days now. Observing your operation and proclivities. The women you choose so selectively. The way you lure them upstairs with your charm and demands and money. The way they cower from your gaze the next morning, so wounded and confused over what did or did not happen. I imagine you like the power of the unknown. That raw animal sense of taking what is not yours."

Abney looked on, speechless, as Straeger placed a shirt and tie on the suit.

"I have two daughters of my own. Grown, of course, but still, I can remember when they were young and I felt this great compulsion to protect them. That feeling is still with me, although I taught them to fend for themselves. Call it parental instinct, or whatever, but a father never really feels safe when their child is out in the world alone."

"I don't, um, understand Mr.—"

"Straeger."

The name and the face finally connected in Abney's brain and fear flushed his cheeks a beet red. "Colonel, I apologize. I didn't recognize you. Why are we talking about your daughters?"

"We're not. I am."

"But…"

"Listen, Mr. Abney. I know this might come as a surprise to you and the little self-centered bubble you inhabit, but those girls you assaulted had lives and dreams and fathers too."

Indignation got the better of Abney. He turned to face the older man with anger teeming in his eyes, but all he saw were Straeger's hard hands slipping a tie over his neck. The expensive silk dug into his trachea and Abney flailed about in a brief struggle to breathe. It was a useless last expenditure of energy. The colonel's half-frozen smile was the last thing he saw before the world dissolved into blackness.

Straeger released the tie and Abney's corpse fell to the

floor with a soft thud. In the spirit of illusion, he attached one end of the tie to a thick walnut cross beam of the four-post bed. Straeger gave it a pull and, satisfied that it held his weight, tied a loop on the other end. Dragging the body over was the simple part. Lifting him up was harder, but Straeger managed. He slipped Abney's head through the loop and slowly eased his weight onto the tie. Miraculously, it held.

The colonel spent another fifteen minutes cleaning up the room. He packed away the bag Abney had taken from Bayless and all the electronics he could find. Satisfied that nothing of interest remained, Straeger slipped out of the room unnoticed and headed to the simple grey sedan he had rented. He planned to dump most of the stuff into the river, but first, he needed to make a call. The phone rang and a familiar twang answered.

"It's done," said Straeger.

"Good. I touch down in three hours. I trust you can find the spot."

Chapter Thirty-Six

A low summer sun danced through the windows and twisted with the curtains at a slow, sensual pace. Its light bounced across the wallpaper like a miniature spotlight. A soft breeze blew across Sherman's face and the combination brought him out of a dreamless sleep. He didn't move at first, but laid there and took it all in. The patterns flickered, and the wind drifted through, but he still didn't move.

Minutes passed before he finally sat up and looked down at himself. His shirt was bloody, not in the horror movies sense, but it was noticeable. Dark brown splotches dotted the front of his shirt and arterial spray decorated his right arm.

Years ago, his mind would have re-spooled the night in one long lecture on what he should have done. After each mission, all the little details and misses would come floating to the surface. Those self-critical moments helped him learn, but they took a toll and his mind had slowly curtailed the process. It could only hold so much carnage.

As Sherman stood up, the bed creaked, and Ruby poked her head in through the open door.

"You look like shit."

"Thanks," he replied.

"Coffee?"

"Yes, please."

Sherman stripped off the shirt. "Can you burn this?"

Ruby looked at him and then at the shirt. The request was not surprising. Nothing much was anymore. "Sure. Oh, Gournsey just left to check his 'email'. Whatever that means."

"Thanks, I'm gonna take a shower. Can you monitor things?"

Ruby nodded and left to look for lighter fluid.

The barista was young and tattooed and anything but Gournsey's mental image of small-town-nice. Her short black hair swayed in unison to the music.

"What can I get you?" she asked.

"I'm open to suggestions."

"Normally, I'd suggest something sweet and frothy, but you look like more of a boilermaker type."

"Kentucky is home."

"Four shot Americano then."

"Sounds utterly extravagant. I'll take it."

The woman turned and started grinding and tamping the espresso. Gournsey stood at the counter and watched her curves shake to some obscure upbeat tune.

She winked while handing over the steaming mug. "Here you go."

"Thank you."

Gournsey took a seat with his back to the wall and an unobstructed view out the front door. He flipped open the cheap laptop and waited for it to power up. The little circle spun in an endless loop as he sipped on the potent brew. The number three popped up over the email application Gournsey hesitantly clicked.

Message one was spam.

Message two caught his attention. It read:

Leave now! Unable to decrypt – DoD level. They traced your IP. Do not contact me again.

Gournsey paused for a sip and to let the information sink in. The result did not surprise him. Sending out the file was a risk. He and Sherman understood that fact but decided that the reward outweighed any consequence.

He looked at message three. The date-time stamp was four hours after the second and only two hours in the past. Gournsey read it once, then twice, then a third time for good measure. The meaning was clear, the threat concise.

"Can I get this to go?" he asked the barista.

"Leaving so soon?"

"Afraid so."

She handed him over a paper cup and lid. "I bartend over at a rafting bar tonight. You should stop by."

"If I'm still breathing, I'll be there."

The woman frowned a little but didn't appear too surprised by the morbid comment.

Gournsey stepped out and wandered around the town, making sure he took a different route back. Somewhere past the Post Office, he tossed the laptop in the trash like a used piece of gum.

Sherman was down to his last shirt. All the others were burnt or trash. Blood had a way of ruining clothing, and he did not have the energy or inclination to scrub.

He was in the living room cleaning Talbot's AR-15 when Ruby walked in. She looked at the gun like it was a bottle of whiskey during a terrible hangover, simultaneously revolting and a potential remedy.

"How's Betsy doing?" asked Sherman.

"She needs treatment from a real doctor."

"You are a real doctor."

"Not anymore."

Sherman paused but let the subject drop. "Your unofficial prognosis?"

"She has some cerebral swelling. Right now, it's stable, but things could turn. She won't survive if that happens."

"And the lacerations?"

"I'm still good enough with a needle and thread."

"Will we know anything soon?"

"If she wakes up, then it's fine."

"And if she doesn't?"

Ruby shrugged. "Probably dead without intensive care."

"Can you get her ready to move?" he asked.

"Is it safe?"

"Let's ask him," answered Sherman with a jerk of his thumb out the window and towards the direction of Gournsey's silhouette walking down the street.

"What happened last night?" she blurted out, wanting to ask him alone.

"I offered her a way out. She didn't take it."

"Did you really offer to let her walk?"

He nodded.

"Why?"

Sherman looked up from the gun while his eyes searched for an answer. "Professional courtesy, I guess."

"That still exists?"

"For some of us."

The door opened slowly and loudly as Gournsey made sure they heard him entering the house. Sherman took one look at him and the conspicuously missing laptop and knew something was wrong.

"Bad news?" he asked.

Gournsey sat down on the couch next to Ruby. "Three-fold."

"No use in waiting," Sherman said as he reassembled the rifle.

"No luck on the decryption. It was DoD level."

"I guess that confirms our hypothesis."

"What hypothesis?" asked Ruby.

Gournsey answered on Sherman's behalf. "No offense but chasing you around for years only made sense if that USB drive carried something flammable. A burn your house down kind of secret."

"I should have trashed it with all of his other shit."

"They would have killed you anyway," added Sherman. "It's good you held on to it. Now we have something to bargain with, assuming they don't know about our failure."

"Unknown, but they found the file and the IP address for the coffee shop."

"And number three?"

Gournsey grabbed a pen and paper from the front desk and wrote out a set of numbers. He handed it over to Sherman and sat back down.

With one glance, Sherman understood the basics of their

situation. The piece of paper contained coordinates. A latitude and longitude somewhere in the southwest, somewhere near Stalworth. He grabbed his phone and typed in the numbers. A satellite image popped up, covered in swathes of green. The location was thirty miles from the B&B in a secluded valley.

"I take it they want to meet?" he asked.

Gournsey nodded. "That was the gist of it, but with more colorful language. They want to meet today at sunset."

"Any incentives?"

"They don't murder us."

"Seems light. No money or diamonds?"

"Nada," replied Gournsey.

"Do you know who wrote it?"

"No. It came from some free email service, but if they found me, then the spotlight is mighty narrow."

Ruby, who had been watching the speedy exchange with growing unease, inserted herself into the conversation. "My ex-father-in-law?"

"Two points for the doc," Gournsey exclaimed.

"Former doctor," she retorted.

"Now, don't ruin my compliment by saying something so silly."

Ruby could not help but smile at the man's country effervescence.

Sherman felt confused. He didn't see any motivation for the meeting. No incentive equaled no action. "If their magnanimity is the carrot, what is the stick?"

"They murder Ruby's family. Her mom and dad were mentioned by name and address and social security number."

"She doesn't like her family."

Gournsey's expression of shock hung somewhere between genuine and contrived. "You don't like them?"

"My father is an abusive asshole, and my mother never had the courage to leave."

"My daddy is a two-bit alcoholic who'd rather barter his measly paycheck away for a gallon of bourbon than buy groceries, but he's still my daddy, and I'd at least try to keep him from a shallow grave."

"He beat your mom?" she asked recklessly.

"Once," answered Gournsey.

"Only once?"

"I broke his arm. He couldn't swing a belt so well after that."

"How old were you?"

"Twelve."

"Were you bigger than him?"

"Within a few sacks of potatoes, but it didn't matter. I hit him with a crowbar."

Ruby looked incredulous. "You broke your father's arm with a crowbar when you were twelve years old?"

"Yes, ma'am."

"My life is blasé compared with yours."

"Don't feel bad," interjected Sherman. "He's got enough stories to fill a decade's worth of reality TV. Besides, everyone's hurt cuts in its own way."

The absurdity of it all made Ruby break down into a fit of laughter mixed with tears. "I suppose, and this is a stretch, but despite all the horrific shit they did when I was young, I don't want them dead."

"I guess we better show up for the meeting then," concluded Sherman.

"It's a trap, Frank. You know that, right?"

"Without a doubt, but they think it's for me."

Gournsey gave his friend a thumping pat on the back. "We better get going. You know they already scouted the place."

Sherman handed Ruby the rifle and added, "Just in case Carl comes back."

Ruby took the gun uneasily and placed it on the couch, then ran upstairs. A small black rectangle stuck out from her fingers when she returned.

She handed over the USB drive to Sherman. "Just in case this plan works."

Chapter Thirty-Seven

Parked in the hotel lot, Officer Carl Ortman pretended to fill in the crime scene paperwork, but his mind was elsewhere. His situation teetered on a dangerous edge. He knew Abney spoke the truth. It all came down to killing Ruby and Sherman and, unfortunately, Betsy. No other options were jumping out at him, except running. What once seemed unthinkable was feeling quite possible. Having smashed in the head of an old woman who fed him breakfast burritos, shooting a couple of outsiders no longer seemed absurd.

The radio in his cruiser crackled to life with an exchange from the dispatcher. A woman in her late fifties named Sue, who Talbot was unwilling to fire despite a growing propensity for forgetfulness.

"Three-Adam-Four, Mr. Harris up on the mountain is requesting assistance for an abandoned car on his property."

One of Talbot's sycophant nephews answered, "10-4. I'll deal with it. Does he recognize the car?"

"Yes. He believes it belongs to some boy named Shaun."

Carl's head snapped up and away from the menial forms in his lap. Even the smallest shreds of hope were drifting away. The car would lead to a stop at the appliance store, which would lead to a search, which would lead to Talbot's body stuffed in the deep freezer. His imagination was a blur of possibilities.

A plan gradually crystallized in his mind. It was a whopper of an idea that made Carl smile at his own ingenuity. Some details remained beyond reach, but the core was stable. He could pin Talbot's murder on Shaun. The body was there. All he needed was a little evidence of motivation. If he got to the house first, planting it would not be a problem.

"This is Three-Adam-One, I knew the family from high school. I'll swing by his daddy's place and see what I can find."

"Are you sure?" asked Sue. "Don't you have enough on your hands?"

"Torres is more than capable of the paperwork and babysitting the county coroner."

"I'll show you en route."

Carl started the sedan and eased out of the Mather Hotel parking lot. A day prior, he would not have considered making such a move without running it by Mr. Abney. With Bayless dead, such niceties felt superfluous. The balance of power had shifted, and he felt good about taking fate into his own hands.

When Carl pulled into the dirt lot of the appliance store, he left the car idling. If his plan were to succeed, he needed to be careful. Knocking down the door and magically finding Talbot's body would draw suspicion. He needed a reason to enter the shop. He needed probable cause or some extenuating circumstance.

Staging a break-in was at the top of his list when the sound of tires crunching over gravel obliterated his concentration. Carl turned around and gasped when Torres parked her cruiser a few feet away.

"Nice try," she shouted through the open windows. "I'm not gonna sit around with a corpse all day while you get to do some actual work."

Carl forced a smile that was way too big and toothy. "Who is at the hotel?"

"Coroner."

"That was quick."

"He was fishing nearby when the call came in."

Carl nodded and tried another smile, this time, less contrived. "I'm sure this is nothing."

Torres stepped out of her car and Carl followed.

"Do you know them?" she asked.

"Once upon a time, Shaun and I were in the same graduating class in high school."

"And since then?"

"We parted ways, but I heard rumors," answered Carl, hoping Torres would bite.

She did and asked, "Rumors of what?"

"Small-time stuff, I think. Pushing a few pills here and there. A bit of herb. The stuff Talbot tolerates if it doesn't go too far."

"The chief didn't haul his ass in?"

Carl gestured towards the quiet afternoon horizon. "It's a small town. People like to leave things as they are. No need to rock the boat."

Torres didn't appreciate the lesson in politics. Not from someone like Carl. She pointed towards the house and asked, "Shall we?"

"Let me," he suggested. "They don't much like strangers in this family."

"I've been here for three years," Torres reminded him.

"They've been here for three generations."

"Fine," she hissed. "Go ahead."

Carl gave her a wink and ambled up the front porch to knock on the door. The hollow thud echoed for a moment in the silence as he manufactured some expectation of answer.

Torres was not paying attention and her eyes had drifted towards the windows. The curtains blocked most of the view, but she caught some tiny glimpses inside. Beer cans and bottles of booze littered the small visible slice of coffee table.

"Both the father and son live here?"

Carl shrugged, "Like I said, I haven't heard from them for years."

"Looks like a bachelor pad to me."

"Oh, see a lot of those on the inside?"

Torres snarled her upper lip. "No one's home."

"We can check the shop," Carl offered.

"Go ahead."

Without a discernible care for time, Carl retraced his steps down the creaky wooden porch and towards the appliance repair shop. The front door was locked, and a CLOSED sign covered with dust hung in the window. Torres started poking around the windows.

"I'll try the back," he offered.

Torres shrugged.

The back door was locked, but Carl already knew that. He had seen Shaun lock it up when they left and hung around long enough to see his friend hide the key between two stack pots.

Carl took a quick peek around the corner to see if Torres was coming. She was not. He retrieved the key and unlocked the door and left it ever so slightly ajar.

"Torres," he called with urgency in his voice.

She came running around the corner with a pistol drawn. He pointed towards the door and they stacked up, ready to enter. Carl went first and cleared right, with Torres on his heels looking left. Any suspense ended almost before it started. Only dust and a few empty shelves remained inside.

"Small-town security?" asked Torres.

Carl shrugged and deliberately took his time looking around the room. "Not much to steal."

"Nothing much of anything," agreed Torres. She gingerly picked through some old electronics. "Unless the thief is from the eighties and needs to steal a VCR."

"I saw an unreturned Blockbuster tape back there. Maybe we can bust him on that," joked Carl.

"The only thing not covered in dust is the chest freezer back there."

Carl followed her gaze expectantly. It had not taken her long to notice. "Yeah, odd place to keep your deer meat."

She walked over and flipped open the lid. A tiny scream escaped before she stifled the rest.

"What is it?" asked Carl, doing his best impression of surprise.

Torres said nothing but kept pointing at the twisted, frozen corpse.

"Holy fuck," yelled Carl. "Is that..." he trailed off.

"It's Chief Talbot," Torres whispered.

Chapter Thirty-Eight

Three brief hours separated them from sunset as the stolen truck rattled down a rutted dirt track. It had taken them almost sixty minutes to reach the remote valley near the Utah border. As they headed south, the green circles of crops slowly peeled away, leaving only dry grass and spindly brush.

Gournsey peered over the steering wheel at the expanding horizon and asked, "Where do you want to stop?"

"A quarter-mile up. We can hike over the ridge from there."

"Are we leaving the same way?"

"Or not at all," Sherman answered.

Gournsey laughed at the casual indifference to death that had categorized his entire time with the team. Long ago, they stopped clinging to that fear. The end would arrive eventually, as it did for everyone. In the meantime, skill was the best way to hide from its grasp.

The dirt road narrowed, and they turned down something only 4x4 enthusiasts would dare consider passable. Neither man so much as frowned. The stakes were low. They were not driving across the darkened deserts of North Africa nor running for their lives in the wilds of Afghanistan. The drive felt pedestrian in comparison.

Sherman soaked in the terrain like a parched landscape, desperate for rain. He memorized the barren ridge, the chalky rocks, the boulder-strewn drainage flowing next to the road, and even the shriveled groves of trees clumping together against the sweeping winds. The ground truth of southern Idaho.

They drove on for another hundred yards until Sherman pointed to a small stand of trees. Gournsey eased the truck between their hardscrabble limbs and turned off the engine.

"Not to be crude, but this place looks like a graveyard."

Sherman stuck his head out the window and agreed, "I don't think it gets any better on the other side."

"Is there a plan formulating under that beard?"

"Grab the Remington."

"I ain't exactly precise with that thing," reminded Gournsey. His bulk did not lend itself to the shadowy world of snipers.

"Let's hope it doesn't come to that."

"And if it does?"

"They'll leave us to the coyotes."

Gournsey left the keys in the ignition and grabbed the rifle as instructed. They set off towards the ridge at a brisk jog. Not much impeded their progress. The ridge lumbered four hundred feet uphill. Grass was about the only vegetation that grew on those windy slopes. Less than a dozen trees dotted the ridgeline like green door-sized tumbleweeds.

On the other side, the valley stretched low and wide with minimal cover. The lack of verticality only accentuated the deep blue sky overhead, which appeared to run right past the edges of the horizon. A lone dirt road ran down the middle before petering out at the base of a pinkish outcropping of boulders.

One way in. One way out.

The two soldiers looked out over the flat, almost featureless terrain and the long valley dotted with knotted clumps of trees.

Gournsey broke the silence. "This is a kill box."

"I know."

"Is Straeger here?"

"Been here for hours."

"No other way to do it," agreed Gournsey.

"Could you find him in time?"

Gournsey glanced over everything in front of them. "No, could you?"

"No."

"You ain't cut out for suicide."

"You see another choice?"

"Run."

"Am I the running type?" asked Sherman.

"Suicide it is."

Sherman pointed to a small slit running down from the ridge. "That drainage is our best bet for getting down to the road."

"Where do you want the Remington?"

"How far out can you be and not hit me?"

"A football field. Anything past that and I'll miss the barn altogether."

They worked downhill with methodical ease. Their slow pace was comfortable and familiar. Both men mentally slipped back into the rhythms of war and the heightened senses it induced. Gournsey tasted faint fragrances in the air, while Sherman felt certain he could hear the trees growing if he concentrated.

Two hundred yards short of the dirt road, a dusty dip in the otherwise flat ground, provided a defilade. The hole was deep enough to crouch in and could have easily served as a makeshift grave. Sherman ripped out a few stubby bushes, all spindly and dry. Stuck in the dirt around the rim, they broke up Gournsey's silhouette as he searched for the danger lurking out there.

"Where would you be?"

Sherman was prone near the edge of the hole. He motioned a thumb across the valley to a pile of rocks that looked like dried clumps of white Playdough.

"That's a long shot," replied Gournsey as he eyed the distant blobs. "I reckon it's a mile or more."

"Mile and a quarter."

The sergeant understood why Sherman had led them down the drainage. It was the only way into the valley that kept them hidden from that angle.

"And if he's not there?"

Sherman shrugged and made a popping sound with his lips.

Gournsey chuckled to himself without moving his eye from the scope. "Your leadership is a boon in trying times."

"Either Straeger didn't see us or Knight wants to have an actual conversation."

"Do you want to talk? The email didn't leave much to the imagination."

"I have a question for him."

"All this for a question. Shit, you'll be lucky if they don't drop you where you stand."

"If that happens, I trust you'll put him down."

"Without a second glance," Gournsey assured.

"Then it's his grave as much as ours."

Shadows stretched out their long tendrils as the men waited for sunset. The sun was warm but not hot, and Sherman felt serene under its rays. Hours rolled by without a cloud in the sky.

Gournsey gave him a nudge as the sun hovered near the horizon like a drunk unwilling to leave the bar. It was not a reminder Sherman needed, but he appreciated his friend's attentiveness. Despite the projected nonchalance, Sherman knew Gournsey was completely focused on the task at hand.

"See anything?"

"The ghosts of Christmas past and a hardscrabble pile of shit with enough dirt to bury Lexington."

Sherman peered through the uprooted bushes and added, "About time I left."

"Don't make me drag you home."

Sherman squeezed his friend on the shoulder as he slithered out of the hole and weaved through the bushes. Gournsey watched him melt into the paltry surrounding vegetation like a lion on the savannah. One minute, he was wading through the grass, and the next, nothing moved but the wind. Al-Qaeda called them *shabh*—ghost in Arabic. Gournsey was no linguist, but he understood the meaning to be both those who appear from the ether and those left behind in the wake.

Ten minutes before official sunset, two tiny pinpricks of light dotted the horizon at the valley entrance. Not full-on headlights, but the running lights of a car that did not let the driver turn them off. Something new and fancy.

Sherman watched them shudder over the rutted road. At that distance, he couldn't see the make or model, but he knew it was an arrogantly-sized vehicle. Something like the FBI agents, maybe a Suburban or Tahoe.

As the lights came within a quarter-mile, he slid out of the bushes and wandered towards the road. He kept his hands over his head, making a very angular 'Y'. As he reached the shoulder, he stopped and took a deep breath.

The lights came closer and so did the sound of a large V-8 engine roaring in the expansive silence. A big black box swayed into view as Sherman's guess came to pass. The Suburban slowed as the driver spotted him off to the side.

Sherman squinted through the light and into the face of the driver. A featureless man with drab eyes and a firm jaw. Ex-army now driving for the highest bidder, Sherman reckoned. Not Straeger.

The SUV stopped fifty feet short of his position. Nothing happened for two minutes, and the occupants discussed something that Sherman couldn't make out. Then the back door opened, and Senator Terrance Knight stepped out. He wore a dark grey suit with a deep red tie hiding behind the jacket. Knight looked younger than his years and projected a virile masculinity refined by expensive haircuts and years without physical labor. Everything about him was sculpted to conform with some myth of the man.

Chapter Thirty-Nine

The senator stood next to the hood and waited. He had no intention of walking towards the strange figure who looked like a homeless man during a confrontation with law enforcement. Knight stood tall, but the Ruger pistol attached to his belt weighed down his pants, and he felt self-conscious about a slight tilt in his posture.

Across the open stretch of dirt, Sherman watched the suit strut like a rooster but kept his focus on the driver. The enormous engine idled. The guy was taking no chances, which meant he was no slouch. Judging by the polo shirt and wraparound sunglasses, Sherman guessed he was a contractor. A deniable and expendable member of some shell company with offshore accounts in non-extradition countries. Once upon a time, he would have stood in Sherman's boots, maybe even outranked him, but something had changed. Hiding behind the wheel, he was nothing more than a hired gun in a golf shirt.

The senator would not meet him in the middle, so Sherman took deliberate steps forward with arms held high and a 'don't shoot' look on his face. The driver's side door cracked open a few inches as he approached. One less thing for the contractor to worry about if the shooting started.

"You got balls, son. I'll give you that," shouted Knight.

Sherman said nothing and took a few more steps.

"That's far enough."

Sherman stopped and lowered his arms below his shoulder, but kept his hands out to the side. The senator was unaccustomed to being ignored. Silence was raising his blood pressure, and Sherman knew it.

"Do you have what I want?" asked Knight.

"What assurances do I have that you'll stop chasing her?"

"None. How do I know you don't have another copy?"

"You don't."

Knight snorted at the absurdity. "How bipartisan of us."

"Isn't that how it's supposed to work, Senator?"

"Who are you, son?" asked Knight, fully expecting no answer.

"Captain Frank Sherman. United States Army."

The senator took the rank with a grain of salt. Truth was such a fluid concept in the age of social media. "What unit?"

"JSOC. Task Force Orange."

"Delta," exclaimed Knight. "That explains this mess you've created. My associate spoke highly of your abilities. We could use a man like you."

"I'm not looking for a new line of work."

"We both work for the American people. Simply different departments."

"If it's all the same, Senator, I'll keep mine."

"You haven't heard my offer yet."

"Is it in any way similar to the one you gave us in the

email, only with some money thrown in there to quiet the little voice screaming NO in the back of my mind?"

"For a young man, you're already a relic, Captain. Wars are not fought by national armies anymore. Never again will a first-grade teacher from Topeka find himself conscripted to fight against tyranny. Those days are done and buried. America doesn't have the stomach to do what is necessary. We've grown soft. A few dead Marines and the public clamors for a withdrawal. Men like Rick over here are the future."

The driver didn't move at the mention of his name.

"Now, do you have the file or not?"

Sherman slowly reached into his pocket, retrieved the USB drive, and held it up.

"How do you know I'm not having the girl killed at this moment?" asked Knight.

"The same reason I know we are not alone in this valley and that Rick over there has an MP7 in his lap."

A look half-filled with surprise and admiration crossed the senator's face. "It's a shame you're shortsighted. We could use a soldier like you."

"I need your word that this hunt for your daughter-in-law is over."

"Ex-daughter-in-law."

"You're a politician. Don't let yourself get bogged down in the details."

"You have my word," said Knight.

"I'll hold you to that," said Sherman as he tossed over the USB drive like a slow-pitch softball.

The small black rectangle landed at Knight's feet with a puff of dirt. He picked it up with immense distaste and tossed it towards Rick, who swiftly plugged it into a laptop. The screen's white light illuminated the contractor's face for a few seconds as he validated the contents before flashing the senator a thumbs-up.

"Tell me, Captain, why go through with all of this? Rick confirmed you didn't open the file."

"No problem can be solved at the level it was created."

Knight squinted at the quote for a moment, grasping for a memory long since lost. "Who said that?"

"Einstein," answered Sherman.

"I prefer fiction," scoffed Knight and awkwardly touched his left shoulder with his right hand as if brushing off some unwanted dandruff. It was a signal of sorts. The kind of unoriginal gesture people who don't signal come up with.

Sherman turned towards the lumpy outcropping of rocks across the valley and held his breath, savoring the brisk mountain air on the edge of autumn. He knew it might have been his last. He knew he'd be dead before pain registered in his brain. One moment, he would be this full version of himself, and the next, he would be a bloody shell sprawled across the ground.

Nothing came.

The senator squinted into the distance with a look of annoyance etched on his face.

Sherman turned around and asked, "How well do you know Colonel Straeger?"

Knight snapped his head towards the sound like a frightened cat.

"I bet you two crossed paths at some point. Maybe at some Pentagon meeting or one of those intelligence trips abroad. You know of his reputation. I mean, who doesn't. The man is a living legend for those with a high enough security clearance."

"What is this?" demanded Knight.

"Just a story," replied Sherman. "But I think you need to hear the ending. See, I've known the Colonel since I was knee-high to a Basset hound. Only, I call him Uncle Charlie. He and my father were in the same unit. The best of friends, as I recall. Get enough beers in them and they'd share some crazy stories. Hell, you might have even met my dad back when he was alive. Major Cal Sherman."

The name registered in Knight's memory like shouts of fire in a crowded theater. The familial resemblance was impossible to ignore. He knew Straeger by reputation, but he knew the major by myth. A surname whispered by those who did the redacting.

"I thought you might know," continued Sherman with his hands still outstretched. In a movement that Knight didn't even see, he pointed to the right with two fingers. Less than a second later, blood splattered across the SUV's interior as a gunshot echoed down the valley.

Rick was dead.

The senator fumbled with his jacket, trying to draw the pistol holstered underneath.

"Don't," yelled Sherman.

It was a useless gesture by both parties. High-ranking officials don't take orders and Straeger didn't miss.

The air snapped and Knight spun around like a top twisted by some invisible hand. He crumpled to the ground, face up with a view of the wine-dark curtain of dusk folding over the horizon. Sherman crouched down, but there was no need to check for a pulse. The bullet hit center mass—a fraction of an inch of the senator's heart.

Sherman rifled through the dead man's pockets and retrieved several items, including a Tom Ford wallet, government-issued iPhone, USB drive, and Ruger pistol. He pulled a thick wad of cash from the wallet and kept the gun and thumb drive, but tossed everything else into the SUV. The driver had no cash, but Sherman took the MP7 for good measure.

"Anything worth keeping?" asked Gournsey, his hulking frame materialized out of the twilight.

Surveying the wreckage of lives lost, Sherman saw nothing worth remembering. Carrying that burden was not worth his breath. The senator died no differently than how he had lived, a pulsing mess of self-aggrandizement.

"Beer money," offered Sherman, and held up the thick wad of cash for Gournsey to see.

"If that was to buy your silence, he came up short."

"The true measure of that man."

"You wanna torch it?"

Sherman was already sliding underneath the Suburban with a knife clinched between his teeth, looking every part a pirate.

"Can you put him in the passenger seat?" he yelled.

Dead weight or not, Gournsey pulled Knight's body through the dirt easier than a bag full of coal. By the time Sherman cut the gas line, the sergeant had already covered up the blood with fresh dirt.

Gasoline mingled with the earthy smell of a cooling night. Sherman lit a pack of matches from *Bedlam Bar and Grill* and the two men watched the blaze consume the Suburban and those who drove it into the valley.

"Who's next?" asked Gournsey.

"Abney."

"Is he the other suit?"

Sherman nodded with concentration.

"He's dead," said a voice from the surrounding darkness.

They turned, not unexpectedly, towards the shimmering blue night.

"When?" asked Sherman.

"After you left this morning. Knight wanted to clean the house."

"You knew?"

Straeger stepped into the soft orange glow. "You're getting careless, Frank. I saw you coming in the back door."

Sherman hung his head at the misstep but didn't dwell on it for long. "Thanks for the heads-up, Charlie."

Straeger heaved his broad shoulders up and down. "The hotel was teeming with assholes. I figured someone would show up eventually, just didn't expect it to be you."

"I thought you retired."

"I was. I am. Bought a little cabin in Montana and planned on wasting away in my old age. Then I got a call from the senator and the money was too good to pass up with Lizzy at NYU and me on an Army pension."

"I hope he paid up front," said Gournsey.

"They always do."

"Thanks for the assist," added Sherman.

Straeger headed back into the envelope of night and waved his hand goodbye. "Don't mention it. Oh, and, Frank, go and visit your mother. She misses you."

Gournsey looked over at him, baffled by the remark. "You said she was dead?"

"It's a long story," Sherman admitted.

"It's a long walk back to the truck."

Chapter Forty

The crime scene technicians from Idaho Falls were still taking pictures well past sunset. Carl sat in the police cruiser massaging his templates, vainly hoping to cure a headache. Having set his plan in motion, it had acquired a velocity all of its own and he could not rein it back in.

First, Sue, the dispatcher, broke down sobbing. Then the coroner showed up demanding extra money for all the overtime. The CSI team was not pleased to receive a call from some town they couldn't place on a map. By the time they showed up, Carl was burnt out, but the worst of it arrived in the form of Mrs. Talbot. She surged towards the body, zipped up in black plastic, as Carl tried to hold her back. She sobbed on his shoulder for twenty long minutes as her grief poured out. Long enough for remorse and guilt to dig their claws into Carl's psyche and start thrashing about.

His mind was still spinning when Torres appeared with an exasperated look.

"What is it?" he asked.

"Mather Hotel just called. They found another body."

"What! Who?"

"A guest named James Abney. I interviewed him this morning." Torres kept talking, but Carl stopped listening.

Something monumental happened without him ever knowing. With Abney dead, he had lost all outside support and any promises of the Chief's chair. Everything was crumbling and even when Carl clawed around to catch a piece of his former life, it turned to ash.

"Did you hear what I said?" asked Torres.

Carl looked up with panic glowing in his eyes. "I need to go."

"What?" protested Torres, but it was no use.

Carl rocketed the sedan across the gravel lot and headed back to town with only one thing in mind—running.

The keys rattled in the deadbolt as Sherman unlocked the front door to Betsy's house. He tried to be loud and purposeful, knowing that somewhere on the other side Ruby had a rifle aimed squarely at his chest. The lock clicked, and he stepped inside with an even stride. It took a second, but he spotted her through the wooden railing above the stairs.

"Damn it, Frank. You could have called ahead."

"I could have."

Ruby sat down and let out a sigh of relief at seeing him in one piece. "Well, don't keep me in suspense. What happened?"

"Coffee?" he asked, pointing towards the kitchen.

"Bourbon," she replied.

"Not yet."

They sat down at the table and Sherman filled three

mugs from the coffeepot that Betsy kept going. It was stale and a day old, but none of them noticed.

"I gave the USB to Senator Knight," Sherman began.

"And you walked away?"

"Yes."

"Wait," said Ruby before connecting the dots. "He didn't walk away, did he?"

"No."

She ran her hands through her chestnut brown hair, nodding slowly at first, but then with increasing speed. "Good riddance. I hated that son-of-a-bitch."

"Abney is dead too."

Ruby pushed back her chair in surprise. "What?"

"Knight had him killed. Loose ends don't last long in Washington."

"Well, shit. Now I don't know if I like him more or less."

"Call it a wash," suggested Sherman.

"What now? Is it done?" She gestured around at her life on the run.

Sherman pointed upstairs where Betsy lay hidden and resting. "Like I said, not yet."

"Carl," Ruby snarled.

"Carl," he agreed.

"I know where he lives," she offered. "Or we could just call in and ask where he's at. I know Sue, the dispatcher."

"No need to call Sue, just give me the directions."

"Now?"

"With Abney dead, I don't think he'll be sticking around much longer."

Ruby grabbed a notepad from the front desk and drew Sherman a map. He studied it for a few seconds, crumpled up the paper, and threw it in the trash.

"How's Betsy doing?" he asked.

"Hard to say without a CT scan. Her pulse is stable, but there is no telling what is going on with her brain."

"You and Gournsey should take her to hospital."

"Is that safe?" she asked.

"It will be."

"What about the guy you saw lurking about? Straeger, right? He sounds ominous."

Gournsey started laughing so hard, he could barely get the words out, "Uncle Charlie."

The inside joke further confused Ruby. She looked at Sherman and asked, "Did he completely lose it?"

"Colonel Straeger is an old family friend. He and my dad were in the same unit."

"Why didn't you say something?"

"I haven't seen him since my father's funeral. I wasn't sure if he saw me or would even recognize me."

"What a catastrophically small world you live in."

Sherman smiled, aware of his own good fortune. "I suppose so."

"Alright, Raylan. Get that big ass of yours off the chair and help me move Betsy downstairs," commanded Ruby with a renewed sense of purpose surging through her.

"Yes, ma'am."

Sherman grabbed the Glock and walked out the back door. The night air was cool and brisk as Idaho flirted with the fringes of fall. At a jog, without stops, he could make it to Carl's doorstep in fifteen minutes.

Light from passing cars shimmered through the living room curtains. With each blast of illumination, Carl's chest tightened. His truck was packed and ready to go. Only a few odds and ends remained. The stuff he couldn't replace at Walmart. Things of sentimental value such as tea set or as his father called them, 'A bunch of queer pansy cups'.

Carl admired the China despite the parental rant. His grandfather brought them back from Japan after World War II, saying it was from the Edo Period. Everyone in the family knew the truth—he'd bought it at some street fair in the rubble of Tokyo for twenty cents. The cups were white with pink cherry blossoms painted ever so carefully around the background of Mt. Fuji.

As a boy, Carl imagined scaling the heights of such an imposing mountain. Many creatures inhabited its imaginary flanks—dragons, ghostly samurai, and even a lost Japanese platoon. Then puberty hit and he lost track of such fantasy delights, being too focused on Audrey Brommer's bra straps.

He placed the tea set inside a cardboard box with a framed photo of his grandfather in full dress uniform. It was the only memory worth keeping. It represented a time when things were clear and good triumphed over evil. Such stark lines didn't exist anymore, not for him, and Carl shuddered to think how his grandpa would view the royal mess he'd created. The photo stared back in judgement. He turned it face-down and kept on gathering the last bits of his life, packing it away in a corrugated coffin.

An empty roll of packing tape lay on the table. Carl picked it up for a moment with an impulse to buy more before tossing it aside. He folded the cardboard top until it stayed shut and took one last look around the house. It was a rental, so no actual loss there. No equity to worry about, other than the deposit and that summed to under a thousand dollars.

A bitter feeling percolated in Carl's gut, and he realized despite being born in Stalworth he had no lasting connection to the town. He owned no property and had few friends. No kids. No wife. Nothing much of anything tied him to the place. It left him feeling adrift and melancholic over leaving without ever having truly arrived.

He picked up the last container and left through the back door. The truck bed was full of boxes and electronics and anything else of value. Afraid of breaking the tea set, he put the box on the floor beneath the passenger seat. He took a deep breath and glanced around, hoping he missed nothing worth taking.

A silhouette caught his attention—singular and out of place. A change where there should have been none. Carl reached for his service pistol, which he had no intention of leaving behind, but it was too late.

Sherman slipped out of the trees so quickly that Carl felt he came from nowhere like a shadow suddenly imbued with weight and mass and inertia. The officer managed a clean pull from his holster, but Sherman caught the wrist with his left hand while striking Carl's neck with the right.

Pain burst through the officer's body as if someone had thrown hot grease on his bare skin. His head, neck, throat, and shoulder throbbed. Then his knees buckled, and before Carl knew down from up, he was on the ground, unarmed. Sherman motioned towards the back door with the barrel of the pistol.

"Get up," he ordered.

Carl struggled to his feet and had to use the door to steady himself. "I'm still a cop," he protested. "That's the death penalty around here."

"Get inside the house."

"No."

"Suit yourself."

Clarity suddenly found him, and Carl realized he'd rather die on something comfy and more dignified.

"Wait," he pleaded. "Inside is fine."

Sherman didn't reply until they reached the living room. "Have a seat, Officer."

Carl did as instructed and sank into his favorite chair—the one thing he wanted to take but couldn't fit into the truck for lack of room.

Sherman leaned against the wall next to a bare TV mount. "I almost didn't come," he began. "I almost turned around."

"You still can," exhorted Carl.

Sherman flashed a thin smile. "I used to think I could walk away from all the madness. Just pick up my bag and leave it all behind. Disappear and run, then keep running. That if I got far enough, it would change. It doesn't change. People don't change."

"I'm sorry," Carl whimpered.

"For what?"

"For Betsy," he admitted and hung his head in shame.

"So, you know why I'm here."

"She preached forgiveness, you know. Not much else she could preach with her choice of husband."

"No need for the past tense. She's not dead."

A look of surprise spread over Carl's brow in tiny waves. "That's good, that's… I just lost it. I shouldn't have done it, but I lost control."

"I know," replied Sherman. "I've done worse."

"Then why are you here?"

"Because people like me don't change."

The single gunshot echoed around the room and out the open back door. Dogs howled at the commotion. An over-attentive neighbor called the police, but Sherman was long gone.

Chapter Forty-One

The incessant beep of hospital equipment and the reek of disinfectant antagonized Sherman's senses. He hated hospitals and had for years, since witnessing his dad waste away from cancer in one of those adjustable beds, too sick to sit up on his own. That death haunted him more than most. Almost more than the friends he lost, but many of them didn't make it to a hospital. They weren't lucky enough for that. Instead, they died where they fell after the first bullet or bomb struck.

Ruby smiled as he entered the room. He handed her a cup of coffee from the cafeteria downstairs. She had not left Betsy's side for twenty-four hours. Not since they arrived, and the CT scan revealed bleak news.

"How's she doing?" he asked.

"She's doing just fine," answered a hoarse but strong voice.

Sherman turned towards the bed with a pleasant surprise. "When did this happen?"

"A few hours ago," Ruby answered.

"Oh, is that all? I feel fine," said Betsy.

"The doctor feels otherwise," Ruby countered.

Betsy sniffed indignantly. "The doctor likes to gamble on the ponies, so I'm taking his word with a shaker of salt."

Ruby stood up and stretched her slender frame, worn thin by stress and time. "I'm going for a walk. Don't overdo it, Betsy."

The older woman stuck out her tongue and held it there until Ruby left the room. Then she turned to Sherman.

"Tell me, Frank. Is she safe? I've grown quite fond of the girl, even if she won't leave me alone."

Sherman took a seat on a faux leather chair slick from overuse. "No one will come looking for her anymore if that is what you're asking. As for being safe… well, that's up to her."

Betsy gingerly touched the cast encasing her arm, then thought for a moment before asking, "What about Carl Ortman?"

"They found his body in an apparent suicide. A self-inflicted gunshot wound. From what I hear, the police linked a weapon recovered at his house to several murders. But, I'm not sure you'll ever know the true extent of his crimes."

A coy smile crossed her face. "Small-town secrets. Who's in charge? Don't tell me it's one of those nephews."

"Torres is taking over as acting Chief of Police."

"Good. Good. She's an honest cop. Big shoes to fill, but honest. Now, what about your friend, Raylan?"

"Last time I saw him, he was driving south to Denver. I believe with a barista from the local coffee shop. He'll head back to Kentucky soon enough. Our leave ends in two weeks."

"And you? Are you planning to stay awhile, Frank?"

"Up to now, there's been nothing I couldn't leave behind," answered Sherman.

"Except the war," she reminded him.

He nodded. "Except the war."

She held his gaze for a moment with eyes full of understanding in a way that made Sherman feel strangely appreciated.

"So, what are you doing for the next two weeks?"

"Maya from the rafting company offered to lend us a boat and gear. Ruby and I are taking a float trip to unplug, unwind, or whatever they call it these days."

"R&R?"

Sherman laughed at the irony of the term already antiquated before the Vietnam War.

"Something like that."

"Promise me something," said Betsy. "When you finally leave, and I mean leave it for good, make sure you don't get sucked back into the mess. Don't make the same mistake Bill did."

Sherman smiled at her sincerity. "If I make it out alive, I won't be looking back."

Next in the Frank Sherman Thrillers Series

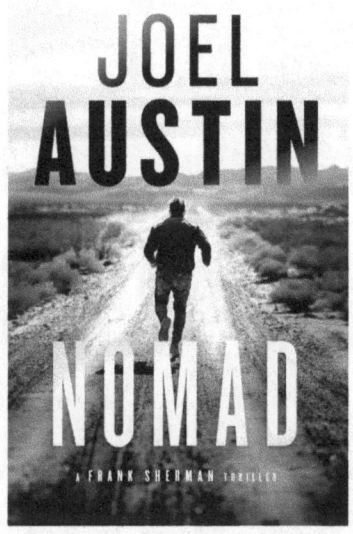

www.vinci-books.com/nomad

A farewell to his dying mother. A friend asking for a favor. A past that won't stay buried.

Frank Sherman is back.

Frank Sherman is returning to California to visit his dying mother. When a friend's request entangles Sherman in an FBI investigation involving missing weapons, he must confront the shadows of his past while navigating the searing heat and treacherous landscape. As the mystery deepens, Sherman discovers that the price of redemption may be higher than he ever imagined.

Turn the page for a free preview…

Nomad: Chapter One

Time was against the three men. A faded day's warmth still smothered the desert sands, and their shirts clung like wet rags. They worked with a quiet concentration that enveloped them deeper than the surrounding darkness. Soft red lights barely illuminated the bed of a dilapidated truck. It held three long wooden crates about the size of children's coffins, which took up the entire area. Large block letters emblazoned the sides, announcing their provenance.

Using crowbars, two of the men pried apart the nails securing the wooden lids, while the third watched the horizon. They worked efficiently, fueled by an abiding sense of urgency. Outside of the packaging, the contents were incriminating. Inside the crates, they would lead down a straightforward path to the death penalty.

"Start laying them out," whispered the tallest of the three men.

The second man solemnly unwrapped the contents. He took them out one at a time and laid them out on the tailgate and truck bed. Thirty new M4A1 carbines glistened in the pale light. The guns smelled of oil and industry.

"Boot, help me with the crates."

The third man swiveled and started tossing the crates into a shallow trench in the sandy ground. Deep enough for a body, the ditch spread out and away from the truck. All three crates went to the bottom before he started shoveling small mounds on top. The sand plopped and spread like a scoop of melting ice cream.

Over the southern horizon, two dots of light appeared, accompanied by the low growl of a domestic engine.

"Contact," barked the tallest man. "Are we clear?"

"Clear," repeated the other men.

"Good. Boot will take the left flank. Hadz will stay with me. Questions?"

"No, sir," they echoed.

A wide country smile stretched across the tallest man's face and his eyes glistened in the oncoming light. "Ain't no sirs out here. Now, let's make some money, boys."

"Yut," they exclaimed in unison.

The headlights swayed like tired dogs across the undulating terrain. From mere pinpricks, they grew in intensity with each passing minute. Audible above the engine noise, a car stereo rumbled across the flatland.

"Deet, who the fuck is this guy?" Hadz asked.

"A local," replied the tallest man.

"And he checked out?"

Deet might have seethed at the comment were the stakes lower, but he gave the question some leeway. "Nothing in the databases and Jones vouched for him."

"Jones is a drunken hack."

"He's a repeat customer."

"I'm just saying, it's a lot of hardware for a first-timer."

"I know."

"And this guy is driving like the Dukes of Hazzard."

Deet's upper lip quivered with anger at the arrival's reckless behavior. "I know."

An ear-splitting heavy metal song poured out of the oncoming truck with enough bass to thump their chests with the pressure change. The driver did nothing to conceal their presence and parked in front of the men with no pretense of discretion. Anyone watching could have seen the odd meeting and the guns lying in the back of the truck. As the vehicle stopped, the giant plume of dust it created swept over them and cast a ghostly ochre pall.

The driver hopped out as the lights flicked off and the screeching sounds faded into the night. Deet eyed him up like a bully on the first day of school. He was average all around. Neither tall nor short, but thin and wiry. He wore working man boots with deep scuffs, and stains of grease covered his Carhartt pants. Shabby, unkempt brown hair fell to his neck and two days' worth of scruff clung to his chin. Compared to the three men standing quietly in the darkness, he was gruff.

Deet stepped forward, frothing with anger. "What the fuck was that entrance?"

"That's no way to greet a customer," replied the driver.

"Are you Steve?" asked Deet, challenging the man to confirm something he already knew.

The driver gave a lopsided grin. "No, I ain't, but I imagine you ain't expecting no Steve."

Deet didn't reply.

"I'm Elmore. What should I call you?"

"D."

"D? Well, that's vague, unless your mama wanted to be mysterious."

"You ain't paying for my family history," Deet said.

"Fine. Don't get your buzz cut in a ruckus. And your friend?"

"H."

The newcomer laughed like a kid with milk squirting out his nose. "Do I get to meet A?"

"No," replied Deet with unequivocal stiffness.

"Live a little," Elmore added with a gesture up towards the starry night sky twinkling above.

"You got the cash?" asked Deet.

Elmore pointed behind them. "If that's the stuff."

Deet nodded towards the tailgate of the much older truck. The one Hadz bought from a salvage place for eight hundred in cash the week before. It was twenty years older than Elmore's ride, but Deet guessed the local's pink slips were legit.

Hadz pulled back the tarp covering the rifles, and Elmore let out a low whistle of joy.

"Hot damn, boys. These look fresh off the assembly line."

"Newer than mother's milk," replied Hadz.

Elmore picked up a rifle and inspected the action with the eye of someone familiar with the design.

"Have you ever shot one of these?" asked Deet with a kernel of suspicion bouncing around his gut.

"And here I thought we weren't sharing our family history."

Deet was in no mood for small talk and moved on with business. "They're three grand a piece, not including ammo."

A frown scrunched up Elmore's face. "Jones said he got them for two Gs each."

"Jones is a repeat customer."

"Maybe I'll just take one as a trial."

"Minimum order is ten," said Deet flatly. "However, we'll throw in the magazines for free."

"But not the ammo?"

"Next time."

"Can I try one out?" asked Elmore.

"Sure, after you buy them and go on your merry way."

Elmore continued inspecting the rifles. "How do I know they're genuine? Fakes are popping up everywhere these days."

"Ask Jones," replied Hadz with a chilly edge in his voice.

"Oh, I did, but one can never be too careful."

"Don't fuck about," growled Deet. "Are you buying or not?"

"I'll take a crate."

Deet and Hadz exchanged a quick glance. They buried the only crates around under the sand, and they wondered how the stranger came to such a descriptive term.

"I've got six Gs on me now," Elmore continued. "I'll get you the rest later."

"This ain't Rent-A-Center," countered Hadz. "You pay upfront and in full."

Elmore looked at the men standing straighter than a pair of two-by-fours. "The economy ain't great now. Things are tight. I can take three off you now for two thousand apiece. I'll come back for the other seven next week."

"Jones said you were good for thirty."

"I am," assured Elmore with a wave of his hand. "But not tonight."

The two men exchanged another look. A litany of felonies passed between them without a word.

"Alright," agreed Deet. "But only because Jones vouched for you."

Elmore smiled and carried three of the rifles back to his truck. Reaching under the seat, he pulled out a roll of twenty-dollar bills held together by rubber bands and tossed it over to Hadz.

"Good doing business with you," he added while climbing into the truck.

"Don't forget the magazines," reminded Deet in a soft voice.

Elmore flashed a self-conscious smile and walked back towards the two men. "Right, I don't want to forget those."

As he reached out to grab them from Deet's outstretched hand, the taller man twisted at the waist and landed a brutal strike to Elmore's solar plexus. The devastating blow doubled Elmore over, and he vomited on his shoes. Before he could draw air back into his lungs, Hadz came from behind and slipped a thick plastic bag over his head.

Panic exploded across Elmore's face. He flailed his legs about, searching for something solid to push against. All he found was sand. It was not enough to budge the man standing behind him. Hadz held firm like an anchor sunk in the seabed.

Unable to move, Elmore scratched at the plastic, hoping to puncture its surface or anything to get a puff of air. Deet stepped forward and locked down the local's wrists with a grip capable of juicing whole oranges. That face with its aquiline nose and heavy black eyebrows was the last thing Elmore saw before the night sky lost all its twinkle.

Hadz gripped the bag for another two minutes until he was sure Elmore was dead and long after the fight disappeared.

"Boot!" shouted Deet.

The man appeared from the gloom with his rifle in hand.

"Grab the E-tool and make some space by the crates."

Boot nodded and started frantically spreading sand with the small shovel. Knowing that Elmore would never wake up, Hadz pulled the body towards the widening gap in the ground. The two worked with purpose. Within minutes, they had a shallow grave into which they rolled Elmore's body.

Deet retrieved the rifles from the dead man's truck and wrapped everything up with canvas tarps. They said nothing until the work was complete and met between the two vehicles. Dawn still waited over the horizon some five hours out.

"We need to get rid of his truck," Deet began. He did not hurry his words, but they came across as urgent.

"I could drive it over the mountain and leave it in the valley somewhere," offered Hadz.

"Do it, but stay off the highways. We don't want any cameras to see you. Boot and I will unload the gear at the shed and then he can pick you up. Remember, don't be late."

The men nodded. They needed no further orders, motivation, or prodding. The risks were abundantly clear.

Nomad: Chapter Two

Shimmering walls of morning heat hovered above the pavement. The distortion twisted the horizon into silvery puddles of nothingness. Captain Frank Sherman shrugged off the temperature as no different from Iraq or Syria or parts of Afghanistan. Each country had its own version of the furnace called summer. The difference that day was one of location and severity. He was only ninety miles from the Mojave Desert and a digital thermometer on the bank sign across the street read 107°F. A heat wave for most of California, but for Buford, it was another Thursday in July.

He did not hurry. No one hurried in that kind of heat. Everything slowed to a crawl as the body coped. The other pedestrians he passed carried a similar look of resignation on their faces. Burdened by their passage, but not unduly.

Twenty minutes earlier, he'd found a decent cup of coffee, but despite the heat, he couldn't bring himself to order it iced. It was a principle of the beverage to be served hot. The cafe also made a decent corned beef hash.

It was more praise than he could say for his motel room,

which had a bed and not much else. The air conditioner ran intermittently with a tepid breeze, but it was clean and cheap. A relic of the fifties, the building clung to the ground like it might be bulldozed for something newer at any moment. Most importantly, it was the closest thing to his mother's nursing home.

The Desert Rose Retirement Village was a star-shaped building with all the dour architectural grace of the seventies. It sat at the end of the street brooding over a dried-out wash optimistically called a river. Back when the paint was fresh, it would have been a pleasant place. Such glory had faded over the decades until only the memory remained.

Sherman waved at the jovial attendant behind the front desk as he walked inside. He could not understand how someone in such a dreary place could stay so positive, but he appreciated the effort.

"Good morning, Stan."

"Hey, Frank, good to see you again. How are things?"

"Still alive."

A sympathetic but morbid smile crossed Stan's face. "Glad to hear it. She just finished breakfast. Go on back."

"Thanks," replied Sherman as he ambled down the dim hall.

His mother glanced up as he entered the room. The year since his last visit had not been kind. Sophia looked like one of those tablets people throw in a glass of water for hangovers, slowly dissolving away at the edges. The fiery Greek mother of his childhood was still there, but dulled and diluted.

Piles of mail and sticky notes stitching together her life covered a small side table next to the bed. A half-eaten plate of gloopy food perched precariously on top. Seeing her like that left Sherman with a profound sense of sadness. He grieved for the years lost and for those lying ahead, already bereft of joy and possibility.

"Franky," she chirped. "There's my boy."

"Hey, Mom. How are you doing?"

She was remarkably lucid and attentive. "Everything hurts and they keep feeding me this goddamn mush, but *c'est la vie.*"

Sherman smiled and took a seat in the threadbare chair next to her bed. The chair belonged to her mother, and she never parted with it even after the fabric disintegrated from years of use.

"It looks hot out there," said Sophia as she took his hand in hers.

"Triple digits," he admitted.

She shook her head in disbelief. "The young man on the news. You know the one I like to watch. He was saying something about how the earth is getting warmer. As if this place can get any hotter."

Sherman smiled. Her relationship with the present tense was fragile.

"Did your father say what time he's off duty?"

There it was. The complete break with reality. Sherman took a deep breath and steeled himself for the conversation.

"Dad's dead, Mom. He has been for years."

Her face flooded with terror, confusion, and a hint of embarrassment as if she should have known such a profound fact. Those beautiful green-orange eyes of hers, the ones passed down to her son, flashed around the room searching for something familiar. Resignation sank into the corners of her mouth in a way that only those suffering from memory loss could truly understand.

"Oh," she began. "I'm sorry. I forget a lot these days."

"It's okay, Mom," he replied and squeezed her bony hand with its knuckles gnarled by arthritis.

A knock sounded on the door and a gentle voice piped through the opening. "Mrs. Sherman, it's time for your vitamins."

The door opened and the nurse slipped into the room. She was slender and short, with tawny skin and big brown eyes that Sherman felt could see genuine joy in the world. Her name was Vanessa, and she had been his mother's nurse for over five years.

"Frank," she said with a wide smile that curved steeply upward in the corners. "I didn't know you were in town."

"I got in late last night."

She handed Sophia a little paper cup filled with a finely woven tapestry of opiates, stool softeners, blood thinners, and cholinesterase inhibitors.

"Well, how have you been? Or better question... where have you been?"

Sherman chuckled, and his mother looked over with genuine interest and clarity. "Not much has changed since I saw you last."

Grab your copy...
www.vinci-books.com/nomad